LEFT

Theanna Bischoff

LEFT

NEWEST PRESS
EDMONTON, AB 2018

Library and Archives Canada Cataloguing in Publication

Bischoff, Theanna, 1984-, author
Left / Theanna Bischoff.
Issued in print and electronic formats.
ISBN 978-1-988732-43-5 (softcover).--ISBN 978-1-988732-34-3 (EPUB).--
ISBN 978-1-988732-35-0 (Kindle)
I. Title.

PS8603.I83L44 2018   C813'.6   C2018-900594-7
C2018-900595-5

NeWest Press wishes to acknowledge that the land on which we operate is Treaty 6 territory and a traditional meeting ground and home for many Indigenous Peoples, including Cree, Saulteaux, Niisitapi (Blackfoot), Métis, and Nakota Sioux.

Board Editor: Anne Nothof
Cover design & typography: Kate Hargreaves
Cover photograph via Unsplash
Author photograph: Stefanie Barton

NeWest Press acknowledges the Canada Council for the Arts, the Alberta Foundation for the Arts, and the Edmonton Arts Council for support of our publishing program. This project is funded in part by the Government of Canada.

201, 8540 – 109 Street
Edmonton, AB T6G 1E6
780.432.9427

NeWest Press   www.newestpress.com

No bison were harmed in the making of this book.
PRINTED AND BOUND IN CANADA

Wordsworth said, "Fill your paper with the breathings of your heart."

For Carrie, Stefanie, and Rachelle—thank you for always being present for the breathings of my heart, both on and off the page.

JULY 2002

Where you used to be, there is a hole in the world, which I find myself
constantly walking around in the daytime,
and falling in at night.

—Edna St. Vincent Millay

ABBY

WHAT WAS THE LAST THING YOU SAID TO ME?

Something about the weather.

Not very poignant, but you didn't know. You thought you'd be back in an hour. I could see the orange Lycra straps of your tank top criss-crossed in the back before you pulled your jacket on and opened the front door. The detective asked me later if I remembered what you were wearing. *An orange tank top*, I told him. *Black leggings, black windbreaker.*

You wanted to get in a run before it started raining. I could always count on you to know the forecast. You'd say things like, "Put mittens in your backpack, Abby. It's going to snow." Or "Don't forget your sunscreen, Sis!" You were always prepared.

In the doorway, holding one foot behind you in some sort of runner's stretch, you said, "You should rest. Pretty soon you can kiss sleep goodbye. When my niece gets here."

"Or nephew." Sitting on the couch, I shifted my belly, pulled your yellow fleece blanket up to my chin. When my OB/GYN had asked if I wanted to know the gender, I said no. It made it too real. You would have found out. You liked to know everything. When I was seven, you showed me your old Ouija board, rested your fingertips lightly on the plastic dial, and told me about how, when you were a kid, you would try to ask the spirits what you were going to be when you grew up, where and when you'd meet the man of your dreams, how you'd ultimately die. Seven-year-old me asked the spirits if Mom and Dad would let me get a hamster—which they totally didn't, because I'm the daughter who forged Dad's signature to explain my missing homework, who ran myself a bath and then got distracted watching TV and let it overflow, who opened my Christmas presents when our parents weren't looking and then tried to re-wrap them.

A niece. You knew. You *knew* you knew.

With the front door open, I could see bruised clouds hanging low in the sky, the sun beginning its slow descent for the summer night. I said, "It looks ugly out." Pregnant at eighteen. Maybe I should have asked the Ouija board some more serious questions about my future.

You slid your windbreaker over your shoulders. Smiled. Zipped. Said, "I can outrun this storm. See you in an hour." You turned. Your dark ponytail swung.

I slept. I dreamed of having a C-section, of doctors lifting out each of my organs, one at a time. Lungs, liver, intestines, heart. Mom wouldn't let you be in the room when I was born, even though you really wanted to. Sorry—my mom, your stepmom. I always forget to word it the right way.

But you, you never forgot anything. You would have remembered all the details—not just the orange tank top, black leggings, and black windbreaker, but the grey running shoes with pink laces, too. You would have remembered that the black windbreaker had a slim silver stripe from shoulder to wrist cuff. You would have remembered the black plastic digital Timex watch you always wore on your right wrist. I didn't remember that stuff until later, after other people mentioned it. And you would probably have remembered the stuff none of us could remember either, like whether you were wearing earrings, and, if so, which ones?

You wouldn't have fallen asleep on the couch instead of waiting up for your sister to come home to have dinner together. Not you.

I awoke to the thick, humid scent of bubbling gravy. My stomach growled. What time was it? Were you late getting home? Had you run for longer than an hour? You'd said, "See you in an hour," right? Maybe you'd come home, but you'd decided to let me sleep. You must have forgotten to turn off the Crock-Pot. You'd gone into your room to read or to make a phone call. You'd come in quietly, not wanting to disturb me. You—

My bladder tightened. I swung my legs over the side of the couch. Stood up. "Natasha?" Squinted. Pushed up off the armrest. Padded into the kitchen.

The light on the Crock-Pot glowed green in the dark. I flicked on the overhead light, lifted the clear glass lid of the Crock-Pot, almost scalding my hand. The lid clattered to the floor. Brown slop had crusted along the edges of the pot; the stew inside had congealed, a sludgy mash. On the kitchen counter sat your cellphone atop a stack of bills labelled with sticky notes in your handwriting.

Upstairs, in your room, your bed was made, as usual, the top edge folded over, exposing the floral under layer of your dark purple bedspread. A lavender lace bra with scalloped edging hung by one strap from the inside doorknob. My own breasts felt swollen and heavy.

My room. Both bathrooms. Down the stairs. I called your name again. "Tash?"

Back in the kitchen, the microwave blinked at me, 12:00, 12:00, 12:00. The storm must have reset the power. I leaned against the counter, rubbed at my belly where some contour of the baby forced itself, probably trying to escape.

Had I missed the storm? Through the blackness outside my window, I couldn't tell. Maybe you'd gone inside somewhere to wait it out. Or maybe you'd come back and then left again. I opened the door to the garage. There was your black Mazda, parked tight against the left wall to leave space for your bike and winter tires.

I got the cordless phone and sat down on the staircase by the front door, staring at the space where I'd last seen you. Dialled.

I hadn't talked to Cameron in eleven days.

"Abby?" Cam's voice sounded thick. "What the fuck? Are you in labour? It's one in the morning!"

One in the morning? A fist closed around my breastbone. "No, I just—I need help, my sister is—"

"I told you not to call me unless you were having the baby." Dial tone.

Back in your room, I found your silver watch on top of the dresser, the watch Greg gave for your last anniversary. You wore it for special occasions, swapping it with the plastic Timex you never left home without. You hadn't worn the silver watch since you and Greg broke up, but you hadn't put it away in your jewellery box, either. *1:17 a.m.*

What?

Work. Maybe you went into work. Maybe you got called into the hospital last minute for a shift. But—without your car? Without leaving me a note? I phoned anyway.

"Natasha Bell? She's not on shift right now." The nurse's voice sounded too chirpy for one a.m., too chirpy for the burn unit. That day, before your run, you'd told me how you'd bandaged the rotting, puss-oozing, third-degree flesh of a drunk undergraduate who'd tripped and fallen face first into a fire-pit trying to roast marshmallows. A not so subtly disguised lesson about substance abuse for your little sis.

"Are you sure?" I felt the hot pulse of my bladder.

"I haven't seen her tonight. But I can page her, hang on."

I shut my eyes, leaned against the staircase railing.

"She didn't answer. If she comes in, or if I see her, I can call you back. What's your number?"

I brought the phone with me into the main floor bathroom and peed a furious stream into the toilet, legs shaking. *Tash, what the fuck? Where are you?* I pulled myself to standing. I put a fist against my chest, inhaled sharply. I reached for the phone, but knocked it noisily into the sink.

I couldn't breathe, but I dialled anyway. The phone rang and rang and rang.

You'd said you weren't going to get back together with Greg. But, where else could you be? Maybe you *did* leave me a note, and I just didn't see it. Maybe it fell behind the counter or something.

Then—Greg's voice, groggy: "Hello?"

"Is Tash with you?" I blurted.

Pause. "Uh, no. Why? What time is it? Is everything okay?"

The baby heaved itself into my ribs.

And I thought of you, at the door, a dark ponytail, a stretchy orange shirt. Your bangs pinned back. Your left cheek dimple. The wisp of a cool summer night creeping through the open door.

Had I even said goodbye?

NATASHA

AUGUST 2001

"We've grown apart." These are the words Greg's mother chose as a way of announcing that she and Greg's father have decided to get a divorce. As though the divorce happened to them, almost by accident.

Why did Greg's parents feel the need to have Natasha there for such an announcement? Because Natasha has dated their son for so long that she's part of the family now? Practically a daughter-in-law, even though she and Greg aren't even engaged yet? Or because Greg's mother didn't want her only child to be alone while hearing the news that his parents were ending their thirty-two year marriage?

Greg's parents have looked the same for as long as Natasha has known them; both husky, pear-shaped, dark-haired. Would Greg's body, still lean and toned from years of swimming competitively in adolescence, eventually follow this trend? While telling their son about their dissolving marriage, Greg's parents looked even more alike, their faces scrunched in concerned resignation, like siblings, together since high school, as though the world had shaped them both, and they'd shaped each other, in the same way. And yet—apart. They'd somehow grown apart.

Greg's mother, Gillian, had reached across the kitchen table and put her hand over Natasha's hand rather than her son's. Greg withdrew his hands from the table and placed them in his lap, even though his mother hadn't actually touched him. Gillian winced, glanced sideways at Greg's father, said, "We've been together so long, I stopped being me." Greg's father nodded. Natasha counted seven tiny rose-shaped buttons on Gillian's pink cashmere sweater. Her stepmother, Kathleen, would have called the buttons juvenile, would have pointed out how the sweater's fabric strained over Gillian's stomach.

Natasha slid her foot over until it touched Greg's under the table, remembering the first time she'd made this gesture, age fifteen, sitting beside him on the couch watching some horror movie about some crazed stalker who phoned his target while she was babysitting and then breathed heavily into the receiver. She remembered that Greg had on a grey T-shirt and Levi's, and he'd smelled like warm pizza; she remembered the electricity—the hum in her foot and her calf as she nudged it slightly over and over and over until her leg lined up right beside Greg's leg, her sock foot and his sock foot, the outer seam of their jeans fitting together like a zipper.

But, at the kitchen table while his parents prattled on, Greg had slid his foot away from hers. He got up and left the table, the kitchen. She heard a door slam.

Now, three months after Greg's parents announced their separation, Natasha stands in her pink satin dress at the front of the church in the four-inch heels her best friend has chosen for all her bridesmaids. Natasha, maid of honour, grips Josie's bridal bouquet and tries to make eye contact with Greg in the rows of guests, but his eyes focus elsewhere. Pink—how cliché. When the vows begin, Jo passes Natasha

THEANNA BISCHOFF

her bouquet of pink and white roses, the look and smell of which remind Natasha of a funeral.

The priest has a deep voice and his microphone volume is too loud, raspy. He sounds like Darth Vader reading the vows. "Solomon and Josie, have you come here freely and without reservation to give yourselves to each other in marriage?" The microphone hisses with each breath.

It's like Greg's parents invented divorce, the way Greg now carries on. Hot black tar bubbles in her gut every time Greg says he doesn't want to talk about it, every time he wants to her to leave him alone, every time he yells at her, "Thirty-two years! Doesn't that mean anything to anyone?" For years, when she'd talked about her own parents' acrimonious split, her father's infidelity and remarriage, her mother's abrupt abandonment of the family, Greg had innocently commented, "Isn't that water under the bridge, now, though?" But now that it's him on the receiving end, he suddenly gets it.

After the ceremony, she can try to find a Band-Aid to put over the spot where the back of her shoe has rubbed up against her Achilles tendon, a blister waiting to burst.

Josie, in her white tulle parachute dress and twinkly tiara, at the front of the church, with Jesus suspended on the cross dangling above her, is acting like she's invented marriage. Josie, who met Solomon after a four-year period of not making it past a second date. Natasha had often comforted herself when another birthday, another Christmas, came and went without Greg getting down on one knee. At least Josie was unmarried, too.

Well, not anymore.

"I, Josie Elise Carey, take you, Solomon Michael McKinnon, for my lawful husband, to have and to hold, from this day forward, for better, for worse—"

Josie barely knows Solomon, the youth pastor at Josie's new church. Greg complains every time Natasha tries to get them to go on a double date, says Solomon gives off a skeezy vibe, which is kind of true, but Natasha has to give him the benefit of the doubt, for Jo's sake. Today, their wedding day, is the one-year anniversary of the day they first met. Has Solomon seen Josie vomit chocolate cherry cheesecake because she forgot to take a Lactaid? Has he had to run to the store to buy emergency tampons? Has he read one of Josie's exorbitant credit card statements? Does Solomon expect Josie, whose biological clock sounded its alarm after her twin brother's son was born last year, to support them financially while he pursues his dream of "ministering to the Christian youth of Calgary?"

They haven't even had sex yet. Does Solomon know that his born-again virgin-white-cake-topper bride, has slept with three different men, including Natasha's cousin Dustin on the day the girls graduated from university? Josie's engagement ring has a tiny cross engraved on the inside, to represent her promise to wait for marriage, as though her virginity could simply grow back.

After the rehearsal dinner last night, Greg had crawled into bed and flicked the lamp off without saying anything, then rolled away from her. He's been so irritable; Josie's wedding is probably triggering feelings about his parents' separation. Be calm, Natasha had thought, be calm. "I'm setting the alarm for seven. I need to meet the other bridesmaids at the salon by eight." No answer. "You okay? You were really quiet tonight." Despite their divorce proceedings, Greg's parents kept inviting Greg over for family dinners, all three of them together. "Love?" Natasha said, again. "You okay?"

Greg yanked his pillow down over his face. "Can we not talk about feelings? For once?!"

Greg's parents were divorcing because they had different interests. Greg's mother was going to take a pottery class and his dad was going to help a buddy renovate a turn-of-the-century character house. Different interests? After thirty-two years of marriage? That couldn't be the only reason— could it?

"You may now kiss the bride!"

Solomon gives Josie a sanctimonious closed-mouth kiss. The guests clap. Natasha scans the pews for Greg. There he is, just behind Josie's parents and twin brother, Jason.

What does growing apart really mean? If anything, Natasha and Greg, together since high school, just like his parents, have grown together, like a tumour wrapping its way around a spinal column. What is she going to do with him? Or, for that matter, without him?

Maid-of-honour-Natasha, big-smile-for-her-best-friend's-wedding-Natasha, passes Josie's bouquet back to her friend and takes her steps down the aisle, linking arms with Solomon's chubby best man. Josie had wanted her brother to be her "man" of honour, letting him and Natasha share the role, but Jason had said he didn't believe in all of Josie's Jesus crap, and then Jo didn't talk to him for a week, after which Solomon said he wanted a traditional wedding and Jason lining up there with all the women would have looked inappropriate. So that was that.

Natasha's face feels stretched. She points her smile at Greg, but Jason catches her gaze instead, grins, rolls his eyes. Her high heel slices at the rawness on the back of her heel. Good thing Josie and Solomon have left the church already and don't catch Jay's cynicism. The last thing this wedding needs is a family feud.

Greg catches Natasha's eye, but looks away. Sticky black tar oozes up her esophagus.

JOSIE

www.findnatashabell.com

I am with you and will watch over you wherever you go, and I will bring you back to this land. I will not leave you until I have done what I have promised you. —Genesis 28:15

MISSING
Natasha Summer Bell
Missing From: *Calgary, Alberta*
Last seen: *July 6, 2002*
Date of Birth: *November 11, 1972*
Age: *29 years*
Sex: *Female*
Height: *5 feet, 6 inches*
Weight: *124 lbs*
Build: *Thin / athletic*
Eyes: *Blue*
Hair: *Long, dark brown, with long bangs*
Race: *Caucasian*

Clothing: *Last seen wearing orange athletic tank top, black leggings, black windbreaker, black digital Timex wristwatch, grey running shoes with pink laces*
Identifying characteristics: *Pierced ears, pale birthmark on back of left shoulder*

IF YOU HAVE ANY INFORMATION ABOUT NATASHA BELL, PLEASE NOTIFY LOCAL LAW ENFORCEMENT IMMEDIATELY.

Two days ago, my lifelong friend and maid of honour, Natasha Summer Bell, went for a run around 9:00 p.m. and never returned. Those of us who know and love Natasha know that she would never leave on her own, and we suspect foul play. Her purse, cellphone, keys, and vehicle were located at her home. There has been no activity on any of her bank accounts since the night of July 6. Police dogs were unable to track her scent further than her front yard. It is possible that the person involved in Natasha's disappearance is not a Calgary resident, due to the number of visitors in town for the Calgary Stampede. Natasha is the kindest, most loving, most generous person I know. Please summon all your prayers for her safe return! WE LOVE YOU NATASHA!!!!

Josie Carey McKinnon

JOSIE AND NATASHA HAD BEEN FRIENDS SO LONG THAT periodic arguments were pretty much expected. Okay, so they had never had an argument of this magnitude, but the timing of it—what with it being their last conversation—was still purely coincidental. One hundred percent. Josie is sure of it.

The whole thing started over coffee. Separately, both girls drank dark roast in the mornings, but together, they indulged in chai lattes, full fat milk, whipped cream sprinkled with cinnamon. None of that half-sweet nonsense. A few sips into her drink, Josie had inquired whether Abby had considered giving her baby up for adoption so that it could have the stable, two-parent home it deserved.

Josie and Solomon had been trying to have a baby ever since their wedding day almost a year ago. At her last appointment, Josie's GP had told her to just relax; apparently, for women under thirty-five, they would not run tests until a couple had been trying unsuccessfully for twelve months, but, in the meantime, she could buy a basal body thermometer and start tracking her cycles. The booklet she'd purchased on natural family planning suggested that she stick her fingers up inside herself and feel for the consistency of her cervical mucus. How embarrassing! She would do whatever she had to do, but creating her new family wasn't supposed to be this hard. Her mother had married in her early thirties (practically elderly for her generation)—and had still conceived naturally only a few months into trying, a set of twins, no less! In a couple of weeks, Josie and Solomon would pass the twelve-month mark and then what?

Josie had wanted to ask Natasha about it, what with her medical background, but Solomon had said, "That's between a man and his wife." He didn't think anyone should announce a pregnancy until after three months, when the possibility of miscarriage decreased. Josie didn't agree—if she did have a miscarriage, she would want Natasha's support. Natasha had been there when she'd had her appendix removed in the eighth grade; when she'd been bullied because an allergic reaction to her band class flute gave her a nasty rash around her mouth; when her mom was diagnosed with breast cancer. But Solomon was Josie's husband, and she had promised to honour and obey him.

The comment about adoption had grown from a tiny seed in Josie's so-far-childless brain; perhaps Abby, obviously unprepared to raise a baby, would consider an older, wiser family friend to raise the child. She and Solomon had opened their hearts to God for a baby—maybe they hadn't had one yet because God was preparing them to be the parents to Abby's little one.

But Natasha was livid that Josie would even suggest adoption, and Josie hadn't even mentioned anything about the fact that she and Solomon were trying to conceive but not having any luck. Natasha said that Abby was maturing a lot, that the baby's father and his family were prepared to be involved, and that both Abby and Natasha were very much looking forward to the baby's birth. The baby was almost here, and Tash didn't want her to grow up thinking she wasn't wanted. Natasha always referred to the baby as a girl even though Abby hadn't found out the gender.

The conversation had only gone downhill after that. But Josie doesn't want to think about that now.

Despite Natasha's vehement *no*, Josie had mentioned adoption to Solomon anyway that night while getting ready for bed.

"Are you serious?" Solomon squeezed a glob of toothpaste onto his toothbrush. "Think about genetics. Nature plays a huge role, you know." He began to scrub at his back molars. Josie sat on the edge of the tub, suddenly shivering. Could he brush his teeth any slower? Finally, Solomon spat into the sink. "Especially a child conceived in sin—and by teenagers, no less. No, I want our own biological children."

"Okay, well what about—?"

Solomon put his toothbrush down on the edge of the sink. "Jesus will give us the family we're meant to have. If He doesn't give us children, then it's not part of His will."

Josie had always figured that they both wanted children, so of course they would become parents however they could, even if that meant adoption or fertility treatments. She felt tears sprout at her eyes. She stood and walked out of the bathroom to the laundry room, tugged the load of fresh white towels out of the dryer, and sat at the foot of the bed, folding perfect rectangles.

Sometimes Jesus' will didn't make any sense. Why would Jesus give a baby to Abby when she was still in high school? Josie's brother and his ex-girlfriend had a two-year-old boy, Finn. Two years old, and Finn already came from a broken home. A cousin of theirs had also had a baby out of wedlock when she and Jason were teenagers, and, last she heard, that child had been suspended from school for getting into a fistfight. It didn't bode well. The sanctity of marriage, of family—these were very important to society. She and Solomon would make excellent parents, committed to raising their child in the Church. So why were they the ones having problems conceiving?

And yet, as she folded the last towel, she felt guilt in her stomach, hot like vomit. Who was she to question God's infinite plan?

ABBY

Orange tank top, black leggings, black windbreaker. She said an hour, max.

What time was that?

Around nine, I think, before the storm.

Does she usually go running by herself that late?

She's a nurse, she works weird hours.

Does she have a cellphone?

She left it here—she never takes it running, she says it's too clunky in her pocket, it bangs up against her hip the whole time...

What about her wallet? Keys? Any ID on her?

I found her purse in the closet, her keys and her wallet were in there. I don't know if she took any ID out.

We'll have a look. When she left the house, where were you?

Here—asleep. Well, I watched some TV after she left, then I fell asleep on the couch. I woke up and she wasn't here. It was past midnight.

You slept through the storm?

I didn't set an alarm! She said she'd be an hour, max!

This is her house? Or your house?

Hers—but I live here with her.

You got a recent picture of her?

Uh, I could find one. I'll have to grab one of her albums. Or maybe on her camera. She takes a lot of pictures, but I don't know if she'd be in any of them—

Where are your parents?

I didn't call them. Should I call them? We're—Natasha and I aren't really talking to them. They're mad because I decided to, to keep it—the baby. Natasha was helping me out, she said I could live here.

Write their phone number down—here, right here.

Her biological mom isn't in the picture. You'd have to ask our dad about that—

Did you call around to any of her friends or anything?

Her boyfriend—well, her ex. I thought maybe she went over there, or, I don't know, maybe—I thought maybe there'd been an accident, she got hit by a car or something.

This boyfriend, what's his name?

Greg.

Greg what?

Morgan. He said he was coming. He's the one who said I should call you.

What's his phone number? Write it too. Address too, if you have that.

I don't know it by heart. When he gets here, you can—

They split up?

She broke up with him—last summer. She wanted to get married, he wasn't ready...

So, a year ago? But you thought she might go there?

I...they were still in touch, sort of—he was a part of the family for so long...

How long were they together?

Since high school. Ten years? Or more, even. You should ask him, he's coming over, he should be here by now—

Does he have a temper? Would he ever hurt her?

What? No! Greg is like, the nicest—someday they're going to get back together. He still loves her. This isn't—she's probably hurt, somewhere. I'm going to be sick.

Did she have any debt? Any financial trouble, vices, addictions, things like that? She on any medication?

No, she's a nurse. She's a health nut. She's always on my case about eating better, working out.

Okay, okay. Now I need you to make a list—people she knows, people she would confide in if she was in trouble. Places she might go if she needed a break or something, if she just took off.

She didn't just take off—she left dinner cooking. I'm having a baby—

What about this breakup, was she depressed at all?

I mean, yeah, she was messed up about it, anybody would…but that's not—

Messed up? What do you mean?

I didn't mean it like—she would never run away or hurt herself if that's what you mean! I'm having a baby! She's really excited about it. She wouldn't just bail, I'm telling you! Something's wrong.

GREG

THE CLOSEST THING GREG HAD TO AN ALIBI WAS HIS VISIT to the walk-in three days prior, a throat culture positive for strep and a prescription for amoxicillin. The consequences, he supposes, of ignoring the first tickle of a sore throat and tromping around in Fish Creek Park with a group of undergrad students collecting soil samples.

On the sixth of July, Greg had called in sick and spent the whole day and night at home. Alone. Four days after Natasha went missing, he had still not yet thrown out an empty Styrofoam container of wonton soup, nor wiped the spilled, now dried soya sauce off his counter. He had not opened or eaten his fortune cookie. Natasha always opened fortune cookies before her meal. On one of their dates when they were both still in high school, she'd once found only a blank slip of paper inside.

"You think it's bad luck?" she'd joked.

"You can have mine," he'd said, sliding his slip across the table to her.

"Ten percent off your next meal," Natasha read. "Clever."

Standing at his kitchen counter, Greg took the uneaten fortune cookie in his palm and crushed it, still inside the wrapper.

"When did you see her last?" the detective had asked.

June twenty-eighth, just over a week before. Greg had been at home, at his kitchen table, trying to fix a pencil sketch of a line of flowers along the Bow River. He was drawing from a photograph, but the shadows looked wrong; he wished he could go back down there to really see it, to get the angles and the light right, but he'd taken the photo at the beginning of April, and the flora would be fuller now, other species would have bloomed in the background. He wouldn't be able to replicate the day's weather, the way the sun reflected off the water. He flipped his pencil over and used the eraser to scrub at a darkened petal just outside the range of the sun.

Then Natasha's number lit up his call display. He'd let the phone ring one extra time, closed his sketchbook, and took a deep breath before answering. "Hello?"

"Greg, thank God—I can't get the cat out of the basement. I'm supposed to feed her like, every hour, she's hiding behind a box in the back of the crawlspace; all I can see are her creepy little eyes. Natasha's going to kill me." Just Abby, having another crisis. His lungs deflated.

He left campus a little early and went over, helped Abby literally sweep Natasha's cat, Larkin, out of the crawlspace with the kitchen broom. Greg held a throw blanket around everything except Larkin's head as Abby pried the yowling cat's jaws open to actually get the syringe of mashed food inside, and even then, Larkin regurgitated a clump of brown pulp onto the carpet before scurrying under the living room couch. Larkin was a bony, grey feral tabby of indeterminate age, with half a tail; Greg had spent full weekends at Natasha's without ever seeing Larkin, who trolled under beds and behind boxes. Did the cat ever eat? Health problems or no health problems, Larkin would probably outlive them all.

"You have to do this every hour?" he asked.

Abby pressed the lid back onto the plastic container of pureed food. "Yes! Natasha took her to the vet yesterday, apparently she has fatty liver syndrome—she won't eat on her own. We have to do this until she starts putting on weight. Tash thinks Larkin is her baby. God help us when she has an actual human spawn..." She bit her lip then, catching herself. Greg remembered a family dinner, Natasha's stepsister, an aspiring psychologist, teasing about how he and Natasha would parent—good cop, bad cop respectively. Certainly none of the Bells had expected Abby to procreate before her much older half-sister.

Greg recalled Abby in preschool making her bedroom furniture "shiny" with Vaseline while he and Natasha made out on the couch instead of babysitting; Abby in kindergarten, trying to pour her own juice and spilling an orange tidal wave across the table; Abby, in grade school, mid-punishment, standing face to the corner in the living room, sneaking glances and sticking her tongue out at them.

Abby put one hand on her lower back, which thrust her pregnant belly out even further. In grey sweatpants and a white T-shirt (clearly Natasha's, given the emblazoned 10K run slogan), she looked like a child in pajamas. A child having a child. "You have to stay," she whined.

Abby turned the TV on to some daytime talk show and Greg zipped out to grab them some lunch and pick up his laptop so he could at least edit his dissertation in-between feeding shifts. His drawing would have to wait—he never sketched in front of other people. Maybe Abby's diversion was a good thing—it would force him to stop procrastinating.

But when he got back to Natasha's, Abby had fallen asleep on the couch, her belly a lopsided mound. Greg put Abby's saran-wrapped sandwich in the fridge, turned off the TV, and stretched a blanket to cover her bare feet. How many times had he and Natasha cuddled under that blanket to watch movies? Every time they went to rent a DVD, she *had* to get red licorice. Did she watch movies without him, now? Or with someone new? He wanted to know.

No he didn't.

Greg lured Larkin out from under the sofa with a bag of catnip and then wrangled a second syringe of liquefied food into her himself, earning a fine slash across one forearm. He watched as beads of blood welled along the linear wound. Larkin scurried back to her safety zone.

He hadn't asked Abby what time Natasha's shift ended, when she might be home. He opened his laptop, paced around while it booted up. When Greg had given his supervisor the last round of edits, his supervisor sent it back heavily marked, red scrawl at the top, *Not up to your usual standards.* Had he brought his laptop charger? Damn. The battery looked pretty low. Oh well. He powered down the computer and slid it back into its case.

He rinsed some of the dishes in Natasha's sink and loaded them into the dishwasher, then wandered upstairs. In the doorway to Natasha's bedroom, he hovered, then stepped inside and made his way to the dresser where Natasha had arranged several toiletries she used regularly. There was the silver watch he'd given her for an anniversary, face up. He'd had the back engraved, but in the moment, couldn't recall the inscription. He picked it up and turned it over. *Until the end of time.* Cheesy. Especially since their relationship had clearly had an expiry date. He set the watch down, careful to leave it in the same position.

Dark hair clung to her hairbrush. For months after they broke up,

Greg had found long dark hairs in his lint trap. He picked up a delicate bottle of perfume and turned it over in his hands. He took the lid off and spritzed the cloudy liquid into the air in front of him. Inhaled. The smell came, too strong, not like her at all.

Something sounded like movement downstairs. Shit. He scrambled to put the cap on the bottle. Now he would smell like it, and she would know that he went into her room, and—

But Abby was still asleep when he went downstairs. Larkin's accusing eyes started out at him from underneath the recliner.

Greg didn't tell the detective about going into her room, about touching her things, about the perfume.

The detective wanted to know if Greg had actually seen Natasha that day. If she'd come home while he was still there. If they'd talked.

Yes, and yes, and yes. Abby had roused, groggy, saying her back hurt. She wanted to take a shower, and said Natasha would be home soon and could take over feeding Larkin. Greg debated going back home, but Natasha's lawn looked like it needed mowing, and he would rather mow a lawn than work on his dissertation. He would rather *anything* than work on his dissertation.

Greg recalled pausing, mid-mow, to wipe the sweat off his forehead with the back of his hand. If Natasha was running late or something, Abby couldn't possibly manage the next dose by herself. She could barely get up and down from the couch, let alone manhandle a writhing feline. He checked his watch: forty minutes before Larkin was due for another squirt. He revved the mower and navigated around the front steps.

Then Natasha's car pulled into the driveway, driver's side window down, music on, the Eagles, "Heartache Tonight." Natasha loved '80s music, kept burned CDs in her car of the top songs for each year of the decade. She made them in university; made him dance with her to "Girls Just Wanna Have Fun" while all the songs downloaded. Who wrote that? Greg could never remember artists or lyrics. Madonna, maybe? Sometimes, he just wanted to listen to music from the current decade.

Natasha quit the motor and the music stopped. She climbed out of her car, still dressed in lavender scrubs, her dark hair hanging around her face in loose waves. "What are you doing here?" she yelled over the roar of the mower, eyes narrowed, hands on her hips.

Greg felt his chest seize. He turned the mower off. Tash's lips looked red, flushed. Red licorice kissed. "Ask Abby," he said, and yanked the lawnmower cord hard, until he felt it go slack as the plug released from the socket. The grass looked jagged now, a large chunk near the sidewalk longer than the rest. He could hardly maneuver his keys with his sweaty fingers. He slid into his car parked beside hers. He tried not to look at her. Could she smell her perfume on him?

After Greg had recapped the story of this day, the last day he'd seen her, the detective had leaned back in his chair, cocked his head, and said, "That's all?" like he knew Greg had left parts out. How many times was he going to make Greg sit through these rounds of questioning? Greg came in voluntarily every time—couldn't the cop ask all his questions in one shot? What was the point of all the stop-start interviewing? As far as Greg knew, they didn't have any new evidence.

The detective was wearing plainclothes, dark jeans and a black T-shirt. He looked bright-eyed and intense, not like the night Tash went missing and he came to her house. That night, his eyes looked bloodshot, and he paced about, going in and out of different rooms but not in any logical order. The T-shirt made him look young—maybe late twenties? Greg's age? Maybe he'd been drinking with buddies at the Stampede grounds when he'd got the call. Or maybe he was just deceptively young, a skilled, senior detective with a baby face. Had he spied the cat scratch on Greg's forearm? Should Greg point it out and say where it came from, or would that just sound like an excuse?

"That's it." Greg realized he'd balled his hands into fists in his lap. He uncurled his fingers and spread his hands, palms down, on the table.

The detective tilted the chair onto its back legs. Abby had a bad habit of doing this; in grade school, she once catapulted herself to the kitchen floor and whacked the back of her skull, requiring stitches.

Greg felt dizzy; he had barely slept since Abby called him to say she couldn't find Natasha. That first night, he'd driven in a spiral, concentric circles widening and widening away from Tash's house, too fast, he'd realized, as he careened crazily into a puddle and bounced up and over a curb while making a wide right turn into a cul-de-sac, his headlights spilling across the wet pavement. All these streets had the same names, too similar sounding. Schooner, Scurfield, Scepter, Scandia... one hour, two hours, four hours, five. The sun curled up over the trees. *You're late*, it said, *a whole new day is here, without her. You're never going to find her. Never never never never—*

The detective leaned his chair back, stared at Greg across the table. Greg's throat felt burnt, blackened, and he coughed, suddenly, overtaken by a spasm. His throat no longer hurt as much, but his stomach felt curdled. A side-effect of the antibiotics? Or just stress? His mother kept coming over with various remedies—Thai lemongrass soup, Neti pots. Then she'd just sit at the kitchen table and cry openly, snot and tears running down her face. He called his father, told him to come get her. He didn't want a stupid Neti pot, he needed something to knock him out. He'd taken double the dose of liquid NyQuil the night before, guzzled it back, trying not to gag, then collapsed onto the couch and slept for a half an hour, after which he just felt lit up and dizzy.

"Excuse me," he said, to the detective, and got up from the table, without waiting for permission. The floor felt dirty, gritty beneath his bare feet as he made his way to the bathroom. Under different circumstances, his mother would have noticed and swept. How long had he worn this same pair of sweatpants? He put his head near the toilet basin and dry heaved.

The detective's questions had started to feel less like information gathering and more like trying to catch him in a lie. He'd asked Greg whether his condo complex had any video surveillance that could prove the time Greg had entered the building, prove he had not exited until Abby's phone call. Greg wasn't sure—he offered up the name of his property manager, though. One of his neighbours had left him a voicemail asking why the cops were questioning the tenants about Greg's whereabouts. So the detective had someone going door-to-door wasting police resources that they could be using to find Natasha. Couldn't they just clear him already?

"So," said the detective, when Greg returned, "Go back a bit—do you have any suspicions that she could have been seeing someone else?" The guy had asked him this before, and would definitely have asked Abby, and Josie, and Tash's parents at some point, probably that first night, and fuck, Greg was so tired, so tired. Where was she? Where was she? Where was she? Greg began to sob; he covered his face with his hands.

"If you had to guess—was she?" The detective asked again.

Was. Greg shook his head. "I don't know. I don't know."

ABBY

WHEN I TOLD YOU I ALWAYS USED PROTECTION, I LIED.

I mean, come on, like I was going to tell you the truth, especially since *you* tried to teach me about birth control in the first place. Maybe I should have paid more attention, filled my prescription when the one you bought me ran out, yeah yeah. But you wouldn't understand, you've only ever had sex with one person who's always loved you.

I'm pretty sure I know exactly when I got pregnant. We didn't use a condom because Cam couldn't find one. He'd probably used them all up with his girlfriend, Jessica the Bitch, my former best friend. Cam and I hadn't been dating *that* long, but it was pretty good, I thought, until *she* swooped in. She was telling everyone they were going to colour coordinate for prom. Seven months in advance, he'd already bought a purple tie.

Perched on the edge of the pool table outside his bedroom, I crossed my arms over my bare breasts, watched him dump the box of empty Trojan wrappers onto his duvet. I never told you that when I got pregnant he was dating Jess, either. I mean, if I'm confessing here, I might as well lay it all out.

I'd climbing up onto the edge of the pool table, still fully clothed, and pulled him towards me while leaning back onto the green felt. I kissed his bottom lip. He tasted kind of like the sour cream and onion chips he'd been munching on in the car on the way home from school. He kissed me back. "Hey," he said, between breaths. "We're supposed to be finishing our project." Serves Cam right for picking me as his partner *before* Jess man-trapped him. Mrs. Augustine said no way when he asked to trade partners mid-semester because he'd traded girlfriends.

"So?" I reached down and fiddled with the button on his pants. He hadn't yet changed out of his school uniform. Before either of us started dating him, Jess and I used to get coffee by the gym where he worked with a trainer on Thursday evenings. We'd stand outside the glass, sipping our lattes. More shoulder presses, Cam, more shoulder presses.

"Last time was the *last time*. I told you, Jess and I—"

I pulled him closer to me. "Has Jess ever fooled around with you on a pool table?"

Okay, I know, you don't want to know the details. But, it was my fault, I came onto him. Not that he really resisted. Much.

Afterwards, he went to roll off me, and his foot got stuck in one of the pockets. In the process, he tumbled off the edge of the pool table and hung there for a second before gravity yanked his leg out of the hole and he collapsed to the ground. It was kind of funny, I'm not going to lie.

"FUUUUUUCCCCCKKK!" he screamed.

I scrambled off the pool table and pulled on my underwear.

"I—fuck! I think it's broken!" He closed his eyes and clenched his jaw.

I reached for his ankle. "Let me see."

He flinched. "Don't! Oh, God, go get some ice or something. Fuck!"

Upstairs in his kitchen, barefoot and wearing only a pink satin thong, thanking God that his parents hadn't come home yet, I found a half-empty bag of peas in the freezer.

That's right, half empty. You would have said, "Half full, Abby. Focus on the positive." You always thought things were going to work out, no matter what shit happened. Look how much good that did.

Anyway.

Cam's face loosened up a little bit once I pressed the cold pack against his ankle. "How's it look?" he asked.

"It's swelling pretty bad. Do you want to try to stand on it?" I helped him to his feet, but when he tried to bear weight, his face contorted.

He leaned against the pool table instead for support instead of me. "Fuck! It kills!"

"We should probably go to the ER. You might want some pants for that, though."

He glared at me, then squeezed his eyes shut. "Not funny." He held the bag of peas and grimaced. "Here's what we're going to do. I'm going to call my parents and tell them to meet me at the ER, and then I'm going to call Jess and tell her I tripped on the—"

I crossed my arms. "You're calling Jess?"

I went into the bathroom while he dialled. My skin looked yellow under the harsh lighting. I sucked in my stomach, snapped one of the elastic bands from around my wrist and pulled my hair into a loose ponytail. I looked crumpled. A used Kleenex. Trash.

I could have left him by himself, let him wait for his parents or Jess to come get him, let him explain to her how he'd injured himself while naked. Instead, I let him brace himself on me and helped him struggle into boxers and sweatpants and drove him to the hospital.

This is where you came in. After dropping Cam off in the ER, I took the elevator to your unit and had one of the other nurses page you. It took you forever to come to the desk; you must have been taking someone's temperature or dispensing meds or something nursish like that. You finally came out wearing your floral scrubs.

"What are you doing here?" You peeled your gloves off and flicked them in the trash. They had a little bit of blood on them. Gross.

"I was studying with Cam," I said. "He hurt his ankle." Both parts true.

"I thought you weren't dating Cam anymore," you said. You checked your watch. Like you had better things to do, like I was wasting your time.

"I'm not dating Cam anymore," I said. Also true. "We have to do a speech for Model UN. We're Uganda. Can you take a break? We could go down to the cafeteria and get a coffee."

"I can't," you said. "I have tons of patients right now." Yeah, yeah. Always busy saving people's lives. You probably also told me coffee was bad for me and I shouldn't be drinking it.

I went down to the cafeteria anyway and bought a plastic container of cold vanilla pudding with the skin on top and a squirt of whipped cream from a can. When I was little, you made me warm pudding in the microwave, heating it slowly to prevent clumps. When I tried to make pudding on my own, I got too impatient, stuck it in for five minutes on high, and it bubbled over and then Mom screamed at me for not cleaning it.

I could have given her away, you know. I thought about it. Not that night with the cold, hospital pudding. I didn't know then. I sat downstairs in the cafeteria with my empty plastic pudding container and tore apart three packets of Sweet'n Low, made a tiny saccharine ski hill on the table. Cam's parents had probably arrived. And Jessica. They were all probably still in the waiting room. They would be tending to Cam's swollen ankle, fawning over him. His dad would be trying to get him bumped to the front of the line, and Jess would be snuggling up under his arm, telling him she hates seeing him in so much pain.

If you come back, I'll never lie to you again. I'll tell you everything. I'll pay attention when you lecture me about strategies for saving money, about how many grams of protein I should be eating a day, about flossing, about packing my bags for the hospital in advance, about how to clean around a baby's umbilical cord.

And I'll actually do it, all of it.

I promise.

JOSIE

JOSIE'S CAR WAS PARKED JUST OUTSIDE NATASHA'S HOUSE. After the detective left around noon on Saturday the seventh, Josie went to get inside her own vehicle to leave, too, but then noticed the pile of cigarettes. She squatted to take a closer look at the pile, crushed up against the curb. Josie reached out to pluck one of the cigarettes to examine it further, then thought better of it, withdrew her hand. What if the cigarettes were relevant to the case? How had Detective Foley missed this?

"Call me Reuben," he'd told her. That didn't sound very professional. Did he even know what he was doing? Shouldn't he have taped off the perimeter? What if whoever had done this to her best friend had sat outside her house chain smoking and waiting for her to come out, thinking about all the evil things he was going to do to her? Josie felt lightheaded. What if these cigarettes had touched his lips, his saliva, his DNA?

Inside Natasha's house, Josie rummaged in the cutlery drawer for a pair of chopsticks and a Ziploc bag. Natasha had an ample supply of chopsticks, still in their paper casing—excellent, sterile! Back outside, Josie delicately plucked each cigarette and placed it inside the baggie.

In retrospect, she probably should have just called Detective Foley and told him to come back to bag the cigarettes himself. But, in the moment, all she could think about was getting the evidence to him as fast as she could.

Plus, when she actually gave the evidence to Detective Foley, he'd sneered. Sneered! Then he'd sort of collected himself, tried to pretend like he hadn't just made an awful face. "You found these where?"

"Right outside the house! By the driveway. In a big pile."

Detective Foley dropped the baggie on his desk. "Good, it's good that you're keeping an eye out."

"You can test these, right?" Josie said. She'd heard that most people who get kidnapped are killed within the first twenty-four to forty-eight hours. Natasha was possibly still alive, then. On TV, a DNA test could get done in a couple hours. They could still find her. But only if—

Detective Foley cocked his head. "There are procedures. The lab can't randomly test cigarette butts you found on the street—we can't just spend taxpayer's dollars unless there's substantial…" he trailed off. "Lots of people smoke. When I went to the neighbour's house to ask if they'd seen anything, their house reeked of cigarettes." He plucked the baggie back up off his desk and held it close to his face. "These are generic, too. I'm sorry."

Josie would not cry. She would not cry.

GREG

GREG HAD TOLD JOSIE HE'D MEET HER BY NOON TO HELP coordinate the search party, so he'd had to leave the station, even though Reuben was still chomping at the bit. This had been the fourth round of questioning in a couple of days. But, as Greg walked out of the station, Reuben had cracked his knuckles and said, "Thanks. I'll be in touch."

Be in touch? Again? Greg shielded his eyes from the sun, scanned the parking lot for his car.

What was your relationship like? Reuben had wanted to know.

Could Greg even answer that question? Thirteen years and then everything that had come after. Even if he put it into words, would the detective understand?

Reuben was the guy's name—Greg had finally memorized it. Perhaps not a fatal flaw, but an embarrassing one, Greg's inability to remember names. When their teacher had first read Natasha's name off the class list way back when, Greg had memorized only the quiet way she'd said, "here," the dimple in her cheek, how she'd tucked her hair over her ear. He'd mentally referred to her by the wrong name for a good week, until he asked a friend of his whether he thought "Natalie from homeroom" would ever go out with him. "Who?" the friend had asked.

Reuben—was that a last name, or a first name?

Josie and her twin brother had dropped by Greg's condo parkade the previous night and the three of them had hauled carton after carton of plastic water bottles for the volunteers, along with boxes of *Missing* fliers from Josie's trunk into Greg's for transporting to the search site. Josie had so much equipment for the search that she could not transport it all in her own vehicle.

Greg hadn't seen either twin since Josie's wedding last summer, shortly before Natasha had broken up with him. Dressed identically in jeans and fluorescent orange T-shirts that bore Natasha's grinning face, the two looked more similar than Greg remembered from when they were all teenagers together. Jason's blond hair had grown out a little bit and Josie had twisted hers on top of her head into an efficient bun.

Josie had plastered the back window of her Accord with Natasha's giant laminate stick-on face and the address of the website her brother had constructed. Josie updated the website continually, even in the middle of the night. She had search parties scheduled in shifts starting at eight a.m. in a matter of days. Days—had it been days, already? Injured and stranded, Josie had insisted. Natasha had to be injured and alone, which meant days—without food, without water, in pain. And this was the best-case scenario.

"Thanks," Greg said, as Jason turned around, empty-handed, having just shoved a box into Greg's back seat. "For all of this—and for the website, too." Why did he feel like he should apologize to everyone? He hadn't done anything. But he was still *the ex.*

Jason looked at Greg blankly, his eyes the same blue as Josie's. "Yeah. Of course," he said.

Josie had boxes of the orange T-shirts for volunteers to wear—to ensure they could spot each other. "I feel like she's alive somewhere, just not in plain view," Josie explained, flipping through the pages of a notebook. "I have teams on the ravine that starts at the top of Scenic Park Crescent, and in the ravine area further west, Twelve Mile Coulee..."

Greg swallowed back a splash of bile. He tried not to look at Josie's car, or, for that matter, at Natasha's grinning face on the twins' T-shirts. Greg didn't recognize the photo, likely taken after their breakup. She looked unfamiliar, like she'd started doing her hair differently, or something. He couldn't quite tell.

Hauling boxes back and forth between the two vehicles, Josie appeared almost manic, moving faster and seemingly lifting more cargo than either of the two men. When they'd finished stuffing Greg's car with all the materials, Josie slammed Greg's trunk closed so hard the car bounced.

"Tomorrow. Eight a.m." Josie seemed to vibrate. She hugged Greg roughly, then jumped in her car with Jason in the passenger seat and peeled around the corner of the parkade, tires squealing.

Natasha and Greg had often fought about speeding, about Greg's tendency to gauge his pace by the flow of traffic instead of checking the speedometer. He could admit that he often drove over the limit, but only by about ten or fifteen clicks, and seriously, driving the speed limit meant contending with irritable honking. How many times had Natasha lectured Greg about the patients she'd seen maimed in motor vehicle accidents? Skin torn away from muscle as they slammed into the concrete, nasty pavement burns. She also lectured him about the fact that he liked drinking Coca-Cola—he had like, three cans a day, the caffeine helped when he had to stay up late working on a paper or something—but apparently this was a "bad habit." They'd shared pop at the movie theatre as teenagers, before she went to nursing school and became the health police.

Okay, so he drove over the speed limit and drank too much pop. But Natasha had a habit of buying expensive items when she could get the same thing for significantly cheaper if she would just wait or look harder for a deal. She'd bought her latest car the day she walked into the dealership.

"It's just money," she would tell Greg, when he chastised her. "And it's money I have, so what's the problem?" Fair enough, she didn't have any debt, aside from her mortgage, and she had a good job and property assets, but Daddy had paid for her entire undergraduate degree—including the rent for her off-campus apartment—so she could focus on studying instead of getting a job. She hadn't even lived with roommates. For obvious reasons, they'd often slept over at Natasha's during those years instead of Greg's bedroom at his parents' house. And Tash had driven when they went to the movies or out to dinner, because Greg's method of transportation was a bus pass.

Had it hurt his ego that his girlfriend had the car, the apartment, the cash? Probably. Even after their bachelors' degrees, Greg had continued on to do his Masters and then Doctorate, taking out student loans and accepting a job as a Teaching Assistant, while Tash landed a full-time job at the hospital and put a down payment on a house in the suburbs. She liked the burbs, said living there was ideal for starting a family. Eventually, he'd thought. They were still in their early twenties when she'd bought the house. Why rush? Ultimately everyone settled down. They would eventually get married, too, have a few kids, at some point. Probably in his thirties. If and when he felt ready.

Okay, so she had a few expensive items and didn't put in the effort to get good deals, but she didn't act spoiled. He couldn't really complain. And he *didn't* really complain, because criticizing Natasha only made her shut down. "Why are you so judgmental?" she would snap, too loudly, even when he used a calm voice and tried to frame his criticism constructively. She had a tendency to keep going, to escalate things. Sometimes, if she had just walked away, cooled down, their bickering might not have gotten so heated. "I'm not good enough for you?" she would say, arms crossed, glaring. "Oh, right, I forgot."

Aside from getting married, which had topped the list of most fought about subject during their relationship from around the time they graduated high school onwards, the second most heated subject had been fighting itself, one of Greg's biggest reasons for not feeling ready to move in together, for not proposing. They bickered too much, Greg repeatedly pointed out, to which Natasha consistently replied, "All couples argue! Fighting is normal!"

Greg's parents never fought. At least not in front of him. And they *never* used the kind of language that sometimes flew out of his and Natasha's mouths in the heat of an argument when he'd accused her of something (sometimes constructively and sometimes less-than-constructively), and when she'd then snapped back about his moral high-horse, his unwillingness to commit. What unwillingness to commit? Had he not been faithful to her since they were teenagers? He hadn't even dated anyone else during their few brief breakups, though he suspected she had. She was unfairly suspicious because of her father's history of cheating.

Greg always regretted when he lost his temper, said something rash, told Natasha she was behaving like a bitch or something. Even though she could spar right back with equal intensity. He always caved first after such a blowout—often with a drugstore greeting card that apologized in prose he himself could have never articulated. One time he'd sketched a picture of her standing in a field of dandelions, her wide eyes, lips slightly upturned, as though about to laugh. But what if she thought it was cheesy or didn't think it looked like her? He couldn't get the mouth right. He'd crumpled the drawing instead.

Natasha's parents' failed marriage and then her father's second marriage with passive-aggressive Kathleen were *not* good examples of marriage. Maybe having grown up exposed to so much conflict—not to mention her biological mother's outright abandonment right at the cusp of Natasha's adolescence—was to blame for the fact that, despite her ability to dish it right back at him, when *he* got mad at *her* for something, she could simply turn off emotionally, crawl inside of herself, stop talking until Greg lured her back out with promises of how much he loved her. How *he* would never leave her. How she *was* good enough.

"Your parents are not normal," Natasha had once spat at him, when he'd touted their successful relationship as something he and she should aspire to. "Don't you ever wonder *why* they never fight?" Uh, no, he hadn't. Because they loved each other. That's why. But when his own parents had calmly announced their separation like they'd decided what to order for breakfast, Natasha had never once thrown it back in his face. She'd tried to get him to talk about it. Stroked his back. Cooked him comfort foods. Didn't protest his wanting to spend nights alone at his condo when he said he needed space. And, instead, *he* had crawled inside of himself. If his own parents couldn't make it, who could? Eventually, undoubtedly, he would lose her.

Greg crossed the police station parking lot to his car, opened the driver's side door to a wave of heat. The July sunshine had become trapped inside, like a greenhouse, despite the fact that he'd left one window open a crack. Now the water bottles for all the searchers would be warm. Useless.

Tip #49
July 9, 2002
*Last week, I went to a baby shower for my cousin
in Scenic Acres and I parked my car on the street
and when I came out from the party my car had been
ransacked and a bunch of my stuff taken, like my CDs
and all the coins in my dashboard! I swear to God
I locked it. I made a police report at the time. It
was June thirtieth, I remember exactly because it
was my brother's birthday. And Scenic Acres is the
same neighbourhood as where that girl went missing.
Maybe it was a botched robbery or something, it
could be connected. You should come dust my car for
prints.*

ABBY

SO WHAT? I HAD UNPROTECTED SEX IN HIGH SCHOOL WITH a guy who had a girlfriend. And one time, I drove home from a house party after having four shots of Sour Puss. And before Cam, Jessica met this older guy in a chat room, and he messaged her to meet up, and she didn't want to go alone, so we got together with him and his friend at Boston Pizza and then went for a walk with them in the off-leash area in Fish Creek Park. Jessica made out with one of the guys, and they could have totally murdered us right there if they'd wanted to—just thrown our bodies into the creek or whatever. Last summer, I agreed to film myself having sex, and I never told anyone about it, not even Jess. And I tried E once. I remember only part of that night and it involved chugging several litres of blue Kool-Aid. I didn't tell you any of this, for obvious reasons.

But I also didn't tell you that I saw a condom wrapper in your bathroom trash only a few weeks before you went missing. You got all lecturey about the fact that I slept with Cam after we broke up, about how I needed to make better decisions. About how in just a few months I would have a baby to think about. You called me "selfish."

I could've had an abortion when Dad suggested it. I swear, as soon as I told him I was pregnant, his hand hovered towards his back pocket, reaching for his wallet. Money fixes everything, right? Would it have been a better decision to spread my legs and let them suck the baby out of me? To just make it all go away?

And why the condom wrapper, Tash? Wasn't it against the rules to sleep with an ex? So much for your clean break with Greg. Did you hook up when I was at a doctor's appointment or something? When I was asleep? How much of everything else you told me was bullshit? How many other secrets were you keeping? Protecting me from things you didn't think I could handle. Things I'm not supposed to know.

You went running sometimes before a shift, at like, four a.m. Running in the middle of the goddamned night, without even taking your phone. Why not just buy a treadmill? You always said you liked running outside, the fresh air, the ability to take a different route but still end up at the same place—home—every time.

Except this time.

Only one detective came that night. He looked bored, like you were just going to show up any minute and this would all be a waste of his time. He told the female officer—a street cop, who showed up first—to go, which seemed to piss her off. I guess he thought he was a bigwig. I was thinking, *don't leave! I need all of you.* All the cops were probably clustered downtown by the bars outside of the Stampede grounds. Last summer, Jessica and I snuck into Cowboys nightclub and watched a guy in a Jack Daniel's T-shirt knock a guy with leather chaps to the ground and stomp on his stomach with the metal heel of his boots.

You only have one life, Abby, you'd said. *You have to take things seriously. I know it doesn't seem like it, but you do. Especially now.*

One detective, Tash. That's all you got.

GREG

CHRISTMAS, SEVEN MONTHS BEFORE THEY BROKE UP, Greg woke up squashed next to Natasha in the double bed in his parents' guest room, before dawn, from a dream of wandering barefoot in a field of snow. Natasha slept on, having pulled all the sheets and the quilt to her side, sprawled with one arm up over her head, dark eyelashes fluttering. Natasha always slept on the right side, Greg on the left. Greg slid out of bed, pulled on his thin plaid robe, and went downstairs to the kitchen.

The first time she'd slept over, when Natasha fell asleep, he'd just stared at her, at the pale, naked curve of her shoulder, her slightly parted lips, her vertebrae like a string of pearls, and thanked God for his parents being out of town. He'd gotten up and wandered into the kitchen for milk. His parents called semi-skimmed milk a symbol of the many conciliations they'd made in marriage: prior to the wedding, his mother had preferred skim milk, his father whole. "When we got married, I gained five pounds," his mother joked. "And I lost five!" his father inevitably added. Why couldn't they have just bought both kinds? His new girlfriend asleep upstairs, teenaged Greg had microwaved a cup of compromise. His mother used to give him a bottle of milk to lie down with to put him back to sleep as a child, a habit he'd later learned from Natasha contributed to inner ear infections and cavities. Somehow, Greg had managed to escape childhood without either of these problems.

"There you are," Natasha had said, the night of the first sleepover, emerging in the kitchen, wrapped in Greg's duvet, her hair tousled and hanging in her eyes, one bare shoulder deliciously exposed.

"Couldn't sleep," Greg said, smiling. "You're dating an insomniac."

She shuffled over, barefoot, the duvet dragging along the floor. "I got cold up there, all alone, without you."

"My parents are coming back tomorrow," he teased, wrapping his arms around both her and the duvet. "Don't get too used to this."

Early that last Christmas morning, though, the only milk in the fridge had passed its expiry date. Greg sniffed the contents before emptying it into the sink. He filled a glass with lukewarm tap water and perched on the edge of the counter, waiting. Waiting for what? How many years since Natasha had woken up, discovered Greg had wandered off, and gotten up herself to find him and bring him back?

Earlier in the day, Greg's mother had made some joke about the possibility that Natasha might *finally* get a ring for Christmas and Greg had scoffed, "Christmas is such an obvious time to propose." He'd put his arm around Natasha's shoulders, but she stiffened.

"Your father proposed to me at Christmas," said his mother.

He took another sip of water. Swallowed. His parents' fridge hummed, its stainless steel face bare of the photos and magnets and grade school art of the old white one they'd had during his childhood. Greg could vaguely see the Christmas tree in the living room from his roost, but his mother had unplugged it before they'd all gone to bed and the lively rainbow lights lay dormant in the dark. A fake tree, garish polyvinyl chloride, so unlike the beautiful pinophyte it was supposed to represent. Pinophyta, or coniferous—cone-bearing seed plants, able to keep their leaves year-round.

He and Natasha had celebrated Christmas Eve earlier in the day with Natasha's dad and stepmom and her sisters, and then made the cross-city drive to Greg's parents' house separately so they'd each have their cars in the morning. Greg followed Natasha until she zipped through a yellow light and left him behind as it turned red. He rubbed his hands together while he waited. The hot air in his crapmobile took forever to get going. The light turned green. He'd lost her. He'd have to catch up to her later, at the house.

Every Christmas, they did the back-and-forth. Natasha had what Greg's mother referred to as a "blended" family, which made Greg think of Natasha and her dad and stepmom Kathleen and stepsister and half-sister and whoever her sisters' temporary boyfriends happened to be all thrown together in a blender, slamming up against each other until the blender tore them all up. Every holiday someone started a fight, usually Abby. Then Natasha would get quiet and say "nothing," when Greg asked what was wrong, but he assumed then that she'd started thinking about her mother, who'd bailed on the family after she found out that Natasha's father had gotten Kathleen pregnant. Still, Natasha idolized her mother.

By the time they'd made it to Greg's parents' house, it was late, almost time for bed, but not late enough that his mother couldn't spoil things by making that ring comment. Greg didn't *feel* ready to get married. So what? He wasn't even thirty, hadn't even finished his Ph.D. Most of his friends and colleagues were unmarried. People could have kids into their forties—why rush?

Natasha went up to the guest bedroom, formerly Greg's bedroom. Greg's mother went to floss her teeth. Greg's father went to the den to watch a cbc documentary. Greg didn't feel tired, but he had a headache, and his headaches often preceded a bout of insomnia. None of the medications Natasha had suggested—Advil, Sleep-Eze, magnesium, valerian—made any difference. He'd simply been an insomniac since childhood, woken by vivid, erratic dreams of his parents dying in a roller coaster accident, of having to perform an '80s fitness routine at a school assembly, of having his legs cut off and having octopus legs attached. And so on.

In the bed, Natasha had stripped down to her underwear and a thin T-shirt. She always got cold in the night and stole the blankets, so why not sleep in sweatpants? Not that he minded, really. That night, she'd crawled into bed without waiting for him, without saying anything. Probably thinking about her mom, still. He slid in behind her and snuggled up to her to keep her warm. Kissed her on the back of her head.

"You're never going to marry me," she said, then. A statement, not a question.

Hours later, wide awake, Greg finished his water. She wasn't coming down. Merry fucking Christmas.

ABBY

YOUR HIGH SCHOOL PROM FELL ON THE SAME NIGHT AS MY sixth birthday and your party dress looked prettier than mine. I threw a tantrum and my mom made me sit on the naughty step during my own party. I just wanted to be exactly like you.

When you hauled your dress out of storage a couple of months ago, you thought it would cheer me up—big sis parading around in her '90s ball gown because little sis was seven months pregnant and refusing to go to her own prom. But I still loved that dress. Blue satin, sweetheart neckline, black lace cross-stitched over the bodice, off-the-shoulder puffy sleeves, crinoline-lined skirt. You still fit into it, eleven years later. You'd even lost weight, toned up since joining the campus cross-country team during your nursing degree. Who *loses* weight instead of gaining the freshman fifteen? You.

By the time I made it to the twelfth grade, vintage was totally in. Had '90s fashion been making a comeback, I could have worn the dress I'd longed for at age six. Except I'd have had to a) not be pregnant *and* b) undertaken one of my mother's celery-juice cleanses to have fit into it.

I can just hear you now: *Calculate your* BMI, *you're totally within normal ranges for your height. You have to stop comparing yourself to magazine covers. Those pictures are airbrushed and unrealistic.* So fine, I'll stop bitching about being fat, except for one more thing: having this baby has totally wrecked my body. Don't even get me started on my stretch marks. They look like the skin graft photos in that presentation you made for a staff lunch-and-learn and made me sit through three times while you practiced. I promise, I will keep pot handles turned inwards on the stove, I will unplug curling irons, I will never go to sleep with an electric heating pad, and I will check that my fire extinguisher is functional on a regular basis by turning it upside down and hitting the bottom with the heel of my hand to make sure the chemical debris hasn't formed clumps. See, I did listen to some of things you told me.

I never really got to thank you for surprising me the night of my prom the way you did, booking us a girls' night at the swanky Fairmont Banff Springs Hotel and indulging me with a dinner of caramel cheesecake and virgin margaritas. *Virgin* margaritas for the pregnant chick. Cue dry laughter. I never really got to thank you because my Cam-loves-Jessica-and-I'm-fat-and-knocked-up funk had shaded my whole world. Can I trade what I feel now for that? Please? Because this feels like a flesh-eating virus.

I woke up the night of my prom to pee—so much for ever getting sleep again—and saw your dress hanging over the back of the desk chair. On my way back from the bathroom, I rubbed my hand over the soft blue satin, the texture of the lace across the bust. You'd hauled that dress all the way to Banff to make me laugh. You put on the dress and we sipped Earl Grey and clinked our tea cups with our pinkies in the air. Cheers to my finishing the twelfth grade. If the baby had been due any earlier, I might not have made it. *You're so smart,* you used to tell me, *don't underestimate yourself.*

Cam and Jess had probably moved on to the prom after-party. When Jess found out Cam had cheated on her with me, they broke up—for like, a week. Did she even have the right to get mad at him? I mean, honestly, he cheated on *me* with *her* first. Technically, Jess was the tit and I was just the tat.

The first day that everybody at school knew I was pregnant, I overheard two girls talking about me while I was inside one of the bathroom stalls. "How stupid do you have to be?" one said. "Like, how hard is it to just use a condom?" And then, the other, "I heard she did it on purpose." The first, again, "Cam definitely traded up." My skull felt as though it had filled with warm fluid. My hands shook. I raised my fingers to the pink metal bathroom stall, touched the black permanent marker letters, YOU ARE A PENIS.

That night at the Banff Springs, the night my prom went on without me, you sat up in bed, maybe woken up by my walking around, or the toilet flushing, or the zipper unzipping, or the fact that the AC in the hotel made it feel like sleeping inside of a refrigerator, even with the baby as my built-in heater.

"You okay?" you asked, and yawned, which made me yawn.

I sat down beside you on the edge of your bed. I used to crawl into bed with you right up until that summer after your prom when you moved out and my mother turned your bedroom into an all-white guest room. White kind of begs a six-year-old to make a mess, doesn't it? Anyway, I sat down beside you on the bed, and the baby kicked, and for a second we could both see the wave of it moving, through my thin white T-shirt. You placed a hand against the bulge.

"Just cold," I said.

"Use one of the hotel robes," you suggested, which I hadn't even thought of. If only all problems could be solved so easily.

Tip #57
July 10, 2002
Uh, yeah, that girl who gone missing, I saw the flier saying to call to report like, suspicious activity and stuff, and there's been a grey pickup, well, bluish-grey, maybe. It's parked illegally beside the fire hydrant on my street for three days.

ABBY

WHEN I WAS A KID, YOU USED TO SAY, "DON'T TOUCH MY stuff!" Poor Natasha, former only child, suddenly having to deal with a stepsister and a half-sister taking your belongings without permission. Remember the time Kayla "borrowed" your denim jacket, then forgot her house key, and when she rang the doorbell after school, she found you on the other side? Priceless.

When I borrowed your stuff, even *with* permission, I somehow always ended up breaking them, losing them, staining them. Honestly, I don't know why you kept trusting me with your stuff, especially not after I came back from my high school Christmas dance minus one of your Tiffany pearl earrings. I'd just found out I was pregnant, but no one could tell yet, and I'd wanted to show up looking hotter and classier and more confident than Jessica.

The night you went running and didn't come back, the detective tried to get me to call Dad. I dialled, but then I just held the phone out, and I could hear Dad answer, saying, "Natasha? Natasha? Hello?"

Greg got to the house first, then my parents. Dad's black dress pants and blue pinstripe shirt looked wrinkled, as though he'd grabbed some clothes from the hamper and fumbled his way into them after Reuben's call. He'd pushed his sleeves up, and his arms looked bare without his thick gold watch.

And my mother—have you ever seen my mother without makeup? Even when she had her gallbladder removed, I visited her in the hospital and I swear she had on black eyeliner. But she showed up early morning July seventh looking blurry and incomplete, her hair spun on top of her head in a sloppy bun, a black cardigan hanging open over a white T-shirt under which a dark bra was visible. Her hair was blonder than I remembered. Police calling equals real emergency. Come-over-quick-or-you'll-look-like-an-evil-stepmother emergency. I could just see the relief wafting off of her, like, thank god it was *you* who disappeared, not me, and certainly not Kayla. Where was Kayla, by the way? I figured my mother would've called her on the drive over. Did Kayla not think you were important enough?

My back ached. I put my hand out to brace myself on a chair. Standing in your kitchen, Mom kept staring at my belly. I hadn't seen Mom or Dad since I told them I was going to keep the baby. You talked to them more than I did, Tash. And I know you wanted me to make up with them, especially after I crossed the three-month mark and abortion was no longer an option. But screw them, *they* rejected me. I didn't want to listen to any of their *we're disappointed in you, but we'll make it work* bullshit.

"Where did she go?" Dad demanded, pacing the length of the kitchen. "You *saw* her leave, Abby!"

"She went for a run! She didn't tell me exactly where." Why wasn't I crying? Why wasn't anybody crying? Greg, sitting at the kitchen table talking to Reuben, looked like a mannequin. What was Greg telling the cop about you? If Dad would just shut up for one second, I could—

"You should have asked her!" Dad said. He slammed his fist down on the counter.

That made the detective and Greg both get up. Greg pulled a chair out from the table, put a hand on my shoulder, and guided me to sitting, but he didn't say anything. I wanted him to tell my dad to shut his mouth. Tell him I didn't do anything wrong. Tell him you would be back any second.

Reuben pulled up a chair in front of me and sat backwards in it, folded his arms over the top of the back rest, leaned in so that his stubbled chin was close to mine. "What about earlier in the day, did anything seem off? Was she acting different at all?"

"No," I said. "I don't—I didn't notice anything…"

Dad's expression reminded me of being spanked as a child. "Think, Abby!" he bellowed. "Detective, we're losing time, here."

"What about the hospitals?" my mother interjected. "Did you call all the hospitals?"

"I've got my guys down at the station checking all of that, Ma'am," he said.

"Kathleen, please!" As though the word *Ma'am* made her sound older than she was. Too bad for you, *Kathleen*, I thought. You're about to become a grandmother.

"Mr. Bell, Mrs. Bell—Kathleen—these situations are undeniably stressful, but if you could please just stay as calm as possible, for now." Reuben turned back to me. "Let's take this one step at a time. What did she do when she got up in the morning?"

It felt like rats were gnawing at my brain. "She was up before me. I got up to pee..."

"What time was that?"

"I don't remember. She was getting ready for work. Maybe seven? I think her shift started at eight, so...she made me breakfast." Oatmeal, blueberries, turkey bacon. You were scrubbing the pan when I came downstairs. You said good morning. I'm sure I grumbled something. You made me breakfast and for some reason I was still cranky. I didn't say thank you. I didn't give you a hug. I plucked a piece of the bacon off the plate with my fingers and ate it. I didn't even use a fork.

"And then..." What if I mixed up the details? "She said goodbye, she left for work. I went back to bed."

Reuben nodded. "Did you talk to her at all during the day?"

"Not until she got home."

"What time was that?"

"...Eight-thirty? She usually works a twelve-hour shift, so...she wasn't home for very long. She was making dinner. Then she changed into workout clothes." You'd said hello to the baby, running your hands along my belly. The baby kicked for you. The baby always kicked for you.

I stood, pushed my chair back. Standing all at once, I felt dizzy. The world looked black for just a second, and then everyone came back into focus, all around me. Mom, Dad, Greg, Reuben. A phone rang, but not the house phone.

Mom lunged for her purse. "Kayla? Oh honey, I'm so glad to hear your voice!"

Reuben turned to Dad. "Okay. Mr. Bell, I want you to get started on this list, calling these people, and I'm going to give a ring to my buddies at the station, check in. It's only been a couple of hours, okay? We'll get this sorted out."

I went upstairs and stood in your bedroom but I didn't *want* to touch your stuff—the lavender lace bra hanging from your doorknob, the hardcover book with cracked spine face down on your bedside table; the laundry basket at the foot of the bed stacked with folded white towels; the empty contact lens case still partially filled with solution; the plastic grocery bag with unopened twelve-pack of toilet paper bulging out the top; a pair of shiny red heels in the corner by the closet, your desktop computer, screen dark, powered down; a scrawled note on your desk, lined paper torn from something, edge ragged, *Dentist 26th 10:30.* The detective would want to see this. That's proof, right there. You intended to come back. You didn't leave me on purpose.

How much time has passed, now? Two nights? Three? My mother has set up a temporary bed for herself on your living room couch, meaning I've had to go back to sleeping in my own room. She doesn't know I can't get comfortable anywhere other than that couch. She doesn't know that my tailbone aches every time I go up and down the stairs. And now she's phoning my doctors and insisting I take strange rainbow-coloured pills shaped like footballs. She forced me to try one, and I gagged on it, felt it stick in my throat. I'm pretty sure *you* know better than her about what vitamins I should be taking. I don't give a shit what my mother's naturopath says. I've never seen my mother sleep on a couch in my whole life. I think she brought her own thousand thread count sheets. And she ambushed me with a hug yesterday, her skeleton arms trapping me, while I just stood there, waiting for it to be over.

I want to go into your room, crawl into your bed like I did when I was little and had a nightmare or Mom and Dad were fighting. You'd rubbed my back, alternating between knuckles, fingers, and the heel of your hand. No matter how much I want to go into your room, I feel like now, I can't touch your stuff. Not *stuff* anymore—evidence. That bra hanging from your door? Not just a bra anymore, but something you touched, something that touched you, something that held your scent, tiny flakes of your skin, invisible traces of your DNA. The cops took your computer. The note you scrawled. The stack of bills on the kitchen counter. Your day-planner. The hard drive from your computer. Your camera. Did any of it tell them anything?

I asked the detective if I could have the mixed CDs from your car. You joked that you would play Queen's "Under Pressure" from your 1981 mix while I delivered. "How about Salt-N-Pepa?" I suggested. "Push It." 1987.

You were supposed to take me to the hospital. We toured the hospital, talked ahead of time about my options, my birth plan. Like me getting an epidural, ASAP. Maybe I should have let you talk me into prenatal classes, but come on, picture me, lying on the floor with my legs spread apart, huffing and puffing and trying to ignore the stares and judgment from the thirty-something mothers with their polo-wearing husbands and their educations and baby registries? It should be *you* having this baby. I know that's what you really want. So let's trade. You come back and I'll disappear.

With my mom on the couch downstairs, I shift in my bed, trying to find a position to ease the pressure, knocking the cordless phone and a glass of water off my bedside table in the process. The glass hits the wall, spilling its contents. A dark stain spreads along the carpet. If I leave it alone, it will dry and disappear, like it never existed. I keep the cordless phone with me at all times, now. Because what if the detective calls? What if *you* call? I take it with me into the bathroom, turn up the volume, just in case.

When I lean and reach to pick up the glass, pain shoots through my lower back, my right kidney. The glass has a fine crack running along the side, but hasn't shattered. I press at the crack until the glass splinters, revealing a long shard extending to a jagged point. I hold the shard between my thumb and forefinger.

"What CDs?" Reuben had said. He didn't ask to look in your car that first night—that first morning, technically. At that point, he insisted you would come back. Insisted that missing people get found, like I shouldn't even worry, like you just needed a break, like you'd just come back, apologetic, when you'd had some time to yourself. I wanted to gag, sitting at the table with him, the kitchen stinking of overcooked beef stew.

"I didn't see any CDs in the car," he said, when he finally went out into the garage and looked again for me, because he hadn't cleared it for me to go in there myself yet. When he came back, he pulled off his blue latex gloves the same way you taught me, by pinching the palm of one hand with the thumb and forefinger of the other hand and pulling the gloves inside out. He said he found "nothing meaningful to the investigation."

I hold the glass fragment with its jagged edge down. Run the sharp point against the inside of my wrist, softly along the skin, again, again. You are gone. You are gone. You are gone. More pressure now. My joints are swollen, my fingers ripened, my ankles inflamed. You are gone, you are gone. Everything hurts. I press harder. This is where people take a radial pulse, you taught me. Don't take it with the thumb, because the thumb has its own pulse. You can feel someone's heartbeat through their thumb. I press harder. Make the first slice. Blood wells in a line. The line burns. It hurts less than I thought.

I need this baby out.

JOSIE

Ms. McKinnon—what can I do for you?

It's Mrs. McKinnon…Maybe I should have called first, but…I have questions about the investigation. I'm organizing all these search parties, and the police aren't telling me anything.

Have a seat, okay? You want coffee? Tea?

No thank you—I don't need a drink, I just need to know, like, why aren't you doing anything? Following leads? Do you have any suspects?

You know we can't really give out details about an active investigation. That's protocol. But, to be honest, we don't have a lot to go on, here. We haven't located any evidence that would point us in any specific direction. Until more evidence surfaces…

What do you mean, surfaces? Do you just expect it to show up by itself? You have to look for it! That's why I'm conducting all these searches and organizing prayer circles!

We've conducted a thorough investigation with the information we have. I know you're frustrated—

Of course I'm frustrated! She's my best friend! She's out there, somewhere. She has to be. Can't you just interview more people? What about her computer? My brother said he could help you with accessing her files, going through her emails—

We have techs down here at the station doing all of that. So far, we haven't found anything relevant.

There has to be something.

Come on, we've been through this. I mean, if you have more information for me, if there's something you've uncovered, or if you think of something—anything—that could be relevant to the investigation, I'm happy to talk to you about that. But we can't just expend a bunch of resources and taxpayers' dollars when there's no evidence. You knew her. Be honest with me, is there any chance she picked up and left voluntarily?

No.

No?

That's why you're not investigating? Because you think she left on purpose? Without telling any of us, making everybody worry like this? No way.

It's a possibility we have to consider. A lot of things were stressing her out.

Is this about the breakup?

Among other things. The baby—

Look, everything stressful in her life would have blown over. Everybody's life is stressful. You don't know Natasha. She wouldn't have just left. And, anyway, she was the one who broke up with him! If anyone had any reason to be heartbroken, it was Greg, not Natasha!

Was he?

Was he what?

Heartbroken?

Well, yeah, I mean, right after the breakup, he called her all the time, he wanted to get back together—

And she didn't?

She did, but what was she supposed to do? He wasn't ready to marry her.

Like, how long did he need, really? If he really loved her, he would want to marry her, especially after how long they'd been together! What kind of person doesn't want that? My husband and I only knew each other for a couple of months when he proposed. When you know, you know. I just don't get why he didn't want to spend the rest of his life with her. She wasn't going to wait forever. She had a house, she had a good job...do you think he had something to do with it?

Hey, now, I didn't say that.

But you keep interviewing him! How many times has he been down to the station now, five? And besides, that's what everybody thinks.

Who's everybody?

My parents, my husband, my brother, people who post on the message board. Even her family—except Abby. But Abby's always loved Greg, I mean, like a big brother. Abby would never think...but if you think Greg had something to do with it—

I didn't say that. I wanted to know what you thought. You know her, you know the dynamics best, right?

Of course. I'm her best friend. We're practically sisters.

Tell me this, that last couple months, or weeks even, was anything different? To do with her and Greg, or even nothing to do with Greg. Anything—even if you don't think it's significant. Was she having any conflict with anyone else?

ABBY

IN THE END, THERE WAS NO WATER BREAKING, NO SUDDEN onset of cramps in the night, no mucous plug in the toilet, no Braxton Hicks. None of the things you told me to watch out for. Just the progressive tightening of a blood pressure cuff around my bicep, extra proteins in my urine.

You would have noticed the symptoms, picked up on the subtle differences between a normal pregnancy and pre-eclampsia before my blood pressure spiked. You would have told me I had to keep eating even when I didn't feel like it, you would have brought me yogurt and stirred it for me because you know I hate the fruit on the bottom. Remember after Cam dumped me for Jessica and you made taco casserole but then forgot to set the timer, and I ranted for so long by the time we remembered, the noodles had hardened into concrete slabs? A hot mess, literally.

You would have asked me more about my headaches, given me a scalp massage. You would have noticed the puffy fingers, the water retention. You would have reminded me about my doctor's appointment instead of letting me sleep through it, caught in a dream where you went for your run, and I followed you, chased you down the street. You ran too fast, I couldn't catch you. The baby was in the way. I couldn't breathe, my lungs burned, *wait! Wait for me!* You didn't even see me. I couldn't catch you. I couldn't stop you. And then I woke up, and just barely got myself to the bathroom before I threw up.

My mother showed up behind me, bent down on her knees and put her hands on my shoulders. I puked again, into the filthy toilet basin and up along the sides. There was vomit in my hair. My mom lifted the strands away from my neck. "Oh, Abby, my Abby." *Stop touching me!* "We're going to the hospital now." *No! I'm not going anywhere with you! Leave me alone!*

By the time they got me up on the exam table, it was too late, too late for prevention, for bedrest, for monitoring. The baby's heart rate dropped. They had to put me under, but I could still feel the first slice. I could see my mother's wide blue eyes over the blue hospital mask that covered her nose and mouth. *Why did you do this to me, Tash? Why did you leave me? I can't do this without you!*

"We're going to do this fast," said the anesthesiologist. "When you wake up, you're going to have a baby." The numbness came, like a high.

A niece. You knew. You *knew* you knew.

Summer Natasha Bell. July 13, 2002. Three-and-a-half weeks early. Emergency C-section. Five pounds, two ounces.

I woke up, and she was here.

Just like when I woke up, and you were gone.

Tip #94
July 14, 2002
Um, I'm calling about that missing girl from
Calgary? I work at a gas station in Kathyrn, I think
that girl came in here. She was driving a black
vehicle—I didn't catch the licence plate. She came
in, bought some snacks. Paid in cash. She had um,
jeans and a hoodie, I think. Don't remember the
colour. I only recognized her after I saw the news
later. [...] Yeah, she was alone. [...] No, we don't
have surveillance. I mean, we have cameras around,
so people don't steal stuff, but they don't actually
work. Real cameras are expensive.

REUBEN

REUBEN GOT THE PHOTOS FROM THE VIC'S CAMERA DEVELOPED prior to heading out, but hasn't looked at them yet. The station said it had a backlog; he could have taken the prints somewhere like Walmart and had a quicker turnaround, but with all the publicity, he didn't want to risk someone making an extra copy and selling them to the media or something. Now, parked out back of the vic's ex-boyfriend's condo in an unmarked car, in full view of the parking garage and the back stairwell exit, Reuben flips on his overhead light and takes the photos out of the package.

Several photos feature the vic's sister. A silly one with her sticking her tongue out for the camera, her belly significantly smaller than Reuben recalls. These must stretch over a few months, at least. A few at a doctor's appointment, lil sis on an exam table—an ultrasound, probably. Further back, there are shots of the vic's sister's birthday, the sister seated at the kitchen table blowing out the candles on a slightly lopsided chocolate iced cake. Reuben bets the vic made the birthday cake herself. He's gotten to know her so well through all the interviews—she's the type to put in the effort and make something homemade. A few more pics of the vic in running gear, shorts and a T-shirt, a white paper bib with the number 603 printed on the front, a 10k medal around her neck. Judging by the weather, probably taken in the last few months.

Reuben's always got a guy tracking the ex-boyfriend, the likely perp, during searches, too. Sometimes a perp—usually a husband or a boyfriend—will deliberately lead searchers to a body, making it look like he stumbled across it by accident. That way, the body gets found, the perp can go from anxious spouse to grieving widower, bury the body (and hence, the evidence), and move forward with their new life. Done and done.

Reuben closes his eyes for a second. His head throbs. It would have been a hell of a lot easier had there been video surveillance in the perp's apartment. According to the property manager, cameras were installed in the elevators, lobby, and the parking garage, but not on the apartment floors. When Reuben interviewed the neighbours, none claimed to have heard or seen anything. Reuben had easily found a pathway in and out of the building via stairwells and a back exit that wouldn't be captured on video. So much for security.

He found the back exit propped open with a rock, surrounded by a scattering of cigarette butts of different types. A couple neighbours whose complexes, like the perp's, didn't have balconies, confirmed that they went out back to smoke, and that they often used rocks to prop open the door so they could come back in without having to go around front and use their keys. The perp didn't smoke, as far as Reuben knew. Reuben briefly thought about having the rock sent for fingerprinting. Maybe his perp's prints would show up, proving he'd touched it recently, perhaps during an escape and re-entry the night of July sixth, during which he claimed to be inside his condo, sick. But that would never work. Even if he got prints off the rock, all it would prove was that the perp had touched it at some point, not when. Same with the back door handle. The evidence would never hold up.

Reuben can only supervise the one door, and physical surveillance keeps him away from the office. He brought paperwork so he could do both at the same time; and he hasn't been completely honest with his boss about staking out the condo complex either. The perp parks underground, which means that, if he exits the building out the front door, it'll be on foot. Out back, he could exit on foot or in his vehicle. Reuben has a hunch that the guy might be trying to cover his tracks. Perps do this sometimes; revisit a scene once an investigation is underway, to hide or dispose of evidence. Reuben can't miss his window—bad guys who clean up after themselves usually do it early on.

Someone exits the condo complex back door, leans against the wall, lights up. Reuben puts the photos face down on the empty passenger seat and squints at the figure amid the exhaled puff of grey smoke. Female.

He's had his guys at the station go through the guy's garbage already and inventory everything. Note anything that even looked remotely like blood. Any cleaning supplies, sponges, or paper towels. He has the list of the guy's trash in his file with him right now. Bathroom garbage: used Kleenex, sock with hole in it, empty pill packets (NyQuil), floss, used razor, crusty toothpaste tube. Kitchen garbage: Ramen noodle packages, two rotting apples, balled up paper towels smeared with ambiguous fluid, mouldy block of cheddar cheese. The guy also recycles—go figure, earth nerd. That bin contained a few empty cans of Coke, some unopened junk mail flyers, a condo notice about the water being turned off, a partially rinsed plastic yogurt container. Vanilla.

How long has he been sitting here now? Reuben turns on the car engine to check the time on the dash. Almost two hours. Fuck. Seven cars have either entered or exited, but not the perp's. He could just leave. But then he will have wasted his time, and he'll feel stupid.

Ninety minutes later, six cars out, two in, and yes! He's got it! Perp's Chevy, headed east. Reuben starts the car, his heartbeat galloping as he follows the car onto a main street and the speedometer picks up.

Asshole! Reuben thinks, as a red Mazda cuts him off at a merge and he winds up a few cars behind the perp. If he'd had his car and siren, this wouldn't have happened, but then, he can't follow a suspect in a squad car. Eventually he speeds up and gets in front of the Mazda and lines up beside the perp, then lags back a little in case the guy recognizes him. Reuben is wearing a cap and sunglasses, but he's still gotta be careful. This perp is Ph.D. educated, seems to know how to cover his tracks well.

Papers slide from the passenger seat to the floor as first the perp, then Reuben, make a right turn. There go the photos, the vic's bank statements, pages of her cellphone and landline bills, and the highlighters Reuben's been using to make notes. Since the vic left her cellphone at home, they couldn't ping it for location. No activity on the credit card or debit card, no weird withdrawals over the last several months, either.

Buddy takes Glenmore to Fourteenth, heads south. None of the searches so far have focused on the south. Vic and sis live North West. Reuben squints and studies the top of the perp's head, the little he can see over the headrest. Take me to her, he thinks. Just take me right to her.

Perp takes the last exit off Fourteenth onto MacLeod Trail and then changes lanes into the far left, turns on Sun Valley Boulevard, and enters a residential area. Where's he going? When they'd entered the South East, Reuben had assumed they'd end up somewhere rural, remote. And yet—

Reuben slows and tails the perp through a playground zone. Asshole drives at least ten over all the way through; Reuben could totally pull him over, but then he'd lose the destination. The guy finally stops at a white house with greyish trim. Whose house is this? Maybe he had an accomplice? He could have hired a hit man to do his dirty work. Reuben continues down the street a little bit, parks where it is less likely he will be noticed. But he wants to see who answers the door when the perp rings the bell. Reuben squints and tries to make out the house number.

A pudgy older woman comes to the door and embraces the suspect.

Reuben groans audibly inside his vehicle. He doesn't have to plug in the address to figure out he's just sat in front of the guy's condo for three hours and then followed him for half an hour across the city to his mommy's house.

Reuben reaches down and gathers the fallen papers from the floor, attempts to sort them back into piles. When he tries to put them back in the envelope, he realizes that a few of the photos had gotten stuck in the envelope the first time he removed them. He pulls out the two photos he hadn't seen the first time through, flips on the car's overhead light, and studies the shots.

There's a close-up of the vic, grinning at the camera. Who took this? Reuben wonders. Her sister? The vic looks awfully fancy, though. He studies the picture more closely under the light. A shiny earring dangles from one visible earlobe. A dangly earring suggests a night out. The person in the next shot, Reuben doesn't recognize, but he holds it for a long time. Is he missing something? No one mentioned a tall, dark-skinned man with close-cropped black hair and a collared shirt. The man looks Indian, possibly Eastern European. Attractive. There's something about the way he's tilting his head, his full smile. It's more natural than posed, like he's staring into the face of someone he loves. If these two photos were at the back, then they were probably the last shots taken. How did he miss them? Reuben thinks. And what else is he missing?

JOSIE

www.findnatashabell.com

The LORD himself goes before you and will be with you; he will never leave you nor forsake you. Do not be afraid; do not be discouraged. —Deuteronomy 31:8

Dear readers—

I implore you to PLEASE join us in the search for my best friend, Natasha Bell, who has now been missing for eight days. A search has been organized for tomorrow, July 15, beginning at 9:00 a.m., and we need all the volunteers we can get. For those of you who are unable to join us, please remain on the lookout for Natasha. Please distribute her photo and spread the word amongst family, friends, colleagues, and neighbours. We need to keep her name in the media until she is FOUND! I believe she is ALIVE! For those of you who never had a chance to meet Natasha, I wanted to tell you what an amazing woman she is. When we were kids, Natasha saved my brother's life. The three of us were playing in the ravine near my childhood home, when Jason, my twin brother, had his first seizure. Natasha stopped him from falling and hitting his head. I ran for help. Jason started throwing up, and Natasha put her fingers in his mouth and scooped out the vomit so that he wouldn't choke. When the ambulance got there, Natasha was holding his head in her lap and he was unconscious. If it hadn't been for Natasha, he could have died. After that, Natasha decided to become a nurse.

Natasha saved my brother's life, and the lives of countless others through her job. Now it is her turn to be SAVED! Hang in there, Natasha! The Lord is watching over you and your family and friends love you!

ABBY

YOU WOULD EASILY OUTSHINE ME IN THE MOTHERING category, Tash. You're the one who set up a high interest savings account for Summer before she was even born. You taught me about crib bumpers and SIDS, about the benefits of breast-feeding, the pros and cons of cord blood banking. You sat down with Cam and his parents and hammered out a child support agreement so we wouldn't have to go to court. You suggested I move in with you when my mom refused to speak to me unless I got an abortion. I mean, what's her problem? Everybody knows *she* got pregnant out of wedlock, too. Not before she graduated high school, but still.

Summer is the scrawny alien sucking my nipples raw; screaming until she can't breathe because she's too tired to fall asleep; vomiting cloudy white fluid over my shoulder; flinging her arms and legs out from her body when she startles; making that scrunchy, accusing stare that makes her look just like Cam; wriggling seal-slick in the bath, making me feel like I'm going to drop her.

But Summer is mine. And fuck anyone who tries to take her away from me.

One night, the week after she was born, I asked Dad if he would hold her, just hold her for half an hour so I could have a nap, because she screeched every time I tried to put her in the bassinet. I couldn't stay downstairs anymore with all the shit Josie set up in the living room, the maps of search locations with Xs all over them in fat yellow highlighter, hundreds of that same photo of you. Dad said, "Sure," and turned away from his computer for a moment, and reached his arms out, took her from me, and then stopped and gazed at her. Had he ever looked at me that way when I was a baby? He said, "Hi, there. Hi."

But when I woke up, I heard voices in the kitchen. My mom and Kayla.

I got closer, stood at the spot where the two walls met, where I could see them but they couldn't see me.

"I just think," Kayla said, "they should consider the possibility more. I mean, she has a number of risk factors."

I could only see the back of Kayla's head, that thick auburn bob, the ends curled under. Clearly she had time to sit and curl her hair before coming over to help look for her missing stepsister. Like mother, like daughter. Even without seeing her face, I could tell right away she was on one of her psychologist rants. Kayla keeps reminding us all that, in about a year, she'll officially be *Doctor* Kayla Shannon. Like she's better than the rest of us.

"What kind of red flags?" asked Mom, and I moved a little closer, pressed myself up against the wall.

"I just think ending her relationship probably triggered a lot of feelings of abandonment—you know, from her childhood, from her mother. I would have recommended she see a psychologist about it. CBT—cognitive behavioural therapy—with a trained professional, of course, would have helped. It has an empirical evidence base."

"Right," said Mom. I could see the right side of Mom's face and the back of her head, her thick, dyed blonde hair pulled into a chignon and held in place with a tortoiseshell claw clip. At her age, her hair probably would have looked better if she let it go back to its normal colour, auburn, like Kayla's. She lifted a mug off the table and sipped from it. The room smelled of coffee, like she and Kayla had come into your house, your kitchen, and made your coffee, and were just having a girl's coffee date, mother-and-daughter-bonding time.

"It's highly likely she met criteria for a mood disorder," Kayla continued. "Her mother had a history of mental illness, right?"

I'd heard comments like this before. "Laurel was extremely unstable," my mother said, with enthusiasm.

"A family history puts her at higher risk," Kayla said. "Plus, the burden of taking care of Abby and a newborn. I think Natasha was in way over her head and everything finally caught up with her."

Then I heard Summer make one of her fussy noises, like a bleating sheep. I moved closer and realized Kayla was the one holding her. Jostling her with one arm, without even looking down. Spread around them were pages and pages of your missing flier. A sideways cock of your head, a curtain of long dark hair, an emerald earring (probably from Greg) sparkling in your one visible ear, mouth partially open as if about to laugh. MISSING stamped across the top. Some of the posters looked faded, like someone's printer had run out of ink. Kayla was using one of the prints as a coaster.

My stomach tightened, like a cramp, like the cramps that came when I tried to nurse Summer in the days after she was born, before I gave up. Sometimes, when I give her a bottle, she sucks like she'll never get enough, like I'll never give her enough.

It's not often that I keep my mouth shut. But I just walked in, took my baby and got the hell out of there, left those two bitches sitting in the kitchen with their dumb guilty faces. I slammed the front door behind me, stood on the stoop, the July air too hot for my sweatshirt and pajama pants. Summer fussed and rooted into my chest. Flowers and teddy bears had accumulated on the sidewalk out front. A fluorescent yellow poster board read WE ARE PRAYING FOR YOU! in purple bubble letters. Praying for who? For Natasha, or for me? A brown teddy bear had tipped onto its back, and its glazed marble eyes stared at me, its upside down mouth in a pout. A car drove by, pulled into an open garage.

Barely dusk, the streetlights had already turned on, bright orbs, like a warning. Neither my mother nor Kayla followed me. What if *I* was running away? What if I laced up my sneakers and ran away from here? Would they look for me? Would Cam look for me? Would anyone look for me?

Then a car pulled up, and a man stepped out, a camera slung around his neck. "Hey, are you the sister of the missing girl? Is that your baby?"

Summer began to wail. Maybe wherever you are, you heard that cry.

REUBEN

DIGGING THROUGH THE VIC'S COMPUTER gives Reuben a headache, makes him want to pass the file over to Grainger. For like, half a
second. He can do this. He's *going* to do this. No matter how fucked
up this case is. The vic didn't reply to this email, but Reuben can
guess what she was thinking. With a family like this, there's no way
she really was as happy-go-lucky as everybody in his interviews keep
saying. Especially after he found the tiny bottle of Celexa under the
bathroom sink, way at the back under all the pipes instead of with the
other vitamins and supplements in the medicine cabinet behind the
mirror. Reuben remembers that first day, asking Abby whether the vic
was on any medications, Abby's vehement no. It's a low dose, but the
vic clearly didn't want little sis to know about her antidepressants. She
was probably keeping other things close to her chest, too.

Reuben re-reads the email.

From: Paul Bell
Subject: Friday
Date: 8 January 2002 5:14:18 AM MST
To: Natasha Bell

I hope you know how ashamed I am of you. Your sister is making terrible decisions and you're supporting them. How is she supposed to learn about real life if you always bail her out? She needs someone to tell her to smarten up, to apologize for the way she treated her mother at Christmas, apologize for ruining everybody's holiday. She needs to give this baby up for adoption, finish high school, and go to University like we always planned. Do you know how poorly this reflects on me? On Kathleen?

We didn't give her everything she could have ever asked for in life just so she could throw it all away. And frankly, I didn't give YOU everything you could have ever asked for in life to have you throw it back in my face, either. Don't come crying to me when you're trying to support a newborn and an out of control teenager. I'm done.

JOSIE

WHEN PAUL INVITED JOSIE AND SOLOMON TO COME FOR dinner on August sixth, Josie thought maybe it had something to do with the fact that it was her birthday. But no, Paul would not have remembered his daughter's friend's birthday even had Natasha not been missing. That, and she'd seen the Bells every day since Tash went running and never returned. Kathleen had ordered an obscene amount of food—lasagna, salad, garlic bread. The water in Josie's glass sparkled. Regular water was not fancy enough, apparently.

The sixth marked an entire month. *An entire month.*

There would be no birthday celebrations this year. Solomon said that celebrating birthdays was egotistical, anti-Christian. He didn't approve of Halloween either. From the third grade until the seventh grade, Josie and Natasha wore matching Halloween costumes: Wilma and Betty from *The Flinstones*, cowgirl and Tiger Lily, monkey and banana. Josie had fantasized about dressing up her own children and taking them Trick or Treating. She and Solomon had not yet conceived, even though they didn't use any contraception because Solomon felt like it was up to God how many children they would have. Josie turned down the glass of wine Paul offered her, even though it was her time of the month and it wouldn't have made a difference. Everybody else was drinking except her and Abby. Josie wanted very badly to hold Abby's new baby girl, but didn't feel right asking. When Abby was a child, she'd gone through a phase of carrying around a grimy Cabbage Patch doll, and if anyone tried to take it away from her, even to wash it, she'd scream like you'd lit her hair on fire.

Seated next to Josie at the Bell's large ovular dining table, Solomon took a large sip from his glass. If she weren't missing, Natasha would have deemed Solomon a party-pooper and would have surprised Josie with a fancy birthday dinner. She would have had the waitress deliver a slice of cake with a sparkler, told her *make a wish!* Natasha never revealed her birthday wishes, but always asked Josie to share hers. Had Natasha not been missing, they would have made up by now, Josie is certain. The two had never missed each other's birthdays since childhood. They unequivocally would have made up by now. Of course they would have.

Josie had phoned Natasha's direct supervisor at work and talked to her for an hour, trying to determine if she'd noticed anything during Natasha's shift that day. Had she tended to any patients that could have become obsessed with her? Angry with her? The nursing supervisor had patiently explained that she could not release information about hospital patients, but had tried to reassure Josie that she had no information she thought was relevant. They all missed Natasha, she said. Several of Natasha's co-workers had helped with the searches, and they had posters prominently displayed in the hospital common areas—cafeteria, nursing stations, waiting rooms, the gift shop. After this phone call, which had, in Josie's mind, yielded nothing, Detective Foley had called her and scolded her for interrogating people, telling her she didn't have the relevant training, that he had already spoken to Natasha's co-workers. "Do you want to mess up the investigation?" he'd challenged her.

There was no empty seat at the table left for Natasha, Josie noticed. In her family, they'd had designated seats. Josie would never have sat in Jay's seat or either of her parents' seats, or vice versa. Solomon passed Josie the crystal salad bowl and Josie plucked some crisp romaine and dropped it on her salad plate. At her place were a salad plate and a bread plate and a dinner plate and a salad fork and a dinner fork and a dessert fork. For the past month, Josie had eaten mostly granola bars, drank mostly black coffee and bottled water. Snacks from the volunteer table, donated in bulk by various grocery stores. Not that there wasn't food everywhere—in the first few days and weeks of Natasha's absence, it seemed like everyone—their church congregation, Natasha's co-workers, neighbours—had a casserole to drop off. Natasha's freezer filled to capacity. Josie had taken some of the excess home and slid them into her own freezer, feeling too guilty to throw them out. Even Josie's own parents had supplied some meals. But she didn't have any appetite. What would all the food solve? Eventually, it would just go bad.

Two days earlier, she'd reached into a child-sized bag of potato chips and discovered a chip folded over on itself with the edges touching. A wish chip, she and Tash had called these, in elementary school. They'd played rock, paper, scissors to determine who got to eat such chips and therefore claim the wishes. The day she'd found the wish chip, Josie had excused herself and locked herself in the community centre bathroom— they'd had to move the command centre out of Natasha's house because it wasn't large enough for the volume of searchers. She wouldn't cry. What good would that do? She closed her eyes, ate the chip in one bite, as per their childhood rule. Otherwise, her wish wouldn't come true.

At the dinner table, Josie slid the salad bowl to Kayla, Natasha's stepsister, and Kayla said, "Thanks," and then went back to a conversation she was having about how one of her bridesmaids had gained twelve pounds. Apparently it was a lot more difficult to take out a dress than to take in a dress. Josie wasn't sure who the conversation was actually with—Kayla seemed to be doing most of the talking. Josie's stomach felt too small for the thick slice of lasagna Kathleen had served her.

Had Solomon even remembered her birthday? Or was his lack of acknowledgement just a reflection of his overall stance on holidays? The first year of marriage was supposed to be the hardest. But they were almost through the first year, now, so things would probably get better. Solomon had helped since day one of Natasha's absence, rallied the parishioners of their church to join the search parties, to start prayer groups, to circulate fliers and emails with the address to her blog. The choir director's teenaged daughter had sung "Amazing Grace" a cappella to mark the opening of their last search, and the words repeated in Josie's head while she and Solomon made love that night. Josie hadn't wanted to—she had too many things to organize, she wanted to update the blog and she needed to call the station—but she made love to Solomon anyway, with "Amazing Grace" knocking around in her brain. *Through many dangers, toils, and snares, I have already come; 'Tis grace hath brought me safe thus far, And grace will lead me home.*

She needed to call the station to follow up about the house under construction down the street from Natasha's. She took a small bite, then another, while Kayla prattled on beside her. There would have been men there, workers, who could have observed Natasha and Abby, two young, vulnerable females, living alone. When Josie lived alone, before she was married, she carried a rape whistle and pepper spray. These men could have seen Natasha go running during the days or weeks leading up to her disappearance. An abandoned home would be the perfect site to hold someone against her will. Detective Foley had said that he'd looked into it, that they'd searched the property as well as a few other houses under construction in the vicinity, but they hadn't found any evidence. Still… Paul and Kathleen's residence was currently undergoing renovations. Coming out of the upstairs bathroom at one point over the last month, she'd bumped into a burly handyman stretching a measuring tape from floor to ceiling. She'd hurried downstairs, her heart racing, and called her brother, inhaling, exhaling, until she felt safe.

According to Detective Foley, K9 bloodhounds had been unable to detect anything further than the curb. Natasha's scent, Detective Foley had explained, would be more concentrated around the house and its immediate surroundings, and then become further degraded, especially given the storm. But had they had the dogs search the partially con- structed house near Natasha's? What if the dogs picked up her scent there, among the skeletal walls? If Natasha had been held there, against her will, at some point, could the dogs not tell? Would her smell not be all over the place, even after the storm? Natasha smelled like fruit and hand santizer. When Detective Foley finished with searches of Natasha's house, Josie had snuck up into her friend's master bathroom, unscrewed the top to a bottle of Natasha's raspberry shampoo, and inhaled. Even if she wasn't in the house under construction *now*, it didn't mean that she hadn't been at some point. She could have been transferred to a second location by the perpetrator or perpetrators.

Only a few bites into her dinner, Josie already felt bloated, but she didn't want to be rude by not finishing. She would eat and then try to find a good moment to talk to Paul—she hadn't had a chance earlier in the day, and she didn't want to bring it up now with Abby right there. When she'd first seen Abby after Natasha disappeared, Josie had questioned her at length, and so had Paul and Kathleen, Greg, and Detective Foley. But afterwards, Josie had felt guilty—Abby was so young, and in shock. Did Abby know about the argument between Josie and Natasha? Would Natasha have said something to her sister? Probably not, but Natasha had gone home that night so upset, maybe she'd vented to Abby about it. Then again, Josie doubted Natasha would have told Abby about Josie's suggestion of adoption for Abby's unborn child. Josie had seen Abby nearly every day for a month and Abby had not let on that she knew that Josie and Natasha had had a fight. No, fight was the wrong word. Argument. Or, maybe *spat*. Had Natasha not gone missing, they would have resolved things by now. Undoubtedly. They'd always resolved things in the past.

Josie felt so *angry* with Christ. Why would He take Natasha away from them? How was that part of His will? What good could possibly come from that? She wasn't supposed to feel angry at Christ, but she did. Or maybe what she was feeling was Christ's anger at her.

At the dinner table, when Kayla fell silent for a moment, Solomon put down his wine glass, and said, "I forgot, your mom dropped off a home video earlier today. She thought you'd want to see it."

Josie forced herself to swallow. "A home video?"

"Of you and Natasha as kids."

Her heart seized.

"Did you bring it?" Abby blurted.

Why hadn't Solomon mentioned it earlier, on their drive over? How could he forget something so important?

He took another swig of wine. "Yeah, it's in my bag."

Josie, Abby, and Paul immediately abandoned their dinner, and Josie retrieved the VHS tape from Solomon's canvas bag. She hunched in the corner of the sofa beside Abby. Abby hadn't let go of the baby throughout the entire meal, holding the sleeping infant in the crook of one arm, picking at her food with the other. Abby seemed to have lost all of her baby weight all at once. Josie would have to check on Abby more, make sure she was eating. Natasha would want that. Paul fiddled with the VCR. Up close, Josie could smell Summer's sweet powdery smell.

"I can hold her, if you want a break," she offered.

Abby shook her head emphatically. "I'm okay." She readjusted the sleeping infant, and Summer yawned, her tiny lips blooming for a brief moment.

And then the TV changed from static fuzz to the kitchen of the home Natasha had lived in as a child. Kids crowded around the table. Josie immediately spotted Natasha, in a pink party dress and a yellow paper crown, the kind pulled from a party cracker. Right beside Tash, she spotted herself, in a blue gingham party dress that matched Jason's blue plaid shirt. Her mother had always dressed the twins alike. A large birthday cake, iced fluffy pink with yellow candles, sat in front of Natasha. A few adults moved in and out of the shot, none of whom Josie recognized. Josie's mother's voice began singing "Happy Birthday;" it was probably her mother behind the camera, Josie inferred. A chorus of voices chimed in, and Josie watched her little girl self put her arm around little girl Natasha as Natasha puffed her cheeks and blew. Everyone cheered. Little Jason sang, "And many mooooore."

Then Natasha's mother stepped into the shot, her dark brown curls fluffed around her face, as was the style then. She kissed Natasha on top of her head before exiting the shot. Josie had so few memories of Natasha's biological mother. She hadn't thought about her in years.

Kathleen stood up and walked out of the room. Abby's eyes, fixed on the screen, looked enormous.

"How does it feel," Josie heard her own mother ask Natasha from behind the camera, "to be nine years old?"

Natasha looked straight into the camera, her moment in the spotlight. "It's the best day of my life!"

Then the screen went fuzzy for a second, cut to a scene of Josie and Jason at Pigeon Lake. Jason's fuzzy shape ran headlong into the water, and Josie, in a purple one-piece bathing suit, licked a strawberry ice cream cone. "Fast forward," Josie instructed. But there were no more shots of Natasha on the remainder of the tape.

When Josie and Solomon got home, Solomon took a long shower, and Josie sat on the foot of the bed, pulled at a loose thread on the marital quilt Solomon's mother had given them. Then she got up, logged into the computer, and checked her email. Jason had sent her a message with an attachment.

> Hey sis tried to call you earlier but I guess
> you were out
> just wanted to say happy birthday from me
> and Finn

When she clicked on the attachment, a picture opened slowly on the screen, loading one line at a time. Their Internet connection was so slow. Row by row, it finally revealed her twin brother's smiling face and the adorable grin of her nephew. Having just seen the home videos, she thought Finn looked a lot like she and Jason had as children.

At least someone had remembered her birthday.

When Solomon came out of the bathroom, a towel wrapped around his waist, Josie went in herself and locked the bathroom door, knelt in front of the toilet and vomited the lasagna that had sat heavy in her abdomen, nagging at her since dinner. The tile felt cold underneath her bare knees.

When she finally went back into their bedroom, Solomon was already asleep. She lay beside him, listening to his breathing, not sure if she wanted him to hold her. Maybe. Maybe not. *Yea, when this flesh and heart shall fail, And mortal life shall cease, I shall possess, within the veil, A life of joy and peace.* It sounded too easy.

NATASHA

AUGUST 2001

The first few seconds after waking—seconds, really, a few breaths, maybe, before it all splashes back.

The striped pattern of the wall—this bed—where?—Right. The hotel. She is at the Fairmont Banff Springs Hotel, it is Monday, she is alone. She stretches out her arms, feels the empty space.

It took three days to line this all up, to switch her shifts, to book the hotel, to come up with a plausible explanation as to where she'd be, why she'd be out of contact. She hadn't planned to call things off with Greg so suddenly. But then, the morning after Josie's wedding, she opened her eyes and looked at him, her brain registering, remembering—the conversation at the reception, the navy velvet sky, her dizzy head. She just started talking, and he just kept looking at her, kept saying, "But what do you mean?"

No one even knows they're not together anymore, yet, unless Greg has told someone, which he probably hasn't. She stares out the window at the clear blue sky behind sharp green pines, the light streaming into the dim room. When she closes her eyes again, the shape of the window burns red behind her eyelids. Too bright.

She has not eaten since yesterday, and even then, she only managed to gulp back some bitter hospital coffee and take in a few bites of slimy green cafeteria Jell-O just to keep her sugars up, to stay alert enough at work to be functional at her job. She lies still, flat, arms at her sides, toes pointed up. Her closed eyelids flutter, a tiny itch tingles at her hairline. The sheets smell of bleach. Has Greg tried to call? Does he wonder why he's only getting voice mail? What time is it? Is he on his way to work, now? Is he singing along to the radio, making up lines to songs whose lyrics he can't remember?

She breathes, in-out, holding back another splash.

She could sleep all day. She could buy a bottle of dark red wine, drink it all. She could change her look—cut her hair short, buy new clothes, get a tattoo. She could spend the day wandering in the mountains. She could wander off into the mountains and never come back. No one knows where she is. Here, no one knows who she is. She can be anyone. She could just leave, like her mother did, eighteen years ago. Run away and never look back. Leave everyone and everything behind.

Josie's grandparents used to have a cabin time-share somewhere nearby, near the Three Sisters mountains, where exactly Natasha can't remember, but she does remember how the drive from Calgary felt so long, her skin sweaty, sticking to the leather seats of Josie's parents' car, playing cat's cradle with Jo using two shoelaces tied together into one long loop, trying to keep their hands steady against the rocking motion of the drive, against Jason's frustrated kicks at the back of Josie's father's seat while he drove: "I'm huuuungry!"

During one of those summers, she'd tripped on a gravel driveway racing Josie to the top of a hill and sheared the skin off her left knee. Josie had gagged at all the blood, so Natasha hobbled over to a patch of grass and picked the tiny rocks out of the wound one at a time by herself, biting hard on the inside of her cheek against the sting. Then she tied her blue windbreaker around her leg like a tourniquet and wiped her bloody hands on her jean shorts. That night, she sat on the ledge of the indoor pool, dangling only her feet into the water, while Jo and Jay and their cousins bobbed and splashed each other, using pool noodles as lightsabers. Natasha had no cousins; had no siblings yet either. During the summers, she pretended to be Josie and Jay's sister. When she grew up, she would have eight children and there would be no need for cousins or pretend families. Natasha pulled her legs out of the pool and pulled her knees to her chest, which made her wound sting again. She kept getting splashed. Kids under fifteen weren't supposed to be in the pool unsupervised, but one of Josie's cousins was fifteen, the oldest girl, and then there was a boy who was fourteen and a half, so maybe that technically counted, since all the adults had gone to the clubhouse to watch a live jazz show. The fifteen-year-old's younger brother had turned thirteen the week before. Josie's aunt and uncle had made a birthday cake to celebrate, a chocolate fudge cake decorated in watermelon Pop Rocks candy, and when Natasha bit into her forkful, the candy exploded in her mouth, sweet and fizzy. Afterwards, she'd played Battleship with the thirteen-year-old cousin. She lost, but it didn't matter. Natasha wondered if someday she might marry him and actually become a member of Josie's family. He was only a little bit older than her, just like her dad was a little bit older than her mom. She liked the chocolate colour of his hair. Maybe her children would have chocolate-coloured hair and be good at Battleship.

How strange—a memory of thinking about marrying someone other than Greg, from before she even knew Greg, the same memory tinged with the craving of an only child for a sibling, before Abby, before she even knew about Abby. Although it occurs to her that, during the summer she'd skinned her knee, Abby had already come into existence, just cells at that point, cells dividing. New life, by accident. Just like Abby's own baby-to-be.

That night at the pool, Jason had lobbed a ball too high, to the far end of the pool, onto the deck behind the deep end. Natasha scrambled to her feet and darted after it. The ball felt slippery in her hands as she passed it back to Jason, who paused for a moment, bobbing on a blue rectangular flotation device.

"Thanks," Jay said. "How's your knee?"

Natasha could barely hear him because of the cousins' shrieks and the way the sound bounced off the water and the pool's high ceilings.

Then she felt a shove in-between the shoulder blades and hit the water hard. She felt a sucking—down, down, like being pulled towards a drain—and she thrashed her arms, her body heavy in jean shorts, the hood of her sweatshirt twisting in front of her face. The water tasted salty; filled her nostrils. Her lungs burned. She kicked up, against the suck. Someone came up beside her, hoisted her from below. She broke the surface and gasped. Then she went under again, but just for a moment. The second time she crested the water, she found herself near the pool's edge. She grabbed on, scrambled up, collapsing on the side, slamming her ragged knee into the concrete in the process.

Josie crawled up onto the deck, water streaming from her long hair seal slicked down her back. "Are you okay?" she gasped, kneeling down beside Natasha. "It was supposed to be funny..."

Who had pushed her? Who had helped her out? Did it even matter? The scab on her knee had reopened, and when she reached down, her fingers came back wet with diluted blood. She could hear the teens laughing. She didn't want to look. Her nose tingled. "It's fine. I'm fine." She clamped her lips together.

In the change room, Natasha stripped her off her clothes and stood still, wearing only a now transparent pair of cotton underwear. Her jean shorts dripped through the grated bench, water forming a slippery puddle underneath. She wrapped a scrawny, bleached-white towel around herself, used some toilet paper to staunch the blood at her knee. When Josie came back with dry clothes from the cabin, Natasha would tell her the push had been funny. She could take a joke. She sat down beside the crumpled pile of her wet laundry and let a few tears come out, but only a few, and just so they'd be gone by the time Josie came back.

In the Banff Springs Hotel, Natasha climbs out of bed and steps lightly, barefooted to the bathroom. She twists the bathtub faucet and water rushes into the porcelain basin. She had fallen asleep in her clothes, exhausted from the drive, from crying. Can she make herself stop loving Greg? Can she choose that? She strips her jeans off now, her T-shirt, her underwear, her bra. Waits.

When it had come time for swimming lessons the fall after the pool incident, Natasha faked a wrist injury and wore her arm in a sling for three weeks while her classmates practiced somersaults by kicking off against the pool's wall and leapt from the tall diving board. She sat up in the highest bleacher with her math textbook and a sixth-grader she didn't know who got rashes from chlorine. Josie had a new neon yellow bathing suit. The bleachers felt safer than the sidelines. Up high, Natasha could see the instructors throwing heavy black rings to the bottom of the pool. One by one, her classmates dunked down to fetch them.

There was, Natasha had reasoned, only so much air in a human being's lungs. If you went far enough under, at some point, you would run out of time, you would run out of breath. And then, even if you wanted to make it to the surface, you couldn't. She watched the kids diving down and popping back up. All of them kept making it. But that didn't mean all of them would always keep making it. That didn't mean she would make it. It only had to happen once.

She turns the hotel faucet off now, steps into the water gingerly, letting her body absorb the swell of heat. She still doesn't know what time it is, but it doesn't matter. She lies back into the water, leans her neck against the hard porcelain of the tub. The heat and the fact that she hasn't eaten have made her dizzy. She closes her eyes. Holds her breath. Slides her back down further. Water slips up over her chin. Her mouth. Her nose.

HIM

I ALWAYS THINK I RECOGNIZE PEOPLE I KNOW ON THE street. Then I get up close and I see their face, and it's never who I thought it was. A human face is based on mathematical proportions and symmetry. Bisect an oval horizontally to find the line where the eyes should sit; bisect the bottom half of the face to anchor the nostrils. Each ear anchors to the face at the first and second horizontal bisects. Section off the top third of the bottom quarter—this line anchors the mouth, one lip above the top line, one lip below. Bisect the whole face vertically to find the dorsum of the nose. Divide the first horizontal bisect into five segments; from left to right, the eyes fall into segments two and four. Did you notice that the space between the eyes is equal to the width of each eye? The bridge of the nose is equal to the width of that third invisible eye. The outer corners of the mouth can be located by running two parallel lines down from the pupils of each eye. People always say eyes are almond shaped, but that's inaccurate. Real eyes lack vertical symmetry. They're shaped like lemons; the part where the rind forms a nub at the end corresponds to the tear-duct. A computer can be programmed to generate a face to exact proportions according to mathematical ratios; you can replicate a person, create an avatar, a graphical alter ego. But a fully symmetrical face isn't authentic. Like how you only have a dimple on the left side of your face.

That first time I saw you out running, I watched you, from the truck. I lit a Marlboro. Seeing *you*, of all people, recognizing *you*—it meant something. Meant things were going to be different. I couldn't just ignore that.

The air conditioner in the truck was broken; whenever I turned it on, it smelled like gasoline. Better to keep the windows down. The truck was so old I had to roll the windows manually. I tapped my cigarette on the window edge to release the ash. I watched you make a right turn. I hit my turn signal. It tracked you like a heart beat. I followed. You had your headphones on. The truck radio was busted, too. Just static fuzz. I wondered what song you were listening to.

2004

THE PICKUP LOOKS WORSE THAN THE AD; AND more blue than grey. Oh, well. John only plans to strip it and sell it for parts anyway. But the guy's listed it pretty high. Dickwad. Maybe John can lowball him. He's already driven all the way out to Airdrie to look at it. Cost him a quarter tank of gas. His own windshield is a mosquito graveyard. The wind has started to pick up. John licks his lips, tastes grit.

"How many kilometres on it?" John asks the guy, opening the driver's side door and climbing in, running his fingers along the dusty dashboard.

The guy comes around the passenger door, leans in through the open window. "Six hundred thou. The engine is pretty shot. It'd need rebuilding, but I dunno if it's worth it. I'd just use the parts."

"You flexible on price?" John asks, checking out the gearshift, opening and closing the glove compartment.

The guy watches him. "I could be."

John swivels, checking out the back seat. The vinyl is darkened in some places. John leans closer. It looks like spilled wine, or perhaps blood. He looks up at the guy, jokes, "You have a dead body in here?"

"My buddy borrowed 'er one weekend and accidentally hit a dog. He tried to get it to the vet in time. Stain never came out."

John averts his gaze, rests his fingers on the wheel. Tries not to think about a dog bleeding, panting, moaning, eyes rolling back in its head. John has three dogs at home—two huskies and a yorkie—the yorkie is his girlfriend's, and it's more guinea pig than dog, but it's grown on him.

He decides he doesn't want the truck. It's not worth negotiating. A long crack stretches across the windshield. John can't even turn the engine on to check any of the features. Who knows what other surprises he might find? He smiles anyway, says, "I think I've seen everything I need to. Thanks for letting me take a look."

The guy says, "No problem."

John steps out of the truck. "I'll give you a call," he says, "if I have any questions." He offers his hand.

The guy accepts the shake. "Yeah, sure. No problem." His hand feels rough.

John starts to walk to his car, then turns back. "That dog make it?" he asks.

The guy shrugs. "Dunno."

JUNE 2008

I want to be cured of a craving for something I cannot find
and of the shame of never finding it.
—T.S. Eliot

REUBEN

REUBEN'S DAUGHTER WET THE BED AND, AFTER GETTING up to change her sheets, he couldn't fall asleep right away, so he took a blanket and a pillow into the den and turned on *World of Warcraft* on his computer. He hasn't been sleeping more than a couple of hours at a time, not since they found the watch. He just can't turn his brain off. Stacy never lets him play *WoW* when the twins are awake—says she doesn't want them to be exposed to violence. Stacy doesn't get it. Violence is already everywhere. Sooner or later, she's going to realize she can't protect the kids.

Probably no one would have realized the significance of the watch had it not been tucked up under the rubber floor mat on the passenger side. It couldn't have just fallen. Someone had to shove it up under there. It was the long dark hair that got noticed. A good chunk of it, the width of a finger, wrapped around the strap. Someone had left it there on purpose.

The doorbell rings, and Reuben stumbles from the couch, his legs tangled in his blanket. He discards the blanket on the hardwood and goes around the corner. Peers through the peephole.

No fuckin' way!

He fumbles with the main deadbolt and the second deadbolt Stacy had installed when they moved in. He flings open the door. The security system starts its low hum.

It's her! The vic! Standing on his doorstep, still wearing her workout clothing, her arms wrapped around herself, her bare skin prickled with goosebumps. She shivers.

"What are you doing here?" Reuben exclaims.

"I'm so cold," she says. But doesn't move to come inside the house.

"Where the hell have you been?" Reuben yells. The security system has escalated to a loud warning tone; if he doesn't deactivate it before the time is up, the siren will start, triggering a call to the system's headquarters, dispatching the police. He really should turn it off, but no way in hell is he going to let the vic out of his eyesight.

"I'm so cold," she says again.

Here's the siren. "Get inside," Reuben says, and reaches out for the vic's arm.

Still, she doesn't move. The siren keeps wailing. "I'm so cold," she says.

"Reuben?" Stacy yells from upstairs.

That's not the siren, that's his son, crying. Reuben rolls over, feeling the rough fabric of the couch against his face. His pillow has fallen to the floor. Fractals swirl on his computer, the screen saver having kicked in. He sits up, lightheaded. Fucking nightmare. Now that they've found the watch, it's like his lungs are just giving up on him. It feels like he's having asthma attacks at random times, watching the coffee machine pee dark roast into his Styrofoam cup. Taking his socks off at the end of the night before a shower. Reuben has been given explicit instructions to—how did his supervisor put it?—stop spinning his wheels and make some real headway. The sergeant even asked that student criminologist who's been hanging around doing her Ph.D. on missing and murdered Indigenous women to take a look at the file, see what they could be missing.

But Reuben *knows* it was the ex-boyfriend who did it. Sick at home, alone, asleep? Yeah right. The fact that she'd started seeing someone else gave him motive, too. Not that the ex admitted he knew about the new fling. Reuben had thought for sure the guy would crack, slip up. All those hours at the station, buddy hacking up a lung, Reuben leaning on him, thinking, *come on, asshole, we both know you did it.* Coming in willingly for all that questioning, offering up his condo to be searched—made him look like the nice guy, the high school sweetheart who would never lay a hand on her.

So what if he didn't own a grey pickup? Of course he'd use a decoy. The pickup means nothing. Could his guys get DNA off the watch? They had her hair in for testing and the watch in for prints. 'Course there was a backlog. 'Course the truck had been dismantled by the time the watch made its way into the right hands, the pieces strewn about, sold, mixed in with other scrap. It had taken awhile for the guys at the scrapyard to figure out the watch's significance. Reuben had guys trying to trace the truck's serial number, but he wasn't holding his breath.

The vic's new guy was a doctor she'd met at work. A step up from the perp, in Reuben's opinion. The doc *did* have an alibi—a whole team of medical professionals watching him assist on a kidney transplant. He'd come into the station voluntarily, identified himself, just after Reuben found the photo, before he even had time to figure out who the guy was. He'd answered all Reuben's questions. Apparently they'd just started seeing each other, but they'd had sex recently and it was getting serious. He asked Reuben not to say anything to the media— didn't want to damage his professional reputation. Not that there was anything to say. His alibi was ironclad. Big guy, six feet, dark skin, dark hair, baseball cap. Cried like a baby, right there in the station. Then he pulled his shit together. Left Reuben his card.

Reuben's pretty sure the family never knew about the new beau. The little sister would have said something for sure. Reuben has kept this evidence to himself all this time. And until the ex-boyfriend trips up and lets on that he knew about the new boyfriend, Reuben's not going to leak it.

When they found the watch, a couple of weeks ago, the sister came down to the station with her little girl to make an ID. They had matching hair, braids twisted all around their heads. The little girl wore pink rubber boots with black stars on them. She had a ring of chocolate around her mouth, like she'd just been sucking on a fudgsicle. The vic's sister turned the plastic baggie with the watch inside over in her hands. Then back to the front. "This means she got in a car, then," she said, monotone.

"A truck, a grey pickup," Reuben said. "Does that sound familiar to you?"

The sister shook her head. "No." She glanced over at the wall behind his desk, at the picture of the vic as a little girl sitting beside her biological mother on a piano bench. She'd tacked up the photo years earlier without asking. Reuben doesn't want it there, but every time he goes to remove it, he gets this tingly feeling, like it's bad luck. Plus, the sister would notice.

Reuben doesn't like to look into the vic's eyes. She was definitely keeping secrets. He imagines her yanking out a chunk of her own hair, winding it around her watch, and shoving the watch under the floor-mat. She'd have to have had a moment to herself to hide this evidence, which makes Reuben think it's the ex even more. He can't see a stranger leaving her alone in the car; too much risk. Had to be someone she knew. She must have known he was going to hurt her. Undoubtedly, he'd hurt her before.

He doesn't buy the theories that she got ambushed by some stranger in town for Stampede, or by one of the construction workers in the area. Her house was too far out there in the burbs, and it was too late for any of the workers to be on the job. He doesn't buy the theory that she ran away or killed herself, either. He leaned that way in the beginning, but not now, after so much time has passed. People who kill themselves usually get found. It's too hard to hide your own body. Even intentionally drowning. Bodies wash ashore unless they're weighted down.

Reuben read all the nasty emails her father sent her, at the time, and again since the case got re-opened. Even though he's an asshole, the father is a wildcard for guilt. Being pissed at your kid is in a different category from filicide. Plus, would he have really taken out all his stocks and savings to put up reward money if he knew his kid was dead? Not likely—the guy was, still is, such as tightwad.

The family had given Reuben heck for his failure to solve the case, too, hired that shitty PI who retraced a few of his steps, dug up some meaningless names, then held out on them for more cash. When all was said and done, the PI ended up making Reuben look good, and Reuben didn't even have to do anything.

That day at the station, the sister kept turning the watch over and over in her hands, like it might look different each time she flipped it. The battery had died, leaving the screen blank. She blinked and looked up, noticed that her little girl wasn't right beside her, started freaking out, yelling the little girl's name. Reuben was taken aback—like, how far could the kid have gone, really? There were cops everywhere! Calm the fuck down!

The kid popped up again right away, sidled up against her mother's leg, stuck her thumb in her mouth. The vic's sis picked her up and put her on her hip. Reuben doesn't even hold the twins like this anymore, and they're years younger than this kid. The kid squirmed a little like her mother was hurting her, holding her too tight.

Early on, when his team found something, he'd think *yes, this is it!* Like the soggy, black, lipstick printed panties in a drainage ditch in Twelve Mile Coulee. Every time a lead like that went nowhere, Reuben wanted to punch himself in the face for getting his hopes up. Those panties could have been anyone's. Teenage lovers sneaking into the coulee to fool around. Someone camping. A drifter. A prank. A totally unrelated sex crime. They couldn't pull any DNA off them anyway. Another dead end.

But the watch, the long dark hair…yes, her sister said, it was hers. The hair was still down in the lab, being tested against her toothbrush.

In Reuben's nightmares, the vic is on the ground, her ex's hand clamped over her mouth, one of his knees on her chest, pinning her back to the cement. She thrashes under his weight, wrenches her head to the side. Her heart wrestles against her ribcage. Her lungs burn. The storm starts to creep in. The sky exhales, giving up. And then hands close around her neck. Hands that have held her and caressed her before. Hands she once trusted. Reuben feels like he's choking, too.

Fucking nightmares. Now, he feels dizzy as he ascends the stairs; puts a hand out to brace himself on the bannister. Upstairs, Reuben finds his little boy sitting cross-legged in his racecar bed. His son stops crying immediately when his father enters the room. He's somehow wearing his pajama pants on his head and no bottoms; a soggy looking diaper sits, open and discarded on the other side of the room.

"You okay, Buddy?" Reuben asks. Parenting three-year-olds is the worst hangover ever. Or this investigation is the worst hangover ever. Both together are going to kill him. When he took on the case, he was only engaged. He didn't even want a baby yet, let alone two.

"Hi Daddy," his son says, grinning. The legs of his pajama pants dangle like inverted rabbit ears. "Wanna play?"

JOSIE

www.findnatashabell.com

The LORD himself goes before you and will be with you; he will never leave you nor forsake you. Do not be afraid; do not be discouraged. —Deuteronomy 31:8

June 2008

Hello blog readers and prayer warriors! We are approaching the sixth anniversary of the date Natasha was last seen. There have been recent developments in her case, including the recovery of a key piece of evidence—the Timex watch Natasha always wore, which was recovered in a grey pickup truck that had been sent to the junkyard. This discovery led to the investigation being re-opened. New searches are being scheduled. It is only a matter of time before more information comes to light. If

*any of you know of anything suspicious that
could be related in any way to Natasha's
disappearance or to a grey pickup truck,
I implore you to please report it to the
authorities, no matter how trivial or
unrelated you think it may be.
Natasha was a beautiful, recently single
woman who interacted with many different
people through her job as a nurse.
Furthermore, Natasha disappeared during the
Calgary Stampede, a time when many tourists
were in Calgary. The person responsible
for this heinous crime could be a complete
stranger to Natasha, but he could be your
co-worker, your friend, your boyfriend,
your brother. If someone you know was
acting unusual during this time, or if you
know anything that you even think could
possibly be relevant, please come forward.*

*We remain convinced that our Lord Jesus
Christ will bring Natasha back to us. While
statistics say that people who are abducted
are often killed within the first twenty-
four to forty-eight hours, there have been
cases of missing people who are found after
months or even years. Take, for example,
the 1990s case of Stefany Beale, a nine-
year-old girl from Toronto who was missing
for three years, presumed dead, until
she was found abducted by her biological
father. Stefany was returned safely to her
mother. We must not give up hope for our
own happy ending.*

*Sincerely,
Josie Carey McKinnon*

ABBY

IN THE BEGINNING, NO ONE WOULD TELL ME ANYTHING. No one would let me help look for you.

That fall, I took Summer for walks in the fancy stroller you bought me. I loved that stroller because, inside of it, Summer faced me instead of the world. During my pregnancy, I wished that the baby would look like you. But, in all honesty, she looks mostly like Cam—fair skin, thin-nish blonde hair and eyes that mottled from navy blue to hazel by her first birthday. Right after she was born, she had these tiny white bumps along her nose and cheeks, like baby pimples, and a rashy scalp. She still has dark, full lips, like she's wearing lipstick all the time.

But, as a baby, she had long fingers, like yours. A nurse who came into my hospital room to teach me how to breast-feed called them pianist's fingers, and I remembered you teaching me how to play "Chopsticks," remembered the picture you had framed in your room, you sitting with your mom at the piano. I started to cry. The nurse said, "I know, it hurts, doesn't it?" by which I think she meant breast-feeding. I couldn't wipe the tears away while holding Summer and holding my breast at the same time. Eventually the tears dried on my face, sticky and itchy, and Summer sucked angrily; my milk hadn't come in yet. I could hear my parents arguing in the hallway, Dad saying, "She doesn't know what she's doing!" I couldn't make out my mom's response. Dad again—"I don't care if she is eighteen. It's not…" More mumbling. "I don't care if he *is* the father!"

The nurse was right—it did fucking hurt.

That autumn, six years ago, Summer and I took long, rambly walks through the nearby parks, stopping to look at any discarded garbage, any bit of fabric or wind-blown plastic bag. Peering into the windows of dented Buicks and rusted station wagons, noticing which ones stayed parked in the same spot for days at a time with licence plates gone past renewal. I wrote down all the licence plates, colours, makes and models in a little notebook. At first, my parents set up camp at your house and wouldn't let me leave, argued that maybe whoever had targeted you would come after me. Here's the thing, though—nobody would want me. Nobody would give a shit. You were the sister that drew people in. And with Dad back at work and Mom helping Kayla with last minute wedding planning, hosting fundraisers in your honour at the country club, and dealing with the home renos they started before you went missing, no one was around to stop me from leaving the house if I damn well wanted to.

On those walks, when Summer got cranky, we'd detour into a gas station bathroom, and I'd mix her a bottle, pinching the nipple shut and shaking to break up the clumps of powdered formula. I know—breast is best—but the swelling, the dry, cracked nipples…I just couldn't do it anymore. My mother never breast-fed me, but I bet yours breast-fed you. Every time I mixed a bottle, I heard your voice, your logical argument, your disappointment. One more screw-up from your little sis to add to the list.

Once Summer had her bottle, I'd buy myself some muddy coffee and we'd head back out. One time, I heard the chopping of a helicopter above, the futile sound of blades trying to rip through the sky, and I looked up, wondering whether someone in that helicopter was looking for you. Another time, I found a tarnished silver keychain abandoned in the dirt of the baseball diamond by the school on Scurfield Drive. An inch-long unicorn with a saddle, front hooves raised, tail swinging, a pole protruding down through its back affixed to a round base at the bottom and to the keychain hook at the top. A carousel horse. A single bronze key attached. What door did the key open?

That day, Summer and I took public transit up to Greg's parents' house where I knew he was staying. We got lost twice because I read the bus schedule wrong and because every house in the suburbs looks the damn same. But what else did I have to do? No job, no college, Daddy footing my bills. You wanted me to be independent. Well, what was I supposed to do, Tash? What was I supposed to do without you?

The clunky movement of the stroller boarding the bus woke Summer, and she spit out her soother and screamed, flailed her fists. A thin, older woman with grey hair and two plastic grocery bags offered to hold her. I said, "No thanks." I unstrapped her, lifted her out, ignoring the irritated looks of the other passengers, and held her against my chest, let her do her protest cry. She knew something was wrong, too.

I could have taken your car, but then I would have had to go back home first, and there was always the possibility I'd find my mother in the living room, although she'd been stopping by less often. I didn't want to drive your car without music, without rocking out to '80s tunes like we used to. My favourite was Wham's "Wake Me Up Before You Go-Go" from 1984, the year I was born. I hummed the tune to Summer as we walked from the bus stop to Greg's parents' place, Summer clutched in my left arm, the stroller empty, propelled forward by my right—but the notes got sucked up by the wind.

Where the hell are your CDs, by the way? Reuben swore he'd searched your car and never found them, and I searched the car on my own, and the garage, and your bedroom, and all the drawers and storage spaces in the house. Maybe you moved them somewhere, before. I remember about a month or so before you went missing you couldn't find 1983 and you asked me if I'd borrowed it. Why would I have borrowed 1983? 1984 was my favourite. You stopped asking me about 1983 so I assumed you'd found it. Maybe you put them all somewhere different after that to make sure none of them got lost.

When I got to Greg's, his mom let me in, and the waterworks started immediately. She reached out her arms as though to take Summer, but I shoved the stroller at her instead. Summer's fingers had found her mouth. I shifted her from over my shoulder to a football hold, pulled the little knit cap off her head, the one you bought her at Baby Gap, grey with tiny mouse ears.

"Your sister saved our marriage," Greg's mom blubbered. What the hell was she talking about? And why should I care?

Greg was asleep upstairs, sprawled like a corpse on his bed. I shook him roughly and pulled the keychain from my pocket. "Do you recognize this?" He had some drool crusted in the corner of his mouth and there was a little bottle of tiny white pills on the bedside table. I would have killed for some prescription relief, killed to knock back a couple shots of vodka or something. Just to put everything on pause for a couple of hours. Dad wanting to talk about your mortgage, about Cam's visitation rights, about me moving back home. Josie's incessant blog posts and press interviews. The fact that she always wore that too-bright T-shirt with your face distorted over her breasts, that stupid cross pendant hanging down over your ironed-on forehead. Reuben's repeated questions, like did you own black cotton underwear with a red lipstick print pattern? Why? Had they found something? How should I know what kind of underwear you wore?

If I was out of it for a second, though, I might forget to feed Summer, or I'd let her roll off the changing table. Accidentally put her to sleep on her stomach and let her suffocate in her crib. Or my parents would say I was an unfit mother and petition for custody. Or worse, Kayla would. Those fuckers. I didn't even let Cam take her for an overnight until she was a year old.

"I...what is it?" Greg took the keychain, stared at it like he was stoned. Cam and I had once skipped school and got stoned, watched *The Price is Right* and ate peanut butter off spoons and laughed with our sticky mouths and poked each other and said, "One dollar, Bob," and "Remember folks, spay and neuter your pets!" Mom and Dad probably smelled the weed on me when they got home—I didn't shower or chew gum or brush my teeth—but they didn't say anything. Either they didn't notice, or they didn't care. Probably the second one.

"I found it in the park," I said. "Is it hers?" Summer began to fuss again, an open-mouthed hungry cry. Earlier, I'd knocked over a container of formula in the bathroom at the Shell station, dusting the countertop with fine beige powder. How much did I have left in the diaper bag? How long would Dad keep buying things for the baby? What if I pissed him off? Would he force me to move back home? How was I supposed to support myself *and* a baby? Could I get an apartment and pay the bills on Cam's child support alone? How much would rent be for a place big enough for me and Summer? You were just starting to teach me this stuff.

Greg's mother came back into the room holding a black cordless phone. "Do your parents know you're here, Abby? They're probably worried about you." When I told my parents the name I'd chosen for my daughter, my mom said, "Summer? It sounds like a stripper!" It was your middle name, I argued. To which Dad said, "Her mother chose that name," like *Satan* chose that name. I filled out the birth certificate anyway.

Greg didn't recognize the keychain. But I still kept it.

It's been six years now, but Josie's twin brother Jason still runs the website and moderates the message boards. In the beginning, there were a lot of posts, mostly comments from people who were sure Greg had murdered you. The theories about *how* he'd done it were super gory. When Josie had the command post set up in the kitchen, I heard Jason telling Josie that he was pretty sure Greg did it, that everyone on the message boards thought so, too, and that Greg shouldn't even be allowed to help with the searches because he'd probably lead everybody in the wrong direction. Josie didn't know I was listening, and afterwards, she told me I shouldn't let Greg around the baby, just in case. Dad and my mom told me this too, and I told them they were crazy except in a way that wasn't so nice.

Yesterday, there was a new post on the message board, just a half hour before I checked.

I worked at the hospital with Natasha and I know for a fact Greg Morgan used to hit her. I saw her changing once and she had a bruise on her arm with fingerprints like somebody grabbed her and I asked her about it and she said her boyfriend had got mad at her. She said it had happened more than once. I told her to break up with him or I would report it and she said she was going to leave him. That was just before they broke up. She told me she was done with him but just before she went missing I saw the two of them talking in the hospital parking lot. He looked angry and he was yelling something but I didnt hear what. Then she walked away. The police questioned me but I didnt say anything at the time because I was scared. He knew me from her work and what if she told him I told her to break up with him and he came after me next?

I closed my laptop and got up and walked into Summer's bedroom. Crawled into bed behind her. Her tangled hair smelled like fake bubble gum, that expensive shampoo that she wanted because the bottle was shaped like Dora the Explorer.

What does dying feel like?

Falling asleep, maybe, a simple letting go—awake and alive one moment, then a light switch just turns off.

Or do you sense it in those moments right before it happens, the permanence of what's coming, like a bad taste in the mouth?

Does the body fight it, like before surgery, when an anesthesia mask closes in? This happened when I had my C-section, when Summer's heartbeat started plummeting and the anesthesiologist said, "Count backwards from ten," and then he pressed the mask against my face, and my heart squeezed, and my brain screamed, *I'm not ready!* but it didn't matter, because it happened anyway—the gas filled my nose, swam into my lungs, and then I was gone. Is that what dying feels like?

You died without reaching your goal to read fifty books in a year;

without putting the load of wet gym clothes into the dryer; without changing the colour of polish on your toes even though your pedicure was half grown out; without hanging the new watercolour you'd just had framed; without finishing the loaf of rye that eventually turned mouldy on your counter.

I *know* you are dead. I would much prefer that you took off to Mexico or something to start a new life, bailed on your old life, even if it meant bailing on me and Summer. Even if it meant you abandoned me on purpose. Even if it was my fault you left in the first place.

And that's a shitty thing to wish for.

GREG

GREG PINCHES THE SKIN JUST ABOVE LARKIN'S SHOULDER blades and inserts the needle, depresses the syringe. Larkin has nowhere to hide in Greg's condo. Not like Natasha's house, now Abby's house, filled with crawlspaces, like the undeveloped basement with exposed insulation, or the shadowy three-inch gap between the carpet and the couch. Greg's bed anchors directly to the floor, a mattress resting on a set of built-in drawers. In the living room sits an individual Ikea chair and a futon too low to the ground for Larkin to slip under. He hasn't even put up blinds.

Greg's condo gives the appearance of student housing, despite the fact that he finally finished his Ph.D. several years ago after a nineteen-month absence. If he didn't defend his dissertation when he did, he would have gotten kicked out of the program, and then how would he have made a living? His mother would love for him to move back in, but she would force him to talk about it. All the time. And she would cry. All the time. He needs to be alone as much as possible. His salary covers the basics, and his loan payments, and allows him to save a little each month, but that's about it. What is he saving for, anyway? He doesn't know.

Greg lets go of Larkin and she slinks off to her food dish. The vet told him she has diabetes and he has to give her twice-daily insulin injections and feed her a specialized kibble. Because of the diabetes, she developed neuropathy in her back legs, so she tends to slide around on the hardwood. Greg has laid down a large textured rug in the living room that gives her some traction.

Larkin grazes for a moment, then saunters off to her safe spot, an orange towel folded into an empty shoebox. She doesn't quite fit inside the box; when she flops sideways, she looks square shaped. She likes the compression, sleeps with her hind leg tucked up by her face.

Greg would never know this was the same cat that prowled unnoticed at Natasha's. But then, Tash only had her for two years and Greg has now owned her for six. In those first few weeks after he brought her home, she cowered in his hall closet behind the metal filing cabinet where he kept the articles for his dissertation. But now she will sit on his lap, and he will stroke her bony skull like a worry stone, her little eyes in slits, her paws and half-tail folded up underneath herself, leaving fine grey hairs along his T-shirts, his navy housecoat.

Tash's dad and stepmom had suggested surrendering Larkin to the SPCA, arguing that Abby had a new baby and couldn't possibly take on a feeble feline, too. One night, after one of the searches wrapped up, Greg had enticed Larkin into her carrier by lacing it with catnip and taken her home, and he had tried not to think about someone enticing Natasha to follow, about someone taking her away, against her will.

Now, after attempting to mark three essays on energy flow in terrestrial communities, Greg could fall asleep right there on the futon with his laptop open and papers spread around him. Teaching summer classes increases his cash flow and keeps him occupied. The year after Natasha went missing, Greg stayed awake for days at a time, eventually crashing into reckless dreams. Then his brain would suddenly turn on, like fluorescent overhead lights, and he would wake, sweating, gasping, strands of dreams like fingers, reaching, remembering slow dancing in the school gymnasium; wrestling for ownership of the remote; sugar and saliva on a swapped straw sharing soda at the movie theatre; Natasha's name lighting up his call display; a door slamming; a bee sting during a Banff hike; the rain; pink shoelaces.

If he could see her one more time, from a distance even, he would then gladly remove his eyeballs from their sockets. If he could hear the trill of her laugh, he would then willingly puncture both eardrums. If he could only touch her again, run a single finger along the curve of her jawline or drape one arm casually over her shoulder, he would readily press his palm onto a hot stove, singe the skin red and raw, melt his fingerprints away.

Now, he takes Ativan every night, but not until nine p.m.; the Ativan blots out his dreams. The more he sleeps, the less of his life he has to live.

If he goes to sleep too early, he will be at the mercy of his insomnia, and he will wake too early, alone in the dark, and be unable to get back to sleep. At first, when this happened, he would simply lie immobilized, helpless, realization rotting him from the inside out. Now, he avoids these black hours as much as possible, and when they do happen, he finds Larkin and settles her onto his chest, where the pain rots the worst, and her purring dulls the ache.

After the breakup, he'd sometimes sketched his way through sleepless nights, painstakingly pencilling individual veins onto individual petals onto individual flowers onto individual bushes that took up whole pages. But he has not drawn since Natasha went missing. Maybe a documentary will keep him awake and deaden the flashbacks. He steps into a pair of pajama bottoms, gathers his students' papers and moves them off the futon, curls himself into a fetal position, then points the remote at the TV. Greg's dissertation supervisor had urged him to consider a career path as a professor following the positive evaluations he'd received as a TA. Greg had originally wanted to consult to the sustainability department of an oil and gas company. But after his year-and-a-half break from the field, his supervisor had slotted Greg in for a dissertation defense date and told him to finish, just finish, just put one word in front of the other, and if he finished in time, he could be considered for the new assistant professor position opening in the department. After his committee had passed him—out of pity? Greg wondered, since his dissertation was probably total shit—he'd bit into the white department store cake in the student lounge, the now severed word CONGRA surrounded by gritty sugared too-sweet blue icing and thought, *she's dead*, and knew in his blood she was.

Greg's supervisor had advocated hard, Greg knew, in spite of the controversy, the fact that many people in Calgary viewed him as a suspect in a disappearance—maybe even a murder. He'd read the message boards on Josie's blog, those who claimed that Natasha had been afraid of him, those who insisted that his anger after the breakup had simmered for a year until it had exploded. Posters theorized that he'd strangled Natasha with his bare hands and buried her in a shallow grave, that he'd beaten her to death and burned her body in the firepit in his parents' backyard. His parents didn't even have a firepit in their backyard, but that image had literally made him vomit. He'd made himself stop checking.

Greg had completed his dissertation under his middle name, Thomas, the name under which he now taught *Introduction to Ecology and Evolution* and *Organic Chemistry*. His undergraduate students filed in daily, reminding him of Abby at that age—fresh, raw, naive. Had any of them put two and two together that Thomas Morgan was technically Greg Morgan, "person of interest" in the disappearance of his ex-girlfriend, despite his new name and new beard?

Greg didn't know if the Calgary police had ever *officially* considered him a suspect, but in all those hours of circular questioning, he'd certainly felt like one. And Tash's family had come out and said they suspected him—to more than one media source. Why? Because of the statistics? Hadn't they seen him interacting with Natasha for years? Didn't they know he would never *ever* hurt her? They'd never accused him to his face. Never given him the opportunity to defend himself. Now that they'd found the watch—Abby had told him she was *sure* it was Tash's, but DNA on the hair was pending—he'd be cleared, right? He'd never once set foot in a grey pickup, let alone driven one.

Ah, there, a documentary about the food industry. Greg has lost almost twenty pounds in the last six years, most of it in the beginning, but weight has continued to slip off. Clothing his mother bought him at Christmas fits looser now. At his last physical, his GP insisted he add twice daily cans of Ensure meal replacement to his diet. Greg sucks his Ensures slowly, trying not to taste them. Sometimes he uses them to toss back his daily Zolofts and his nightly Ativan, though he takes so many pills now, he could swallow meds dry if he wanted to. His GP will probably admonish him again at his annual physical, try to get him to give grief counselling another shot. He wouldn't go back, except that he has to, to get his prescriptions refilled.

Greg always liked how Natasha, despite how health conscious she was, would still devour a cheeseburger and fries on occasion while they watched a hockey game; the fact that she once won a contest amongst their friends to see who could consume the most "Gut Incinerator" hot wings; the fact that, while cooking, she measured by feel and laughed at herself if her concoctions did not turn out as planned. "Everything in moderation," she used to tell him.

Greg's cellphone rings. It's Reuben. It's 9:30 on a Sunday night. What the hell is Reuben calling him about?

"Hey," Reuben says, as if they are old friends, as if this is just a casual call. "I'm going to need you to come back into the station tomorrow, if you don't mind."

If he doesn't mind? Greg feels dizzy. He already went in last week, after they found the watch, talked to Reuben for two-and-a-half hours. Reuben has a beard these days, too. It looks like hell. Greg's beard probably looks like hell, too. Hopefully the only thing they have in common.

"Why do you want me to come in again?" Greg says. He's never asked why before. He's always just said *sure*. Sure, ransack my apartment. Call me all hours of the day. Ask me the same questions over and over. Go door to door bothering my neighbours. Ask my mother whether I ever tortured the family pets. Call my colleagues, ask if I ever hurt her. If I ever cheated on her.

"Why?" Reuben repeats, and his tone sharpens, sarcastic. "Uh, I dunno, Greg, why don't you tell me?"

REUBEN

REUBEN HAS WATCHED THE TAPES OF THE VIC'S EX-boyfriend being interrogated weekly since the day he first answered the radio call. Since the post accusing Greg of domestic violence popped up on the message board, he's watched the tapes over and over, pausing and rewinding. He doesn't have tapes of the first two interrogations because he'd conducted them in homes—the vic's, that first morning, and then the perp's, to see if he could spot anything suspicious in the vicinity.

The ex played it smart, though. Voluntarily allowed Reuben in his home, let him conduct an informal search of the premises, let him look inside his car. And he never changed his story. Didn't mean it was true, though. He probably killed her and dumped her somewhere remote. Reuben doesn't have a warrant to search for fingerprints or DNA, but even if he did, the vic's DNA would be all over the perp's house and car, anyway. Easy argument for a defense—they dated for so long, kept in touch afterwards.

Reuben had started with basic information gathering, rapport building. If a suspect likes a cop, feels they have some camaraderie, he'll find it harder to lie. Reuben always tries to find some common interests. But what the hell does he have in common with a guy with a Ph.D. in plants or some shit? Who does he think he is, David Suzuki?

At the condo, when the perp went to use the bathroom, Reuben flipped through some paperwork and notebooks sitting out and found a book full of sketches. Page after page of the same thing—trees, flowers, bushes, leaves, branches. Reuben paused on a single page and peered more closely at the details. Was he imagining things? Or were there tiny eyes embedded in the bark of the tree? All of them, staring at him? He heard a toilet flush; closed the book.

In retrospect, Reuben probably should have brought the perp down to the station from the get go because he could record the sessions, and also because it would have given him home team advantage. The interrogation room is set up specifically to lure a confession. Small and soundproof, no decoration, uncomfortable seating—all designed to make a perp feel isolated, uncomfortable, crowded. Now, Reuben only has notes from those first two sessions, and he wasn't paying that much attention to body language at the time. Serves him right for assuming the case would be open 'n shut.

He'd asked *everyone* about domestic violence. But this vic had her secrets, like the antidepressants—just because no one had seen any bruises didn't mean she didn't cover them up. Her best friend had alluded to some pretty bad fights, though she'd said to her knowledge they'd never gotten physical. Clearly things were going on behind closed doors. Whoever this colleague of the vic's was, she isn't coming forward. Still scared, likely. The post came in anonymously, and the guys in IT could only track the IP address to a public library with no video surveillance.

Reuben had assumed the case would be his big break. His senior partner, Grainger, would have told him to let the street cops handle it. Would have made him stay at the precinct to catch up on paperwork. But Grainger had been in the Kootenays with his second wife at the time.

Normally, the General Investigation Unit doesn't go in on cases like this until twenty-four hours have passed, but something felt off about this one. Reuben had heard the call come through, heard one of the street cops, Pendleton, pick it up. He'd stacked his paperwork to finish later, grabbed his keys. The teenaged, pregnant sister was the kicker. This was GIS material. He could use the novelty, and a case like this had the potential to turn into extra hours, overtime, especially with Grainger dicking around in BC. Reuben just hadn't expected the case to stretch as long as it had.

After rapport building, step two was to ease into more serious questioning. Reuben had tried asking the same questions in different ways, trying to trip the guy up on details. In the videos, the perp fidgets like he needs some serious Ritalin. In the first couple interviews, the ones not on tape, he did the same thing—got up and down from his chair, went back and forth to the bathroom or to get a class of water or a Kleenex. Maybe trying to emphasize the flu angle as part of his alibi. In the tapes, he keeps changing position in the metal folding chair, crossing and uncrossing his ankles, jiggling one leg up and down, leaning back, putting his elbows on the table. Licking his lips, cracking his knuckles, looking up at the ceiling. Like he's got guilt crawling around under his skin.

At one point, tape number four, 72:13, he finally asked for a drink, and Reuben thought, good. Reuben needed to piss. He'd been drinking shitty vending machine Cokes without offering the perp anything for a good hour. Tryin' to make him thirsty, uncomfortable. The fact that it took this guy over an hour for a drink makes Reuben more convinced this guy is a planner. Some people kill on impulse—heat of the moment. Then they wig out, dump the bodies. Those shitsacks usually get caught because they leave their DNA everywhere or they don't hide their tracks. But with this vic, Reuben's got nothing. No body. No crime scene. Obviously the perp covered his tracks well, just like he covered up the DV. If Reuben had to profile this guy, he'd pay attention to his intelligence, his delay gratification, his ability to keep secrets. He waited a year after the split to off his ex, for Christ's sake. Had to get all his ducks in a row. Serve her right for breaking things off.

Aside from needing to pee, Reuben had also needed to stretch his legs, clear his head. Reuben couldn't grill the guy too hard—they both knew that he could walk out at any moment. Pressuring him could backfire—make him stop cooperating. Maybe the guy needed a moment to himself, a smallish glass of lukewarm tap water. If he wet his lips a little bit, maybe he'd be ready to go another round again. Plus, leaving a suspect alone behind a one-way mirror sometimes yields good info.

Watching the video, Reuben recalls how, at first, after he left the room, the guy just put his head down on the table like he was frickin' exhausted. The videotape stays on him the whole time—each time Reuben watches it, it's like reliving the questioning all over again. The perp didn't show much emotion except for during the one interview at his place, when Reuben pressed him about whether the vic was seeing anyone else. He had a hunch—beautiful, single, late twenties vic—in all likelihood, she'd re-entered the dating game and her ex had found out about it. Perfect motive. Only when the subject of a possible new fling had come up did the perp start to cry. Pretty telling. He probably beat the shit out of her for trying to move on.

Reuben remembers how, standing outside the one-way mirror, he couldn't wait any more, his bladder was about to burst. He asked another detective to just watch for a sec while he peed, got the perp his water. Let the video capture anything he missed. His colleague had smirked, stood up from his desk and sauntered over, taking his sweet time. "Sure thing, Tuesday."

Alone inside the bathroom stall, Reuben stood in front of the urinal and unzipped his fly. Ruby Tuesday. Fuck. He'd once told Grainger that his mother had named him after her sister, his aunt, Ruby. You have to walk a fine line with partners—tell them enough so that they have your back, but keep your guard up at the same time. Grainger, a big Rolling Stones fan, had come up with the nickname. This was the thing about Grainger, always needing the upper hand. But then, what do ya know, Grainger had gone off to BC and a hell of a case had just landed in Reuben's lap. His perfect chance to prove himself. Level the playing field a bit.

Only Grainger hadn't shown any interest when he got back from vacation. Said he had better things to do than to chase some runaway. Grainger had even told Reuben it was a waste of their time. Worry about more relevant cases. Whatever. Grainger didn't know what he was talking about.

Reuben's mother kept a framed photograph of Aunt Ruby on the mantle, her dark hair draped over one shoulder. Aunt Ruby who didn't get a chance to even be *Aunt* Ruby. Reuben hadn't told anyone that his aunt had died before he was born, murdered in her late teens, by—surprise, surprise—her then ex-boyfriend, who—surprise, surprise—had a history of roughing her up. Reuben had, as a kid, gone to the library and looked up the old microfiche and read about it, and then, once he'd joined the force, got the evidence box out of storage. Ruby's ex-boyfriend had raped her, left her in the field outside their high school with her skirt hiked up, her shirt yanked up over her face. Reuben had stared at the photos in the file—at Ruby's white school-uniform socks, still pulled up to her knees, and her tangled cotton panties at her ankles, the bruises on the insides of her thighs. The guy got convicted of manslaughter and spent only fifteen years—out for good behaviour. Good. Fucking. Behaviour.

Reuben watches now, on camera, the perp sitting alone in the interrogation room, reading the back of Reuben's empty can of Coke. Reuben has watched this clip so many times. Why the hell was the guy reading the back of a Coke can? What was he expecting to find back there? A good alibi? And then the guy actually started crying! Like, tears actually coming out of his eyes, face in his hands crying. About a can of pop? He could conjure up more emotion for the empty can than he could about the vic! Seriously twisted. Reuben watched as the guy suddenly stopped crying, wiped his face, glanced around the room and then wide-eyed at the mirror.

He knew they were watching.

Now, Reuben hits pause and stares at the screen. There's nothing new on this tape. He's got the victim's watch, but not the vehicle where it was found, and a witness statement but no witness. Fuck. Fucking fuck. He's called the perp back into the station, but what makes him think he's going to get anything out of him this time? This asshole is steady as a rock. A rock he'd like to pick up and throw through the fucking window. Reuben stands up and paces. He pulls his cellphone from his pocket and stares at it for a moment. Then dials.

"Hey," he says, when the ringing stops.

And the answer. "Hey, Bro. What's up?"

CAM

THE HAIRCUT IS GOING TO BE HARD TO EXPLAIN.

I had some time to kill because Summer was napping when I went to pick her up. Abby said Summer had a bad dream last night. I didn't want to wake her up, so I went to the mall to wait, to do some errands. My hair was getting too long, anyway. I needed a trim.

It sounds believable enough. Plus, Reuben point blank asked him to spend more time with Abby and her family. Asked him to see if he could get the inside scoop, incognito. As a kid, Cam told everybody he was going to grow up to be a cop, just like his big brother. Okay, so technically Reuben wasn't his biological brother. For all intents and purposes, Cam is an only child, an IVF baby—his parents were high school classmates who reconnected after their twenty-year reunion and had trouble conceiving. Cameron Christopher—their miracle baby. But before all that, Cam's father was married to Rebecca, and Rebecca had a son from a previous relationship, Reuben. Reuben had been pretty little when Cam's father married Rebecca, and had raised him like a son until he'd divorced Rebecca when Reuben was almost an adult.

Reuben wasn't around much by the time Cam was born, but there were pictures of him around the house, like one in his uniform posing with Cam's dad. One Christmas, Reuben had bought him a *Star*

Wars Millennium Falcon replica bigger than his head. And one time Reuben picked Cam up for lunch in his police cruiser and they went for Happy Meals. All the kids in his class were totally jealous. Cam went as a cop for Halloween three years in a row until the year his teacher took away his plastic nightstick because he whacked another student with it. Come on, he was a kid! They were just playing.

Cam was just being helpful when he went over to Abby's. Cam recalls the probe of Abby's fingers against his scalp, the slight tug on his hair as she measured the evenness of the strands. The steady vibration of the razor against his neck.

From the back seat of his car, Summer asks, "Is Jessica going to be there?" Summer had sat quietly from the time he picked her up until this. Cam hits the turn signal and makes a right. Summer never calls him Daddy. She doesn't call him Cam or Cameron, either. She doesn't call him anything, really. Just looks at him with her furrowed brow. Where did she get that quiet stare? Not from him, and *definitely* not from her mother. Abby can't stay quiet for more than a couple of minutes before mouthing off some opinion.

"Yup, Jess will be there," Cam says. Why does Summer always ask this question? He and Jess have lived together for two years now. "She's making spaghetti," Cam adds. "You like spaghetti." Does she actually? He's seen her eat it before, sure, but what is she *really* thinking? What does Summer really think about anything?

Summer presses a button and rolls the window down, removes a dull glob of pink gum from her mouth. Her fingers flutter at the gap for a moment before the gum is released to the wind.

The first time Abby put newborn Summer in his arms, Cam held her away from his body, like he was giving her away. She'd squirmed, balled her fists, and shrieked. He'd thought he was going to drop her.

"Jeez!" Abby had said. "Hold her like you mean it!" She stood up and winced, her stomach still saggy, the top of a white bandage visible against the waistband of her low-rise sweats, covering her C-section scar. Cam had not been in the room while they'd sliced her open. Thank God. Abby readjusted Cam's arms around his daughter, and he let her manipulate him, like a mannequin.

Were babies supposed to scream this much? "She doesn't like me," he'd blurted. Shit. Why did he say that?

"Neither do I," said Abby.

Well, Cam thought, the feeling is mutual.

Was that six years ago? Almost. Summer sits quietly again as Cam slows for a stop sign. Maybe after dinner, he'll drive Summer by the new house he and Jess just closed on. Or, he should say, the new house *he* just closed on, because technically Jess's name isn't on any of the paperwork, but he's told her, "it's *our* house, Baby." Even though the money came from him selling the condo that his parents bought him after graduation, and the top-up funds they added to "help him out." Cam told Summer about the new house last week, and how she can pick whatever colour she wants to paint her bedroom walls, but she hadn't mentioned it since.

So, he doesn't know for sure if Summer likes spaghetti, but he wouldn't say she doesn't like *him* anymore. They've hit a groove. It's not like when she was two and he didn't cut her hot dog lengthwise and she started coughing and choking and then threw up on the kitchen hardwood. Not like when she was four and he took her to the splash park but forgot to put sunscreen on her and she burned lobster pink, dead skin peeling from her shiny shoulders for a week.

He's hit a groove with Abby, too. He pays child support, sees his kid pretty regularly. In the beginning, his parents paid child support for him until he finished his B.Comm, but so what? He was eighteen, and Abby probably got knocked up on purpose. Plus, she didn't even put his name on the birth certificate. He could have just walked away. Easily. Six years later, he hasn't told his parents that his name isn't on Summer's birth certificate. It's just better not to push Abby, not to get her back up. Cam takes his daughter for dinner, goes to her school plays and stuff like that, pays child support on time. Is civil with Abby when they do the drop-off and pick-up.

Cam pulls up to his house, quits the ignition. His head throbs as though Abby's fingers are still massaging his scalp. He feels the little bits of hair, like whispers, falling to the kitchen floor. "I got a haircut at the mall while you were sleeping," he says to Summer, opening the driver side door. Summer should know the party line before they walk into the house and Jess quizzes him about his new hairdo. Summer glances at him with eyes like Abby's and scurries out of the car. Her quiet personality isn't like her mother, but those judgy looks are. Still—she was asleep the whole time. She won't rat him out.

Rewind a couple hours. He'd arrived at Abby's to pick up his kid, but Abby came out front before he'd even made it up the steps. "She's sleeping," Abby explained. "I didn't want you to ring the bell. She had a nightmare last night and was up from two to four. She crashed about half an hour ago. Probably won't sleep for much longer. You can come in and wait if you want." Abby had on a low-cut black tank top and jean shorts. Cam could see the nude-coloured straps of her bra.

"I was fixing the sink," Abby said. "Sorry, I look like shit."

Did she add that part about looking like shit because he'd looked at her weird or something? She looked good, actually. Flushed. Hair twisted into a ponytail. Her pale freckles came out in the summer, across her shoulders and in the cleft of her breasts.

"Okay," he said. Swallowed. Followed her inside. Usually he just rings the bell, stands and waits in the doorway until Summer comes out. He's going to have to get used to this if he's going to help Reuben out. It's win-win, really, if he solves this case. One, he'll get a lot of attention in the media. He'll be a local celebrity. Think of all the chicks he could get with—wait, no no no, he's engaged. Oops. Anyway, Reuben would get some of the credit, too. And Cam would look good in his big brother's eyes.

Plus, solving the case would be good for Summer. This house is creepy—how much of this furniture had belonged to Abby's "missing" sister? Natasha was clearly dead, Cam had thought—no one just doesn't show up for six years. His little girl was being raised in this mausoleum. It's about time this whole thing gets put to rest so Summer can be a normal kid. And also, Reuben scared the shit out of Cam by telling him that Abby let Natasha's ex-boyfriend, Greg, babysit, and that a witness had come forward saying that Greg had been abusive to Natasha way back when. That could mean his kid is being babysat by a killer. Greg looks like a wimpy dude—could he really have killed Natasha? Reuben seems so sure.

"Do you want juice?" Abby asked, already moving towards the kitchen.

Cam sat down on the edge of the couch. She didn't wait for him to answer, now did she? What was Summer's nightmare about? Should he know these things? Abby would know what Summer was afraid of. Monsters or bumblebees or some cliché shit like that? Maybe she's having nightmares about "Uncle Greg."

When Cam was a kid, he had this recurring nightmare where he was alone inside a candy store, eating handfuls of sugar-crusted jujubes, chocolate-covered malt balls, banana-shaped marshmallows, stripy hard-candy mints, squishy gummy worms. The candy was so plentiful that it spilled from the containers. Cam licked his lips and stepped over it, licked a giant yogurt-covered salted pretzel that hung suspended from the ceiling. Mmmm. He ducked around behind the counter and scooped a cold chunk of strawberry ice cream with his bare hand, put the frozen sludge to his lips and slurped. His mother only let him have ice cream on special occasions, and even then, it was the shitty kind, reduced sugar, low lactose. He slurped the last sweet pink drops from his palm.

A lone pear sat beside the cash register. Cam wiped his sticky hands on his jeans, stood on tiptoe until he was at eye level with the pear. The pear sat on a white paper napkin, on which someone had scribbled, DO NOT EAT.

Do not eat? Cam licked his lips. Why not? He picked up the pear, turned it over in his hands. It felt soft, round. What was it doing there, with all the other goodies? Cam held it closer, inhaled. How subtle and delicious it smelled, better, suddenly, than all the candy, all the chocolate, all the—

He bit into the pear's side. Juice squirted into his mouth, splattered across his cheeks. He bit into it again. Again.

His lips tickled. Then his tongue. Cam felt his fingers tickling where he'd touched the pear, an itching that spread across his cheeks and prickled its way down his throat. He dropped the pear at his feet, into the rainbow mess of splattered candy. His tongue felt thick in his mouth. He tried to swallow. Gasped for air.

Cam darted to the door, yanked on the handle. Locked. He raised his fists, slammed them against the glass wall that looked out onto the empty street. Where was everybody? He clutched at his throat. His hands and arms had speckled with an angry rash. His stomach tightened. He heaved for air, grasped at the windowpane, smearing the glass. Black spots danced in his line of vision. Help me! Help me! I'm sorry! I'm so sorry!

Abby came back into the living room with a glass of something purple. "Grape. Summer's new thing." When she leaned forward and put the juice down in front of him on the coffee table, he snuck a peek at the dark hollow of her cleavage. Even when he hated Abby, even when she was nine months pregnant and he couldn't talk to her without wanting to put his fist through the wall, he still wanted to have sex with her. Once you've had sex with a woman, you can't look at her and not want to have sex with her again. Not after having the kind of sex Cam had with Abby. Abby used to chide him that sex with her was better than sex with Jessica. Wilder. She was right, and she knew it, and she knew Cam knew it.

Ever since Cam proposed, Jessica has been on this new weight-loss kick so that she looks "hot" in her wedding dress, even though they haven't set a date, and even though she doesn't need to lose weight. Jessica was beautiful, where Abby had been *hot*. Abby had come on so strong at that house party, her breath smelling like tequila, pulling him sloppily into the bathroom, taking his hands and sliding them up her shirt, up under the wire of her bra. He remembers the way he'd grazed his thumb along her nipple, crushed his lips into her neck.

He'd actually thought Jessica didn't like him at all, to begin with. Then that one pool party all three of them were at, Hurricane Abby stormed out because Cam had done something to piss her off, he didn't remember what. Did she expect him to follow her? He'd offered Jessica a ride home, because technically Abby was Jess's ride. Jess's long dark hair was wet, and she twisted it to the side to wring it out a little bit, let it fall over her left shoulder, over the strap of her cherry red bikini. He'd never seen Jessica in so little clothing before. Compared to Abby, she always looked chaste, buttoned up. When he pulled up in front of her house, she thanked him for the ride, apologized for Abby's impulsiveness. Oh man, did he want to kiss her then. She had little wet spots on her white cotton T-shirt where her breasts still hid behind her bathing suit. He liked taking care of her.

Now, Jessica has replaced Cam's regular milk with almond milk. She comes home from the farmer's market with acai, matcha, quinoa. She does squats while blow-drying her hair. At night, Cam feels like he's curled up beside a skeleton. Jess leaves at five a.m. for spin class and does CrossFit two evenings a week. Cam can never remember what night she's doing what. He thought tonight she'd be at CrossFit, but then she started yakking about how she bought gluten-free pasta and was going to make Marinara sauce and maybe give Summer a manicure. What's wrong with gluten? What's wrong with a C-cup and a nice ass to round things out?

Sitting on the couch, Abby watched him take a sip of his juice.

"What?" he said. It tasted surprisingly good, like a melted popsicle. He had to figure out some kind of question to ask, some way to get the inside scoop without making it obvious he's trying to get the inside scoop. Why was she looking at him like that? Did she already know his secret agenda? Back when Abby's sister went missing, Reuben made Cam swear he wouldn't let on to anyone that they knew each other because it could get him kicked off the case. Cam had, so far, kept this promise.

Abby kept staring at him. "Where do you get your hair cut?" she asked.

What was wrong with his hair? "Her name's Rachel. She works in Westhills—why?"

"It looks crooked." Abby pulled her own hair out of its elastic, letting waves fall loose around her shoulders. Abby could have gone to university, she was smart enough, probably even smarter than Cam, if he was being honest. Her parents were livid about the fact that she'd studied cosmetology instead of getting a real degree. She probably refused university just to piss them off. Abby's own hair changed practically every time he saw her—colour, length, curl—but it always looked good, even today, like she'd just woken up this way, just rolled out of bed in short shorts and sexy hair to fix a sink.

"Crooked?" Cam touched the back of his neck.

Abby sat down on the other arm of the couch, retied her ponytail. "Yup. Plus, you've had the same style since high school. You should go shorter. Your hair is so thin."

Did she mean *balding* thin?

Jess has a way of nagging him without it sounding like nagging, except it's clearly nagging. "We should do a fitness challenge," she'd said, a few days before. "Keep track of our calories. Set healthy goals. The first person to reduce their percent body fat…" bullshit bullshit bullshit. Jess likes to announce things this way, things that *they* should do, meaning things she wants him to do. *Do you think **we** should figure out what to get your mother for her birthday?* Or *It might be a good time for **us** to have the cars detailed.* Can't she make a single decision or do a simple errand by herself? He didn't know if Abby could actually fix a sink, but she was doing it anyway.

The house felt creepy and hot and he hadn't been this close to Abby in a long time. He couldn't remember the last time he'd actually sat and talked to her, not just hi/bye/what time are you dropping Summer off. So far, he wasn't doing a very good job at solving the case. "My hair is *not* thin," Cam said, and took the last swig of his juice.

"It is," Abby said, and slid the plastic glass away from him, stacked it with her own, disappeared into the kitchen again. "Summer gets her thin hair from you," she called out. "Your hair's thin and uneven." He heard the tap start to run. "Aha, sink's working!"

"You think you could do a better job?" Cam challenged.

Abby returned, wiping her hands on her shorts. "Yeah, I could."

Afterwards, he had to admit, she was right, his hair did look better shorter. And, at the end, she'd squatted in front of him, held his face in her hands, stared at him, taking it all in, making sure everything was even. Her fingers vibrated hot against his jawline. Then she let go, and Cam could hear his daughter waking up in the other room. He stood up, brushing the hair, like evidence, from his T-shirt.

Now Summer lingers at the front door to his house, waiting for Cam to let her in.

"Your mom said you had a nightmare. What was it about?" Cam asks her. His daughter squints at him, putting one hand to her forehead to shield the sun. They do kind of have similar hair.

"I didn't have a nightmare," says Summer.

So much for that. "You like spaghetti, right?" says Cam. "With tomato sauce?" He won't be snobby and call it Marinara.

But Summer darts ahead of him, making her way inside the house, and doesn't hear the question.

NATASHA

DECEMBER 1988

Looking over the railing down onto the party, Natasha spies Greg by the dessert table, choosing a Nanaimo bar. She feels like a child sitting in the grass, having discovered a ladybug on her arm, wondering how long she can sit there, holding still, before the wings eventually perk and the ladybug lifts up, into the blue sky, away from her.

She and Greg are ten months and three days old.

Natasha has come to Josie's family's New Year's Eve party every year since she met Josie and Jason in the second grade, but this is the first year she brought a boyfriend. She reaches up and touches the thin silver chain with a small, hollow heart pendant at her neck, her Christmas gift from Greg. She loves that he's chosen to wear the sweater she bought him for Christmas to the party. He looks great in forest green, she thinks, as he takes a bite of his dessert.

Her first time at Josie's family's annual NYE party, eight years ago, Natasha had come with her mom but not her dad because her parents had had a big fight. Natasha had helped her mother pick a nice red sweater and long black skirt for the party and stuck her arms into all Mom's pantyhose until she found some without runs. It wasn't fair that Dad screamed at Mom—Mom hadn't been feeling good ever since she had surgery for her knee. She still had to take medicine for it. Sometimes Natasha helped her get the medicine from the hiding place in the tampons box and brought her a cup of water to help her swallow. Natasha chose to wear her Christmas dress with the red puffy sleeves. She and Mom matched. Mom told her to get some of the cookies they'd baked earlier in the day from the fridge and put them on a little plate to take to Josie's house, and then her dad had come in, slammed the front door, went to the bedroom, slammed that door, came back out, slammed another door. Natasha picked shortbread with powdered sugar and some chocolate with peppermint chips and licked the crumbs off her fingers after she put them on the plate. At Josie's house, the grown-ups let them stay up until midnight, and the grown-ups started counting down ten, nine, eight—and then everybody said, "Happy New Year!" and all the grown-ups kissed their husbands or wives except where was Natasha's mom? Natasha couldn't see her.

Natasha stands at the railing for a moment longer, watching below—look, it's her boyfriend at the party. Her boyfriend takes a bite of his Nanaimo bar. Her boyfriend picks a Styrofoam cup and moves towards the punch bowl.

Kathleen had actually had the nerve to ask Natasha if she would stay home this year to babysit Abby, because the sitter they had lined up had decided to go to a party and cancelled last minute. When Natasha complained to Greg, he said they could be alone together at the house and make out. Except no way was Natasha going to skip out on her first annual holiday event with a boyfriend. Instead, she'd brought her little sister with her, let Abby eat too many treats and play with some of Josie's younger cousins. Then, she'd fed Abby warm milk and tucked her into Josie's bedroom. The last time Natasha checked, Abby was still asleep, one thumb in her mouth.

Twenty minutes to the countdown.

"What are you doing up here?" Jason asks, coming up behind her. Jason has on grey sweatpants and a black T-shirt. Jay had a seizure on the twenty-eighth and dislocated his shoulder—he'd had to go to the hospital for a couple of days while his neurologists reworked his meds. His arm hangs across his chest in a sling.

"Just checked on Abby," Natasha says. "She fell asleep in her dress." She glances at Jason's sling. "How are you feeling?"

"Better question. Why are you at this party?" Jason scratches at his sling arm with his opposite hand. "If my brain wasn't so fucked up, I'd be anywhere but here." He follows her gaze down to the partygoers. "New boyfriend?"

Not new, she thinks. Ten months and three days, a long time, almost a year.

"Hey," Jay says, "can you do me a favour? Bring me up a plate of snacks. If I go down there, my parents are going to trap me and make me be social."

"Okay," Natasha says. Better get this over with, since the countdown is going to start soon. Greg has left the table. Natasha goes downstairs and plucks goodies off the various trays and assembles a plate for Jay, fills a red plastic glass with punch. She carries the plate back upstairs quickly, but carefully, so as not to spill.

"Thanks," Jay says, and bites into a cookie. "I can check on the kid for you if you want."

Natasha glances back down the stairs. "Nah, she's okay. I uh—I hope you're feeling better."

"New meds. So far, so good." Jason smiles. "You can go, you know. You don't have to stand here making small talk with me when you have a new boyfriend downstairs to make out with."

All boys ever think about is making out. Natasha blushes. "I—"

Jay jabs her in the hip with his good arm. "I'm kidding."

Natasha can't find Greg, but she finds Josie talking to some older girls she doesn't recognize on the front steps. Both of the older girls hold lit cigarettes; one has unnatural looking black hair, permed and puffy, and the other has short blonde hair, like Princess Di. She's noticeably pregnant, her belly a red silk mound protruding from her unzipped winter parka. Natasha wrinkles her nose as the pregnant girl takes a drag and exhales smoke into the cool night air. Josie's mother pokes her head outside with a tray of cheese cubes on tooth-picks. She oohs and ahs over the pregnant girl, gives her belly a little rub. Tells the girls that they should come back in soon, tells them it's only minutes to midnight.

"Have you seen Greg?" Natasha asks Josie. What if she misses her first midnight New Year's Eve kiss? Who are these girls? And the pregnant one—doesn't she know smoking is bad for the baby? Natasha just saw an ad for this, about "breathing for two," it's what the new studies are showing. She's probably only smoking outside because Josie's parents made her.

"I think he went to the bathroom," Josie says. "Tash, these are my cousins." Josie goes on to give their names.

Josie and Jason have so many cousins, Natasha can't keep track. She says, "hi," and goes to extend her hand, but both girls kind of wave their cigarettes in the air instead. The pregnant one finally extends her opposite hand and shakes Natasha's limply, sneers, like who shakes hands these days? Natasha pulls her hands inside the sleeves of her dress to keep them from freezing. "I'm going to go back in."

"Your boyfriend is cute," says the not pregnant one.

"Thanks," Natasha says, her hand hovering over the doorknob. Did they not just hear what she said? She doesn't want to be rude, but she's going to freeze to death and probably miss her first midnight kiss, all for these girls she doesn't even know.

"Does he work out?" the pregnant one asks, tapping her cigarette and releasing ash onto the front steps.

Josie chimes in—"He's a swimmer."

The pregnant girl takes one last drag, drops her cigarette to the ground, snuffs it out with her rhinestone-studded high heel. "Hot."

These girls can't be more than five years older than her and Josie. And the pregnant one—where is her husband? Natasha looks at the girl's hands—no ring. "Um, thanks," Natasha says, because what do you say to that? She turns the front doorknob.

"Use a condom," the non-pregnant one says, smirking.

Natasha feels herself blush. Her icy fingers fumble with the cold metal knob. Josie giggles.

"Yeah," says the pregnant one, reaching into her purse and procuring another cigarette. "Or you'll end up like me." She leans in, and the other girl lights the tip with her Zippo.

Great. Natasha is going to reek of smoke when she kisses Greg at midnight. When she and Greg get pregnant, they'll be married, and they won't go partying for New Year's Eve, they'll sit at home and watch *It's a Wonderful Life* even though Christmas is already over, and Greg will rub her swollen feet and she'll fall asleep by the fireplace.

Before she can go back inside, the door opens and it's Greg! Thank God. "Hey!" he says, and puts his arm around her waist. "Abby woke up and she's crying."

Oh, Abby—not right before the ball drop!

They head upstairs, Natasha taking the lead, to the bedroom where Abby, her party dress crinkled, her puffy ponytail askew, sits perched next to Jason on the edge of the Josie's bed.

To Abby, Jay says, "Cheer up, kid, it's all good."

Natasha can hear counting downstairs. Ten, nine—

She hates her father, she hates Kathleen, and in this moment, she even hates Abby. Why can't she be a normal teenager?

Abby snuffles and Natasha forces herself to go over and pick up her sister. She feels like a robot, Abby heavy in her arms. She hears the cheers downstairs. The moment is gone.

"There goes another shit year," Jay says. Clearly he doesn't care at all about swearing in front of a little girl. "See ya, kid," he tells Abby, on his way out, and Abby snuffles and wipes her snotty nose on her sleeve, buries her sticky face in Natasha's shoulder.

Greg puts his hand on the small of her Natasha's back, but she cannot see his face. "Happy 1989," he says.

GREG

MAYBE GREG SHOULDN'T HAVE CONFESSED SO MANY DETAILS about Natasha in all those police interviews six years ago. But Reuben kept asking and asking. Kept saying all they needed was that one fact. A single piece of information could give them the insight they needed to crack the case wide open. He'd actually said that, those exact words, "Crack the case wide open," making him sound like a cheesy, television cop, the kind who solves the mystery, catches the bad guy, all within the span of an hour-long episode, not including commercials. Reuben probably thinks this bullshit post that showed up on the message board is exactly the piece of info he's been looking for. Even though it's a complete lie. Greg never touched her. Never.

He hadn't even seen the post until he went back into the station—again, voluntarily—and Reuben slid a printed version of it across the table at him. "Anything you want to tell me?" Reuben had sneered.

Reading the words, Greg had felt his stomach seize. He looked up and met Reuben's gaze. "I want a lawyer."

What if, he had thought so many times, after all the interviews stopped, what if something he said had thrown the investigation off track somewhere? What if all his rambling just made things worse, reinforced their theories? This thought, this regret, plays often during moments like this, moments he can't numb with work, or TV, or sleep, or meds.

And now his car has finally crapped out. In the mechanic's waiting area, Greg pops a stale-tasting honey-flavoured donut hole into his mouth and braces himself for the estimate. He'll just wait here. When he arrived an hour ago, the mechanic did a quick walk around of Greg's Chevrolet Craptastic and noted the dented right rear. "You want us to fix this, too? Or just the engine?"

Greg has held off on having the dent fixed since March 2002, since the night it happened during a snowstorm. That night—or, morning, more accurately—four months before she went missing, Natasha had phoned him at two a.m.. He couldn't tell if she sounded drunk, or just upset. Or both? "Can you come get me?" she said, "Please?"

Of course he would go get her. But what was she doing downtown at two a.m. on a Thursday night? And why was she calling him? She'd broken up with him almost a year ago, and had refused all his pleas to give him another shot.

They both had weird schedules; he could arrange most of his graduate research when he wanted, and she had such irregular shifts. This had created an ideal situation during their relationship—his flexibility allowed him to work around her timetable. They'd joked about getting great seats at movies because they went to matinees; they could get into their favourite restaurants without reservations because they went on weeknights instead of weekends.

Was she in trouble? Hurt? He'd kill anyone who...

He was getting ahead of himself. His car's gas gauge hovered near empty. Unsure which gas stations in the vicinity might be open all night, he pulled his car out of his condo's underground parkade and into a swell of fresh snow. He drove up the ramp and made a right turn, squinting against the blur of wipers and fog on his windshield.

Five minutes into the drive, he spotted a gas station. He rolled down his window to see whether the pumps were open. No luck. He put the car in reverse to back out, shoulder-checked. This kind of situation called for a rear wiper, he thought. Then—crunch!

He quit the ignition and got out of the vehicle, ran around to the back. Sure enough, he'd hit a concrete pillar with his rear right corner. He wiped away mud and snow from the point of impact with his bare hand, Natasha's voice in his head telling him to be more prepared, to carry gloves in his car, and an emergency kit—blanket, flashlight, granola bars, that kind of thing. He couldn't fully assess the extent of the damage. He'd probably wasted more gas taking this little diversion, and he still didn't know whether Tash was even okay.

The car was still driveable, just dinged up. Back in his vehicle, he inched forward, turned his wheels, and backed out properly, avoiding the post, and pulled onto the main road, hoping for no more road-blocks—literal *or* figurative. He'd have to get gas once he had Tash safely in the car—she would probably know where the twenty-four-hour gas stations were. If anyone would know, it would be Natasha.

There she was, standing outside, waiting at the corner she'd identi-fied on the phone. Snow had collected in her dark hair and she had her hands jammed into her coat pockets. She darted forward upon recog-nizing his car, and he unlocked the passenger door for her. What now? Should he give her a hug?

"Thanks," she said, and she sounded a bit stuffed up. But at least she seemed calmer than when she'd initially called him. Her seatbelt made a little *click* as she did it up.

"No problem," he said, and leaned back into his own seat. Awkward! "I'm just glad you're okay." But was she? "What happened?"

"Nothing." She looked out the passenger window. She turned back towards the dash. "You're out of gas." Her cheeks and nose appeared flushed.

"I know." Greg nudged the heat up. "I just...is everything okay? When you called, you sounded—"

"There's a gas station about two minutes ahead...just turn right at the intersection."

Of course she knew where it was. He slowed at the stop sign, and then made the turn as instructed. The snow had started coming down harder as he pulled into the station. He ducked out and filled the tank a quarter, then got back in. "So am I just taking you back to your place? Or did you leave your car somewhere?" Was she okay to drive? Had she been drinking? Why had she called him instead of just calling a cab? Had it not been for the time, he would have suggested they go grab a coffee, maybe push a little more for her to tell him what happened.

She sniffled. Smudged some of the fog off the passenger window with her parka sleeve. "Can we just go back to your place?"

Really? Most of the time, they'd hung out at her place, what with her having a big fancy house and him still renting a condo. But Tash had taken Abby in; they had stayed in touch enough after the breakup for Greg to know about the pregnancy. Abby would be at the house, probably asleep. Okay, so they would go to his place. But then what?

When he glanced over, Natasha looked like she was biting back tears. She rubbed one of her eyes, smudging her purple eye makeup.

"Um, okay," he'd said, waiting for more. Did she want to talk? Why wouldn't she just tell him why she'd called? Did she want to get back together? No, *she'd* been the one who called it off, and Natasha rarely changed her mind.

They'd driven back to his place, and Natasha said she wanted to take a hot bath. Pretty standard. She often took hot baths before bed, and Greg couldn't stand the water as hot as she liked it, so he had always sat beside the tub while she lounged, her feet up on the tub's edge.

But sitting beside the tub felt too weird. Seeing her naked was off the table, now, right? Greg paced around the condo while Tash bathed, and then she came out already changed into one of his T-shirts, wet hair falling over her shoulders, and she started crying, asked him if he'd hold her. He'd agreed, still waiting for an explanation, and they'd climbed into bed, but she'd cried herself to sleep. And he eventually fell asleep, too, but only after he was sure *she* was asleep. It felt so good to hold her again. She felt warm, her skin soft from the bath, her bare legs tangled with his. Her breathing was slow and even. She would tell him what had happened in the morning, right? He'd actually slept that night, no nightmares, no migraines. Miracle!

Reuben probably didn't believe this story, at least not completely. Greg had told it to him that first week. When Greg finished giving up the details, Reuben had drummed his fingers along the table. "So she *never* told you what happened? Why she was so upset?"

"It's not like I didn't ask. In the morning, she said she wanted to go home. She wouldn't talk."

"And you just let her go?"

Greg clenched his jaw. "She wanted to call a cab, but I drove her home. I insisted." She'd actually called the cab already when he woke up. The night before, she'd stood out in the snow waiting for him, and then, in the morning she couldn't leave quick enough.

The way this story ended hadn't been good enough, during all those hours of questioning. "And?" Reuben had leaned forward, clasped his fingers across the table.

Greg remembered how his mouth had felt so dry. "I drove her home. It was awkward. She said, *thanks*, and she got out of the car. I was just doing what she wanted."

He didn't want Reuben to think he hadn't done everything he could. It would be wrong.

Right?

REUBEN

"HEY, BRO," WAS EXACTLY WHAT CAM SAID THE FIRST TIME Reuben asked him to come into the station. Thank God he'd said it *after* Reuben shut the interrogation room door.

"Listen," Reuben had said, spinning a chair around and sitting down on it with his chest against the chair's back. He did this sometimes when grilling suspects so he could tilt the chair forward and get closer across the table. "You can't be calling me Bro anymore, okay? You can't tell anyone that we know each other." Might as well get right to the point. "I could get kicked off this case."

Cam raised his eyebrows. "Why?"

"Because, technically, you're a suspect," Reuben said. He remembers the vic's stepmother pulling him aside, a day or so after Natasha went missing, telling him they should look at "the baby's father," because "we never liked him."

"What's his name?" Reuben had asked.

"Cameron," the vic's stepmother had said. "Cameron Olsen."

And Reuben had felt a wave of nausea. Was it possible that there was more than one eighteen-year-old Cameron Olsen in Calgary? Likely not, not with Reuben's luck. Could his former stepfather's spoiled teen-aged son really be a suspect? Maybe the whole thing would just blow over. Maybe she would just show up. That's what he'd told the family, anyway.

Still, he had to cover his bases. So he'd called Cam down to the station. He had to admit—Cam had motive. He'd knocked up the vic's little sister and the baby's birth was just around the corner. Little sis had filled him in—the vic had gone to Cam's house to talk to his parents, to determine how involved Cam planned on being, and to ensure the baby-to-be would be financially supported. It was a flimsy motive, though—that was months earlier, and Cam's parents had already agreed to financially support their soon-to-be grandchild. If money or the baby was the motive, it would have made more sense to murder Abby. Why kill the person who had planned to assume a large part of his parental responsibility?

But when Reuben told Cam that he was technically a suspect, the kid actually smiled, like the whole thing was cool. Reuben groaned inwardly. "I need three things from you. An alibi, so I can clear you, any information you have about the victim and her family that might be relevant, and your word that you won't say anything to anyone about how we know each other."

"What if Dad says something?" Cam pointed out. "Is there a vending machine in this place?"

"I'll talk to Dad," he said. Reuben had called Cam's father *Dad* for years, though technically the man wasn't his biological father and had never formally adopted him. Since he'd divorced Reuben's mother, he had no responsibility. Still, Cam's father wouldn't want to jeopardize Reuben's career. He could keep his word. Cam, on the other hand, Reuben would have to watch.

"Tell me the truth," Reuben said. "Where were you the night of July sixth?"

Cam looked like he was trying to stifle a smile. Sometimes suspects smile when they're nervous. In Cam's case, though, it looked like he thought the whole thing was one giant joke. "I was at home with my girlfriend," Cam said. "Ask her."

"I will," Reuben said, "but it's still a weak alibi. Partners lie for each other all the time."

Cam shrugged.

"When's the last time you saw the victim?" Reuben took the glossy photo of the vic out of the file and slid it across the table with one finger.

"When she came to my house that one time to talk to my parents."

"Not since?"

"No."

"Walk me through what you did Saturday night. Start at dinner time."

Cam looked up and to the right. People do this, Reuben knows, when they're trying to recall information. "We went out for dinner," he said. "Pizza, I think."

"You have that receipt?" Reuben asked.

Cam scoffed. "Who actually keeps receipts?"

"I'll take that as a no."

Cam shrugged.

"Keep going," Reuben urged. "After dinner..."

"We came home. Watched a movie."

"What movie?" A lack of specific details can be a clue someone is lying.

"*Die Hard*," Cam said, without missing a beat.

"Your girlfriend sat through *Die Hard*?"

Cam grinned. "What can I say? She likes me."

God knows why, Reuben thought. He knows Cam was cheating on his girlfriend when he conceived his soon-to-be child. When Reuben was a kid, "Dad" was still making his money. They played basketball at the YMCA and "Dad" taught him how to fish. Cam has a basketball hoop on the front driveway. Not that he ever uses it. Last time Reuben went over there—Cam must have been twelve or thirteen—Cam played some sort of handheld videogame the whole time and threw a tantrum when his parents ordered pizza without mushrooms. As a little kid, Cam had worshipped Reuben. By thirteen, he barely looked up from his game to acknowledge the presence of his "big brother." They hadn't seen each other in a couple years, if not longer.

Reuben kept going. "And after the movie?"

Cam smirked. "My parents were out of town. What do you think?"

Sex was the kid's alibi. For fuck's sake.

"Like you didn't do the same thing when you were my age," Cam continued. "Gimme a break."

Reuben crossed his arms. "Abby called you before anyone else. The media could come down pretty hard on you."

For a split second, Cam actually looked worried. Then he said, "Doesn't that phone call prove I was at home that night?"

Reuben shook his head. "Timeline doesn't match up. You could have had time to—"

"We both know I didn't do anything," Cam interrupted. The two made eye contact across the table.

"If I were you," Reuben said, "I'd try to dig up anything you can that strengthens your story, just in case. And I mean what I said." He gestured between the two of them. "This whole brothers thing doesn't exist. As far as anyone else is concerned."

It took Cam two full days before he called Reuben back and coughed up the computer files. "I can't get in trouble for this, can I?" he'd asked, refusing to make eye contact. "I swore I never showed them to anyone."

There were five in total, dating back just over a year, all video format, recorded directly to his hard drive. Reuben had watched about ten seconds of the most recent one—the one Cam said proved his innocence—before realizing what it was. Cam had filmed the encounters on his webcam. What was he going to do with the videos? Watch them and jerk off? Share them with his classmates to brag about his conquests? No way was Reuben going to watch his "little bro" go at it for the full twelve minutes and twenty-four seconds. He'd requested Cam's laptop, handed it and the USB upon which Cam had copied the files over to the guy in IT.

"Kid's a perv," the guy had told Reuben, afterwards. "He had a bunch of other porn downloaded on his computer. But the file itself seems legit. It would have taken someone very skilled to change the time stamp." He'd paused. "The first two aren't the current girlfriend. They're the vic's sister."

Reuben didn't want to know, but he had to ask. "He doesn't do anything creepy, or—" he swallowed. "Aggressive?" Thank God the IT guy didn't know Cam was Reuben's "bro."

"Not unless the missionary position and some dirty talk count." The IT guy chuckled. "The kid's a quick shot. If you know what I mean."

For fuck's sake. "Did they know?" Reuben asked. "The girls, I mean."

"That they were being filmed?" The IT guy nodded ruefully. "Yeah. They knew. How he got two different teenage girls to volunteer for that, I don't know. The first girl, the vic's sis, seemed more into it."

Reuben covered his ears. "Don't need to know."

"It's been a long time since I was in high school. They both over eighteen?"

"They are now. Probably not when the...*home movies* were made. But then, neither was he." Cam is stupid, but lucky. So long as he's telling the truth about not showing the tapes to anyone else—and there's no evidence, as far as the IT guy can find, that he did—the tapes fall under the 2001 Supreme Court ruling on intimate photo exception, meaning they were made by two willing partners over the legal age of consent, and they were kept private, therefore, they're not considered child pornography. Later, Reuben had given Cam a serious lecture so he wouldn't pull this kind of shit ever again. And he deleted all the porn and videos off the laptop before giving it back.

Asking Cam, of all people, to help with the investigation was asking for trouble. Not to mention unprofessional. If his boss or his partner found out, they'd lose their shit. He would probably get fired. But what other choice did he have? It wasn't like he was giving Cam any case details that weren't public. The post was there on the message board for everyone to see. Reuben just wanted Cam to spend more time with the family, get to know Greg better, take him out for a drink or something, loosen him up, get him talking. If the videos and *Die Hard* were any indication, Cam had a way of talking people into things. Plus, it was in Cam's best interest—Abby, still insisted Greg was innocent and let him spend time with Summer unsupervised. Even after Reuben had questioned her about the post.

An innocent, smooth-talking kid that nobody would suspect had any agenda could be the way to go. That is, if Cam could pull it off. Which was anyone's guess.

CAM

IT WAS *NOT* CAM'S FAULT. ABBY PROBABLY WORE THAT SKIRT on purpose. Who wears a skirt like that to a meeting at an elementary school?

The whole day was messed up. First, Abby called to tell him she was going to Summer's school because she got a call from the principal. Abby almost never calls him—usually she just sends him a text message with the date and time of Summer's school plays or about when to pick Summer up. One time Summer had bronchitis and Abby took her to the ER in the middle of the night, and she told Cam after the fact, offhand, like, oh, I took our kid to the ER, she got put on antibiotics. Usually Abby acts like she's Summer's only parent, even now that he's been hanging around more to keep a closer eye on his daughter. But this time, Abby actually *invited* Cam to join her. Getting the inside scoop for Reuben would be easy if Abby invited him along. It wouldn't look as weird as it would if all of the sudden he just started hanging around more.

When Abby called, Cam was still at the office. He could pack up work a little early; one of the many benefits of working for his father's company. This was an important meeting about his *child*, that took precedence. Plus, he could work in some snooping for Reuben. Detective work sounded much more fun than processing invoices.

Cam called Jessica on the way to the school to let her know, even though the night before she'd locked him out of their bedroom, effectively making him sleep on the couch with only a throw blanket and one of her stiff decorative pillows, the one with all the sequins. Yes, sequins. He'd flipped it over, but the back had a zipper across the middle. Lose-lose. Jessica had come home mad because one of her colleagues had planned a baby shower the same night Jessica had planned to invite people out for her birthday, and apparently the colleague knew all about Jess's birthday plans even though Jess hadn't sent out the invitations or something blah blah blah and Cam was a terrible partner for not listening to Jessica's feelings, and something something he never listened to her feelings.

Aside from the crappy pillow and the fact that his neck now had a weird kink in it, Cam didn't mind the couch, because he didn't have to listen to Jessica's alarm go off at five o'clock, that stupid, supposedly relaxing pan flute bullshit that made him feel like a tiny leprechaun was sneaking up on him every morning. He wanted to shove that stupid pan flute right up that leprechaun's ass.

Cam didn't technically have to tell Jessica about the meeting. Summer was *his* kid, not hers, and she still hadn't apologized for their fight, which was totally her fault for overreacting. When she heard where he was going, she started harping about how she wanted to go, too, throwing around words like "co-parenting" and "team effort." Calling Abby controlling. Seriously? Jess calling someone else controlling? Cam hung up on her.

When he got to the school, Abby was already there, waiting in the office, wearing a denim skirt that would definitely *not* have passed their high school dress code. He'd never been to the salon where Abby worked, but maybe this was how she attracted male clientele. In high school, Abby had rolled over the waistband of her pleated school-uniform skirt to make it shorter, unbuttoned the top few buttons of her blouse. Such behaviour often got her in trouble, both with administration and with boys, which, in retrospect, was probably exactly what she wanted. Okay, maybe not the pregnancy per se. But all the stuff leading up to it.

On the wardrobe front, Abby's pregnancy had caused logistical problems at their high school given its uniform policy. Jessica had snickered about Abby having to order the same size shirts as the kid who was three hundred pounds and sat at the back of the classrooms at a table because he couldn't squeeze into a desk. Cam hated the fact that Abby walked the halls with his shame so visible. Of course she told *everyone* he was the father.

Abby had her hair loose and wavy around her face, with blonde streaks, like she'd just come from the beach.

He hadn't yet asked what the meeting was for. Was Summer in trouble? Cam had never *voluntarily* visited a principal's office, though he'd gone many times against his will. Typically unjustly. He recalled receiving detention in the seventh grade when his teacher handed out pencil crayons and a map of the world and asked them to colour. Seriously, this was the first-class education his parents were paying private school tuition for? "I already know how to colour," he'd said, crossing his arms. "How about you teach me something relevant?" Yeah, that got him a lunch hour in detention, which was bullshit, just like his teacher's justification that colouring a map helped consolidate a blueprint of the world into the students' visual-spatial memories. Were Summer's teachers this stupid? Cam felt his heart rate increasing, his body revving up for a debate about his daughter's education, about his daughter's rights, about all the money he spent on her tuition. Okay, so technically his parents were funding Summer's education, but same thing. Whatever she was in trouble for, Cam would defend her.

A middle-aged woman with a sort of reverse mullet—longer in the front than in the back—and the school logo on her sweater emerged from an office behind the front desk. "Mr. and Mrs. Bell?"

Oh man.

Abby totally smirked, too.

"We're not together," Cam said, gesturing at Abby but avoiding making eye contact with the woman. Secretary? Principal? If it was up to him, he would have named Summer something that didn't make her sound like a hippy, and given her *his* last name, Olsen. He liked his mother's name, Alexandra—naming his baby after his mother would have probably salved the wound of his getting some girl knocked up while still in high school. At least a little. And "Alex" would have been a cool nickname. But Cam knew better than to try to assert his will with Abby—it just made her assert hers back twice as hard. And then, with everything that had happened in the week or so leading up to Summer's birth—what kind of asshole would he have been to argue about the kid's name, especially since Abby had supposedly named Summer after her sister?

She'd actually called him the night Natasha went missing, but he'd just assumed it was a disguised plot to get back together, which is what Jess had told him Abby wanted. Jess had been lying right beside him in the bed and he'd sworn to Jess that he wouldn't talk to Abby except once the baby was born and then only about their child. So he'd hung up.

He hadn't wanted anything to do with Abby or her whole family drama. At eighteen, he'd figured they could just pass the kid back and forth—like, he'd have Summer sometimes, and then the rest of the time Abby could do whatever, and they wouldn't have to mix. And yet, somehow, six years later, he's being called Mr. Bell and his brother is breathing down his neck, trying to get him to dig up information.

The lady with the school sweater was, in fact, the principal, and she didn't seem to care that she'd butchered Cam's name in the most humiliating way possible. She just ushered them into her office and shut the door. Cam took the empty chair beside Abby, on the opposite side of the principal, who sat upright in a leather desk chair and folded her hands on top of her desk.

"Thank you both for coming. As I mentioned on the phone, there was an incident yesterday regarding Summer and another child in her class. The parent of this other child phoned to complain that their child came home upset, talking about kidnappers and police and people who go missing and never come back. This parent asked their child where they'd heard this kind of information, and the child identified Summer. When I spoke to Summer about this, she reported that her auntie was missing and, I quote, 'A kidnapper got her.'"

Cam glanced sideways at Abby, who crossed her arms. Would she have invited him to this meeting if she'd known *this* was going to be the topic? Was any of this information useful to Reuben?

"I did some research," the principal continued, "and I understand the uh…circumstances. And we recently had a policeman come visit the kindergarten class to speak about safety, which may also be an inciting factor. But I'm concerned about Summer in all of this—I have a Masters degree in child development, and I'm not sure whether she's processing this information in an appropriate way. I'd like to refer her to our school psychologist. We have an excellent—"

"I'll handle it," Abby interrupted. "I appreciate you looking out for her, and I'll take her to see someone, but I want to handle this privately."

Cam could tell that the principal wasn't thrilled with the idea by the way she sort of leaned back in her chair, scrunched her eyebrows together. Probably looking at the two of them, wondering how old they were, estimating the likelihood of their ability to fix this problem on their own.

"Abby's right," Cam said. Did he actually just say those words, *Abby's right*? Had hell frozen over? And how many times had he worried about Summer, still living in Natasha's house, attending the yearly candlelight vigils, hearing stories about her long lost auntie, her picture in the paper, the baby named after the missing girl, as though *his* daughter was

Natasha reincarnated. How many times had he, too, wondered whether Summer was processing all of it in an appropriate way? What if she ended up telling the psychologist something incriminating about Greg? Or someone else? Nah, she was just a kid. The whole thing had gone down before she was even born. She couldn't possibly know anything. But, if his brother was right, Summer was regularly hanging out with a creep who beat up and eventually offed his ex-girlfriend. Who knows what else Greg was capable of?

Cam kept going. "It's so close to the end of the year. And if my daughter's going to see a psychologist, I'd rather choose that person myself." That part was true, yeah. He'd find his daughter the best psychologist his parents' money could buy. Maybe he could even go, he and Abby, to learn strategies for better co-parenting. Jess would want to come, but it would be best for him and Abby to go alone. He and Abby had a lot to work out between the two of them, especially if he was going to be hanging around more, trying to get information out of her and her family. They were twenty-four now. They could be mature and go to counselling together. And maybe even for coffee afterwards. To discuss their daughter, of course.

"I agree," Abby said. She uncrossed her arms.

"I know of a good child psychologist," Cam said. Not true, but maybe it would get the principal to lay off.

Once outside the school, Cam asked, "Should we just hang around until school's out and pick Summer up?" They had only a half hour to wait. Abby's short skirt and high-heeled sandals made her legs look long and toned. "The three of us could go for ice cream," he suggested.

"She has a play date with Kenzie," Abby said, retrieving her keys from her purse. "Kenzie's mom is picking them up."

"Who's Kenzie?" Cam asked, before thinking about it. Clearly Kenzie was one of Summer's friends. But the comment made him look like a shitty, absent father.

"Her best friend..." Abby said, smirking, which made Cam feel even worse. "This week," she added, which made it a little better.

Cam squinted into the sun. Well, now he'd have to go home. To the master bathroom toilet he still had to unclog, to the lawn he had to water and mow, to renewing his driver's licence and paying the gas bill. To Jessica and her feelings.

And what would Reuben say? Wasn't this a prime opportunity?

"Thanks for backing me about the psychologist," Abby said, then. She reached out and touched his arm. Her fingers made his skin feel hot, even though he was wearing a long-sleeved dress shirt.

"No problem." Cam swallowed. He felt sweaty. He undid his top button.

Abby fiddled with one of the multicoloured hair elastics looped around her wrist. "Well, I guess I should go."

"Yeah," Cam said, and then, "I'm still craving ice cream, though." He'd once taken Abby on a date for ice cream, and they'd walked by the Bow River the opposite way of all the cyclists and runners. It had been so hot that Cam had taken off his shirt and they'd dangled their feet in the water and licked each other's cones. Right now he craved Rocky Road: chunky dark chocolate, walnuts, springy marshmallows. Plus, he could ask Abby more about Greg. And stuff.

"Stop!" Abby chided, smiling. "Now you're making me crave it."

"We should go, then," Cam said.

Cam had only cheated on Jessica three times. First, with Abby, when they were still in high school, the brief affair that led to Summer's conception. He couldn't really be criticized for that one, given the combination of his age and how aggressively Abby had pursued him (even more so once he'd officially coupled up with Jessica).

After that, he'd behaved himself for almost two years, the remainder of high school, and throughout most of their first year of university. Both pursuing business degrees, he and Jess had enrolled in most of the same courses. Cam's father had promised him a junior position at the company once he completed his degree. And, with Jessica around, he had *consistent* sex, an okay trade for the varied but irregular hook-ups his friends were having. He and Jess were still living with their respective parents.

"We're saving for a house," Jessica had told a classmate their freshman year. Oh they were, were they? When had their life together become a foregone conclusion? Sure, Cam wanted to own property—it was a smart investment. And his parents would help him substantially with a down payment. At some point.

Still, he liked the fact that he had his own room in the basement, a new-ish car (2002 Audi A6, a graduation gift), a hot tub just out the back door. Some of his buddies were living in the campus dorms, sharing a single room with two coffin beds, having to take showers in a communal bathroom, use a swipe card to buy lunch from a cafeteria. Not that Cam cooked. But he could make a mean baseball cut sirloin on the BBQ. His parents also helped a ton with Summer—he could still go out on dates or with his buddies; his daughter hadn't hampered his social life at all, because his parents loved having her. Living with his parents made hooking up difficult, but only a little—both his parents often travelled for work. Plus, his buddies in the dorms didn't have it any easier, what with their roommates' beds literally right beside theirs.

Anyway, after the saving-for-a-house comment, Cam just needed a night to get obliterated, like a normal college kid, not a guy with a baby and a "wife." At the campus bar, The Den, beer was cheaper by the pitcher. The bathroom contained a giant urinal that stretched all down the wall, like a trough, and every so often some guy would toss a Loonie in there to see who would be dumb enough to reach in and grab it. He stumbled out of the bathroom and into Luna.

Luna. With a name like Luna and skin like caramel, how could he help himself? Two years older, Luna had her own apartment. They had sex three times that first night, but technically it was only *one night*. A one-night stand. A one-time deal, a one-time oops.

The third time was a little more involved. Cam had heard of the seven-year itch, but was there such a thing as a three-year itch? For their anniversary, Jessica wanted an engagement ring. Cam had told her he had no intentions of getting engaged until they graduated. But he'd stupidly bought her a promise ring in high school after she'd agreed to give him another chance after his indiscretion with Abby, so he couldn't buy her a promise ring *now* to hold her off a little bit. Maybe she'd settle for a puppy. Except where would they keep it? Her dad was allergic, his parents already had a dog, Harrison.

He had to give Jessica props for loyalty. Would any other girl have stood by him after his infidelity led to a pregnancy? Sure, girls fawned over him when he took Summer to the park, especially when her hair got long enough to put into a little stick-straight-up ponytail on the crown of her head. But a single dad in his early twenties...no girl really wanted that. And Jessica was beautiful, and she bought him little gifts just because, like those honey-roasted peanuts that he always craved. And she always looked good, put together, classy makeup, sexy little lace bras and panties under her sweaters, her tight jeans. She'd never gotten sloppy, didn't wear sweatpants or leave her retainer around or something like that. They went on great trips together, like to Maui and Mexico. His parents got along with hers. She even looked beautiful when she cried, her brown eyes filling up with glossy tears, her wet eyelashes like the points of little stars.

Still.

So, he had a fling with Erika, a waitress at the restaurant where he and his buddies went because the waitresses there were babes. He and Erika hooked up for about six months, usually after her shift was over, in her car, behind the restaurant. Her car was old and grungy, but it had more legroom than his Audi. Around Christmas, Erika got a boyfriend and stopped answering Cam's texts, but no hard feelings or anything. And Jessica never found out. It was just a fling, and after it was over, he actually appreciated Jessica more.

When he came over to see Jess after his last hook-up with Erika, she was in the kitchen making stir-fry, and he could smell the sweetness of the sauce as he entered, but she didn't see him at first, her back to him as she worked away at the stove, singing along with the radio. Sweat prickled along the back of his neck and his stomach curdled. Maybe he should just confess. She didn't deserve this. But then—that would just ease his conscience and hurt her even more. He hated seeing her cry. He'd already devastated her once. Abby had been the one who dropped the bomb about her pregnancy, phoning Jess after school. Cam had watched Jess answer the phone and he had known, just by the look on her face, the way she sat down really slowly. She began to cry. He'd expected her to be mad. He'd only ever seen crying like that from his mom, at his grandmother's funeral.

He was such a shit. The worst boyfriend ever. He'd make it up to her. He'd think seriously about proposing. She turned around, gave him a big smile, still holding the wooden spoon. "Hungry, Babe?" she asked. He might be the kind of loser that would cheat on a girlfriend, but he was *not* the kind of scumbag who would cheat on his fiancée. He would never hurt her again.

"I'll drive," Cam said to Abby, eager now for ice cream.

JOSIE

TECHNICALLY, JOSIE GOES TO ACUPUNCTURE EVERY WEEK for her migraines, not infertility. Her company health care policy covers only three hundred dollars a year; the rest they pay out of pocket. Josie takes care of their finances—organizing their statements, paying their bills, selecting where to invest their RRSPs, paying their taxes. It makes sense, with her accounting background and the fact that she makes over double Solomon's salary. Solomon probably wouldn't have noticed if she'd started seeing an acupuncturist without telling him. But that would be dishonest. And she *does* have migraines, headaches that only started in the last five years or so, screws that drive themselves into the base of her skull, twisting sharpness radiating up over her scalp and into her sinuses. Last year, she had to take several unpaid sick days. The acupuncture has helped a little. But some days, nothing she does, not even lying as still as possible in their bed with the lights off, helps. She simply has to wait them out. *Be still for the Lord and wait patiently for him.*

Lying on her back on the acupuncturist's table, a thin sheet drawn up underneath her armpits, tiny needles protruding from the middle of her forehead and from her arms, legs, feet, and hands, Josie shivers, but tries to be still. She hates this part—the waiting—letting the needles do their work. Her acupuncturist says stress contributes to her migraines, and possibly to her infertility. She lectures Josie weekly about self-care, as though Josie can just choose to eliminate certain stresses in her life. Like she can just choose to stop having nightmares about Natasha being locked in some rapist's basement.

Josie hasn't told Solomon that she has started asking her acupuncturist to treat her for infertility as well as for her migraines. The research is wishy-washy about to what extent acupuncture can influence fertility. Her cycles are regular—they have been, since her first period at age thirteen. Natasha got her period first, which made Josie jealous, until hers came along and she realized just how awful cramps felt. Her cycles are regular, her Body Mass Index is in the appropriate zone. She eats a healthy diet, takes a prenatal vitamin, doesn't drink or smoke, doesn't have a family history of infertility or miscarriage. Her thyroid levels tested normal, her iron tested normal, her FSH and LH tested normal. She still has cramps, but nothing two extra strength Midol and a Snickers can't fix. Josie's charting suggests that she ovulates nearly every month. Recently, she made the switch to all natural makeup, organic meat and produce, and BPA free Tupperware. None of that has made a difference, except financially—why are healthy choices so expensive? She had to adjust their budget in some other areas to accommodate, especially with Solomon planning another mission trip, this time to Romania.

Solomon knows how badly she wants a child. And he wants a child, too—he's told her he does, anyway. But when she suggested they pursue fertility testing, he didn't speak to her for three days, and then he said she was messing with God's plan.

Be still for the Lord and wait patiently for him.

Josie feels a little guilty every time she goes for acupuncture, but it's not like she started taking Clomid, which her GP had suggested as a possible avenue—though she said Solomon would have to have his sperm tested first. On Clomid, her GP teased, Josie would have a higher likelihood of conceiving twins. Josie *already* had a higher likelihood of conceiving twins, being a twin herself.

Speaking of higher likelihoods—her migraines could be stress related, but they could also be something more. Josie has never had a seizure, but she knows her risk is higher because Jason has epilepsy. When the migraines started, she'd had an MRI and an EEG, but neither revealed any abnormalities. Sometimes she feels her heart rate quicken when she does one of the activities that doctors caution people with epilepsy to avoid, like driving or taking a bath. What if epilepsy is just lying dormant inside of her? She could, at any moment, get into a car accident or drown.

Josie would take a set of twins—she'd take children no matter how they came—but, as a twin herself, she'd prefer her children to come one at a time. Most people thought having a twin meant an automatic partner for life, never feeling left out, having a built-in protector. In elementary school, she'd wished Natasha was her twin; Tash had spent as much time at Josie and Jason's house as at her own.

In grade four, Jason had found the picture of a ballerina the girls had painstakingly drawn for art class and added a tiny mustache and caterpillar eyebrows. He'd bet the girls they couldn't both fit inside one of the kitchen cupboards, then slid a hockey stick across the handles and left them in there until Josie's dad finally came in from mowing the lawn. In grade five, he'd given Natasha a note he claimed was from Tyler Kirnbauer that read *Do you want to go out with me?* Natasha wrote a reply on the back in pink ink: *You are a nice boy but I think grade 5 is too young for going out.* Tyler had made an awful face, crumpled the note, threw the ball of paper back at Natasha, and sneered, "I never wrote that. You thought I wanted you to be my girlfriend?"

Lying on the table in the cool room forbidden to move, Josie wills her acupuncturist to come back, to let her change positions, make some small talk. Anything.

Her brother had been a pain as kids, but now, she doesn't know what she would do without him helping with the searches, with the social media presence, with manning the blog and the message boards. He has really matured, stepped up to the plate. She's loved watching him with his little boy over the years. He's such a natural father, whether he be down on the floor playing Thomas the Tank Engine, building Finn a spaceship out of a cardboard box and tinfoil, taking Finn to the water park and running through the sprinklers alongside him, or volunteer coaching Finn's summer baseball league. Twins wouldn't be so bad. Plus, she knows a lot of Jason's teasing was because he had low self-esteem because of his epilepsy; at least, that's what her parents always told her.

Maybe Solomon's reluctance to undergo fertility testing is about self-esteem, too. Maybe, deep down, he feels ashamed of his inability to give Josie children. She knows how important it is for men to feel masculine, to provide. Solomon does such amazing work with the youth group, with his ministry—but she still brings home the bulk of their income. Does he feel inadequate? What overtures could she make to help him feel more valued?

Her acupuncturist enters, then, grins at her, approaches the table and begins to pluck the needles from Josie's exposed skin. "Were you able to relax?"

Josie forces a smile. "Yes."

"Good." Her acupuncturist plucks the last needle from her foot. "Good, good."

ABBY

PSSSSST. I HAVE A SECRET.

I went out after work with some of the girls and I had some wine, half a bottle, or more than half, I don't remember exactly. I don't even like wine. I haven't had a drink in so long. Don't worry, Summer's at her dad's and I got a ride home. But I'm soooooo wasted.

No no no, that's not the secret.

I never once saw you trashed. Never ever.

And also, you know what? In all your lectures about safe sex—STDs and condoms and date rape and how some boys just want you for sex and as soon as you give it up they won't call you again—you never once said anything about the *good* sides of it. Like how your whole body gets tingly when someone *chooses* you, can't stop touching you, pulls your shirt over your head, pulls you right up against them, skin to skin. When someone wants *you*, just you. Has to have you. Why didn't you ever tell me about that?

In high school, when I had sex with Cam, and that other guy— who, actually, I never told you about, but it was only a couple times so it doesn't really count—I never had an orgasm. Which Cosmo says is actually not that unusual, apparently something like fifty percent of women never achieve orgasm, and I'm not going to kid myself and think I'm in the lucky half.

Anyway, that was then, this is now. The other night, Cam was doing this thing where—

Oops. Well, I guess you know my secret now.

Judge all you want to.

Yes, he's engaged. Yes, he totally rejected and humiliated me when we were teenagers. Yes, he's my ex and he's my daughter's father, and I swore I wouldn't date anyone until Summer was much older because I didn't want her to ever feel like you did when Dad started dating my mom.

But this is different. This isn't about wanting him to be my boy-friend. This is just about sex. Really good, toe-curling, Cam-has-to-have-me-now kind of sex. Maybe now that he's older, he's just better at it, he's had more practice. This is just about two people who have this crazy hot connection.

And you're not here to tell me not to do it again.

NATASHA

MAY 2002

Natasha spends longer than usual in the shower, squeezing raspberry shower gel onto her purple loofah and running the lather up and down each of her arms, across her breasts. Most mornings, she showers quickly, ties her hair into a ponytail, throws on a pair of scrubs, and drives to work while it's still dark. The sun has been rising earlier, now that it is spring. Sometimes she catches the violet dawn blossoming across the sky on the way to the hospital. Not having to deal with rush hour most days is certainly a job perk, as is comfy clothes and shoes. All Natasha has to do is grab a pair of cotton scrubs and her sneakers and go. Sometimes, when she has extra time, or when her shift starts later in the day, she puts on a little mascara. She's been wearing more makeup lately, carrying mascara and blush with her in the car and applying them in her rearview mirror before she leaves the hospital parking lot to head inside. Depends whether a certain attending is on call.

Natasha closes her eyes and lets the hot water run over her one more time before turning off the spray. Tonight, she'll wear her hair down and loose. She would ask Abby to curl the ends for her—Abby's always been good with hair and makeup—but then she'll have to deal with Abby's questions, and she's not ready for that yet.

Last Christmas, Kathleen gave Natasha a pricey bottle of *Chanel Gardénia*. Kind of a useless gift. Natasha isn't supposed to wear perfume at work, given her patients' sensitivities and allergies. In high school and university, she had faithfully spritzed her wrists and neck with *Blue* from The Gap; she knew Greg loved the smell. Personally, Natasha prefers the smell of the *Gardénia* to the *Blue*, despite the fact that she can't wear it often. Perfume always reminds her of the day she got her period. Kayla was with her dad that weekend and Natasha's dad was out of town, and Abby was at daycare, so Kathleen took Natasha for pedicures, followed by drinks at the Glencoe Club (a cocktail for Kathleen, a mocktail for Natasha). Kathleen had given her two Midol for cramps and then offered her a spritz of *Chanel No. 5*. Natasha recalled her own mother applying perfume to her wrists and rubbing them together. When Natasha had copied this gesture in front of Kathleen, Kathleen had said, "Oh, no, never do that. It crushes the scent." Kathleen had then lifted Natasha's hair and spritzed just under Natasha's earlobe, telling her, "The key is to spray it where you want to be kissed." Kathleen squirted the bottle towards her own ample cleavage. Were Kathleen's breasts real? Natasha knew her stepmother would never admit to having had an augmentation, even if Natasha asked.

Now, Natasha drops her towel, spritzes some of the *Gardénia* into the air, and walks naked into the mist. She has never really dated like this—getting dressed up, planning ahead, surprise reservations. When she started dating Greg, they'd first eaten lunch together in the school cafeteria, then hung out in a big group, then hung out with a small group of friends, then hung out at each other's homes doing homework… Each claimed that the other had initiated their first kiss, which Natasha actually recalled as awkward and chaste, neither of them opening their mouths. At some point, she'd opened her eyes. At what point were you supposed to pull away? Should she let him pull away first?

THEANNA BISCHOFF

Her first kiss with Greg had been her first kiss with anyone. "Mine, too," Greg had said. But a year or so into their
relationship, he admitted that he'd actually kissed two girls
before, one girl he hadn't wanted to kiss at a spin-the-bottle
party, and one he had wanted to kiss at a dance in the eighth
grade. The kisses didn't bother her, but Greg's lie did, the
fact that their first kiss had now somehow lost some of its
magic. Greg didn't think it was such a big deal, and when
she got upset he told her he regretted confessing after all,
which just made it worse. His confession had led to one of
their first blowouts, followed by her freezing him out. This
lasted a week, after which Greg had called Josie and asked
Josie to give Natasha a letter in which he'd asked her if she
still wanted to be his girlfriend.

How juvenile this all seems, now, as she steps into a set
of nude-coloured nylons, stretches the sheer fabric up the
length of one leg before spotting a run, several inches long.
Since splitting with Greg, she's been asked out numerous
times, and each time, it's felt like someone asking her to
strip naked so they can examine her bellybutton or the
creases between her toes. At Solomon's last birthday party, a
party she didn't want to go to but did because she couldn't
let Josie down, a male friend of Josie's from church had
touched Natasha's elbow and asked her whether she believed
in Christ. Josie had made eye contact with her across the
kitchen and winked. Yuck! Natasha had snuck into Josie's
garage for a break from all the evangelizing and stumbled
into Solomon, hunched over on the garage stairs. He stood
and swirled around, a stubby cigarette pinched between his
first and second finger, a trail of ash dripping from it onto
the concrete floor.

He looked at her, eyes wide. "Don't tell Jo," he said. "I—I
used to, um, when I was a teenager, and I quit, but then,
when my grandfather died, I guess, the smell reminded me
of him..." He dropped the cigarette to the floor, stubbed it
with his shoe, kicked the remains under the garage stairs.
"Everybody has vices." Solomon reeked. Josie had probably already caught on to Solomon's new vice—if she hadn't,
she was super naïve. It was like he wanted to be caught,

huddling with his cigarette less than a metre from the door, where his wife could enter at any minute.

So much for sneaking off for some fresh air. She turned to go back into the house, and Solomon reached out and grasped her arm. "You shouldn't wear tops like that," he said. "You'll attract the wrong kind of attention."

She looked down at her pale pink, long sleeved, V-neck sweater. Tops like what? Was it the neckline he had a problem with? It barely exposed her chest—only the tiniest hint of cleavage. Or the fact that it was snug against her body? Either way—he should mind his own business. And stop touching her. She shook him off and went back into the house, found Jo, told her she had an early shift the next day, and hurried down the street in the cold to her car.

Then, when Jason came by to fix the Internet and set up the baby monitors, they'd been having such a nice chat, and then he'd had to wreck it by asking her if she wanted to grab dinner afterwards. "I never told you this, you know, because of Greg," he confessed, not looking directly at her, but rather, at some wires he was twisting into place, "but when we were kids, I had a crush on you."

She'd known. Jason was also recently single, having split from his son's mother. Seriously, all these people who were not fit to be parents were having babies—first Jason's girlfriend, then Abby. Natasha saw pregnant women and engagement rings everywhere she went.

A few days after Jason asked her out, Natasha had gone to Starbucks to do some budgeting in anticipation of her niece's birth. She'd asked a guy who looked like he was probably in his mid-thirties if he would watch her spot while she went to use the washroom. Later, when she'd gotten up to leave, long after the guy had left, too, she found he'd scribbled a note and tucked it in her belongings—his name and phone number, and a line saying he thought she was beautiful. She'd sat there beside him for how long, with this note there, in between them, her not knowing. She'd balled up the note and slipped it in the garbage on her way out. Next time, she would make coffee at home.

Pav had asked her out one night in the cafeteria with Melissa, and Melissa had answered, "She'd love to!" before Natasha had a chance to say, "I just got out of a long-term relationship..." Only later did she realize she might actually be excited about going.

Now, she discards the ragged nylons into the trash and reaches for a new pair. She could probably go without—but there's something sexy about wearing nylons, and since Pav insisted on keeping the name of the restaurant a surprise, it's better to err on being too formal versus not formal enough. Greg's idea of romance was a cheesy card plucked from one of the aisles at the grocery store. He always signed his name at the bottom, never wrote his own words. The other day she was rifling through all the compartments in her car looking for a CD she couldn't find—1983, which Abby swore she hadn't borrowed, but was for some reason missing from its sleeve—and found an old card Greg had once given her. She'd stared at the card, a red lollipop emblazoned on the front, and bubble letters, "I'm sorry, I suck." She couldn't remember what he'd done. Sometimes Greg had just seemed like a little kid trying to get his TV privileges back.

A couple of years ago, Natasha's unit held a black tie fund-raiser to purchase new hospital equipment, and Natasha had brought Greg as her date. She'd worn a long mauve dress and put her hair up. She'd introduced Greg to many different co-workers that night, and can't remember whether Pav was one of them, whether the two men actually talked. Shy, introverted Greg, had shaken hands with all these strangers, sipping his wine and nodding, but not adding to the conversation. Had Pav brought a date or a girlfriend? She recalls Pav at some point joking about her seeming taller because she'd worn heels and he'd only ever seen her in sneakers. Was Greg standing next to her when he made that comment? Does it matter now? Probably not. Just weird to think about. Greg will probably eventually find out about Pav, likely through Abby, if they keep seeing each other, that is. She doesn't necessarily want Greg to find out, and she doesn't want to know if Greg is seeing someone new, although she keeps changing her mind on this—some days, she does want to know, or, at least, a masochistic part of her wants to know. But if Abby knows something, everyone knows it, too, and Abby treats Greg like a big brother.

What if Greg is seeing someone else? Greg will, eventually, end up with someone easy to love, someone who looks confident in a sweatshirt, hair a messy pile atop her head. Someone who will join him in the swimming pool, in a shiny blue one-piece and goggles, instead of watching from the stands. Someone who accepts an apology with a kiss, who cooks like an artist, who goes hiking sans makeup and tips her freckled face to the sky with a genuine smile, needing nothing more than that moment. Someone easier to love than her.

As a little girl, Natasha's mother read her *Anne of Green Gables* chapter by chapter each night before bed. Later, Natasha tried to read it to Abby, but Abby didn't have the patience for long bedtime stories, so they never finished. "Tomorrow is always fresh, with no mistakes in it," Anne's beloved teacher had said to her, in the story, and then added, "Well, with no mistakes in it yet." The quote offered little comfort when she would awaken next to Greg in the morning and stare at her sleeping boyfriend, all their history, all the mistakes, all the things she couldn't change, flooding over her.

After splitting with Greg, she'd boxed up all the clothing that reminded her of him (pretty much her entire closet) and sent them off to charity. Then she'd blown through an entire paycheque replenishing her wardrobe. She hadn't had an opportunity to wear the black Calvin Klein sheath she'd purchased last summer after the saleswoman had told her how great she looked in it, how she couldn't pass up such a classic little black dress, one that would never go out of style. "Perfect for a first date," she'd added. At what point had she started giving off a single-girl vibe, having been practically married since high school? Practically, but not actually married, she'd reminded herself, and slid her credit card across the counter. A vital distinction. Natasha slips the dress over her head. Is it worth it, trying again? Starting from scratch? The dress is almost a year old, but it still has the tags.

REUBEN

SHE SHOWED UP AT HIS CUBICLE WITH COFFEES, ONE IN EACH hand. "Can we chat?"

Is he supposed to know who she is? Clearly she knows who *he* is. She puts one of the coffees—a large to-go Starbucks—down on his desk, and moves to take a seat.

"Uh…" Reuben has a stack of files on his desk, a meeting with his sergeant in an hour. "Now's not a great time…"

"I'm Sylvie," she says, "from the university criminology department? I had a chance to look over the Bell file. Larsen asked me to share my thoughts. And I brought you an Americano."

Now he knows who she is. And despite the fact that she clearly asked someone what kind of coffee he likes, he already hates her. Does she think she knows something Reuben doesn't? Does his boss, Larsen, think she knows something Reuben doesn't? Her thesis is on missing and murdered Indigenous women, and last time he checked, his vic is as Caucasian as they come. Larsen must think Reuben is a fuck-up if he's asked some student to audit Reuben's work.

Reuben gets a whiff of the coffee, can practically taste the dark roast. Almost erotic, since he's so used to the horse piss the station machine spits into his Styrofoam tumblers every couple hours. Reuben reaches out, wraps one hand, then the other, around the white paper cup. So warm.

Sylvie drags a nearby chair over to Reuben's desk. Up close, she's quite striking. Large blue eyes, long lashes. Apple cheeks. Her top is tucked into pale jeans. A visitor pass hangs on a lanyard around her neck, between her ample breasts. A thick honey-coloured braid hangs down her back.

Reuben takes an overeager sip of the coffee, which scalds his tongue. Fuck.

Sylvie sits, crosses her legs, pushes her sleeves up. "Okay, so I'm just going to get right to the point. I reviewed the file several times, and I'm leaning away from Morgan as the perpetrator."

Reuben crosses his arms. First she taunts him with real coffee, now she's flat out trying to discredit everything he's been working towards for the past six years? His tongue feels fuzzy. "And why is that?" he challenges. She hasn't even brought the file with her. She's just flying by the seat of her jeans.

Sylvie gives Reuben a small smile, like this whole thing isn't her fault. Like she wishes she could just agree with him. "Cases like these— it's usually the boyfriend, or the ex, or what have you. I'm aware of the stats. But sometimes that view can be too narrow—"

Reuben feels a hot flare in his gut. "Narrow?"

Sylvie leans back in her chair. "I'm just saying there are alternatives that might warrant a closer look."

Oh really. She thinks he hasn't covered all his bases. Thinks she knows better than a seasoned detective who's been wearing this case like contact lenses for the past six years. "Like who?" he says, between clenched teeth. Can she feel the rage wafting off him right now? He reaches for the coffee and takes another sip. Burns the roof of his mouth. Fuck! Why does he keep doing that? As he sets it back down, some of the coffee sloshes through the lid and down the side of the cup.

Sylvie takes a measured sip of her own coffee, shows no signs of having just been singed. "For starters," she says, "the construction workers in the neighbourhood. They certainly had opportunity."

"What about motive?" Reuben can barely feel his mouth.

"Any one of those guys could have been a sexual predator," Sylvie says. "That's plenty of motive. And we've got the pickup truck now. A pickup screams handyman to me."

We've got the pickup, she says, like they're working together, like it's her case, too. "I checked that angle—" Reuben starts, but Sylvie cuts him off.

"Back in '02. But, like I said, we've got the pickup now; I think it warrants a second look. And if it *was* a sexually motivated attack, the perpetrator has probably reoffended. We could do a search for similar cases, run background checks on the guys who were working at the time. See if any of them have a record now, even if they didn't have any priors."

Reuben plucks the lid off the felonious coffee, releasing steam into the room. Is she seriously telling him how to do his job? "The bulk of the evidence suggests the ex," he insists. "We've got an informant who says he was abusive—"

Again, Sylvie cuts him off. "I think that post is bogus." Her lipstick has stained the lid of her coffee. "Natasha wore short-sleeved scrubs to work. Her arms were bare all the time. There are pictures in the file of her, that spring, in a running race, wearing a T-shirt and shorts. No bruises whatsoever. She went for a physical every year—did you ask her GP if he saw any evidence of physical abuse? I doubt you'd find any. Not to mention that none of her co-workers owned up to writing the post."

She's making it sound like victims of DV walk around with bruises and black eyes twenty-four-seven. Doesn't she get how calculated this perp is? Emotional abuse, intimidation, these kinds of things don't leave visible scars. Maybe he got rough once or twice; that wouldn't show up in photos or be detected at a doctor's appointment. Some criminologist. Reuben's mouth tastes sour. "DV is complex. Subtle. You should know that. And whoever wrote the post is too scared to come forward."

Sylvie waves her hand. "If you believe the post really came from one of the nurses, then you should be running identification analyses. Check writing samples, like running notes; did you notice the poster failed to use proper punctuation in the word *didn't*?" Reuben hadn't. But before he can retort, Sylvie continues. "Even her family and her best friend don't have any evidence of Morgan getting physical with her. They all think he killed her, too, but they can't come up with any examples of him being aggressive. Not one."

"Doesn't mean he wasn't. And DV isn't just physical."

"Of course," Sylvie concedes. "But even if Morgan has motive, you've still got to consider other possibilities, especially this long after. Think about Chandra Levy. The congressman was the obvious perpetrator—older man, position of power, secret affair—"

"I know the case," Reuben says. Does she think he wouldn't know the details of such a prominent murder? What kind of detective does she take him for? Levy's body had been discovered in May, 2002, only months before Reuben's own vic went missing. Police had ultimately arrested an illegal immigrant who'd waited in the park for victims and then assaulted them.

"Or, if you want a Canadian example," Sylvie continues, rambling off the details of a case of a woman who went missing out east in 2005. Reuben's obviously familiar with this case, too. Cops had leaned heavy on the boyfriend, especially after he refused to take a polygraph and was arrested for DUI in the days after the disappearance. But then a wildcard had confessed—the next-door neighbour.

"These cases aren't the norm," Reuben argues. "I could give you a hundred examples where an intimate partner snapped."

Sylvie smiles, shrugs. Like, she just can't help herself. "I know," she says. "But what if this is the one in a hundred?"

JOSIE

THE METAL FOLDING CHAIR UNDERNEATH HER IS THE MOST uncomfortable chair Josie has ever sat on, and the church basement is so drafty. Josie shifts her weight, crosses her arms, cranes her neck to see around the six-foot something blond man in front of her. *Man* is a bit generous—he can't possibly be much older than twenty. Between his chair and the chair of the girl beside him dangle their intertwined hands, the female's adorned by a single solitaire bauble, probably less than a carat. Josie rests her hands in her lap, twists her own engagement ring and wedding band around on her finger until the diamonds—a set of three—face the opposite way. She clenches her fist and feels the gems press into her palm. Three diamonds chosen by Solomon to represent the sanctity of a true Christian marriage—husband and wife on either side with the Lord in-between.

At the front of the room, Solomon paces as he talks. Josie hasn't attended one of his sessions in awhile, but because this particular talk is focused on marriage, he asked her to come. The audience is made up of recently engaged members of the congregation. Why do they look like teenagers? Josie was in her late twenties when she and Solomon tied the knot and she'd felt like an old maid at the time, but when she looks at her wedding photo, she and Solomon standing on the front steps of the church, her chapel-length veil lifted by an errant wind, she thinks they look so young. She is over thirty-five now, which puts her in a higher risk category for fertility. She can practically feel her eggs shrivelling up. Can she still refer to herself as "mid-thirties?" Or, now that she's crossed the halfway point, is she "late thirties"? These couples have so much more time than she does. It isn't fair.

Solomon reminds the audience of Ephesians, Chapter five, reads aloud from his worn Bible with the dark green cover. "Wives submit yourselves to your own husbands as you do to the Lord. For the husband is the head of the wife as Christ is the head of the church, his body, and is himself its Saviour." Josie stretches both legs, tries to distribute her weight across the chair's stiff seat. Solomon paces as he talks. "Set concrete boundaries about your physical intimacy during this time, and discuss a plan for helping you maintain your purity."

He passes around a role of scotch tape, tells each participant to tear off a strip. He then asks the participants to approach members of the opposite sex and stick their tape to their bodies, remove it, repeat the process. Josie takes this opportunity to stand and walk, observing the exercise as the couples whisper and giggle, pressing the tape against each other's shirtsleeves and chests, peeling the strips away. Solomon then asks them to find their own fiancé or fiancée and to try to make the tape adhere one final time. The blond who had obscured Josie's view presses his strip against his fiancée's shoulder and runs his palm up and down its length several times, determined to get it to stay.

The exercise ends, and Josie reluctantly returns to her seat as Solomon explains how the tape represents their own purity, and how choosing to give away one's heart and body prior to marriage can leave one with less virtue, could lead to divorce. The couples hold their ruined strips. The blond fidgets with his, while his fiancée lets hers dangle limply from her open palm.

Solomon returns to his Bible. "He might present the Church to himself in splendour, without spot or wrinkle or any such thing, that she might be holy and without blemish." Josie can't see the faces of the audience members in front of her, but several bob their heads, nodding along. *Amen.*

Solomon had proposed so quickly into their courtship that Josie had not yet confessed her prior relationships—in particular, her tryst with Natasha's cousin. She hadn't felt guilty about it at the time. Dustin was still, if she's being honest, the best sex she'd ever had—from a purely physical standpoint. Since their wedding night, she has, obviously, told

Solomon that *he* is the best she's ever had, which is technically true because of their emotional connection and commitment.

Josie had chosen to begin attending Mass regularly as an adult. The mistakes she made prior to fully committing herself to Christ were not entirely her fault. Her parents did not guide her appropriately. She'd been planning to tell Solomon when the time felt right and when she could muster the courage, but he'd taken her out for dinner, and then back to his apartment and, just inside the front door, by his shoe rack, got down on one knee. Her first thought was, *I'm not worthy*. He stood up and began sliding the ring onto her finger before she'd had a chance to speak, and then from inside the apartment, his parents appeared, and then her parents, and their remaining grandparents. He'd even flown her Nana out from Saskatchewan. Her Nana, a Catholic, and the most religious of all her relatives, had always attached a plastic, coloured rosary with each gift or card she'd ever given. She and Solomon aren't Catholic, but Josie still keeps a pink rosary in the console of her car, fidgets with it at red lights.

Maybe most of the audience members are virgins, maybe not—but, either way, none are without wrinkle or blemish. All have certainly made mistakes in life, sexual or otherwise. All have likely yelled at their partners in the heat of the moment, turned away from a hug because of busyness or distraction, fallen asleep without saying *I love you*, forgotten a partner's birthday, shared too many details of their partner's personal life, disagreed with their partner about the number of children to have or who to invite to the wedding, drank too much alcohol and behaved inappropriately.

To say that Solomon had been disappointed by her previous sexual encounters would be an understatement—but he'd already known about how late in life she'd come to find Jesus, and she'd been twenty-eight when they started dating, he a year older. She would not have faulted him for being intimate prior to having met her. But Solomon insisted that *he had certainly not* done anything of the sort and told her to go back to her own apartment, said he'd needed to think. Because she had had premarital sex, or because she had insinuated that he might have? She wasn't sure. They'd planned brunch with Natasha and Greg the next day to celebrate the engagement—Josie had considered calling Natasha to tell her about their argument, but what if that made things worse? She fell asleep on her couch only to wake up at five a.m., at which point she felt too upset to go back to sleep, but it was also too early to call and attempt reconciliation.

She had sorted through her kitchen for ingredients to bake cookies. Stirring raisins into the thick, oatmeal dough made her feel temporarily better. She brought the still-warm cookies on a plate and drove back over to Solomon's, rang his doorbell. When he answered, wordlessly, she felt at once so childish, so small. She'd had so many things she planned to tell him but couldn't remember any of them. She held out the still warm plate, blurted, "Do you want your ring back?"

He'd shaken his head. "I've decided to forgive you," he said, but his face still looked angry, his features contorted into a scowl, even as he took the plate of cookies from her and pulled her roughly into a hug. He could forgive, she surmised, but probably never forget.

Up against the right side of the church basement room stands a folding table, upon which sits various platters of squares and cookies. The smell makes her stomach coil, makes her regret not eating one before sitting down. It would be impolite to get up and take one now in the middle of his talk. She should make herself wait.

She had waited so long for a husband! When the boyfriend Josie dated through university had broken up with her just before finals, Natasha had feigned an illness to get out of a family obligation and had, instead, taken Josie to the bakery in Parkdale where the two sometimes studied and shared a single dessert. Josie blotted her tears with a stiff white paper napkin while Natasha returned with a tray. Two mugs of steaming chamomile tea—Josie preferred coffee, but Natasha said tea would be more calming for her nervous system—and *two* generous pieces of chocolate cake. "Devil's food," Natasha had said, setting down the tray and offering Josie a metal fork. "Some days, we need two."

Josie has replayed their argument in her head so many times since Natasha went missing. She's probably blown it way out of proportion. Natasha probably wasn't *that* upset, Josie tells herself. Just sleep-deprived from her two back-to-back shifts, stressed about Summer's impending birth, which had already stretched her both emotionally and financially.

Solomon concludes his lecture. Josie stands, claps limply, and wanders over to the dessert table. Mini cinnamon buns, flaky croissants, lemon squares. A carafe of coffee, probably cold by now. Will Solomon care if she skips out on the socializing before he can show off his wife, brag about their seven year marriage? Probably—but these days, he's usually annoyed at her about something already anyway. She interrupts a young couple thanking her husband for his wisdom, tells him she is not feeling well. The young couple make concerned faces; the man pats her on the arm, and Solomon, thankfully, tells her to go home and rest. Genuine benevolence? Or just because they are in public? She offers to return and pick him up if he calls her when he's ready to go, but the young couple volunteers to drive him home and he accepts.

The bakery she and Natasha frequented in university closed down years ago. Josie parks the car at the Co-op grocery by their house and makes her way to the cool glass display case that contains the baked goods. There—chocolate cake by the slice, whorls of icing on top so dark it is almost black, gritty the way Natasha liked it. Josie orders two slices, takes them to the register and pays with cash, crosses the parking lot back to her car. Opens the first plastic container.

She forgot to ask for a fork. Oh well. She reaches in with her bare, unwashed fingers, plucks a generous glob of cake and frosting and stuffs it into her mouth. The icing feels slippery. She consumes more of the confection, crumbs falling down her blouse. She wipes her fingers on her black skirt, where the stains won't be detected.

She could bring the second slice home for Solomon. Her husband has a sweet tooth—she remembers going to various bakeries to choose their wedding cake together, linking arms and feeding each other small cubes. She'd wanted that silly, uninhibited moment at the reception of shoving cake in each other's faces, kissing it off—but Solomon thought it was cheesy. He'd chosen strawberry shortcake, which reminded him of birthday cakes his mother had made for him as a little boy. Since their wedding, she's learned to make Solomon's favourite shortcake with cream cheese icing and concentric strawberries on the top, cut in half, like hearts.

Maybe she should go back to the library and check out *The Seven Principles for Making Marriage Work*. She read it about a year ago, but could probably use a refresher. If she bought it, she could refer to it any time she wanted, but every little bit of savings counts for their budget. The first time she read it, Solomon was away on a mission trip in Uganda with his church youth group. Alone in their marital bed, Josie had felt awash with guilt as she devoured the chapters on turning *towards* each other, making sure to respond to bids for attention and affection. More than once, Solomon has accused Josie of being pre-occupied with her work, uninterested in sex, unenthusiastic about his ministry, obsessed with her blog about Natasha, obsessed with timing intercourse to achieve a pregnancy.

Now, her fingers sticky with chocolate cake, she thinks she should have stayed at the church. Truly turning towards her husband would mean listening intently to his lecture instead of fussing about the chair, letting her eyes wander to the snack table. Turning towards would have meant standing beside him afterwards, putting her hand on his lower back, smiling and nodding as he spoke to the young couples. This is just a slump—the seven-year itch. All marriages go through slumps every now and then, but theirs doesn't have to. She should drive home, put the second piece of cake on a plate, fill a glass with milk, and put it on his bedside table. She should run a warm bubble bath, put on her white cotton nightgown with the spaghetti straps. And when he comes home, if he turns to her in the bed and initiates intimacy, she should turn towards him, even though it is too late in her cycle for it to count— and if he doesn't initiate tonight, she should offer him a back massage. Maybe God is making her wait all this time for a baby to teach her a lesson. She needs to focus on more physical expressions of love for her husband. Maybe if she relaxes, she will get pregnant. Children will be a natural expression of their love. She pictures herself rubbing Solomon's tense shoulders, feeding him the cake, kissing his mouth, tasting the chocolate on his lips.

But how will a detour to the grocery store fit with her story of feeling ill, of going home to rest?

She pops open the second container and reaches in. Places a generous mound in her mouth and lets it sit there, on her tongue.

When both slices are gone, Josie opens the car door, takes the plastic containers and crosses the parking lot again to the nearest trashcan. Her tongue feels tingly and her head suddenly aches with the onslaught of sugar and selfishness. The bin overflows with trash, but she stuffs her own garbage down until she cannot see it anymore.

GREG

GREG HEARS THE VACUUM BEFORE HE UNLOCKS HIS
apartment door. He should not have given his parents a key. And he
should have known better than to let two phone calls from his mother
go by without at least a text back. His parents had completely freaked
out over the message board post. His father said he'd thought Greg
should have asked for a lawyer on day one, and his mother just kept
repeating, "Why would somebody write this? Why?" His father had
actually suggested doing a press conference to "set the record straight."

"No," Greg had insisted. "Please, no." Good God, what if his lawyers actually thought a press conference was a good idea? His father had
been the one to hire the lawyers in the first place—Cooper and Lau, two
females, a good strategy, his father insisted, given the domestic violence
accusations. He needed to have women on his side. Who knew what
the cops were going to try to pin on him next? Greg has started having
diarrhea, and yesterday he noticed a speckled rash in the crook of his
right elbow. He will *not* mention these things to his mother, because she
will undoubtedly drag him back to the doctor. The other day she practically tried to force-feed him perogies—she'd actually lifted a forkful
dripping with sour cream to his mouth.

Now, as he opens the door, the vacuum powers down, and his mother ambushes him with a hug. She's gained weight; the buttons of her navy blouse strain over her breasts. Greg can see the chain of the pendant she's worn around her neck ever since Natasha went missing, a single silver cursive letter N, but the letter itself hides under her shirt.

"I made dinner," she says, releasing him. He smells something hearty. The toilet flushes, and his father emerges, wiping his hands on his jeans. "Pork casserole and garlic bread." His mother moves into the kitchen and opens the oven, releasing a waft of heat and garlic into the apartment. Larkin has occupied the Poang chair, curled herself around a blue pillow Greg's mother brought over on one of her last visits in an attempt to make the apartment more homey.

Greg kicks his shoes off. "You know, I have a bunch of papers to mark—"

"What's the topic?" Greg's father rummages through the cabinets. "Do you have any salt?"

"You're too busy to eat?" His mother wraps the vacuum cord around its base. Greg doesn't actually own the vacuum. So little of his condo is carpeted, and also, he doesn't care. His mother must have hauled his parents' vacuum over herself. "Do you know how much cat hair this thing picked up?" she asks. Was it reasonable, he wondered, for his mother to expect that, on top of keeping up with his work deadlines, keeping Larkin alive, dealing with his lawyers, dealing with Reuben, and remembering to take all his meds, he should also keep a clean and homey house as well? Sometimes, during a panic attack, he stares at the vials on his nightstand and imagines unscrewing the childproof caps, emptying the pills into his palms like candy, gnawing the capsules into fine white powder, sharp and vile on his tongue. Chewing would get the drugs into his bloodstream faster, and then he could just go from sleep to nothingness. The quicker the better.

"What's the topic?" his dad asks again.

Greg looks away. "It's...they have to identify risk factors for flooding..." Is he really going to get into it? How much of this will his parents actually understand? When he told them about his proposed Ph.D. thesis topic his mother's eyes had completely glazed over. Doing a Ph.D. in the first place had been Greg's mother's idea—she'd shaken him awake one morning as a little boy and told him she'd had a dream of him becoming a scientist. She liked to tell him about the time in junior high that she and her brother had gone fishing and discovered the dead carcass of a one-eyed frog. She'd taken it home, wanting to preserve and study the birth defect, but her mother had screamed, thrown the corpse immediately in the trash, and told her if she ever brought home any wildlife again, she could go without dinner. Despite the memorable one-eyed frog, she'd majored in English and never finished her degree. Greg wondered how his parents would have felt if he'd decided to study art in university like he really wanted. But then, he would have actually had to show his sketches to someone.

"Like what risk factors for flooding?" she asks, now.

"Like...logging...forest absorption...you know, all of these things could cause runoff, potentially raise the water levels in Kananaskis River, which flows into the Bow."

Greg's dad leans forward and sniffs as his mother takes the bread out of the oven. "Better loosen my belt!"

How quickly could Greg get through this dinner? Tomorrow is Tuesday, and on Tuesdays he watches Summer after school so that Abby can work late at the salon, so he won't be able to get his marking done then either—and he's supposed to post the grades by Wednesday.

"What's runoff?" his mother asks, playfully swatting Greg's father away with an oven mitt and grinning. Seriously, these two people almost got divorced six years ago? Now teasing each other in the kitchen like newlyweds?

Greg looked away. "Excess water...you know, the soil can only absorb so much, so it gets infiltrated to full capacity, and then the surplus...it has nowhere to go."

His mother leaned back down into the oven to remove the pork dish. "So where does it go, then?"

"It just...spills over everything, causes water damage, flooding. Especially if it's polluted. After it rains, for example..."

Rain. Natasha, running. Running in the rain. All the peripheral damage. "Just—give me a second," Greg says. He steps around the vacuum and into the bathroom, closes the door behind him. Turns on the fan. Sits on the edge of the tub. Puts his face down between his knees. Feels the pressure building behind his eyes.

Make it stop. Make it stop.

His phone vibrates in his back pocket. He blinks, retrieves the device. He doesn't recognize the number, but what if it has something to do with Natasha? He hasn't not answered an unknown number since 2002.

"Hello?" he mumbles.

"Hey," comes a male voice. "Is this Greg?"

"Yeah. Who's this?"

"Oh, hey! This is uh, Cam—Summer's dad?"

Why on earth is Cam calling him? No no no no no…"Is Summer okay?" Greg blurts.

Cam sounds surprised. "Uh, yeah, man, she's great. Listen, I was just wondering if you wanted to like, hang out some time? Go for a beer or something?"

Greg can hear his parents laughing outside the bathroom. One of them has told some kind of joke. He takes a deep breath.

ABBY

YOU MADE ME PROMISE I'D GO TO UNIVERSITY. TOLD ME IT would set a good example for my future child. Told me I had the potential. Told me university was different than high school, that I could choose my classes, study what I wanted. You swore I would like it.

So I promised. What choice did I have? You'd opened up your home to me, bought me a crib and a changing table, made sure I had child support. You'd even set up a savings account for soon-to-be-Summer so that *she* could go to university someday.

You were kind of a snob about that kind of thing, you know. Like, what's wrong with people who go to community college or trade school? Or people who get a job after high school, like waitressing or admin assisting, and just stick with it forever? If you'd been alive when I got offered the scholarship to go to college for hair and esthetics, you would have shit your pants. I would have got one of your serious big sister lectures, complete with hands on hips, pacing, creased brow, pursed lips. Words like, "seriously," and "vital," phrases like, "setting your life course *forever*."

But that's a moot point, isn't it? Because if you were still here, I wouldn't be the poor uneducated single mother whose sister went missing, and therefore, I wouldn't have been offered the full tuition scholarship in the first place. You always knew you wanted to be a nurse, but I never knew what the hell I wanted to do with my life. I didn't even really want to be a hairstylist. I just wanted to piss Dad off, since, at the time, he was in the business of withholding my trust fund unless I went to university and got a *real* education. I wonder where you got your academic snobbery from. Eye roll.

You always knew you wanted to be a nurse, ever since your heroic childhood rescue of Josie's brother in the ravine. Every time I heard that story growing up I wanted to throw something. Like, who could possibly live up to that? You had to set the bar impossibly high, didn't you? I didn't have a chance.

Anyway, I'm thankful for that scholarship, not only because I got to give Dad the metaphorical middle finger, and because now I can make a decent enough living for me and Summer, but also because I actually like doing hair. Let's face it, I was never going to be the kind of person who could sit behind a desk all day. And I'm way too much of a fuck-up to have a job like yours with real responsibility. I know I got the tuition offer because you went missing and it made the college look good in the press. But I'll take whatever scraps I can get.

When people sit in my chair, they tell me things. Like how their brother is an alcoholic. How their spouse cheated on them. How they're too scared to get a divorce. How they hate their mother-in-law. How they went to their grandfather's funeral but couldn't cry. And they let me rub shampoo into their scalps, fringe their bangs, create soft layers that frame their face. And when they leave, I hope they leave a little bit better.

I cut Greg's hair and Josie's hair for free in exchange for babysitting. Dad would have a fit if he knew I let Greg babysit. Fuck that. I know whoever posted that lie is a shit disturber. People post all kinds of stuff on Jason's message board and none of it is true. You loved Greg and Greg loved you and if none of this had happened you would have gotten back together. It was only a matter of time. Nobody ever loved me an ounce of what Greg loved you. To be honest, you leaving him was a huge mistake, Tash. When you have that kind of love, you don't let it go. I wouldn't have.

Last year, Greg was sitting in my chair, after hours, and I was brushing the strands of hair from his neck, when Summer printed her name for the first time with the S the right way—a major deal. Greg and I cheered and Greg hoisted her up onto his shoulders and paraded around the room and banged into my co-worker Shayna's station and knocked over her hot rollers and a box of bobby pins.

Summer laughed and laughed and laughed.

You should have been there.

GREG

USUALLY, GREG LEAVES HIS OFFICE DOOR CLOSED, EVEN though he doesn't have a window. Initially, his mother tried to decorate the office, mounting his framed doctoral degree on the wall opposite his desk, bestowing him with a cactus, the only plant, she teased, that could grow in a room devoid of sunlight. Sometimes Greg gets caught up in his research and doesn't realize the passage of time; he has, several times, left his office to find the university hallways empty, the parking lot barren. His degree hangs crookedly now, covered with a layer of dust.

Early on, Greg made an implicit deal with the cactus. He would not require it to maintain its appearance, nor to bear the burden of making his office appear homey or inviting. He would, in fact, not water it. He would simply allow it to die as opposed to suffer. Greg can't help but pity this stoic Cactaceae, spines out, defenses up. What is it protecting itself from? Why should it have to live out the rest of its miserable existence under a dingy 1970s light fixture with Greg as its only other living companion? Still, years have passed, and despite Greg's refusal to water it, the cactus remains steadfast, barely shrivelled.

Over the summers, Greg sometimes lets his office door hang open. There are so few students wandering the halls, and it can get so hot without a window to crack. The door hangs open, but she knocks anyway, and Greg startles.

"Oh," she says, "sorry!" She has long, thick, caramel-coloured hair, flushed cheeks. She must be lost.

"Uh, no problem," Greg says. Did he shower today? This is why he shouldn't leave his door open. "Can I help you?"

She smiles. "Uh, yeah, can I come in?"

Greg looks around. There is only one other chair in his office, a stiff metal folding chair currently serving as a resting place for a stack of textbooks. "Okay," he says, and goes to clear her some space, toppling the books in the process. Is she like a new department admin or something? Maybe with some sort of complaint? Shit.

She reaches down to help him re-stack the books, and they each apologize over top of each other, until she eventually sits, and crosses her legs. Smiles at him again. "I'm Sylvie. We haven't met, but um, I'm a doctoral student here, well, not in this department but—" she stops. "Let me start again. I'm Sylvie—I'm doing my doctorate in criminology."

Greg's stomach drops. It's been a long time since he's had a voyeur, especially since he grew out his beard and started using his middle name. He used to get phone calls, even, somehow, after he changed his number; letters requesting interviews or blasting him for his supposed guilt; or condolence cards, usually of the religious variety, fluffy clouds and blurry doves and silver crosses, all of which reminded him of Josie. One letter had, oddly, not referenced Natasha at all, but been, instead, a bullet list of the writer's transgressions, in shaky, smudged penmanship. Unsigned.

What does this girl—this *criminologist*—want now?

She must have seen something in his face change, because she looks embarrassed, starts to apologize again, rushes to explain. "I've been working at the police department on my thesis, and I was asked to look at Natasha's file…"

She keeps rambling. Something about Reuben. Will Reuben never leave Greg the fuck alone? But Greg's brain sticks on that one word—Natasha. Natasha Natasha Natasha Natasha. Almost nobody says her name anymore. Beautiful syllables like three keys on a piano played in sequence, a little trill. Na-ta-sha.

He takes a shuddery breath.

"He's wrong," she's saying. "I told him flat out. Of course, he didn't want to believe me, but I thought you should know that I—that someone—advocated for you. What he's doing—it's like victimizing you all over again. And it's preventing the case from being solved. In my opinion." She shakes her head.

"We should close the door," Greg says, and stands to do so, almost tripping over the books. What if someone walked by and heard all of this? He's been having nightmares since he heard about Tash's watch, her dark hair tangled around the strap. During their relationship, they'd given each other scalp massages while cuddling in front of the television, using a timer to designate turns. When she wasn't looking, he'd twist the timer knob so he could get a little bit of extra love, feeling her gentle fingers probing the sore spots at the base of his neck and just above his ears. "You're so tense," she used to tease. A few nights ago, he'd dreamt that he'd been giving her a head massage, but then her dark hair began to fall out in clumps, into his hands. Her scalp exposed and bloody. Her blood on his fingers, underneath his nails.

The girl—what was her name again?—blushes. "I'm sorry, this is so awkward. I just wanted you to know."

"Thank you," he says. He looks up, into her eyes. Blue, where Natasha's had been brown. Her eyes seem genuinely sad. He's not sure what he's thanking her for, but what else can he say?

NATASHA

November 1983

Dear Diary,

Today is my golden birthday! It's November 11 and I am eleven. Plus its extra special because November is the eleventh month. I thought my golden birthday was going to be the best birthday ever accept that this is the worst birthday ever because my mom wasnt here. My dad told me she wasnt coming home for my birthday and she isnt coming home for even CHRISTMAS. she didnt even call. She missed my birthday party last weekend and the stupid person who lives at my house now who's name I wont say got a store cake. I didnt want a stupid cake from a store. I wanted my mom to make me a cake like always. So I wrote my mom a letter that said PLEASE PLEASE PLEASE PLEASE COME HOME and I MISS YOU. I was crying and I put some of my tears on the letter so she would see how sad I was. But I didnt know where to send it and Dad wont give me her address or her phone number. I HATE HIM. I ripped up the letter and flushed it down the toilet. Im 11 now. I need to tuffen up and not be a cry baby.

THINGS TO DO TO NOT BE A CRY BABY
by Natasha S. Bell

1. start running laps around the block so I can get super fast and strong

2. watch the saddest videos ever and make sure I DONT cry and if I do I have to watch them again like old yeller and bambi and the yearling and dumbo and sofies choice

3. walk to school past the house with the scary pit bull

4. if I feel like being a cry baby again listen to happy music like the tape I got for my birthday from Jason and also eye of the tiger

5. think of more things to not be a cry baby

THEANNA BISCHOFF

GREG

EVERYTHING GREG KNOWS ABOUT CAM, HE'S HEARD FROM Abby or Summer. According to Abby, Cam is an inconsistent parent, sometimes surprising Summer with expensive gifts, other times cancelling on her with little notice. Most of the time, she's told him, Cam shows up fifteen to thirty minutes late and seems quick to get going, ruffling Summer's hair at the door, saying, "Come on, Kiddo." His partner, Jessica, who Abby hates, either doesn't come during pick-ups, or waits in the car. Cam doesn't typically come to Summer's birthday parties, though Abby makes the point to invite him. He and Jessica host their own parties. Greg remembers Natasha telling him about how, every year on her birthday, some part of her kept expecting her mother to just show up, to walk through the front door. But then, Natasha had had her mother and father together in her life for ten years, whereas Summer has always known her parents apart. And Cam has stayed around—Greg has to give him credit for that.

Summer rarely talks about her father, but her comments tell a story similar to Abby's—"My daddy bought me this bike," or, on the occasion when Abby calls him, panicked and in need of a sitter because Cam has come down with a very sudden flu or Jessica booked a surprise weekend away, "Daddy couldn't come play with me tonight."

Greg isn't at all surprised when Cam shows up to Swan's Pub twenty minutes late, but seemingly in no rush. Cam pulls up a chair to Greg's table and waves down a waitress, says, "Corona?"

"Sure," says the waitress, and grins at Cam. Seriously? After he flagged her down and didn't say hello or please or anything?

"Sorry I'm late." Cam takes his jacket off, drapes it on the back of the chair. But he gives no explanation as to his tardiness.

"No worries." Greg has been aimlessly sipping Coca-Cola for the past fifteen minutes. His tumbler is almost empty.

Cam gestures towards the drink. "Rum and Coke? Nice. Want another?" Before Greg can answer, the waitress returns with Cam's beer, and Cam tells her, "He'll have a refill. On me."

"Thanks," Greg says, though he still feels guilty when he has more than one pop, Natasha's voice still in his head. As the waitress heads for the bar, Greg excuses himself to go to the washroom. Cam says, "Sure," and immediately pulls out his cellphone.

Greg pees, even though he doesn't have to, and, on the way back, sidles up to the bar and catches the waitress's attention. "Hey," he says, "would you mind making all of my drinks virgin?"

The waitress screws up her face. "What do you mean?"

She can't be more than twenty, Greg thinks. "Like, any time that guy—" Greg glances towards their table, "—orders me a drink, just make it without alcohol."

The waitress glances down at Cam's beer and the drink Cam ordered for Greg, already prepared.

Greg adds, "I'll still pay for the alcohol. Just add it to our tab." How can he explain that there's no way he's getting drunk with Cam?

The waitress shrugs, slides another tumbler under the tap and fills it with regular Coke. "Whatever," she says, and hands Greg his pop and Cam's Corona.

Back at the table, Cam puts his smartphone down on the table, but face up. "So," he says, and smiles. Does a head bob kind of thing. "What's new with you these days?"

Greg forces a smile. "You know…just keeping busy with work and stuff."

Cam smiles again, takes a sip of his beer. "Yeah, me too. Daily grind."

"Right."

Cam takes another sip, and so does Greg. Cam does the head bob thing again.

Finally, Greg says, "So, what'd you want to talk about?" Might as well get it out in the open. Might as well get this whole thing over with.

"Right," Cam says. Another sip. He's downing his beer awfully fast, Greg notes. Or is this just how young people drink now?

Cam continues. "I guess I just wanted to like, get to know you and stuff, because I know you babysit Summer sometimes."

Sometimes is a bit of an understatement. It's more like twice a week. But Greg knows better than to open up about the true frequency— Abby's family would freak if they know how involved he was in Summer's upbringing, especially now, given the message board posting, given that he's lawyered up. It all makes him look guilty, but the Bells have assumed he's guilty all along. He has no *necessary* ties to Natasha's family anymore. He could just refuse to babysit, avoid fueling the fire. Just avoid Natasha's family altogether, cut off all contact. But he knows that's not what Natasha would want. "What do you want to know?" he asks Cam.

Sip. "I guess—well, did Abby tell you about the incident at Summer's school?"

Greg assumes he means the referral for Summer to see a psychologist. "Yeah."

"Okay. Well, I guess I'm just worried. I mean, you're around them together, does she—does Abby talk about Natasha a lot in front of Summer?"

All the time. "Sometimes," Greg chooses. "Summer knows who her aunt is." Is? He thinks. Should he have said was?

"Right. But it's not like, scary stuff?"

Summer has memorized her address, their home phone number, Abby's cellphone number, Greg's cellphone number, her grandparents' cellphone numbers. They have a safe word—mozzarella—so that, in case of an emergency, Summer can tell if the person is safe and Abby has vetted them ahead of time. Abby has told Summer that, if someone ever tries to grab her and she can't run away, to sit on her bum, kick her legs, and flail her arms, making it harder for a person to get ahold of her. Told her that, if she's ever placed in the trunk of a car, to try to kick out the tail lights. Abby wanted Summer to practice this maneuver, but Greg stopped her, saying Summer looked scared. Abby capitulated in the moment, but Greg would bet she made Summer rehearse it after he left.

Still. "She's talked to her about safety. Stranger danger. That kind of thing."

"Right. Okay."

"Are you going to take her to a psychologist then?" Greg asks. It couldn't hurt. But then, would it do any good? Greg saw a psychologist twice, about six months after Natasha went missing. About half an hour into the first session, he knew he was beyond help. The second session was just a formality to try to appease his mother. Back when his parents had separated, Natasha had suggested he see a psychologist—even offered him a name of someone a friend of hers had gone to. He'd torn the business card up in front of her, told her there was no way he was talking about his feelings with a total stranger. Now, he leans forward and takes another sip of his virgin Coke, feeling the saccharine guilt slide down his throat.

"I'm looking into it," Cam says. "My fiancée says I should. She's really pushing me on it." He rolls his eyes. "You know, women. No matter what you do, you're doing something wrong." Cam has already drained half of his beer. "You want to order food?" he asks Greg. "Wings? Onion rings?"

"Whatever," Greg says.

More small talk. Cam flirts with the waitress, orders both appetizers when the girl can't decide which to recommend. Cam tells Greg that Summer refuses to take the training wheels off her bike, which Greg already knew. That Jessica wouldn't let Summer paint her bedroom orange, which Greg also knew. That he wants Summer to come to Kelowna with him and Jessica for the August long weekend, but he thinks Abby is going to say no. "I think Summer would love it, though," he says. Not true. Summer has told him she doesn't want to be away from Mommy for so long. But it's probably easier for Cam to just blame Abby. The food comes. Cam is doing all the talking. He's ordered another round of drinks. Greg's stomach acid grumbles, hisses. Has he even eaten today?

Cam talks with his mouth full, complains that his fiancée is controlling and wants him to set a wedding date. Why propose, Greg thinks, picking the batter off a limp onion, if Cam doesn't seem to want to marry her? "That was the deal with you, too, right?" Cam says, red barbecue sauce on his upper lip as he sucks the meat off another chicken wing and puts the bone down on his plate.

"What deal?"

"You know, Natasha always pushing you to get married and stuff."

Where has he heard this information? Abby? Her parents? The media? "She wanted to get married, yeah," Greg concedes.

Cam raises his hands in a small surrender. "Hey, man, I'm with you. Why settle down, am I right?"

Cam is engaged, has a child. How is he not settling down? "I guess," Greg says.

"Cuz you don't want kids, right?" Cam asks.

Present tense, as though having kids is still a possibility for him. "No," Greg said. Not anymore, anyway. When he was with Natasha, he wasn't sure. Tash thought this ambivalence meant he just didn't want them *yet*, but actually, he wasn't sure if he wanted them *ever*. Sometimes now, when he babysits Summer and they play Yahtzee, or binge watch '90s sitcoms, or make hot fudge sundaes, he thinks, *I could have done this.* Even, *I could have liked this.* Sometimes even, *I would have liked this.* But then, Natasha's own mother had walked out after *ten years*. And never even called. So, who's to say he wouldn't have been an equally shitty parent? Can he steer Cam away from this conversation?

"You going to eat that?" Cam gestures towards the last crusty onion ring on the platter. Greg shakes his head. "Cool," Cam says, and puts the whole thing in his mouth. "You wanna play darts?"

How long is this night going to go on? "I'm not very good," Greg says, "and I—"

"Me neither. Come on, it'll be fun."

Yeah right. Greg excuses himself to go to the bathroom again. He didn't eat very much, but he feels nauseous. In the bathroom, he kneels on the floor of a stall and attempts to vomit. Nothing comes up. He scratches at his elbow rash through his shirt.

By the time he makes his way back to the table, Cam is at the darts board, giggling with the waitress, who, Greg realizes, has been invited to play. Maybe he can make his exit, let the waitress distract Cam for the remainder of the evening. As he approaches, Greg realizes a tray of clear shots has been ordered. Cam holds one out to Greg, who shakes his head, feels another wave of nausea. "Gotta pace myself," Greg says, and Cam shrugs, clinks shot glasses with the waitress, sucks back the booze. Cam scrunches up his face and snatches a slice of lemon up off the table, pops the juicy end into his mouth and then gives the waitress a citrus smile, the rind as his teeth.

"Your turn," Cam tells Greg, and hands him a dart.

"How do you guys know each other?" the waitress asks.

Greg is about to say, *friends of friends*, but Cam interrupts—"Okay, get this, my daughter's mother is the little sister of Greg's ex-girlfriend, and she's *missing*. Like, *kidnapped*."

Fuck.

The waitress's eyes bug out. "Are you kidding me?"

Cam nods, suddenly serious. "I know. Tragic."

"Oh my God!" the waitress says.

"Six years ago," Cam says, his eyes wide. "They still don't know who did it."

Greg's stomach lurches. Natasha has become Cam's pick-up line.

"Oh my God!" the waitress says again. "I hope they catch the bastard!"

"Me too," says Cam, and puts his hand on the waitress's shoulder, like he's consoling her.

"I need another drink," she says.

"Agreed," says Cam, and the two reach for the tray of slimy shots, each tips one back.

Greg feels faint. His legs refuse to move. His tongue feels thick. Make it stop. "Show her a picture of Summer," he tells Cam. Anything, anything to change the subject.

"Oh yeah!" Cam says, and slides open his wallet, procures Summer's school picture, over which the waitress swoons. The waitress procures her own wallet to show Cam a picture of her nephew, but instead, encounters one of her ex-boyfriend.

"He dumped me last month," she says. "I forgot this was in here."

Cam suggests they pin it to the dartboard, give the asshole what he deserves.

"Yes!" the waitress exclaims. She and Cam do another shot. Isn't she supposed to be working? Cam is looking a little stumbly as he aims his first dart at the boyfriend's photo. The dart hits the wall. Cam laughs like this is hilarious.

"Your turn," he says, to Greg, who manages to pluck the dart from Cam's outstretched fingers.

Greg looks into the eyes of the ex-boyfriend, affixed to the dartboard with a thumbtack. Maybe the guy is an asshole. Or maybe not. Maybe Natasha's parents have done similar things with Greg's picture— at the very least, they've wanted to. Especially since the message board post. Who wrote that, anyway? Some twisted sicko looking to stir up trouble? What happens if Reuben finds something on the watch that he can link back to Greg? Greg must have touched that watch hundreds of times over their relationship, his fingers intertwined with hers, their wrists pressed up against each other. His lawyers have said that even if the cops pull Greg's DNA from the watch, they won't be able to argue anything other than casual contact. The watch could give them some- one else's DNA, they pointed out, could clear him. So far, though, Greg's heard nothing in this respect. Not that Reuben shares details of the investigation with him. But if they'd detected DNA from an unknown, it would get back to him, wouldn't it?

Greg could play one round, then say he's beat, let Cam drink himself stupid with the waitress. Get into whatever trouble he's going to get himself into. But Cam's still Summer's father.

"Come on!" Cam urges. "We don't have all night!" He reaches over for another shot.

Greg aims at the board. Lets the dart loose. Misses.

CAM

CAM HAD FOLLOWED ALL OF HIS BROTHER'S TIPS FOR GETTING
Greg to talk. Start with light conversation. Empathize. Make him think
you're on his team. Use alcohol to lower his inhibitions. Do something
active so he's focused on something else. All of these tactics are equally
effective in seducing women.

And yet, he's somehow ended up spending the night on *Greg's*
couch. His head throbs. He rolls over. This futon is so fucking stiff.
Did he puke last night? He has a vague memory of the cold tile floor
of Greg's bathroom. And yes, there's a garbage can on the floor in front
of his face. And there —Greg's cat, seated on a nearby Ikea chair, paws
tucked under itself, glaring at him, not moving, but very clearly plot-
ting Cam's death.

Cam sits up, almost pukes in his mouth. More spotty memories—
darts missing the corkboard; Greg helping him into a cab; the knock-
ers on that waitress. Cam fumbles for his phone. There it is, on the
floor beside the garbage can. He reaches for it; the cat's eyes trace his
movements.

Six texts from Reuben, two from Abby. Only one from Jess. Cam
has cheated on Jess enough to know that you have to make up an excuse
when you're going to be out late drinking just in case. He'd told Jess he

was going to hang with a buddy and possibly crash on his couch, drive home in the morning. Be safe. There was that one time he got pulled over and given a breathalyzer and blew just under the limit, so the cop had to let him off. He didn't want to risk that again. Cam had no idea how late he'd be out with Greg, and thought maybe he'd head over to Abby's afterwards. Jess's one text reads, "Good night baby! I love you!"

Cam can only imagine Reuben's texts—probably demanding answers, wanting to know why Cam hasn't responded. It feels like he's back in high school, slinking in the back door after a night of partying, his parents with their arms crossed, questioning where he'd been.

Or maybe Reuben thinks Greg has murdered Cam by stabbing him with darts.

Five minutes into his conversation with Greg, Cam knew he had nothing to do with Natasha's disappearance. The guy was way too pansy. Cam has this thing where, when he's watching *Law & Order* on TV, he can always tell who the killer is in the first fifteen minutes. It drives Jess crazy. She's always saying, "Stop ruining it!" It's not Cam's fault if he's smarter than her. Anyway, in Cam's opinion, Reuben's spidey sense about Greg are off. The killer is probably a total stranger, which is why nobody can solve it, because nobody knows the guy.

Cam shouldn't have downed so many shots. But that waitress was so hot. Greg was drinking, too. How did they even get home? Where is Cam's car? Where the eff is Greg anyway? Is he going to come strolling out in a robe and offer Cam some scrambled eggs or something? Cam needs coffee—badly.

Cam cranes his neck over the edge of the couch so he can see into Greg's bedroom. The door hangs open; Greg is sprawled face down, one arm dangling off the side. No shirt. Does he have underwear on underneath that blanket? What if he sleeps totally naked? Is he going to wake up if Cam starts moving around? Is Cam just supposed to slink out like they just had a one-night stand and Cam doesn't want to stay and cuddle? Should he just twiddle his thumbs until Greg wakes up so they can have an awkward goodbye? Or should he deliberately make noise but pretend it was an accident? *Oh, I'm so sorry, I'm such a klutz.*

Or…he could snoop around the house and uncover some dirt. Cam said he'd play undercover cop, so he might as well, even though he's pretty sure Greg had nothing to do with Abby's sister's murder. Greg looks like he's dead himself. This is going to be reeeeal easy.

Cam gets up off the couch, stretches, scrolls through his texts. Abby has sent him a couple about Summer. Well, their daughter may be the content, but Cam gets the underlying message. She wants him. She's been texting him *way* more since they hooked up. Always about their kid, of course.

Cam texts her back:

```
not feeling well this am
need some sexual healing
can u get babysitter for summer?
will be it worth it xxx
```

Cam glances from the cat to Greg's bedroom door. Greg still hasn't moved. Cam walks slowly to the kitchen, and the cat's eyes follow him. Here's Greg's mail—some envelopes opened, some not yet opened, spread out on the kitchen counter closest to the door, as though he dropped them on his way into the condo, hasn't yet come back to open the rest. Could Greg's credit card statement tell him anything? Cam slides the pages out of the envelope, flips to Page 1. Okay, so the guy has zero credit card debt. What a keener. He probably doesn't have a rebellious bone in his body.

What about his more private things? His secret stash? Cam's bedside table contains condoms; a picture of the first girl he kissed in junior high; a Michael Crichton novel—the sequel to *Jurassic Park*; a photocopy of his first paycheque; spare Euros from a high school family trip; his orange belt from karate from when he was twelve; that pair of cufflinks he thinks are ugly but has to keep because they are family heirlooms; a couple dirty magazines. From what he can see, Greg doesn't have a bedside table. But he can't see the whole room from here.

There's a closet in the hallway off the main room. Maybe he's one of those guys who keeps things in a shoebox tucked way at the top in a back corner. Cam once, way back when, asked Reuben whether it was true that murderers and rapists kept trophies of their victims. Reuben said, "Sometimes." Cam eases open the closet door, hoping it won't squeak. If it wakes Greg up, he'll claim he was looking for his coat. Was he wearing a coat last night? Hmmm…

Anyway, Greg doesn't wake up. And the closet is basically full of filing cabinets. Cam slides the top one open. What are these, articles? Nerdy science papers. Cam slides open the next two drawers. More of the same. Boring!

Cam slides his hand up to the top shelf, above where he can see, stands on his tiptoes and reaches back, gropes his hand blindly around until he hits the back wall. Nothing. His fingers come back dusty. No secret stash. Not even a shoebox of baseball cards or some hidden porn. Not here, anyway.

When Cam looks back, Greg hasn't changed position, but the cat has somehow moved from its spot on the chair to the kitchen counter, beside Greg's mail, without Cam having heard it.

What time is it, anyway? He could leave, but he has no idea where in the city Greg lives. He could be in some random suburb where it's impossible to get a cab. Cam could walk until he finds a street corner with designated signs and then call a cab back to his car. There's no point in being here anymore. Cam looks back at his phone. Maybe Abby has texted him back. She'll know where Greg lives, maybe she could come get him. Maybe he'll get lucky.

Three missed calls? In the last five minutes? Really? Cam checks—they're all from Reuben. And several new texts, too.

CALL ME RIGHT NOW
I'M SERIOUS

Cam can practically hear his brother yelling at him. He's way too hungover for this. Wait, are these texts from Reuben or Abby? Cam sees his message to Abby a few lines above Reuben's all caps.

His stomach sinks. Did he accidentally—

Ohhhhh shit.

REUBEN

CAM IS SLEEPING WITH HIS VIC'S LITTLE SISTER. AKA THE LAST known person to see her alive.

What a fucking idiot! Reuben's hands shake on the steering wheel. He couldn't sleep last night when he didn't hear from Cam; and then this morning, when there was still no message, he couldn't sit still. He nursed a black coffee and told Stacy he'd go get groceries just so he'd have something to do. It's his day off—he just wanted to sit around watch TV, but Stacy planned this whole family outing, taking the kids swimming. He'd argued that they could wait a couple hours, go to the outdoor pool when it got a bit warmer. In the meantime, he'd go for a drive, clear his head. Come back with some apples or something. Anything.

He hadn't even gotten to the grocery store when the texts came through, all in a row.

```
not feeling well this am
need some sexual healing
can u get babysitter for summer?
will be it worth it xxx
```

He had to pull over. His shithead little brother's silver-platter life has no consequences. Reuben slams his fist down on the steering wheel and the horn blares.

He needs a beer. He needs a beer he needs a beer a beer a beer a beer—

He has not had a beer—or any alcohol, for that matter—since his early twenties, since he joined the force. In college, he drank himself to the point of blackouts more than once until Stacy gave him an ultimatum.

He flings the driver's side door open, gets out of the car. His whole body is vibrating. He could get suspended for this—or fired. Cam has thought this whole investigation is a cool game or something from the very beginning. Greg is a *violent offender* for fuck's sakes. Reuben took a gamble and ended up making everything worse.

He presses the release button on the trunk and it springs open. Inside, Stace has stacked the kids' swimming shit. It smells funky, like she threw the kids' towels and water wings and stuff in there when they were still damp. The twins' pool noodles—one pink, one blue—criss-cross over top of the other swim stuff. Stacy's on a kick to get them to learn to swim without lifejackets. The thing about a lifejacket, though, is that you don't have to keep your eyes on your kids every second they're in the pool. When they're floating around on some sort of flutter board or hanging onto a pool noodle, they could just let go and drown.

Reuben should have fucking known better than to let Cam get involved. Correction—he didn't *let* him get involved, he *asked* him to. Practically begged.

Reuben grabs his daughter's pink pool noodle from the trunk as though it's a baseball bat. Swings it once in the air, then slams it against a tree. The thwack of foam against the tree is weak. Not particularly satisfying. Reuben swings again. Again.

The hair tested positive. He's got the vic's DNA, but he can't trace the fucking vehicle. He's got a witness who claims she knows about domestic violence, but won't come forward, an IP address that hit a dead end. He pushed his perp too hard and the guy's not talking, has a whole team of lawyers making sure he never gets questioned again. And now his one in with the perp is ruined. And some know-it-all with big tits at the station is trying to talk him out of his hunch. Probably talking to all his junior detectives, too. Making them question whether Reuben even knows what he's doing.

Whack! The pool noodle splits in two. Reuben pants, trying to catch his breath. His blood pressure is probably sky-high. He looks down at the broken half of the pink noodle, still clutched with two fists. The other half lies limp on the grass beside the tree. Some weapon.

HIM

I DIDN'T EVEN HAVE TO TRY THAT HARD.

"Hello?" Your little sister sounded like she'd just woken up.

"Uh, yes, I'm calling from Scotiabank Mastercard, can I speak with Natasha Bell please?"

"She's not home right now."

"Is there a better time to phone? Perhaps this evening?"

"She gets home around eight-thirty."

"Alright, thank you, I'll call back then."

"No problem."

I mean, I used a pay phone just in case she remembered the unusual call and mentioned it, in case anybody ever tried to track it. But it didn't matter. She didn't remember anyway.

Same thing with the message board. When you're dealing with stupid people, you don't even have to try that hard to cover your tracks. I just had to distract them a little bit, get them to stop thinking about the watch.

You thought you were so smart, didn't you? Stashing your watch under the floor mat like that, with a chunk of your hair. I hope it hurt when you ripped it out.

2009

KATIE CAN'T HOLD IT ANYMORE. SHE SHOULD HAVE peed at the gas station, but she didn't anticipate getting lost. At least she'd filled her tank up an hour ago, she tells herself. At least it's light out. Sooner or later she'll find her way back onto the main road. But not before she pees.

She pulls over, exits the car, walks around so the car shields her from the road and unzips her denim shorts, slides them and her thong down over her hips. She squats, leans forward. God forbid somebody show up in the middle of nowhere right as she's baring her ass. Pee quickly, she tells herself.

What's this blue plastic thing on the ground? Katie yanks her shorts back up, then bends to pick up the item. A baby's soother—caked with dirt.

It's not like there are garbage cans anywhere near here. Katie brings the soother with her back into the car and drops it into the empty paper coffee cup in her cup holder. She'll throw them both out later. When she finally figures out where the hell she is.

JUNE 2013

The rain to the wind said,
'You push and I'll pelt.'
They so smote the garden bed
That the flowers actually knelt,
And lay lodged—though not dead.
I know how the flowers felt.
—Robert Frost

TRACY: I'm here tonight with the family of Natasha Bell, who was just twenty-nine years old when she went missing in 2002. With me is her father and stepmother, Paul and Kathleen Bell, her stepsister, Dr. Kayla Cox, and her best friend, Josie McKinnon. Next month marks eleven years since Natasha was last seen. Paul, for those viewers who are unfamiliar with your daughter's story, can you give us a recap?

PAUL: Thanks for having us, Tracy. Well, it was a beautiful night during the Calgary Stampede, there were many visitors in town, everyone was in good spirits. Natasha was at her home with our younger daughter, Abby, who was spending the night. Natasha left to go for an evening jog—she lived a very healthy lifestyle, she was very athletic. Anyway, after some time, Abby became concerned because Natasha had not returned. This was very out of character. Abby called the police, and they began an investigation. But, you know, it was an extremely frustrating case, right from the get-go, because we had virtually no leads. Initially, there was no evidence of a crime, because she left the house, and no one knows exactly where she went.

TRACY: Tell us about the new evidence uncovered in 2008.

PAUL: Well, basically, her watch was found in the remains of a vehicle—a grey pickup truck—that had been sent to the junkyard. It was reportedly found underneath the vehicle's floor mat, which aroused suspicion for two reasons; one, because it was somewhere that it could not have fallen—it would have had to have been placed there deliberately—and two, there was a large quantity of hair alongside it, which also seemed to have been put there deliberately. The hair tested positive for Natasha's DNA. This was the first real evidence we had that we were dealing with a crime here, although it was something our family really knew all along. To me, it's clear that she knew she was in danger, and she left evidence behind in the hopes that it would be found and could lead to her recovery.

TRACY: And tell us, Paul, what happened with that evidence?

PAUL: Unfortunately, by the time the watch was located and reported to police, the vehicle had been dismantled. All we know was that it was a grey pickup truck. Because it had already been taken apart, we were not able to test the rest of that vehicle for evidence, such as blood or fingerprints.

TRACY: That's so unfortunate! You know, back when this tragedy happened, I read that there was some suspicion that Natasha's ex-boyfriend could be involved. Is there any truth to that?

PAUL: The police looked hard at him, Tracy, because Natasha was the one to end the relationship, and, in cases like this, it's usually a male who was in an intimate relationship with the victim. He certainly had a motive.

TRACY: That motive being—

PAUL: It's possible he tried to get back together with her and she rebuffed him. We will never know because she hadn't talked to us about it. They started dating when they were teenagers. I wish I had been more involved. Asked her more about how things were going, if she had any concerns. I always had a funny feeling about him, that something was not quite right. Also, in 2008, there was an anonymous tip that he had been violent towards Natasha prior to her disappearance. This tip was left on the message board that we still run—

TRACY: Yes, we have that link running on the bottom of the screen now, findnatashabell.com.

KATHLEEN: Hindsight is 20/20. He claimed that the information was falsified, and he acquired a team of lawyers. We asked him to take a polygraph, but he refused. I mean, why would somebody just make something up like that? It doesn't make sense.

TRACY: He refused a polygraph? On what grounds?

JOSIE: Because they're inadmissible in court. But I still feel he should have taken it. For Natasha. For us. I mean, why not take it if you have nothing to hide?

TRACY: Now, Josie, you are Natasha's best friend. The two of you go way back, is that right?

JOSIE: Yes, since childhood, that's right. We were extremely close. She was always there for me, through—[…] Sorry, I still cry whenever I think about her.

TRACY: Understandable. I hear you were instrumental in the case in the beginning, orchestrating searches, soliciting donations, maintaining a presence in the media. Tell me what you've been told about the investigation, where it stands at this point.

JOSIE: At this point, we're not very much further than where we were in the beginning, and I think the relative lack of evidence—

KATHLEEN: —complicated by police incompetency—

JOSIE: Without a crime scene, we didn't really have any specific area to focus, to really search. When we did obtain leads, like the discovery of her watch, it almost made things worse because it would get our hopes up and then just…go nowhere. And the more time that goes on, the more frustrated and devastated we become. Without her.

KATHLEEN: It's been such a strain on our whole family. It has really just hurt us all, so so much. Really. I still have panic attacks, I have been prescribed anti-anxiety medication. I see a therapist regularly. No one has any idea the kind of pain I have been through.

TRACY: Of course, of course. Undoubtedly this has been such a tragedy. Mrs. Bell, can you elaborate on the, uh, the police incompetency, as you say?

PAUL: I can speak to that. From the get-go, we were disappointed by the lack of police presence. That first night, we had a missing, endangered young woman, and the Calgary police sent a single detective to the house.

KATHLEEN: Not to mention our eighteen-year-old daughter was the last known person to see Natasha before she went missing, and I feel like the police should have had a psychologist present during that interview. She was very vulnerable at that time.

TRACY: How is she doing today?

KATHLEEN: Wonderful, she's wonderful. Of
course it was awful for her to lose her sister—they
were extremely close. But through it all, she went
to college, she's raising her little girl—our beautiful
granddaughter, Summer—here's a picture of her, isn't
she adorable?

TRACY: So precious! Let's zoom in on that. Thanks
for sharing, Mrs. Bell.

KATHLEEN: Thank you. We just love her to death.

TRACY: Now, let's go back, then, to the
investigation. You say you feel police mishandled
some things?

KATHLEEN: Yes. And we were kept out of the
investigation, which was so frustrating. We hired
a private investigator, but that didn't give us any
more information than we already had about her
abduction.

TRACY: Her presumed abduction, yes.

KAYLA: Not to mention we were taken advantage of,
by the private investigator, you know, financially. When
you're in this position, you really have no resources.
You're completely exposed. Everyone is a vulture. We
eventually fired him. So that was money wasted.

TRACY: It must be exceedingly frustrating—ten,
going on eleven years later. Tell me, each of you, what
do you think happened to Natasha? In your heart of
hearts?

KATHLEEN: You know, I really, really think that
she's gone. It kills me to say that, but I just feel,
deep down, that she's no longer with us. Maybe it's
mother's intuition.

TRACY: And how about you, Paul?

PAUL: I just—I'd rather not speculate.

KAYLA: I have to agree with my mother. And, I think statistically, when someone has been missing for this amount of time, that's usually the case. We have to face the facts.

TRACY: Yes, statistics can be sobering. And you, Josie—you've been so active in the investigation from the beginning—do you have any feelings or suspicions, based on what you know, about what has happened to your friend?

JOSIE: You know, I have to disagree with Kathleen and Kayla. I just feel strongly that…you know…there are always exceptions. There have been several cases recently, in the States and in Europe, where missing people have been found after years and years, having been imprisoned, or held against their will. There is also the possibility of sex trafficking. I don't want to assume I know what happened until I know for sure. I want to follow all possible leads. Leave no stone unturned.

ABBY

REMEMBER WHEN MY MOTHER USED TO DRAG ME HOUSE hunting? Every summer she tried to convince Dad we needed an upgrade. Seriously, what kind of kid wants to wander around someone else's abandoned mansion trying not to touch anything or leave footprints on the newly steam-cleaned carpet?

I was mad at you for having a tennis lesson, or a date with Greg, or whatever else it was that allowed you to have fun while my mother tortured me, asking realtors questions about square footage and ensuite bathrooms, always ignoring my whining about how much longer before we could go. One time, I said I needed to go pee and I snuck into the family's den, stole a Sharpie, and doodled an angry face with Xs for eyes and a zigzag mouth onto the underside of the desk where probably no one would see it until they moved.

This is what Cam and Jess's McMansion reminds me of. Ruining things.

Parked out front, I spit on my thumb and wipe a smear off the dashboard, as though this somehow makes my car clean, somehow negates the breakfast bar wrappers in the console, the dark stain where I once spilled wonton soup on the passenger seat, Summer's smelly dance leotard and duffel bag strewn in the back.

Most of the time, I *hate* Cam. And even when I don't completely hate Cam, I hate that I have to share my daughter with him, that she goes over to his house and the three of them—Summer and Cam and Jessica—eat dinner together like a little family, and I sit in my car, waiting for her to come out, waiting to get her back. I wonder if someday she'll want to spend time with their family versus just with me. A real family—a mom and a dad and a kid—not an accidental, split family. Not just her and I eating penne noodles with butter and Parmesan and watching reality TV, me doing her hair.

I don't want to marry Cam. I don't even want to be with Cam.

No, seriously. I don't.

I just want to sleep with him whenever I want. Because I can. And because I'm pretty sure Jess still doesn't know, although I've heard him arguing with her on the phone, and he talks about her like they fight all the time. Like he doesn't even like her. So maybe she suspects something. But it's been five years, on and off. So maybe she's just naïve and stupid. He tried to call things off with me after the wedding, and I said, "Yeah, good luck with that," and then two months in, they had a big fight, and surprise surprise…guess he can't resist.

Anyway, he was mine first.

Yesterday morning, when the alarm went off, Cam rolled over and hit the snooze button before I could. I deliberately set the alarm with a cheerful tune, thinking I wouldn't wake up so cranky. Now, every time I hear "Sweet Home Alabama," I want to strangle someone.

"Get dressed," I whispered. "I'm going to wake up Summer."

He groaned. "I don't have to work today. Why am I up this early?"

I rummaged beside the bed for my T-shirt. "Why don't you have to work today?"

He stretched, yawned a morning breath yawn. "I took a personal day. I have to pick Jess up from the airport at three; our place is a mess, I forgot to book the cleaner, I have to—"

I stood and slid my T-shirt over my head, reached for my crumpled bathrobe. "I'm going to wake up our kid and I don't want her to know that you're here. So put your clothes on."

Most times, Cam doesn't mention his wife. Most times, Cam doesn't sleep over, either. But Summer had the flu last week and Cam had a work deadline and we hadn't hooked up in over a month, and with Jess out of town, it was just easier. Still, I made him park down the street. Summer could recognize his car. I'm not putting her in the middle of this. Someday maybe I'll start dating someone for real, and kick Cam to the curb, and she'll never have to know. Or maybe he'll leave Jessica. It could happen.

"Stay," he said, and reached out, lazily, grazed my thigh with the back of his hand, hooked his pinky into the waistband of my panties. "You know, if we sent Jess and Summer out *together* some time, we could do this more often."

I yanked my hand away. "Uh, no. No way am I going to let *your wife* bond with *my child* just so you can—"

He narrowed his eyes. "So I can what?"

I pulled my robe tighter, tied the belt. "You should go."

Maybe Cam slept with Jess after he picked her up from the airport and before he picked up Summer from school. Maybe he slept with both of us in the same twenty-four-hour period. He told me once, "Remember when you were a kid, and your parents let you stay up past midnight like, *one time*, and only because it was New Year's Eve, and you knew you better enjoy yourself because it could very likely *never* happen again? But then you're so fucking exhausted that you don't even want to stay up for it? That's what sex is like when you're married." True? Maybe. Or maybe just what he thought I wanted to hear. How would I know? I'm not the marrying type. Nobody would want me that much.

I'm the same age now that you were. Well, technically, you were twenty-nine years, seven months, and twenty-five days. Next year, people will ask me, "How old are you?" And I'll have to say, "thirty." And it will hurt, every time. Because you never got to be thirty. Or thirty-one or thirty-two or thirty-three or thirty-four…

My Summer-girl springs from the door of her father's house, her hair in waves hanging around her face. Did she curl her own hair? Or did Jess? Dear God, she looks like a teenager already, even though she's not even eleven until next month. I unlock the car door and my daughter slides in beside me.

"Ready?" I say.

She clicks her seat belt into place. "You know what's gross?"

I turn the key in the ignition. "What?"

"Dad has to go get his sperm tested."

"What?" I pull the car out into the street.

"I heard them fighting about—" She digs around the dirty napkin and empty coffee cup in the console. "Do you have any gum?"

"They fight in front of you?" Those assholes. A guy in a red SUV honks; I've drifted into his lane. "Maybe. Check my purse."

"They don't fight *in front of me*." Summer rolls the window down a little, rifles through my bag. "They were in their room and I was in my room, but like, I could still hear them."

"Why is he getting his sperm tested?" I ask, as Summer searches. But why does someone get their sperm tested except because they're trying to have a baby and it's not working? And is Jessica stupid? Cam *has* a child. If anyone is infertile, it's her. Maybe it's because she's such a coldhearted—

"Jess wants a baby." Summer tosses my purse onto the floor in front of her, pops open the glove compartment.

"I don't keep gum in there," I tell her. "How do you feel about it?"

"About gum?" She hums a line along with the radio.

"About your dad...if he has another kid."

She shrugs. "I dunno."

The music blares. I nudge the dial down a few decibels. "Are you worried he won't love you as much if he has another baby? That maybe he won't spend as much time with you or something? A baby could change a lot of things, you know."

She rolls her eyes. "I dunno. Whatever."

JOSIE

WHY WAS IT SO HARD TO LOVE SOMEONE? TO BE LOVED? Josie had even asked Natasha this question, once, in university, when Tash and Greg had had some sort of argument—about what, Josie can't remember, because they were always fighting about *something*. Josie and Natasha had taken the long route around the university to where Josie had parked outside of the kinesiology building because Natasha knew Greg's schedule and thought they might run into him if they took their regular route. As they walked, Natasha explained the story of the most recent fallout. Josie couldn't even keep up with the relationship politics at the time, let alone in retrospect. She remembers, though, that she had interrupted—"Why does it have to be so hard?"

Natasha stopped walking, glared. "What do you mean?"

"Like..." Josie felt flushed. "Shouldn't love be about feeling happy all the time, when you see that other person? Feeling like every day is better because...because you have that person in your life. It should feel like..." At that point, Josie was still waiting for the guy who would show up and surprise her when she was having a bad day and bring her jelly beans with all the black ones picked out. The guy who would read Robert Munsch's *Love You Forever* to his kids every night. The guy who would draw a heart on the mirror in the fog left behind from her shower. The guy who would ask her father's permission to marry her. The day before, she'd gone to her parents' house for Sunday night dinner, and her dad had cooked because her mother hadn't been feeling well, and when her mother had come to the table, her father had pulled the chair out for her, kissed the top of her head. "It should feel like…" how could Josie explain?

"Like sunshine and roses?" Natasha crossed her arms, clearly sarcastic. "Like unicorns and lollipops?"

Josie fidgeted with her keys. "That's not what I meant."

"Real love isn't like that," Natasha insisted. "Real relationships are frustrating. Sometimes you want to give up. Sometimes you have to sacrifice your own needs for the other person. And sometimes they have to sacrifice their needs for you." Her voice had raised in pitch and people kept looking over at them. How embarrassing!

But Natasha kept going. "Sometimes you feel totally in love and sometimes you don't. Sometimes it feels like they're going to love you forever and sometimes it feels like you could lose them any second. Me and Greg, we're connected, all the time, by a string, an invisible string running from my heart to his heart, and sometimes the string pulls really hard and it hurts like hell. And sometimes it gets tangled up and I have no idea how I'm going to pull it all apart. It's all knotted up. I'm not easy to love. Like, at all." She looked up. "You know?"

No, Josie had thought, she didn't know. Or, she didn't really agree. "I just want you to be happy," she said. She passed her keys from one hand to the other. "If that means being with him, that's what I want. But if you'd be happier without him…"

"I know." Tash started walking, which was probably a good sign. They both stayed silent until they hit the exit and stepped out into the crisp winter sunshine, the unseasonal breeze of a chinook, floating over from the mountains. In a day or so, they'd be back to minus thirty.

Now, over a decade since that conversation, Josie lies very still in bed beside Solomon as he snores, one arm sprawled above his head. An entire other person could fit in the space between them. In their wedding vows, the minister had spoken about how, if Jesus was not the centre of their relationship, their marriage was in danger. They had promised each other to always make room for Jesus. Josie rubs her three-diamond engagement ring with the pad of her opposite thumb. In this empty space between them, Josie doesn't *feel* God. Only Solomon's words from hours earlier, his hands on the table, palms up. He sometimes held his hands like this in prayer, as though making an offering up to the Lord. He'd said, "I have feelings for someone else."

He had not, he assured her, acted upon these feelings, not physically. He had not committed adultery, but he was guilty of coveting. He had spent a lot of time with the daughter of the church's former choir director—the young girl who had sung "Amazing Grace" so many years ago at one of the searches for Natasha. She was in her twenties now, the new choir director (her father having retired), and she and Solomon had worked closely together for the past two years. *Two years?* Josie thought.

These feelings confused him. He was struggling to push those feelings down, to stay true to his marriage. Okay, once—they had kissed, once. But it had been a moment of weakness, he was a flawed child of God. And while he felt remorseful, while it was technically a sin, the kiss had made him feel peace in his heart, it had been a genuine moment of connection, of joy.

As he'd said this, Josie felt a buzzing in her ears, across her cheeks. A dissolving from the inside out. Perhaps she would simply cease to exist.

The feelings were mutual, he told her, as though he'd anticipated the questions she couldn't bring herself to ask. He and this…girl… could no longer suppress these feelings. He needed some time to think, to decide what he wanted. He wanted to open his heart to Christ to lead him in the right direction. He wanted to spend more time with this girl, to explore a relationship, to determine the best path to proceed, before breaking his marriage covenant. He had to be honest, he reminded Josie. *Thou shalt not lie.*

This girl—she made him feel *majestic*, he'd said. *Majestic?* Was he serious? He kept going. She made him feel like he could do anything, be anything. She made him feel admired. Desired. Grand. "She pays attention to me," he said. "When I talk to her, she listens. She cares about what I have to say."

STOP! Josie had felt like screaming. She was a good wife. She did the best she could. Had Solomon—God forbid—been the one to disappear, she would have done everything she could. Just as she had done—just as she was still doing—for Natasha. How could she not?

She glances sideways at her husband's sleeping form, his seemingly peaceful sprawl. He looks as though a load has been lifted. He probably feels relieved. He probably feels *majestic*.

He's moving out, he told her. He doesn't know for how long.

What if this is the last time they share a bed? The last time they sleep in this house together as husband and wife? What if this is like the last time she saw Natasha, only this time she knows it's a *last time* instead of thinking it's just a regular day?

The whole thing had started over coffee. Where had it gone so wrong? Could she have stopped it, had she only realized? Can she stop this from happening to her marriage now? And if so, how?

"I just meant," Josie had struggled to explain, that day at the coffee shop, her best friend and her sweet chai in front of her, "a two-parent home is more ideal. Obviously. You know?" All she'd wanted was for Natasha to understand why she'd suggested adoption for Abby's baby in the first place. She hadn't meant to offend anyone.

Natasha had raised her eyebrows and glared. "Obviously?"

The coffee shop had felt unusually warm. "I don't mean it in a bad way," Josie said.

"What other way could you mean it?" Natasha had crossed her arms. "*I'm* not from a two-parent home."

"You're taking this personally." Remnants of Josie's pale pink lipstick had smeared along the rim of her paper cup. She'd swiped absently at her mouth with the back of her hand. Couldn't Natasha just calm down? People could hear them! "I remember what you went through when your parents split up and your mom left. You would have been happier if—"

Tash cocked her head, arms still crossed. "If I'd come from a family like yours?"

Josie shrugged. "Maybe." Why was Tash being so hostile? Had they not spent most of their childhood playing at the Carey's where they didn't have to worry about anybody screaming or calling names? Natasha's mom leaving had traumatized her. Natasha herself had said, more than once, that she wished she and Josie were sisters.

Natasha had leaned back. "Okay, well then, what about Jason?"

Josie felt a little jolt. "What *about* Jason?"

"He came from a—" Here, Natasha raised her hands and formed air quotes with her fingers, "*stable, two-parent home.*"

Low blow, Josie thought. Since Finn's birth, Jason had made some really good strides. He was an excellent father, even if he and Finn's mother weren't together anymore. It wasn't ideal, but he was making the best of it. Plus, he had epilepsy. "That's different," Josie had challenged. "There are medical factors. It's harder for him."

"The epilepsy doesn't excuse everything," Natasha interrupted. "The drugs, the fights—he has his problems, Jo. I know your parents would like to think it's just because he has seizures, but I think that's a cop-out. Lots of people have epilepsy and function totally fine. How people turn out—it's more complicated than just black and white, medical issue or none, one parent or two, married or divorced."

Josie had tried to change the subject. She still hadn't brought up the fact that she'd been offered a promotion at work. She wanted to take it, but what if she got pregnant right away? Would it be fair to take the position, only to go on a maternity leave nine months later? But then again, she and Solomon could use the money, especially if they got pregnant. Babies were expensive. Maybe Tash would have some insight.

She remembers Tash looking pale, with dark circles under her eyes, her ponytail slightly greasy. Has Josie exaggerated Natasha's fatigue and frazzled appearance in all the years of rehearsing this memory? Natasha had arrived at the coffee house fifteen minutes late, unusual for her, apologizing, saying she'd worked a double shift and had been having trouble sleeping. Josie had decided, in the moment, to forgive the comments about Jason. And yet—Josie wonders now if, in the moment, she had really let it go. Maybe she had simply stuffed her feelings down. Why had Tash's criticism of Jason bothered Josie anyway? Tash was typically more sympathetic to Jay, despite the lack of familial relation. Was this where the conversation had taken such an ugly turn?

Natasha wouldn't let it go. "It's not like all two-parent families are stable. Just because a couple is married doesn't mean they're able to provide a stable home for kids."

Was that comment some sort of dig at Josie's marriage? When she and Solomon had taken pre-marital counseling, their pastor had encouraged them not to air their dirty laundry. But sometimes Josie slipped and shared details about her relationship with Natasha, just as she had in high school and university. Except those men—those boys, really—were not her husband. And Natasha always seemed to dislike Solomon. Maybe she was just jealous. It wasn't Josie's fault that Greg hadn't proposed.

The week before that coffee date, Josie had shared an incident in which Solomon had chastised her in front of another couple from their church during a dinner party they'd hosted. She'd served his favourite, steak and potatoes, but apparently set the table with the wrong knives. Solomon, seated at the head of the table, had asked her to go back into the kitchen to retrieve the proper cutlery. Josie had obliged—despite the fact that Solomon's seat was technically closer to the kitchen, and wouldn't it have just been easier to get the knives himself, given that he knew exactly what he wanted?

When she'd returned with the new knives, Solomon had practically sneered. "Not those ones. The ones with the serrated edges." Didn't all knives have serrated edges? It had taken her three tries to find the "right" knives, each time forcing a smile for her guests while Solomon redirected her back to the kitchen like a petulant child. When she'd finally found them, she'd taken her seat beside her husband and he'd reached for her hand, gesturing that they should all hold hands, in a circle, to pray before they ate. As Solomon led the prayer, thanking Jesus for their meal, and for their fellowship, Josie hung her head and closed her eyes, painfully aware of Solomon's large hand enclosed around her small, sweaty one. When she'd told Natasha this story, she'd felt herself redden all over again, especially when Natasha had raised her eyebrows and said, "Why didn't you tell him to get up and get them himself?" As though it were that easy.

It wasn't fair to judge a marriage from the outside. Josie had promised to love Solomon for better *and* for worse. Nobody was perfect. That day in the coffee shop, after Natasha's comment about a stable home, Josie felt the words spilling from her lips before she had a chance to edit them. "That's not fair. You don't know anything about marriage."

What if, Josie wonders now, in bed next to Solomon, Natasha's comment about marriage had nothing to do with her? What if, that day long ago, she'd overreacted, taken it personally, lashed out for no reason? Or what if Natasha was hinting about Solomon because she could see the cracks in their relationship long before Solomon started to have feelings for the choir director? What if Natasha was just trying to protect her, and instead, she'd gotten her back up? Which was worse?

That day, Natasha had looked at her across the table, her skin pale, her eyes blank. She didn't say anything at first. Then, quietly—"Are you trying to push me over the edge?"

Josie hadn't known how to respond. Why didn't she say anything? Why didn't she apologize or ask for clarification? Why didn't she run to the other side of the table and give her beloved friend a hug, tell her that she was worth more to Josie than some stupid argument? Why hadn't she *known* something bad was going to happen? Why hadn't she had some sort of premonition?

They'd both sat there, for a second, saying nothing. And then— "Seriously," Natasha said, still quiet, too quiet. "Do you think I haven't had enough to deal with over the past year? Do you really want to jump on me about marriage right now? Knowing everything I've been through? Do you want me to just give up? Or have a complete breakdown?"

Josie remembers feeling stuck to the chair, her words stuck inside her mouth. Natasha had stood and pushed her chair back. Leaning forward, she held her fingers in front of Josie's face, her thumb and forefinger about an inch apart. "Because I'm *this* close," she said, and walked out of the coffee shop, abandoning her latte and Josie.

Now Solomon is leaving her, too.

GREG

WHEN HE WALKS INTO THE KITCHEN, GREG SEES THAT SYLVIE has left breakfast for him on the counter, even though she's already eaten, and even though she's still technically upset with him. Sylvie eats whatever she feels like, regardless of social conventions, for breakfast, lunch, dinner. The other night he came home late and she was eating a slice of pineapple upside-down cake; this morning, she's left him a plate of Triscuit crackers and some thick slices of cheddar cheese, alongside orange juice in a floral coffee mug. She often leaves him a helping of whatever she's having, but doesn't push him to eat. Today, he chews on a salty cracker and washes it down with some OJ. His stomach snarls at the slosh of acid. He's still not a breakfast person.

Sylvie's upset with him, and he's not entirely sure why. The house is quiet. Has she left for work already? No, it's Saturday. He opens the door to the dishwasher and is met with a sour stink; dishes are loaded, but not yet washed. He fills the caddy with chalky soap and starts a load. Nibbles another cracker. Pads down to the basement in his bare feet.

There's Sylvie, in child's pose, on her yoga mat, face to the ground, legs tucked up underneath herself, arms outstretched. Larkin stretches out this way sometimes, too, arms out in front, like a swan dive. Maybe he should go for a swim this morning, clear his head. He started swimming again a couple years ago, after he and Sylvie bought the house. At first, it made him feel old, out of shape, out of breath. He'd wake up the next morning, shoulders aching, skin itchy from the chlorine. Now, his muscles know the pattern of his strokes, his lungs no longer scream from the lack of oxygen when he holds his breath and goes under. He knows to rinse off the chlorine afterwards and to keep granola bars in the car so he doesn't get dizzy. Hypoglycemic, Natasha would have said.

After the day Sylvie came to his office to tell him about her conversation with Reuben, they'd occasionally met for lunch in Mac Hall, the campus hub. She was still finishing her Ph.D. then. They'd go early, before the line-ups got too long. Sylvie went through a phase of ordering a Vietnamese sub every day, after which she would give the owner, a sweet, middle-aged woman who drew smiley faces on the napkins she wrapped around Sylvie's sandwiches, a large tip. Greg got into the habit of ordering the same thing, minus cilantro. Often they took the food back to Greg's office to eat. One day, Sylvie had glanced over at the cactus and run one finger through the dry dirt at its base. "Do you ever water this thing?" she'd asked.

Greg had shrugged. "It's managed to survive this long."

"Well, *I'm* going to water it," Sylvie announced, retrieving a plastic water bottle from the side pocket of her backpack and tipping the remaining contents onto the dry dirt.

Sometime later, maybe a couple of months, Sylvie had been with him when Abby called, needing a last-minute sitter, and so he'd introduced the two women, and then he, Sylvie, and Summer all had Vietnamese subs together when Abby left for work.

Maybe a year into their friendship, Sylvie finally defended her dissertation, and to celebrate, planned a trip to Prague to spend some time with her brother, a married expat living in Paris with his husband and their adopted son. Prague had always been on Sylvie's bucket list since she was a kid. Greg had asked what else was on her bucket list. Tash had goals she'd talked about, but, to Greg's knowledge, she'd never formalized them into a list. She'd simply wanted to marry, to have two children, to someday get her Masters in nursing, and to start a charity to support women burned by acid attacks in countries like Bangladesh and Cambodia. She hadn't been big on travel, which had suited Greg fine. In grad school, he hadn't had the money to travel, even if he'd wanted to.

Sylvie had showed him her bucket list, which she'd saved on her computer; a list preserved from her childhood and added to over the years. Hold a snake, take a cooking class, walk a suspension bridge, get a tattoo, milk a cow, keep a journal every day for a year, eat ostrich, go two weeks without spending any money, sing at an open mic night, send someone an anonymous gift, take a photography class, donate blood, research family tree, be present at a birth, donate hair to a cancer charity, grow a tomato garden, learn CPR, read an entire encyclopedia, wear a kilt, enter a pie-eating contest.

Several items had already been crossed off. She'd asked if he had a bucket list. Finish his Ph.D. had been the sole goal in his mind for so many years. He'd accomplished that goal years ago. Now he had no direction really, other than going through the routine motions of taking a shower, going to work, not killing himself. But Sylvie's list made him think, and that night he'd told Summer about it, and she'd started one. Over the next few weeks, they'd crossed off a few items together. Learn to figure skate. Taste sushi. Get a picture drawn by a caricaturist. Summer added *get a kitten*. He'd have to work with Abby on that one. He wondered if Abby had a bucket list.

Greg had offered to drive Sylvie to the airport for her flight to Prague, and she'd accepted; when he pulled up at her apartment in his still dented Chevy (he'd never had the heart to fix the damaged bumper), she'd emerged with a large backpack slung over one shoulder. Her hair! She'd chopped it all off. It looked good, but whoa!

"Your hair!" Greg exclaimed.

"Oh yeah!" She'd reached up and touched her bare neck. "Abby cut it for me. I thought it'd be easier for travelling. I've had long hair forever. I needed a change." She didn't ask his opinion. He wondered why Abby hadn't mentioned that she cut Sylvie's hair. Were they friends now? Did they hang out without him? Had Sylvie donated her thick, fawn-coloured locks to a cancer charity? He could see Summer adding this goal to her own bucket list—Summer was such a bleeding heart, donating her allowance to the SPCA, befriending the child in her class who had cerebral palsy and was in a wheelchair, volunteering to pick up trash at recess for her school's environmental club. Greg was particularly proud of the last one. Still, he wished sometimes that she would have a thicker skin—if she hurt so much for other people, she would undoubtedly hurt badly when life's traumas came her way, which they inevitably would.

He popped the trunk for Sylvie and offered to load her backpack, but she said, "I got it," and slung the sack into the trunk herself, climbed into the passenger seat beside him. Patted her small handbag. "Ready."

He suddenly didn't want her to leave. Anything could happen to her in the next three weeks. What if he never saw her again? He leaned over and kissed her.

After a second, he could feel her kiss him back. When they broke apart, she smiled. "About time."

On the drive home, he wondered—now what?

And what about Natasha? Had she kissed anyone since him? The person who had taken her—did he kiss her? Did he force his lips up against hers? He pictured Tash's beautiful lips—licorice sweet. It could be anybody. He doesn't know—he won't know—who kissed her last. And if it had hurt.

The other day, Sylvie mentioned that it'd been four years since she defended her dissertation. Which means four years they've been together now. Greg's memory has always been shit, but especially since Tash disappeared. Sylvie doesn't seem to care, though, about noting or celebrating anniversaries. Greg suddenly remembers—he can't go swimming today, he promised his mother he'd have breakfast with her. Usually, they have breakfast on Sunday mornings, Sylvie included—his mother hovers less when they have a routine—but his parents are driving to the Okanagan tomorrow morning, so he'd agreed to move it a day earlier. He hadn't told his mother about Sylvie for almost six months after they started dating, unsure of what to really say. He and Sylvie had never really talked about it. He didn't even know if Sylvie ultimately wanted to get married or have children. Sometimes he wanted to know, but still, he just kept his mouth shut.

Why Sylvie was with him, he didn't know. He was probably—definitely—a terrible companion, a hollow shell of a human. What did he have to offer?

But then they'd had their first argument—his memories about the details are blurry, but it was the first time he'd seen Sylvie cry, and it had made him sick to his stomach. Of course, she would leave now. Whatever illusion she'd had about him, about them, was shattered, right? He'd blurted everything to his mother that day.

"Do you love her?" his mother had asked.

Did he? Was he even capable of love? And, if he did love Sylvie, should he be telling his mother before telling her?

Luckily, his mother hadn't waited for him to answer. Instead, she'd said, "You need to think about what kind of life you want—if you want her in it or not. If you want her in it, you let the little things go. And sometimes you let the big things go. I can't believe I ever thought about leaving your father. I was so stupid. And selfish. When we lost Natasha, I realized, it wasn't about me being happy or fulfilled or enlightened all the time. It was about just showing up every day, on the days when everything about him made me feel warm and fuzzy, and on the days when he couldn't do anything right and I was furious with him. If, at the end of the day, as I was falling asleep, I could hear your father's annoying snore beside me as I drifted off…" She'd reached across the table and taken Greg's hand, then sang, off-key. "Love is not a history march." She looked up. "You get it?"

He'd nodded. But—what? History march? Did she mean he should never have let Natasha go, because they had so much history?

He thought he recognized the tune from one of Natasha's '80s CDs. As he had a million times since that July night, he wondered where the hell her CDs had gone. He found an '80s station on the radio and let it play whenever he was driving or alone in the house for the next three days, the music so painfully reminiscent of Natasha it felt like he'd sliced a vein shaving, blood and melody spilling and mixing, unable to clot. On the third day, he'd almost had enough, almost couldn't tolerate it any longer, but then, there it was. The same tune his mother had sung.

He'd heard her wrong. Of course he had. It was victory, not history. In mishearing the lyrics, he'd missed her point entirely.

She'd meant, there was no sure thing, no clear right answer, not a test you could pass. When the notes filled the room, he was at once back in Natasha's car, listening to her sing along to the suddenly familiar song. He could practically smell her hair.

Tash had used to tease him about always getting the words to songs wrong. He hummed along quietly. How much else had he gotten wrong without even realizing it?

HIM

WAS IT HERE? THIS STREET, WHERE WE TURNED OFF? OR THE next one?

The third left? Or the fourth?

That night, when I got home, I couldn't stop shivering. Like I could still feel the rain in my bones. My muscles ached. The skin on my hand felt raw from where I'd gripped the shovel. You gave me a fuckin' blister.

I staggered to the shower, stood under the hot water, still in my boots, my jeans. Dirt and grit swirled around the drain, disappeared.

And then I peeled off the wet clothing, one piece at a time, left the hot water running. Stepped naked out into the bathroom. Swiped my hand across the foggy mirror. Looked into my own eyes.

Now, whenever I come out here, I get frickin' allergies. My lungs seize up and my eyes start to water. I'm like, wiping my nose with my sleeve trying to focus, trying to remember if it was this tree or that tree.

Everything looks different now, with the houses going up. They're closing in. Back then it was just the middle of nowhere. I wasn't paying attention to directions that night. I didn't think it through. You got me so riled up. It was your own damn fault.

NATASHA

OCTOBER 1984

Yesterday, Natasha stayed home from school with a bad cold. Her dad was at work, and Kathleen took baby Abby to the pediatrician, so Natasha was home alone. She fell asleep on the couch, but then something made a rumbly noise outside, like a garbage truck going by, or maybe a robber breaking in. Last time Natasha went camping with Josie, Josie's dad told a story about an old man who lived at the end of a dark street, and some kids went trick-or-treating at his house late one Halloween night, and (he put his flashlight under his chin) "they were never heard from again." Josie's mother said, "Brian, cut it out, you're scaring them!"

Natasha couldn't sleep after the noise, especially with her runny nose. She took a roll of toilet paper back to bed with her because it would probably last longer than Kleenex, even if it was scratchier. She wished for some pop to sip, but Kathleen had a rule—no "soda" in the house, too much sugar. Natasha's mom used to make root beer floats; the foam from the ice cream and pop mixed together always tickled their noses and made them laugh. That was before Mom hurt her knee from slipping at the skating rink and had to get surgery. After that, Natasha made the floats and brought them to Mom in bed and sometimes brought her her medicine, too. One time, Mom's hands were so shaky, she spilled root beer in the bed. So sticky! Natasha liked taking care of her mom. Mom called her, "my little nurse." Natasha needed the cough syrup. She tried to reach it at the back of the medicine cabinet, but when she pushed a chair over and climbed up, she got dizzy and had to get back down.

A couple of times she has snuck into baby Abby's room at night to hold her. She has to be careful not to wake her sister. One time, this happened, and Kathleen came rushing in all crazy with her pink silk bathrobe a little bit undone, and her makeup smudged.

"I heard her start to cry so I got up to rock her," Natasha said, her heart beating really fast. But Kathleen actually wasn't mad; she told Natasha if she wanted she could feed Abby some formula. "Two scoops with hot water. But not too hot. Test it first." So Kathleen went back to bed, and Natasha went downstairs and made a bottle and squirted a little bit on her arm, then came back upstairs and fed baby Abby in the rocking chair.

Natasha and Josie don't go to the same school anymore because, for grade seven, Natasha's dad moved her to a private school where she wears a uniform and knows nobody except Kayla, who is now her stepsister, but they don't like each other. There are a couple of girls in her homeroom that invited her to eat lunch with them, Nicole B. and Nicole P., and they both have mood rings. Most of the kids at her new school have gone there since kindergarten, except there are a few who moved later, like Patrick and Penelope Lam, who are a brother and sister from China, and Gregory Morgan, who moved from Vancouver last year, and who both Nicoles think is cute. Natasha might have a crush on him, too. She hasn't decided, she kind of thinks Robbie Palmer in French class is cuter. The Nicoles think baby Abby is adorable, even though Nicole P. swears she's never going to get married or have kids, and Nicole B. says she's going to adopt after they had to watch that video in health class of a woman giving birth.

Before, when Natasha was sick or upset, her mother would tell her the story of the night she was born, how her dad fainted because of the blood, how her mother waited too long and had to push Natasha out without any medication, how her father went to A&W to get her mother onion rings and a root beer float because she was so hungry after the labour. Kathleen doesn't eat fast food.

This morning, when Natasha went back to school after having been sick, Robbie Palmer came up to her at her locker and said, "I have the notes from French class if you want them," and he looked really cute in his Adidas jacket.

Natasha strokes the top of baby Abby's baldy head. Uncurls one of Abby's fists, inserts her finger. Baby Abby's fingers curl again around Natasha's, and she makes a small sucking noise in her sleep. Natasha puts her face close to her little sister's head and inhales. "Robbie Palmer talked to me today," she tells the baby. "Josie says she's not going to date until she's fifteen. I wish Josie and I went to the same school." The baby feels warm, smells like baby bum cream. Abby's little chest in her pale pink onesie pulses up and down, up and down, as she breathes.

SUMMER

LAST WEEK I HAD TO GO TO A FUNERAL FOR AUNTIE JO'S twin brother Jason. It was the first funeral I ever went to. I had to miss school for it, because it was on a Monday, which meant missing French, my favourite. A lot of kids in my class had gone to funerals before me, for their grandparents and stuff. But my parents had me really young, so my grandparents are young, too. For grandparents, I mean. Some of the kids in my class have parents who are practically the same age as my grandparents. Also, I'm the only kid in my whole family, so I think sometimes all the grown-ups forget that I'm here when they talk to each other, which means I know all the gossip, all the things I'm not supposed to know.

Like, I know that everybody's saying Jason died of a seizure, but also I heard Mom on the phone with Auntie Jo saying something about an overdose, and maybe it was accidental or maybe it was on purpose. Overdose means drugs, and on purpose means suicide. I met Jason's son once at Auntie Jo's house a long time ago, like first grade or something. His name is Finn, and he's two years older than me except my mom says boys aren't as mature as girls. It's really sad how Finn doesn't have a dad anymore. Even though my parents aren't married to each other, I still get to see both my mom and my dad.

I feel like getting married is bad luck, because everyone in my family and also most other couples that I know aren't even happy anymore, or maybe they were never happy. Like, according to my mom, Auntie Jo's husband Solomon is a douchebag and Auntie Jo really wants a baby and she tried for a long time but now she's almost forty so it's probably not going to happen. P.S. What does douchebag really mean, anyway?

Auntie Kayla is almost in her forties and she already got divorced once and she is a doctor, except not the kind that does medical stuff. She's a shrink. I don't think she has time to have any kids because she's too busy having a career. I was supposed to be the flower girl for her last wedding, to Uncle Drew, but my mom said, "yeah right," and we didn't even go. The last couple of times we had a family dinner, Uncle Drew didn't even show up. Like, twice in a row. So, I'm pretty sure they're fighting a lot, too. Also my dad and Jessica fight a lot, even more now because she has to give herself all these shots so she can get pregnant, and my dad yells at her that the hormones are making her psycho! My Grandma and Grandpa Bell got separated last year, so now technically both of them have been married twice and it didn't work out either time. Pretty much nobody I know has a happy relationship, except maybe my friend Celeste's parents, who go for walks around the block holding hands, even when it's snowy out. But maybe that's a lie. Adults do a lot of pretending everything is fine.

I was kind of worried at the funeral that I would have to look at Auntie Jo's brother's body in the casket, but apparently he got cremated, so I only had to look at a picture of him at the front of the funeral home. The picture had Finn in it, when Finn was a baby. Real Finn sat in the front row with Auntie Jo. Finn has blond hair like Auntie Jo, except curly and a bit long and one of the curls kind of sticks up on his forehead. He's kind of cute—if he went to my school, Celeste would probably have a crush on him. I don't know why I had to go to the funeral, because I didn't even really know Auntie Jo's brother, but my mom said we were going to support Auntie Jo, and that she supported us a lot when I was a baby and when Aunt Natasha went missing. Also, Jason was a computer nerd, and when my mom was pregnant with me, he came over and rigged up a whole baby monitor system so that my mom and Aunt Natasha could hear me in every room of the house and he did the MISSING website for Aunt Natasha for so many years.

Auntie Jo has a blog on there that she's been doing since before I was born. I wonder if anybody except me reads it anymore. I read it all the time, even though nobody posts much these days. I read the old stuff over and over, like how my mom watches reruns of her favourite

TV shows. My favorite posts are when Auntie Jo puts memories up there, about when she and Aunt Natasha were kids together. Like, how they used to play this game called "Roommates," where they would pretend to be university students and they made their own little apartment in Josie's basement with old furniture and Josie's mother's old purses and shoes, and a New Kids on the Block calendar. My mom said New Kids on the Block were kind of like One Direction except in the '80s, and then she played me some of their music and we had a dance party.

Celeste and I never played any games like that. When we were younger, I always wanted to play "Detective," where we took walkie-talkies around in the park and looked for evidence in trashcans and solved crimes. One time, I found a toonie, and another time I found someone's ID card for their job at Staples. Then Celeste said it was a stupid game and refused to play anymore. Now all she wants to do is have nail parties—she even bought little brushes so she can paint designs on our nails, she gives me pedicures with polka dots and stripes, but it's so boring to have to sit there while it dries. Speaking of detectives, the detective who is in charge of Aunt Natasha's missing case is called Reuben, and he got split up from his wife, too.

At the funeral, my mom cried, which I thought was kind of funny since she didn't really know Jason very well, so how could she miss him? I asked her afterwards why she was crying, and she said, "Aunt Natasha never got to have a funeral." We were in the little McInnis and Holloway room after the service was over having snacks and punch. Everyone was telling Auntie Jo and her parents and Finn they were so sorry Jason died and what a good man he was. Maybe when you die everyone thinks you're a hero and it doesn't matter what you did when you were alive.

"Do you want a sandwich?" I asked my mom. I picked an egg salad bun off the table and made it into a little mouth, made the bread open and close at her. "Hello," I said, making my voice silly. "Please don't eat me."

That made her laugh a little bit. I hate it when my mom cries.

NATASHA

MARCH 2002

Sometimes not picking up the phone to call Greg involves physically leaving the house. Lacing up her sneakers and running as far away from the house as she can. If she runs long enough, sometimes exhaustion turns into euphoria, a runner's high, endorphins and the cold air surging through her lungs.

Which is worse? The waiting? The constant waiting for Greg to feel ready to marry her, to have a baby? Or the craving— the constant craving to call him, to hug him, to hear his laugh, to drink hot chocolate together in front of the fireplace, to drop him off on campus and kiss him goodbye, to snack on his homemade pepperoni and pineapple pizza, to sleep in one of his white cotton undershirts, to argue over which late night TV host is funnier, to raise eyebrows at him during a family dinner, to steal his sunglasses while out for brunch, to boil raw ginger into tea when he has a cold, to flip through his sketchbook when he's asleep...

On Thursday, she caved.

A middle-aged woman and a teenaged girl had come into the ER following a car accident. Natasha had attended to the girl, who'd been burned when flames began to lick up the car from the asphalt. No head injuries or signs of organ damage, but, from the sounds of it, the driver hadn't been so lucky. The girl's polyester pants had melted into her flesh; she had to be put under general anesthesia so that the team could pick the fragments out of her molten skin. Her face had been spared, but the severity of the burns meant she would have to learn to live with ridges of scars, mottled, mismatched skin. She would likely require multiple surgeries, grafts. The pain would recede over time, but dull into pins and needles, itching, tingling. She would likely go to college self-conscious about wearing a bikini, about undressing in front of a lover.

When she roused from anesthesia, the girl moaned like an abused animal. If she hurt this bad now, tomorrow's procedures would shave a whole other level off her soul. Natasha had never personally experienced true burn pain before—just minor sunburns and, once, a nasty scald on the underside of her chin from a slip of a curling iron. But after years of working on the unit, she could gauge pain tolerance by the level of analgesic requested by patients in combination with the hollow, hopeless notes of their cries.

Natasha had asked the girl if she needed more pain relief.

"No," the girl whispered, her voice hoarse. She reached a bandaged hand up and looked at it, where the IV fed into fragile skin.

"Lie still," Natasha instructed. "Your grandparents are on their way." The middle-aged woman was the girl's mother. The girl's father was not in the picture.

"Is my mom okay?" the girl asked.

Hospital policy dictated that information about other patients could only be released by certain personnel and under certain circumstances. Since her patient was under eighteen, Natasha could not divulge anything about the mother's condition without a guardian present. Bad news delivered at the wrong time, in the wrong way, could be detrimental to a patient's recovery. Then again, she knew what not knowing felt like. What it felt like to wait for her mother to call, to send a postcard. Anything.

Natasha tried to make her voice as calm as possible. "Dr. Kennedy and Dr. Singh are looking after her," she said. "They're the dream team. If it was my mother—" She swallowed, before concluding, "She's in the best hands possible." Small brown flecks speckled the left thigh of her pink cotton scrubs. Natasha usually wore brightly coloured scrubs, having read studies that suggested they put patients at ease more than sterile white or traditional cornflower blue.

The girl's eyes looked like an overcast sky. "Can you check?" she pleaded.

Natasha averted her gaze to the girl's chart. "Okay. Let me see if they know anything yet." She rode the elevator down a few floors.

Sometimes her mother had slept in Natasha's twin bed, the two of them squished together, Natasha up against the wall. Natasha's mommy had blue silk pajamas, and Natasha smooshed her face up against the cool silk of her mommy's back while mommy slept. She didn't like it when her mommy was so sick, but she liked cuddling. She used her fingers to untangle one of mommy's curls very carefully without waking her up.

At the nurse's station a couple of floors down, Natasha asked whether anyone had seen Pav or Mitch or one of the assisting nurses. They'd gotten out of surgery early, she was informed, they'd have to be paged. Then Mitch had come around the corner, wringing his hands like he was washing them the way they all had to do so many times a day. Natasha had noticed that she herself did this sometimes, when stressed, or when having an intense conversation.

"Female, forties, MVA," Natasha probed, then felt guilty for identifying the victim—someone's daughter, someone's mother—by her trauma. "I have the daughter upstairs. How'd surgery go?"

Mitch shook his head, looked down.

Fuck.

Back upstairs, Natasha poked her head in the girl's room, forced a smile. "I couldn't find anyone yet, sorry, sweetheart." The girl's hopeful face collapsed. She took a few shuddery breaths. "You'll keep checking, right? You'll tell me as soon as you know?"

Natasha's face felt like stretched plastic. "Sure."

As Abby's pregnancy advanced, Natasha typically didn't accept invitations to go out for drinks with her colleagues, but she had the next day off and she didn't want to feel anything. She'd gone straight from work to the pub downtown, carpooling with Melissa, having changed into a pair of dark jeans and a silky black top. She left her car in the hospital parkade. She could ask Jason to drive her back to get it later, since he was scheduled to come over to help set up the baby monitors and fix the Internet connection, which, for the past week, had been flickering in and out like a spotty pulse. Thank God for knowing an IT expert.

Her first beer tasted like soap, the second like the aftertaste of vomit. She sipped at the foam, feeling lightheaded, listening to Melissa and Danielle gossip about Danielle's cowboy-themed bachelorette party, scheduled for the second Friday during Stampede. Melissa had gotten married at twenty-two, but she'd recently separated from her husband, and, she confessed, was casually seeing one of the new residents. "You know who I'd really like to bang?" she declared, after a round of shots. "Dr. Kennedy."

"Mitchell Kennedy?" Danielle squealed, twisting her diamond solitaire back and forth. "Seriously? He's *ancient*!"

"Silver fox!" Melissa chortled. "Plus he's probably loaded."

Natasha pictured Mitch coming around the corner, scrubbing at his empty hands. "He did a surgery on my patient's mom today," she said. Her friends looked at her like *enough with the shoptalk!*

Danielle grinned, slapped the table with both hands. "We need more shots!"

The two subsequent shots made the inside of her mouth feel numb. Natasha excused herself and went to the bathroom, threw up neatly into the toilet. The stall smelled sour; toilet paper littered the floor and the toilet basin appeared discoloured. Goosebumps dotted her bare arms. She cupped her hand under the faucet and spilled some water into her palm, wiped it across her mouth. She just wanted someone to warm her up. She needed a hot bath. Memories stumbled into her brain, then; her mother's long fingers rubbing shampoo into her hair, wrapping her in a giant bath towel; vanilla bubble bath, legs tangled up with Greg's, trying to fit both of them in the bathtub, someone knocking a row of tea lights into the water, extinguishing the flames. Their wet hair on the pillow afterwards, his arms wrapped around her. She dialled, clumsily. "Can you come get me?"

ABBY

I WOULD HAVE BEEN YOUR MAID OF HONOUR WHEN YOU AND
Greg got married, right? I know you and Josie were the same age and
technically you knew her longer than me. But we're *sisters*. Plus, I would
have thrown you a way better bachelorette party. We would have started
at the spa, then had a 1980s dance party at your house while getting
ready to go out. We would have had a red velvet cake, a classy one.
Double-decker with a sparkly crown as a cake topper, and the words,
Future Mrs. Morgan! We would have toasted you with champagne. For
you, we would have taken a limo, all worn silver dresses, and you would
have worn something smokin' hot, like a white sequin dress with a low
back. If you got it, flaunt it, right? I sure don't.

Doesn't that sound better than what Josie would have planned?
I remember the list of rules Josie gave you when you planned her
bachelorette party. No strippers, no alcohol, no lingerie, no novelty
genitalia. No fun.

Other than being super bored, I remember only a few things about
Josie's wedding. Like how cheesy and pink it was. I'd wanted to wear
your blue silk dress. You finally said yes, even though it was expensive,
but then I couldn't get the zipper to do up. So I ended up wearing one
of my old dresses and sitting at the kid's table listening to the violinist

and staring at a display of framed wedding photos near the entrance—her parents, her grandparents, Solomon's parents, Solomon's grandparents. Even a set of great-grandparents. What show-offs.

One time, you showed me a photo you'd stolen from your parents' wedding album when they split up. Dad looked so young—but also kind of like a pedophile, with big 1970s glasses and mustache and pleated cummerbund. Your mom's dress wasn't too hideous, given the year. But she should have ditched the long sleeves and high neck. I haven't seen that many pictures of your mom over the years, other than her wedding photo and the picture of the two of you on the piano bench, the one I made Reuben put up so that he wouldn't see you as just some missing girl, but as a real person. From that one photo, I can tell your mom was gorgeous. That picture was your favourite memory, you told me. You and your mother watching Princess Diana's wedding to Prince Charles, eating homemade scones and sipping tea, playing the wedding march on the piano. It's not fair that you loved weddings so much but never got to have your own. And it's not fair that you wanted children so badly but never got to sit on a piano bench sipping tea with your own little girl.

There are no pictures of my parents' wedding, at least none that I've seen. Apparently they just went down to city hall one day and made it legal. You, Kayla, and I weren't even there. Well, technically I was, since Mom was pregnant with me at the time. They were probably too embarrassed to host a big country club shindig with five hundred something guests. They're separated now, anyway, although they pretended not to be for that awful TV interview they did two months ago. Of course, Kayla volunteered to do it (that bitch). Dad tried to get me to do it, too. Apparently it's better if a family presents a unified front. Better for who? Dad said viewers would be more sympathetic if Summer was there. I said, "Over my dead body," and he flinched.

Honestly, I don't know whether my parents will ever actually file for divorce—probably too expensive. Dad has softened without my mother, though. He came to Jason's funeral, which was kind of weird, since Dad has never been the sentimental type, and I didn't know he was coming until I ran into him there.

"Jay was a good kid," he said. "He helped a lot when Natasha..." He wiped his nose with his thumb and forefinger and looked away. Was he crying? "Anyway, life is short, right?"

Life is short. Actually, for a lot of people, life is agonizingly long, like eighty years of fuck-ups one after the other, eighty years of bad things happening to them. Maybe life is better short. Because I will probably spend the next sixty or seventy years waking up every morning to the same punch in the gut: you are still gone.

After the funeral, Dad and I were sitting with Summer, eating appetizers, and then Summer went off with Josie for a bit, and Dad said, "Do you think we should have a memorial for your sister?" Technically, we should have been mourning Jason. But I couldn't stop thinking about you, either. How we never really had a chance to say a formal goodbye.

"I don't know," I said. A few years ago, my mother asked whether we should have you declared legally dead. I don't think their marriage ever really recovered from that. Or maybe it had started unravelling long before and her suggestion was just one of those strings near the end, you tug and the whole thing unravels, but the sweater was already ruined anyway. I know how much your parents' divorce crushed you, Tash. But when mine finally pulled the plug, I just thought, *whatever*.

After enough bad stuff happens to you, new bad stuff doesn't make a difference. It's just like scab forming over scab. At the funeral, Josie's mother came over to us, and my dad stood up and gave her a hug, and then she hugged me, too, and then got sucked back into the crowd of people probably all saying the wrong thing at the wrong time. Like, *everything happens for a reason*, which more than one person said to me when you went missing. Like there was a good reason you disappeared from my life without any warning. Like maybe I deserved that.

I remember when Mrs. Carey had breast cancer, when that was the worst thing that had ever happened to their family. Then they'd lost you, and you were like a daughter to them. And now, they have to mourn Jason. Like I said, scab over scab, scar tissue over scar tissue.

I spied Summer across the room, chatting with Finn. What will Finn remember about his father? If I die, what memories will Summer have? Was I a good enough mother when she was little? Is being a good enough mother even possible when you're just a shell of a human being?

What did you remember of your parents, of your mother, before she left? You mentioned how much they'd argued, but only a few times, when you slipped up, when you weren't on guard trying to protect me from the big bad world. The odd time, you'd mentioned that your mom had been sick, near the end. A chronic illness, maybe? Or depression? Had she sensed our father was a cheating bastard about to leave her for his mistress? These moments happened so rarely, though—you always recovered pretty quickly, made a joke, changed the subject. I never got the full story.

NATASHA

JUNE 2002

In the aftermath of the breakup, Natasha resigned herself
to the fact that, if she were ever to have sex with anyone
other than Greg, it would, for the remainder of her lifespan,
always feel like cheating. She imagined her sex life with Greg
like a slow bell curve; an awkward start, followed by a gradual incline, a peak in their early-to-mid twenties, followed
by a gradual decline. She continued taking her birth control
pills, but felt a hot flare in her gut every time her period
came. She was pretty sure if a pregnancy did happen, Greg
would finally propose, move into her house, put his hand on
her growing belly to feel the baby's outlines and curves, just
like she sat with Abby, her hand resting under Abby's belly
button, feeling the rush of joy as the baby kicked, followed
by the hot letdown. She could only feel the baby from the
outside in—Abby got to feel the baby from the inside out,
Abby got to be "mama."

Natasha would never, ever deliberately get pregnant until Greg was on board with the decision, but if life were to make that choice for her...

She and Greg had waited a long time to have sex, over a year. Greg had unwrapped the condom, the first she'd seen out of its wrapper, a slimy, collapsed balloon. "Promise me you'll tell me if it hurts," he said. "I'll stop. I don't want it to hurt." Natasha had the bedding pulled up under her armpits. Greg had seen her bare breasts before, touched them, put his mouth on them—they'd fooled around plenty of times— but this felt different, a plan in motion from the time Greg's parents won a weekend at a B&B at the school silent auction. If she had wanted to take it back—which she didn't think she did—but if she had wanted to take it back, it was probably too late.

It had not, actually, been that painful. Not pleasant, but not unpleasant. Better than some of the first-time horror stories she'd read in *Seventeen* magazine. When Greg had fallen asleep, Natasha eased out from where she'd tucked up under his sweaty armpit and went to the bathroom and peed, which was what you were supposed to do to prevent urinary tract infections. She looked at herself in the mirror, smoothed her hair, wrapped her arms around herself. Her dark hair, tousled and wild, reminded her of her stepmother after a visit to the salon, her hair teased and blown-out. How old was Kathleen when she lost her virginity? Probably really young. She probably bragged about it afterwards.

Natasha had never showered in Greg's bathroom before. She turned on the water and waggled her fingers underneath it until the temperature felt just right, then stepped in. She bent and retrieved a bottle of body wash from the shower's tiled floor, squirted a small amount of the bright blue fluid into her open palm, and smelled. Wrinkled her nose. So sharp and woodsy, Greg's smell, but too concentrated. She held her hand towards the stream of water and let the blue syrup wash away down the drain.

She had not, she realized, prepared a towel. She turned the tap off and hesitated, watching the steam slowly seep out over the open glass of the shower door. She opened the door a crack, then all the way. Stepped out and stood on the linoleum, water pooling at her feet. In the cabinets below the sink, she could not find a towel—they were probably in some linen closet down the hall or something. Now she was naked, wet, and cold.

The first time with Pav, though—

She had not expected it to happen so fast, not expected how gentle his large hands would feel as they slipped below her lower back as his body hovered over hers; not expected the heat of his mouth on her nipples, between her legs; not expected how much she wanted him, wanted just that moment. Not expected to feel so...

So full.

CAM

THE FIRST TIME ABBY LET HIM TAKE SUMMER OVERNIGHT, CAM had tried to soothe his daughter to sleep by walking her around the house, jiggling her in his arms. She'd arched her back, pounded her little fists on his chest, leaned her head back and roared. He could feel her damp pajamas, soaked with tears and saliva. His mother had suggested he just put her in the crib and let her cry it out, but when he laid her down, she'd thrashed her fists, slammed her heels into the mattress, into the tiny grey elephant pattern of the nursery motif his mother had chosen. He'd stood outside the door for only a few minutes before he couldn't take it anymore. He'd strapped her into the car seat and driven from one end of the city to the other and back with the radio playing The Black Eyed Peas.

At some point, she spat out her soother and somehow wrenched it free from where he'd clipped it to her jammies, but he didn't dare stop and pull over to retrieve it. Eventually, she'd fallen asleep sucking on the neckline of her shirt, and he'd turned around to head home, simultaneously more exhausted and more hyperalert than he'd ever been in his life. He could feel his heart drumming in his chest, even when he pulled up to the house and turned off the engine, and with it, the thudding bass stereo. He unstrapped Summer very slowly and carried her back into the house, but hesitated before putting her in her crib. Instead, he'd eased onto the couch and settled his sweaty, defeated daughter into the crook of his arm. Smoothed the whorl of fine blonde hair on top of her head. He didn't dare reach for his cellphone or for the TV remote. It felt like he was holding Summer against her will.

Now, in the doctor's office waiting room, Summer wheezes into the crook of her elbow and leans against him. Cam glances up from his smartphone. Thinks about whether he should sweep some of the hair away from her eyes or put a cool hand against her forehead and check her temperature. Honestly, Cam has never mastered this fever detection technique—there's hot and there's not, determining severity is a thermometer's job. Summer gets colds easily—probably, their pediatrician says, because of her premature birth. Her hacking made Abby worry this could be turning into pneumonia, but Abby was supposed to be doing hair trials for an entire wedding party so she'd asked Cam if he could take Summer to the doctor. If Summer has to stay home from school tomorrow, Cam will book the day off and order her udon soup. His own mother had stayed home from work when he was sick and made him homemade chicken stew. Cam can't cook, but udon is the next best thing. Summer hates missing school. She definitely did not inherit that from him or Abby.

For Summer's tenth birthday, Cam asked her if she wanted to go to Disneyland, and she said she'd actually rather have a party at home and, instead of presents, her friends could bring donations for an orphanage in Africa. It was kind of cool, honestly, that he had a kid who would rather give to charity than dress up like Cinderella. He'd agreed to come, despite the inherent awkwardness, and he'd shown up with a big donation *and* a big present—a new iPad with a glittery purple case and two hundred Apple dollars for all the apps, songs, and movies she could want. Abby seemed pissy about it, telling him he shouldn't spoil Summer, but whatever, he could—and would—spoil Summer as much as he wanted. Abby was probably just ticked that his gift was better than hers. Also, sometimes he liked making Abby mad; they had really awesome hate sex. Summer raised a thousand bucks for charity, and Abby sculpted a huge volcano out of Oreo ice cream cake and used strawberry and chocolate syrup for lava. Cam had eaten two pieces.

At the clinic, a chime signals that the door has opened, a new patient has come in. Summer lifts her head from Cam's shoulder. "That's Reuben!" she whispers.

Cam almost forgets that he still has to pretend he doesn't know his big brother. As far as Summer is concerned, his only connection to

Reuben is that he's the detective guy from Natasha's murder case. Okay, technically not a murder "officially"—Cam has to remind himself not to say murder around Summer (and especially not around Abby). But come on. Everybody knows.

"Can I go say hi?" Summer whispers. Reuben probably doesn't want to say hi, Cam thinks. Reuben hasn't said hi beyond an obligatory Christmas card, probably sent by his now ex-wife, in five years, since Cam got involved in the whole investigation and, as Reuben put it, "royally fucked up." It wasn't Cam's fault Greg got a lawyer and Reuben isn't able to question him anymore. If it'd been Cam in Greg's shoes, he would have lawyered up on day one. And it wasn't Cam's fault that Reuben's only good leads—Natasha's watch and the message board post—went nowhere. But will Summer think it's weird if they don't go over and say hello?

Before Cam can answer, Reuben's son, Hunter, starts a full on tantrum—"But you *said* I could! I hate you!" Hunter is only a couple of years younger than Summer—probably too old to be having public meltdowns, but what does Cam know? Summer had some freak-outs as a toddler, but rarely in public, and she hasn't had a meltdown in Cam's presence in a couple of years at least. Abby says, "Wait until she's a teenager," which Cam doesn't want to think about, especially given who her mother is. He just hopes Summer won't have a psycho phase. One time, he'd run into the grocery store to pick up some things for dinner, one of Jess's last-minute errands, and he'd offered Summer a treat because he felt bad dragging her along on such a boring chore.

"Anything you want," he'd said.

And Summer, sweetly, had said, "Can I have a green apple?"

Hunter took a swing at his dad, socking Reuben in the stomach. Jeez! Good thing the kid had little fists. Reuben said, "That's it, I'm taking away your Game Boy!" The kid swung again.

Summer and Cam exchanged a look that said, *awkward!* Cool, Cam thought, a 'moment' with his kid. He smiled, gave her a look to say, *thank you for never doing this to me.* How would he handle things if Summer was a brat? He was, at the very least, an *okay* dad. He looked up, trying to offer a sympathetic glance to his big brother, who'd finally wrangled his son into a waiting room chair. The kid slumped in the chair, scowled, folded his arms, like he was going to seek revenge later.

Reuben didn't catch Cam's eye. Had he even noticed Cam's presence? He staggered to the receptionist's desk, pulled out his wallet, procured some documents. A health card, probably. Maybe, Cam thought, Reuben should inquire about some meds for his little tyrant. Or some valium for himself.

As he made his way back, Reuben finally noticed them. "Hey!" he said, giving an uncomfortable smile. The cheery tone was probably directed more at Summer, Cam thought.

"Hi!" said Cam, too loudly, sounding like an idiot, even to himself. "Reuben, right?"

Reuben made a move to extend his hand, but then Summer coughed loudly, into her sleeve, and Reuben withdrew. He glanced back at his little dictator. When Abby had first announced her pregnancy, Cam had hoped for a boy. Jess had told him he might finally get a son. She'd gone full steam ahead with pills and hormone shots, without really asking him his opinion. But kid-wise, he'd hit the jackpot on the first pull. Why try again? Why ruin a winning streak? And really, did he want to start all over again just for a boy? No.

Reuben gave Cam a look like he wished Cam would spontaneously combust. Seriously? Still? After all this time? It was Reuben's own fault he hadn't been able to solve the murder, Cam thought. He should stop focusing so much on Greg. There was a killer out there, walking free. Plus, it wasn't fair for him to be mad about Cam sleeping with Abby. Cam's sex life was his own business. He'd slept with Abby way before the whole investigation thing. Summer was proof.

Fortunately, the receptionist called Summer's name.

HIM

PEOPLE ALWAYS USE SUCH STUPID ONLINE PASSWORDS. So easy to hack. One in six people use the name of a pet. That's always a good guess. I tried that first for your email. *Larkin.* Got me right in.

> From: Dr. Paval Singh
> Subject: Friday
> Date: 13 June 2002 6:31:08 PM MST
> To: Natasha Bell
>
> Hi you!
> Hope you have a good day off tomorrow.
> My surgery is scheduled for 8 AM. I know
> you're working late tonight so I won't
> phone and wake you up, but I'll try to call
> when I'm out. Hopefully by 2 if all goes
> well. Miss you. Looking forward to Friday
> night. I've got a Prosecco up my sleeve.
> I've learned my lesson after last weekend's
> Malbec incident!
> Cheers,
> Pav

From: Natasha Bell
Subject: (No Subject)
Date: 14 June 2002 12:04:31 AM MST
To: Dr. Paval Singh

I want you. You know what I mean. ;) I
can't wait until your shift is over.
XOXO
Natasha

NATASHA

OCTOBER 1983

October is probably a bad month to run away. Especially at night. Not that Natasha has much of a choice. Even though there's no snow, it's still cold. Dad hasn't got her winter clothes out of storage yet. That's usually Mom's job.

Her fingers, curled around the pages of her library book, have started to tingle. She needs gloves. Her book, a novel about a group of orphaned children living independently inside a boxcar, is due back in three days.

If she goes to Josie's, then Josie's parents will call her dad and send her back home. Unless her dad hasn't noticed she's gone, which is possible. He might not even be home from work yet. He works late all the time. Or maybe he just doesn't care that she ran away. He probably hasn't even called around to her friends to find out where she is.

Natasha dog-ears her paperback and stands up, rubs her hands together. Her baby brother or sister is due in May, and Natasha already counted back nine months. Her dad and his "girlfriend" could have told her about it back when it was still warm out. Would have made running away much easier.

"Does Mom even know you're a SLUT?" Natasha had screamed at Dad. Normally, she doesn't say words like slut. Dad won't even tell her where Mom is or a phone number to call her.

Natasha could try going around the back of Josie's house and throwing rocks at her bedroom window, or tapping on the screen door at the back. Natasha slides her hands into her sleeves. This is probably her best option, unfortunately. She doesn't know of any abandoned boxcar, and she doesn't have any siblings to live with. She doesn't have siblings, but only until May.

Natasha met her dad's "girlfriend" Kathleen only once, at the school Christmas concert last year. Was her dad having s-e-x with Kathleen way back then? Kayla and the other girls from grade four had done a hand-bells performance to "O Holy Night." Hand-bells are the stupidest instrument ever. Natasha's mother plays piano; Natasha loves to watch her mother's long fingers dance over the keys, especially to Beethoven's "Für Elise," which has no words but is still the saddest song ever. Natasha's mother keeps her fingernails short because of her piano playing. But when they ran into Kayla and her mom later in the hallway, Natasha's dad said, "Oh, this is Kathleen, she goes to my gym," and Natasha could not stop staring at Kathleen's long, glossy red fingernails. How could Kathleen work out without wrecking her manicure?

Josie doesn't live very far away—maybe a ten-minute walk from the ravine. Natasha walks quickly because of the cold. She pulls the little string that opens Josie's family's side gate and goes into the backyard. From here, she can go around the side, where Josie's bedroom window faces, and—

She sees Jason's face in the window. He waves at her and smiles. Jason almost never smiles. He pops out the back door. "What are you doing here?"

Natasha scoots up close to the door. "Is Josie home?"

"No. My parents took her for pizza because she got an A on her report." He leans back inside. "Come in, it's cold."

She does. His parents aren't home, good. She's safe, at least for now. "How come you didn't go?" she asks.

"Grounded," he says. "Fuck them. I'd rather stay at home and play video games, anyway."

Natasha has never said the word fuck. But why not, after what her dad has done to her? Her fingers tingle as they warm up. "I hate my dad," she says. "Fuck him, too." It feels good.

"Why?" Jason says, and they go over to the couch, sit down. Natasha unzips her jacket. Jason has a video game on the TV. On the screen, a little person in blue stands in a field and holds a gun. The gun is big compared to the guy. Maybe a bazooka.

"My parents are getting a divorce," she says, the first time she has said this out loud. "My dad cheated. And he kicked my mom out. He won't tell me where she is." Her eyes sting. None of her friends' parents are divorced—not even one. Sitting here with Jason feels kind of weird, because Natasha keeps picturing when he started falling down in the ravine, and how he had been standing beside her, and she just kind of caught him, like a reflex, or maybe he just fell on top of her and her saving him from hitting his head was just an accident. He'd started twitching, his eyelids fluttered, and his jaw started opening, closing, opening, closing. Then he went limp, his head in her lap. His eyes jerked open. He heaved, and puke started spewing out, down the front of his T-shirt, all over Natasha's T-shirt. His eyes looked glossy, staring straight up, straight into hers. He started to gag. What if he choked? She twisted his head forward so his mouth was pointing down and reached in with two fingers, started scooping. If his jaw started clenching again, he'd probably bite her. Maybe he'd bite her fingers right off. Where was Josie?

"Are you okay?" she'd kept saying. What a stupid question. Jason was clearly not okay.

When Josie's parents got there, they said, "You saved his life!"

On the couch, Natasha looks away, trying not to remember the glazed look of Jason's eyes during his seizure. Jason got diagnosed with epilepsy and the doctors put him on medicine. When he got out of the hospital, Jason and his parents sent Natasha flowers, a huge bouquet of yellow lilies and purple snapdragons. So beautiful! The lilies had orange powder on the insides that sprinkled on the table and made her fingers dusty when she moved the vase to change the water.

"Your dad cheated?" says Jason, his face contorting into a scowl. "What a jerk!"

"I know." Pressure builds in Natasha's chest. Does she actually want to tell Jay about the baby before she even has a chance to tell Josie? "And guess what?" She can't keep this secret anymore, her father's dirty secret. "They're having a baby. My dad and his...mistress. And he's going to marry her." The tears start coming, fast, all down her face, making her vision blurry. Why did she have to start crying in front of Jason? All that time in the ravine, alone, reading her book, she didn't cry. So why now? So embarrassing!

"Here," Jason says, and he thrusts something into her hands. The video game controller. "Press this button. It makes him shoot. I like shooting stuff when I'm mad. Makes me feel better."

Natasha has never played a video game before. She blinks and focuses on the screen. Mad—is that what she's feeling? She presses the button to make the gun shoot—pt pt pt pt pt pt pt! This guy is just killing everybody.

"You're a natural," says Jason.

ABBY

THE OLDER MY MOTHER GETS, THE BLONDER SHE GETS.
I kept the salon open for her after closing because, as she put it, she
desperately needed her roots done. With her hair in foils, I begin to
tidy the salon while she sips her venti latte and flips through a trashy
magazine. Summer lounges in one of the pedicure chairs, having
turned on the auto-massage function. She has her headphones in. At
first, I thought she was doing homework, but when I passed by with
my bottle of Windex, I realized she was sketching a floral scene from
a snapshot paper-clipped to the top of her notebook. Uncle Greg has
been teaching her a thing or two. Early this spring, the two of them
started a garden in our backyard. Last month, the flowers sprouted,
rainbow colours in no particular pattern, like someone sprinkled
Skittles in the dark black dirt. Neither you or I had a green thumb,
Tash. But I bet you'd like it.

My mother flips through her magazine, then scoffs.

I put my rag down. "What?"

She turns the page to show me: an older male celebrity is having
an affair with his children's twenty-something nanny. "Disgusting," my
mother adds.

I raise an eyebrow. "Uh, you're one to talk."

My mother scowls. "Kevin and I were separated *before* I started seeing your father."

"Technicality." I glance at Summer. Headphones still in. "And what about Dad? You married a cheater, so…"

My mother closes the magazine. "Your father was *not* unfaithful."

I roll my eyes. "Natasha was there, okay? He was still living with Tash's mother when you got knocked up."

"Yeah, for good reason! She was crazy."

"Yeah, sure."

She looks over at her granddaughter. "You don't know what you're talking about."

I spritz again, wipe the rag across the back of my chair. "Whatever."

She's stuck in the chair because of her highlights, but she looks as though she'd like to march across the salon and give me a spanking. Send me to my room. "You shouldn't speak negatively about your father," she says, between clenched teeth.

Clearly, I've hit a nerve, even though they're separated. "What do you care?"

She rolls the magazine. "Your father is a good man. He busted his butt for your sister, especially after her mother died. If you think for one second—" And then she stops, because it's out there. She cannot take it back.

My breathing quickens. "She *died*?! When?"

My mother's face has turned crimson. She shakes her head slowly. At me, or at herself?

"Tell me!" I demand.

She looks down. "Right after—right after she left." She sighs. "Your father should be the one having this conversation with you."

My hands clench around the rag. "She's been dead this whole time?!"

She reaches up as though to fiddle with her hair, then remembers the foils. "She was—she had problems."

"Her husband was screwing another woman," I spit. "Of course she had *problems*."

"She had an addiction to painkillers," my mother hisses.

We both look over at Summer, who doodles away, seemingly in her own little world. She's *my* kid though—it could all be an act. Maybe she's got the volume off and she's listening to this whole show. "Natasha never told me about that," I say.

My mother crosses her arms. "Well, it's true. It was after a surgery she had. She was prescription shopping with different doctors. Your father caught her driving under the influence—with your sister in the car. She refused to go to rehab. He told her he wanted a divorce, but he couldn't just move out. It wasn't safe to leave Natasha alone with her mother."

I don't want to believe her. "So he kicked her out?"

"He didn't have any other choice." She crosses her legs. "Your father told her she needed to get help or she couldn't see Natasha. He didn't hear from her after that. A couple of months later, the cops called. She'd been in a car accident. Drove headfirst into a tree."

Summer keeps drawing, seemingly unaware.

I ask, "Was she—"

"High?" My mother grimaces. "Yup."

"Does Reuben know?"

My mother rolls her eyes as though this is a stupid question. "Of course. We told him everything."

My blood feels hot. "But you never thought it would be a good idea to tell Tash? You just let her keep believing her mother abandoned her? For the rest of her life?!"

She crossed her arms. "She'd already been through so much. It was right before Christmas. She would have been devastated."

I lower myself into the chair at reception. "She thought her mother didn't want her. That she didn't love her. She grew up thinking that."

She unrolls the magazine. "*We* loved her," she insists. "That should have been enough."

NATASHA

OCTOBER 1983

With Jason's pointers, Natasha is actually pretty good at the video game until they hear the front door open; it's Josie and her parents coming home.

"Hide!" Jason whispers. The two of them squeeze into the basement storage closet. Jason's face is so close, Natasha can feel his hot breath on her cheeks.

Mrs. Carey calls, "Jason! Come upstairs!"

"Stay here," Jay instructs, slipping out and shutting her inside.

It takes a few minutes for Natasha's eyes to adjust to the dark. She doesn't want to start crying again. She hopes Jason will tell Josie and Josie will come down and bring her a peanut butter sandwich and then they will figure out a plan. Her stomach grumbles. She didn't think to bring any snacks when she left school, and now she's missed dinner.

It takes a long time before Jason comes back, and he has Doritos. He huddles in beside her and tears open the bag. "Shhhh!" Natasha hisses. She plucks a few chips and tries to chew as quietly as possible. But they taste so delicious, and she is so hungry. "Where's Josie?" She helps herself to another handful.

"Dad's helping her with math," Jason whispers. "I told her I wanted to show her something downstairs and she said 'get lost.' I'll have to wait until she's alone. I think it's going to be awhile."

Natasha's heart rate quickens. She wipes her cheesy hands on her jeans. How long is she going to have to stay in this closet? Why can't Josie just come rescue her? She's eaten too many Doritos too fast. Her mouth is so dry. Should she ask Jay to get her some water?

Jason munches on some chips. "It's pretty cool that you ran away," he whispers. "It'll show your parents who's boss."

Natasha can feel the spittle and the crumbs as he talks. "It's so unfair!" she whispers. "Why'd this have to happen to me?"

Jason keeps chewing. "Sometimes bad stuff happens to good people. Bad stuff happened to me before, too."

"Like what?" Natasha can feel tears brimming again. The cheese smell from the Doritos has started to stink up the closet. She's too hot with her jacket still on. The Careys have a garage out back—maybe she can hide out there. Except then what will she do in the morning when Josie's dad goes to get his car for work?

"Like..." Jason hesitates. "Swear you won't tell anyone?"

Natasha nods.

"One time one of my older cousins came over, and she said she would show me some magic tricks. She had a whole set, like a wand and trick cards and this long rainbow scarf she pulled out of her sleeve. She made me lie down on the floor and she tied my arms to the chair with the scarf. Then she said—presto, change-o, I'm going to make you feel good. And she started touching me, like, down there."

Natasha stares. "Are you serious?" At school they learned about stranger danger, and about how nobody is supposed to touch kids in their bathing suit area. This wasn't a stranger, though—this was his cousin, actually, and she was a kid, too, kind of, a teenager, but still—Natasha's gut tells her it's wrong. "You have to tell your parents," she says.

Jason scowls. "No way!"

"That's sexual abuse!" Natasha whispers loudly.

"No it's not—my cousin's a *girl*." Jason crosses his arms. "She's older than me, she knows stuff—"

"So?" Natasha had heard that sexual abuse was from creepy old guys. But... "Kids aren't supposed to do sex stuff."

"Shut up!" Jason hisses. "I made it up, okay? I was just trying to make you feel better."

"You're lying." Natasha feels lightheaded.

"No I'm not!"

"Jason?" Mrs. Carey calls from upstairs. "You better not be playing video games down there unless your homework is done."

"I'll be right back," Jason says, and scrambles out of the closet, closes the door behind him before Natasha can say anything.

Alone, Natasha feels so sick she might throw up. She shuts her eyes and takes a few deep breaths, picturing Jason's older cousins, the ones they'd gone swimming with at the cabin. She'd always assumed it was one of the boys who pushed her into the pool, but Josie and Jay had a lot of cousins. Should she say something? She needs to get out. She can sneak out the back before Jason comes back down. Maybe her dad will kill her for running away, or maybe he hasn't even noticed. She will make him tell her where her mom is. But what if her mom actually doesn't want her? What if her mom moved out to make a fresh start, and she is breaking up with Natasha's dad *and* Natasha?

It's too much—being in the closet like this. Trapped with her secrets, his secrets. She's just a kid.

Just as she's made up her mind to sneak out, Jason pops back in.

Natasha scrambles to her feet. "I'm gonna go home."

Jason looks less angry. "I swear that never happened to me. It was from a movie I saw. I just said it so you'd feel better." Okay, maybe. But he'd seemed pretty serious. Natasha twiddles with the frayed edge of the rainbow friendship bracelet from Josie on her wrist.

"My cousin doesn't even have a magic kit," Jason adds. "If you tell anyone, you're just going to get her in trouble. You could mess up her whole life saying she did something like that. I swear!" He puts his hands on her upper arms and squeezes. "I swear!"

"Okay," Natasha says, and wriggles away. She doesn't want to get anyone in trouble. "I won't tell."

ABBY

I KNOW IT'S REUBEN CALLING WHEN MY PHONE RINGS JUST as Cam is getting close to orgasm. Reuben's number is the only one with a ringtone that sounds like a home security system going off. When I got my new phone, I set the ringtone to the loudest, most obnoxious one for Reuben so that I would never miss it. He hasn't called in so long. The last time my phone sounded the alarm, I was driving down Crowchild Trail, and I grabbed for it in the console but missed, knocked it to the floor. I braked hard, veered into the right shoulder, flung open the door as cars hurtled by. All he wanted to tell me was that he'd been contacted by a journalist wanting to do an article on missing person's cases in Canada and he thought it could be good publicity.

I know it's Reuben calling and I know it's bad. I just feel it.

I slam both palms into Cam's bare chest, heaving him off of me. I scramble naked off the bed. "Where's my phone?!" I fling the blankets and sheets off the mattress. I can hear it, but I can't find it. "Where's my phone?!"

"What the hell?" Cam can barely catch his breath.

There it is! I grab it up from the floor. "Hello?"

Cam moves closer. "Are you okay?"

I push him away, trying to make sense of what Reuben's saying.

Cam starts getting dressed. Goosebumps prickle my bare arms, breasts. I squeeze the hand that's not holding the phone into a fist, nails into my palm.

"What's the matter?" Cam asks.

I can't say it, but I do. "They found my sister's body."

JOSIE

WHILE SUMMER AND FINN SET UP JOSIE'S OLD MONOPOLY game at the kitchen table, Josie goes to the window and stares out at the rainy street. At work, they sent around an email that some communities were being evacuated due to possible flooding and power disruptions, but Josie's home was outside of that range, as was Summer's private school, so she hadn't paid much attention. Now things seem more dangerous. But then, she knows how dangerous a small storm can be, too.

July 6th, 2002—the storm had come and gone so quickly. Josie had spent that evening at choir practice and had stayed late to straighten up the church, to practice some of the songs alone, to listen to her solo voice carry throughout the empty pews. *Our God is an awesome God, he reigns from Heaven above, with wisdom, power and love, our God is an awesome God.*

Father Tucker, their new, thirty-five-year-old pastor, had wandered in and asked what she was doing there so late, and he'd said, "You have a beautiful heart for Jesus," and then, "And a beautiful voice." Josie had blushed. It *was* late—almost ten. When she'd exited the church, the sidewalk looked wet, but the air felt warm, deliciously humid. She drove home with the radio off, still singing hymns. When she got home, Solomon asked where she'd been so late, and when she told him about Father Tucker's compliments, he'd accused her of flirting.

Why hadn't she called Natasha to say goodnight, to hear her best friend's voice one more time, instead of listening to her own voice echo inside the empty church? Why had she let their spat drag on instead of calling to extend an olive branch?

She hoped Summer and Finn could be friends. Finn would turn thirteen soon, but it didn't feel like she'd lost him to adolescence just yet. He helped her do the dishes, told silly knock-knock jokes, invited her to shoot hoops with him and was patient with her when she had no idea what a three-pointer was. Neither Summer nor Finn had ever actually played Monopoly before. Summer unfolded the rules to read them, while Finn fiddled with the silver playing pieces and kept getting up and down from his chair, first to get a glass of water, then to check his cellphone. Seriously, a cellphone at thirteen? Josie was starting to think maybe he had AD/HD, like his father—although his report card this semester had come back all As and Bs.

She'd convinced Finn's mother, Angie, to enroll Finn in Summer's private school starting in September by offering to pay the full tuition. Now she'd have to convince Angie to let the school psychologist do some tests—or pay for a private assessment, that would be faster. Jason had been so smart—always getting into trouble, but still *so* smart. Her parents hadn't wanted to "label" Jason—they'd blamed all his problems—how long it had taken him to get his college diploma, his experimentation with substances, his rocky relationship with Angie—on the epilepsy.

For many years now, Jason had been third in her nightly prayer sequence, after first thanking the Lord for her abundant blessings, and then praying for Natasha to be found. She prayed nightly to absolve herself of the guilt she felt for not being more supportive of her brother, for feeling superior, for having her education, her job, her marriage, while he struggled. After Jason passed, she'd prayed for Jesus to have mercy on her brother's indiscretions, to welcome him into the loving arms of Heaven.

Some nights, she prayed for Solomon. Some nights she didn't. The nights after she didn't pray for Solomon she prayed twice for Solomon, and for absolution for the sin of not praying for her husband in spite of his transgressions. She and Solomon were still married in the eyes of the church. She'd made her vows for better *or* for worse. She'd phoned Solomon in tears the night Jason died, but he'd refused to come to the funeral, stating that he was taking private time to let God speak to him.

He'd left his job and applied for employment insurance, but the payments weren't much. A life in the ministry was a calling, Solomon often said. Josie would have liked to pursue some of her own callings, but someone had to pay the bills. Solomon's extra apartment was going to cost them fifteen hundred a month. After he refused to come to the funeral, Josie hadn't prayed for Solomon for three days. Mercifully, Angie had allowed Finn to come to see his father put to rest, though Angie herself had declined.

"It's raining cats and dogs!" Josie joked, moving away from the window as Summer distributed colourful bills. The kids looked blankly at Josie; clearly they'd never heard this expression before. When did she get so old?

"Do you want to play?" Finn asked.

"No, you two go ahead." She should probably check the forecast again, wait for the rain to let up before making the drive across the city to take Summer back to Natasha's. She still thinks of the house as Natasha's. Will Abby ever get her own place? And, if so, what will happen if Natasha ever comes back? No one else believes this is possible, but there was a recent case in the States where a young girl was finally rescued after being held prisoner for almost two decades. Maybe Josie is the only one still holding out hope, but someone has to. She searches Calgary weather on her phone.

Evacuations? Possible flooding? Not good. Josie examines the map on the city website. Thankfully, her house is outside the zone, as is Natasha's. Abby's not the safest driver, and poor visibility makes Josie nervous. Josie tries to figure out if she could take a different route to Natasha's and back without crossing through any red zones, but it doesn't look good. Not only that, but the rain seems to have intensified. Maybe Summer could borrow one of Josie's T-shirts and stay the night. Josie is babysitting Finn for the weekend anyway, maybe for the last time, since he will be old enough to stay home by himself, soon. He and Summer could keep each other company.

Abby answers Josie's call right away, but asks, "Did you talk to Reuben?" before Josie can ask about the rain. Josie immediately goes into the other room, not wanting the kids to overhear. Abby keeps going—they've found skeletal remains in a park.

"Is it her?" Josie asks. Her body goes numb. It can't be.

Abby bursts into tears. "Reuben says it'll take awhile to know for sure, they haven't found the...the head...but they might postpone the search because of the weather. What if the rain washes everything away before they find...? I want to come get Summer and go down to the station. Maybe he'll tell me more in person. I *know* it's her."

"They're closing roads. Have you been watching the news? That's what I was calling you about. It's not safe to drive right now. I think Summer should stay here."

"I want her with me," Abby insists. Sometimes Abby treats Summer like a best friend instead of a daughter. Last Halloween, the two of them dressed up as ketchup and mustard, which reminded Josie of the matching costumes she and Natasha used to wear.

"She's safer here." These bones must be someone else's, especially if they were just found now. A more recent skeleton, someone else's missing loved one, even though Josie isn't aware of any missing Calgarians in recent years. "Where did they find the skeleton?" Josie asks. "What park?" She paces over to her bedroom window, peeks through the blinds.

"Fish Creek Park!" Abby says. "A dog found her, under some plants."

Fish Creek Park? The exact spot Greg and his students tromped around collecting soil samples? If Josie were the type to swear, to take the Lord's name in vain, now would be the time. She reaches for her book of daily devotions, rifles the worn pages back and forth with her thumb. "Abby," Josie says as calmly as possible, "are you alone?"

"No. I have...a friend is here."

"Is it Greg?"

"No. Should I call him?"

Josie rifles the pages again. Of course Abby hasn't made the connection. Abby never doubted Greg, not even when the accusation about domestic violence came out. "No, don't do that. It's late. Wait until we know." Josie needs to talk to Reuben right away. "Stay there," she tells Abby. "I'll call you right back."

NATASHA

AUGUST 2001

Natasha barely has time to talk to Greg at Josie's wedding, what with her maid of honour speech, having to hold up Josie's hoop skirt while she pees, shaking hands with the guests, many of whom Natasha doesn't even recognize. Solomon's family and their new church congregation, probably. When the dance floor opens, Natasha sneaks away from the head table and pulls up a chair beside Greg at the table where Josie has seated him with the partners of the rest of the wedding party, all of whom are already married, one of whom is visibly pregnant.

"Want to dance?" Natasha asks Greg. Rarely does Greg get dressed up. She is so used to seeing him in jeans and T-shirts, clicking away on his laptop, or rain boots and his hooded black windbreaker, tromping around in some forest or marsh. Fish Creek Park is his favourite site for gathering data—he trekked down there regularly and brought home test tubes filled with soil samples and river water. He'd describe the flowers that lined the creek, but never picked them for her, not wanting to disturb the ecosystem.

"I think I'm going to head home," Greg says, fiddling with his linen napkin. He looks so handsome in his navy jacket. She had once fantasized about what he would wear on their wedding day—a grey, three-piece suit, probably—and the smile that would split his face open as she walked down the aisle towards him. When did she stop having this fantasy?

She lets out a long exhale. He will not stay, even if she begs. Begging will probably make it worse. His parents' separation has closed something inside of him permanently.

They take a flight of stairs down to the main lobby and go out the front door. Natasha pushes the rotating door and they both squeeze in. Greg kisses her goodbye, but it's haphazard, like an obligation. She watches him get into a cab. As she turns to head back in, she sees Jason coming out.

"Hey," he says. "Greg leaving already?"

She nods, as Jason sits on one of the concrete steps that lead up to the hotel doorway. Natasha lifts the A-line skirt of her pink satin gown a little bit to avoid stepping on it and sits beside him.

"I hate weddings," Jay says. He's unbuttoned the first few buttons of his shirt. He smells skunky, like rotting coffee in the heat. He pulls his wallet from his jacket pocket and shows Natasha a picture of his little boy posed in front of a blue-iced birthday cake with a single candle, a blue pointy hat atop his blond curls.

"Cute," Natasha mutters. Jesus, even Jason has managed to secure a relationship and a kid. She knew about Jason's little boy, but this photo is like scratching a scab open. She wants to scream. "Angie didn't come tonight?"

Jason says, "She left me."

Natasha exhales. "I'm sorry." Maybe misery does love company, even Jason's company. She met Angie once before at one of the annual Carey family New Year's Eve parties. She doesn't go every year anymore, but the New Year's Eve right after Josie's mother had her mastectomy, they all went to be with her. Angie and Jay must have been "on," then—four years is a long time to be off and on. Maybe they're off permanently now. Natasha doesn't blame Angie—Jay isn't the kind of guy she would choose for her child's father, not by a long shot. But then, she didn't have the greatest impression of Angie, either. Natasha tries to remember what Angie looks like, but thinks instead of the first New Year's Eve that she was dating Greg, standing out on the front steps with Josie's pregnant cousin, the chain-smoking one with the Princess Diana hair. Whatever happened to that cousin? Her baby would be ten or eleven now.

Jason reaches into the pocket of his jacket and pulls out a joint. "Want a hit?"

Seriously? On the night of his sister's wedding? In public? Do all the passersbys assume he's smoking a regular cigarette? They probably can't smell it from the street, too caught up in their own lives.

"I don't smoke," Natasha says, as he lights it. She knows all the statistics about marijuana—she's lectured Abby about it. She's never smoked a joint in her life, not even in adolescence when her friends experimented—even Josie, once or twice. Solomon probably doesn't know about that, either.

Jay snickers. "Yeah, I know. But right now, you look like you could use something to take the edge off."

Her head feels cloudy. Maybe Greg will change his mind and come back. Or maybe when she gets back to the hotel, he'll be apologetic, and she'll give him a real hug, and he'll let himself soften into it instead of bracing himself against her.

No, she tells herself, *stop it. You're just setting yourself up for disappointment.* "Okay," she tells Jay. "Hit me."

Jay laughs. "It's not blackjack."

The first two hits make her gag, make her feel dizzy. After a couple more, she leans back on the stairwell, hangs her head back, looks up into the black August sky. Who the hell is she anymore? "Greg is never going to marry me," she says—to herself?—after what seems like a long silence.

"Greg's an idiot," Jason says, and takes a drag. "Seriously. What's his problem? You should just leave him."

Maybe it is that simple. She will just leave. She is a star, twinkling in the night, a shooting star, free from anyone, anything. She can release herself from all of this, any time she chooses. "I'm going to," Natasha says, then. "I'm going to leave him."

GREG

GREG HAD ALWAYS KNOWN WHAT KIND OF RING NATASHA wanted. Not a traditional, solitaire diamond. A navy blue, oval sapphire surrounded by a halo of smaller diamonds on a white gold band. She'd given Greg a magazine picture of Princess Diana's engagement ring, which he hadn't kept. It'd be pretty easy to find another picture of Princess Di's engagement ring if he ever needed it. Of course, he'd never be able to afford anything close to Diana's in size. Who was Natasha kidding?

At age seven, Tash had watched Princess Diana's televised wedding with her mother, a memory she often talked about, one that predated her father's affair, Abby's birth. Tash had an out-of-focus photograph of her and her mother poised on the piano bench, a snapshot probably taken by her father, back when it was just the three of them. One year for her birthday, Greg had slipped the photo out of Tash's album, hoping she wouldn't notice its absence, and had it duplicated, converted into black and white, and framed. It hadn't even come out looking very good, what with the poor quality and blurriness of the original photo, and the store's inability to enlarge the photo very much before it started looking pixelated. But the present had made Tash cry—in a good way—and, when bragging about how amazing her boyfriend was to friends over the years, she'd referenced the photo as opposed to several other gifts he'd given her. Natasha idealized her mother, which made Greg wary, but he'd never told her that. Whatever happened to that photo?

Tash remembered every momentous date in the history of their relationship—first date, first kiss, the date they became "boyfriend and girlfriend," the date they lost their virginities to each other, the date they started dating again after that breakup that neither one of them wanted but somehow happened anyway. Who's fault was that? He can't remember—Tash said it was his and he felt it was hers, but Tash had the better memory. Tash sometimes announced "anniversaries" with little notes or gifts—a lipstick kiss on the mirror, a smile drawn into the snow on his car window, a Twix bar with one chocolate half for each of them, etc. She probably wanted *him* to remember these dates, probably felt like the fact that he didn't meant that the memories weren't as special to him, or *she* wasn't as special to him as he was to her. He made mental notes to write the dates down somewhere each time she left one of these tokens but then he would forget again. No one had a memory like Tash's anyway. No guy for sure. She often reminded him of other significant dates, too. The first year after they'd split, she'd sent him an email reminder of his mother's upcoming birthday even though they weren't together anymore.

Like the photograph, there are other mementos Greg thinks of, at times, wishing he could still have items that probably got thrown out at some point because no one other than he and Tash would have understood their importance. Silly, seemingly insignificant things, like plastic spoons she'd saved from their first date for frozen yogurt that she kept tucked together ("spooning" she joked) in her jewellery box. His beloved childhood stuffed panda he'd let her keep as collateral when he went to camp that one summer, a vow he wouldn't fall in love with any other girls. Her '80s CDs—he had grown so sick of '80s music while they'd dated, and yet, now, when a song came on the radio from that decade, he would freeze, tense his hands around the steering wheel, or stop in the middle of the mall. He could almost hear her singing along.

He'd ended up with Larkin, and Larkin was the best possible memento, but sometimes he feels like asking Abby whether certain trinkets still exist. Only he doesn't want to find out they've ended up in a trash bag somewhere.

He knows Sylvie knows more about Natasha's case than he does, since she had access to the files all those years ago. She's asked him more than once if he wants her to share the details. The last time she offered, he said, "She was seeing someone else, wasn't she?"

And Sylvie had said, "I will tell you—but you have to be sure you want to know."

He could tell the answer was yes. Natasha had been seeing someone else. She had moved on.

He told Sylvie no, don't answer that. Natasha hadn't told him, so it wasn't fair for Sylvie to.

Sylvie had said, "Okay," and gave him a kiss, and got up and started doing the dishes.

Maybe Natasha's trinkets, and the magic or meaning Tash insisted they held, are out there, somewhere. Like the magic of the photograph, and the magic of that day, Tash and her mommy, Princess Diana and Prince Charles. Tash's mommy disappeared, Princess Diana and Prince Charles divorced, Princess Diana died. Greg remembers Natasha talking about Princess Di's car accident, remembers her saying, "Do you think she *knew*?"

"Knew what?" Greg had asked.

"That she was going to die. When they were pulling her out of the wreckage. She was still conscious, you know, when the paramedics got there, apparently she was still talking, she didn't go into cardiac arrest until—"

"I don't want to know!" Greg told her. Accidents and hospitals and needles and all that stuff freaked Greg out.

Prince William had ended up with Diana's sapphire engagement ring, and when he gave it to Kate in 2010, Greg thought it would have been easier to find one for Natasha if he'd been looking then instead of when Josie got engaged and Tash really laid on the pressure. Yes, he'd actually gone to jewellery stores and enquired about the price of a sapphire, what the hell a carat was, how long a custom ring would take, what kind of payment plan could be procured for a starving graduate student with a girlfriend with expensive and nontraditional tastes.

He'd even thought about how he would propose, if, or when, he actually felt ready to. He had a variety of different scenarios. Surprising her at the door after a long shift at work, when she was least expecting it, having spelled WILL YOU MARRY ME? in red licorice across her kitchen table. Or creating a treasure hunt around the city, leading to the top of the Calgary Tower. At sunset, if he could pull it off.

Only one time had he actually come close to proposing—it had been *after* she'd dumped him. That night of the snowstorm, the dented rear bumper, picking her up downtown and going back to his place. Lying in bed, his arms wrapped around her, her wet hair tickling his face. He'd almost blurted it out then: *I want to marry you.*

But he'd stopped himself. Did he really feel this way? After all they'd been through? Or was it just having her in his arms again, how comfortable that felt, how he knew all her grooves and contours, how nicely she fit into his own grooves and contours? Was it just his impulsive unwillingness to let her go all over again? He couldn't propose now, he thought, not like this. It had to be special. He would have to have a ring. He would have to go back to one of his plans, map it out a little bit. She deserved more than just a reckless blurting in the middle of the night. And he didn't want to wake her up, anyway. In the morning, he'd see where they were at, tell her he wanted to get back together. That he was sorry. Except, he'd have to figure out how he felt about kids—he knew that was part of the deal for her. Maybe it wasn't the right time, not quite.

And then, in the morning, she'd been so formal, gathering her things, blushing as she handed him back the T-shirt she'd worn the night before, folded. Like she'd just tried it on in a change room and it hadn't fit quite right.

Greg had told Sylvie he was going for a swim, a lie he hopes she'll appreciate. Now, he holds the simple, antique gold band in his left palm. It feels so light, though it is a thicker ring than most. In the light, it looks almost pink. Rose gold, the jeweller had told him. There is no centre stone. He doesn't know why he's chosen it—it just seemed like Sylvie to him, the first time he saw it. The band itself is intricately carved, twists that blend into each other and wind their way around, connecting beginning to end and end to beginning. Inside, the band is smooth, an inscription once engraved there now faded by time and use. He cannot make it out. Perhaps it was a love story in only a few lines. *I belong to you. You belong to me.* Or maybe it was simply an etching from the jeweller, way back when. A serial number, nothing more.

"Thank you," he says, and looks up, meeting the eye of the jeweller, an older, heavyset woman with a purple cardigan and a warm smile. "It's perfect," he adds.

"You're welcome," the jeweller says. She plucks the ring from his outstretched palm and tucks it between the velvet folds of the box, closes the lid. "I hope she likes it."

"Me too," Greg says. He puts the small box into his jacket pocket.

The jeweller glances out the window of the shop, and Greg's eyes follow. The rain is coming down heavily now, unrelenting streams against the window. Greg pulls the hood of his jacket up over his hair.

The jeweller raises her eyebrows. "Some people are saying the river's going to flood. I hope this doesn't ruin any of your plans!"

Greg offers a half smile. "It won't."

NATASHA

June 2002

Happy Father's Day, Dad! I know we haven't talked in awhile, but I couldn't let Father's Day go by. You'll see I put Abby's ultrasound in the card. I'll let you in on the secret. It's a girl! Abby doesn't want to know, but I couldn't help myself—I took the ultrasound to work and had one of our techs read it for me. I thought, for Father's Day, you should know that there's going to be another little girl in your life. And, even though she wasn't planned, I'm pretty sure there is a bigger plan for her life. Everything happens for a reason. So get excited about it!

Love,

Your first little girl

CAM

YESTERDAY, WHEN CAM STEPPED OUT OF THE SHOWER, Jessica said, "Are you cheating on me again?"

Not really a fair question before 7 a.m. He wasn't even really awake yet. "What makes you think that?" he'd asked. Normally, when the alarm goes off, Jess rolls over and nudges him, says, "Fifteen more minutes, Baby," and then goes for her shower, comes back with a towel around her hair and says, "Now it's *really* time to get up!" And then he drags himself out of bed and into the shower himself. She won't kiss him good morning until he's brushed his teeth.

"I have a feeling," Jess had replied. She'd gotten up early, before the alarm, showered, dressed in a sheer white blouse, tight grey skirt just above her knees, black pantyhose. Nylons are so sexy. She'd even curled her hair, as though she wanted to look 100% before making such an accusation.

"You just have a *feeling*?" Cam repeated. That had to be bullshit, right? Did she actually have some real evidence? Had she seen something? He grabbed a towel, wrapped it around his waist. "Seriously? You're going to just accuse me of cheating on you, out of the blue, because you have a feeling?" His voice kept rising. "You're sure it's not the hormones?" He tugged the towel tighter around his waist.

Jess looked briefly in the mirror. Was she going to cry? Cam wondered. She turned away before he could tell. "I'm going to work. Then I'm going to my parents' until I decide what I'm going to do."

Is Jess's *feeling* about Abby? Or about Hillary, the girl he met at Hudsons the night of his friend's bachelor party? Hillary, as it turned out, just got a summer internship in the office building across the street from his, which made meeting for sex super convenient. When Jess said she was going to stay with her parents, she wasn't bluffing. She hasn't come home and she hasn't answered any of his texts.

Now, he's in the middle of a breakdown at Abby's because of the phone call about her sister. Even during their biggest screaming matches, he'd never seen her like this, sobbing into her hands, unable to say anything.

The rain was coming down so hard, Abby couldn't go pick up Summer. Good—Cam didn't want Summer around while her mother went batshit. He'd convinced Abby to go take a shower, said he'd stay until the detective phoned her back. Abby kept saying she was *sure* it was Natasha, she had a feeling. How did he end up like this, surrounded by all these women and all their feelings?

The whole skeleton thing creeped him out. How long had Natasha's body been lying there, decomposing? Cam had met Abby's sister only once, when she and his parents had ambushed him with a meeting about child support payments and stuff. Natasha sitting in his kitchen with a budget and some blurry sonogram pictures made it so real, and his parents had nodded solemnly and shot him disappointed glares. His mother had told him to walk Natasha to her car, and she'd slipped him one of the ultrasound photos and said, "Congratulations, by the way." He'd stared at the snapshot. His child. He was going to have a child. Holy shit.

When Abby comes downstairs, she has a towel wrapped around her hair and is wearing a pair of sweatpants and a thin white T-shirt through which he can see the outline of her bra. He rarely sees her without makeup. Her eyes look bloodshot. She looks like a teenager as she plops down on the couch and releases her wet hair from the towel.

Cam sits beside her on the couch. "Didn't you *want* something like this to happen? I mean, this could be the break you were waiting for."

"You don't get it," Abby says. "This means she's really gone."

Of course she's really gone. She's been missing for eleven years. She's probably been dead this whole time. It's pretty much mathematical certainty. Do the bones really change anything?

"She was the only person who ever—" Abby paces over to a window she's left open and slides it down. "You should go home."

Cam gets up. He pulls his phone from his pocket. *R U safe?* Jess has texted him. If he owns up to cheating, especially with Abby, she will probably leave him for good. He texts back, *Yes. Hope you're safe too.*

JOSIE

THERE, IN THE TREES, A FLASH OF ORANGE. A DARK PONYTAIL.
Josie pushes branches out of her way. She can barely see through the rain.
"Wait!" she calls, but Natasha doesn't stop. Mud sucks at Josie's feet. "Wait!"
she yells, but the rain masks the sound. She can't catch her breath.

Natasha scrambles down a small embankment. Josie follows, her paja-
mas streaked with mud, her hands raw and red. In her orange tank top and
black leggings, Natasha is much more equipped for this trek. When Josie
finally catches up, her friend kneels on the ground, digging under a small
bush with her bare hands. Josie's soaked cotton PJs cling to her skin.

Natasha stops digging, looks up. Wordlessly, she unties the black wind-
breaker from around her waist and passes it to her friend. Josie fumbles as
she slides her arms into the coat and struggles with the zipper. She pushes her
wet hair out of her face. Natasha reaches deep under the bush, deep into the
hole she has dug there. When she emerges, she holds a naked, squalling baby,
a little boy. "Here," she says, and she hands the baby to Josie.

What is Josie supposed to do with him? The baby is so little, so cold, so
slippery. With one hand, she gropes to undo Natasha's windbreaker, then
tucks the baby inside, pulls the zipper back up, clutches the baby to her
chest. "I'm so sorry!" Josie sobs. "I didn't know! Will you forgive me?"

RAIN POUNDS AGAINST THE BEDROOM SKYLIGHT. JOSIE opens her eyes wide in the dark, stares up against the square of glass. The skylight was how she knew, when she and Solomon first got married, that this was the right house for them. That little square right above where they would sleep, open to the sky, to Heaven. In the morning, the sun would come in like a hug from God.

Now, the glass is blurred by the incessant rain. Before Solomon, all those years she spent single, Josie slept sprawled in the middle of the bed, hoarded all the pillows to herself. Now she sleeps neatly against the right, the other half of the bed empty. Josie flicks on the bedside lamp, pushes herself to her feet, plucks her glasses up off her nightstand, along with her phone, in case Reuben calls her back, and paces into the kitchen. She tried him three times before going to bed. Fish Creek Park. Greg, all along.

"Auntie?" comes a small voice.

Josie had forgotten about Summer—wrapped in blankets just hours ago, on the couch, since Finn was already set up in the spare room. She sits down at Summer's feet. "Did the storm wake you up?"

"Do you think they're going to cancel school?" Summer asks. Just waking up, she looks younger than almost-eleven, lost in one of Josie's faded T-shirts.

"Probably," Josie says.

Summer's brow creases. "I'll have to call my mom."

"In the morning," Josie says.

Then a key turns in the lock. Josie tenses, feels Summer tense beside her, and before she can stand, Solomon staggers into the house. Water splatters to the floor as he pulls an umbrella closed.

Josie's heart races. "What are you doing here?"

Solomon raises his eyebrows. "My neighbourhood was evacuated. I'm going to stay here until I get the all-clear from the city."

Josie stands and approaches him. This soggy, pathetic man, standing in a puddle in her doorway, is her husband. His hair looks greyer than she remembers, though she knows, rationally, that this can't be true.

He didn't come to Jason's funeral, she thinks, in Natasha's voice. "You didn't come to Jason's funeral," she says.

Solomon's eyes look behind her, and she turns, aware again of Summer. "Go into my bedroom, Honey," Josie says—so calmly. "I'll be there in a second."

As Summer leaves, Josie and Solomon maintain their positions in the doorway, and then Solomon starts to unzip his coat.

"You can't stay here," Josie says, and takes a step forward. "The children are here. And I want a divorce."

NATASHA

JULY 6, 2002

Standing on the front step, Natasha pauses before she starts her run, breathes in the crisp night air, the stillness. She feels on the cusp of something, like at the top of a roller coaster, the pause right before it descends. A relationship is beginning. A new life is emerging. She checks her watch and places her headphones on her ears.

Parked right out front is a bluish grey pickup truck. As she descends the few steps to the sidewalk, she realizes she knows the driver. That can't be right. He's not supposed to be driving, not within six months of having a seizure.

He rolls down the window.

"What are you doing here?" she asks.

He leans over and unlocks the passenger side door. "Can we talk?"

Natasha inhales. She doesn't want to hurt his feelings. Okay, she thinks. Just for a second.

And when she opens the door to the truck, she notices the other person in the back seat.

HIM

THE FIRST TIME WAS MY HALF BIRTHDAY. FEBRUARY SIXTH, 1983.
We used to celebrate half birthdays in my family. That's how fucking happy we were. My mom inflated fifty helium balloons and let them float to the ceiling all over the house—like in my bedroom and in the family room and even in the kitchen—the strings hanging down like tails. I got to eat Pac-Man cereal for breakfast and watch cartoons and then my aunts and uncles and cousins came over for dinner. Hawaiian pizza, my favourite. I ate six slices and nobody said anything because my parents were distracted looking at pictures of my auntie and uncle's trip to Las Vegas, and I felt a bit sick, and my cousin said, "Hey, want to go play in your room?"

This doctor my parents took me to see as a kid told me that anger is like a monster inside of you, trying to get you to do bad things. I imagined my monster as a swamp monster—black and slimy, like a bad guy from a video game. He'd open his sludgy mouth in a lopsided grin; teeth lined with metal braces; nasty breath. He didn't have any eyes. Just gaping holes, hollow sockets. When he expanded in my stomach, I felt like I was going to puke, like the puke was bubbling and bubbling up in my throat and just going to explode.

The psychologist was like, "Call me Dr. Jack." He made me sit in this chair and practice taking deep breaths, making my stomach rise and fall. He said taking deep breaths would keep the angry monster from making me do something bad, like hitting somebody or throwing the snow globe in Dad's office into the wall and making it break into a million pieces. I had to clean up the mess that time and it reeked like antifreeze. I thought I would inhale the fumes and die, but I didn't, even though I wanted to.

Dr. Jack had curly brown hair and big glasses that were kind of dirty up close. He said, "Imagine your tummy is like a balloon, fill it right up," and then he reached over and took this limp blue balloon off his desk, put it to his lips, and started blowing. The balloon got bigger and rounder right in front of my face. It made me think of all the balloons hanging from the ceiling, about lying down and watching the balloons bobbing up against each other. I was supposed to be happy, it was my half birthday, and the whole time, my cousin was saying, "Doesn't that feel good?"

The balloon was getting bigger and bigger. It wouldn't stop!

I took a swing—hit Dr. Jack right in his stupid dirty glasses. The balloon shriveled up and fell to the floor and Dr. Jack stared at me, his eyes wide, a little bit of blood trickling from his nose.

Wow, I thought. *I* did that? Dr. Jack was a real grown-up, and I made his nose bleed. It felt kinda good.

Except Dr. Jack was the only doctor who actually tried to help me. It wasn't him I was mad at, really. All the other ones didn't even try to teach me tricks to make the anger go away. They just slapped me with a bunch of labels. ODD, ADD. Not one of them ever asked me where the monster came from. Not one ever thought to ask, why'd he get all those letters? What I didn't get was, why did I have to have the monster inside of me? I didn't do anything!

You're the only one I told, Tash—you know that, right? I thought you would get what it was like to be broken. Lying there, tied to the chair, looking at those balloons, I was thinking, I'm different now. "Before" ten-and-a-half and "after" ten-and-a-half. That kind of thing, you can't change. I only told you about the first time, too, because you started freaking out, saying I would have to tell. She came over again at Easter, and then in the summer she started coming over all the time to tutor me in math. One time, she was there and you were there and you asked her to curl your hair, and she said, "Okay," and I thought good, I won't have to deal with the monster today, but instead of going to play I just sat there, watching her wrap your hair around the hot curling iron, thinking, if she hurts you in any way, I will break her neck.

It kept happening even after I told you. Like, the day before your birthday party, she was babysitting, and I flooded the toilet by putting a T-shirt down it so that my mom and dad would have to come home early. Except they were at a work thing for my dad, so they didn't actually come home early, they just called a plumber, and then they grounded me for a week and I wasn't allowed to go to your birthday party. I hadn't talked to you since the night in the closet. But you made me feel like maybe it wasn't my fault. Maybe you would be a goody two-shoes and tell even though I told you not to.

I made you the best birthday present ever—a cassette tape of songs I recorded from the radio on dad's ghetto blaster. I had to be sneaky about it, too, because I wasn't supposed to touch the ghetto blaster. I put eleven songs on because you were turning eleven, and I stole some of Josie's stickers to decorate it. I gave it to you the next day at school—do you remember that? You were totally psyched—you said, I remember this exactly, "I *love* it!"

Also, in case you were wondering, the night I plugged the toilet, my cousin made me play with her in the basement in the dark and I could hear the furnace hissing at me, like my monster, laughing.

That Christmas, she and her brothers stayed for a sleepover, and I couldn't fall asleep. I kept thinking she was going to come into my room any minute. But then she didn't. And it just stopped. I don't know why. I guess she just figured I wasn't worth it anymore, I don't know. But even when she stopped, the monster stayed.

Sometimes I could make the monster shut up for awhile by playing video games. Sometimes, that put the monster to sleep. But then, when he woke up, he was bigger than before.

I thought I could love you. I thought I could make love to you and not feel the monster slipping and sliding around inside of me. Not feel the puke rising and rising.

I thought you were broken, too. Your mom abandoned you—left you behind. And then Greg broke you, too. I could see it in your eyes—like all the light went out. Sometimes I wondered how you put your monster to sleep. And then I watched you running, listening to music I couldn't hear, and I knew. Your '80s music. It probably reminded you of being an innocent little kid. Probably reminded you of your own "before."

At least, I thought you were broken. Then I saw your emails. *I want you. You know what I mean.* You filthy slut.

You sounded just like her.

JOSIE

IT'S FINALLY SAFE ENOUGH FOR ABBY TO DRIVE OVER TO PICK up Summer. With the kids downstairs watching TV, Josie stands at the window waiting for Abby to pull up. The rain has stopped. For now.

"I'm getting a divorce." She says it aloud, alone in the empty room. The words taste so unfamiliar. She remembers the sweetness of *I'm engaged!* And *I'm Mrs. McKinnon!* The bitterness of *it's negative* and *my mom has cancer.* The numbness of *my best friend is missing.*

There's Abby, coming up the walkway—and, behind her, is that Greg? Abby didn't say he was coming, too. Fire rises up Josie's throat like reflux. She throws open the door and pushes past Abby, makes fists with both hands and slams them into Greg's chest. He stumbles back a bit, his mouth open.

"How dare you?!" Josie screams, her heart galloping.

Abby tries to get in-between them. "What the hell?"

But Greg has already put his hands up, as though surrendering. "What's going on?"

"Fish Creek Park!" Josie spits. "All this time! All these years!" She's crying now. Her arms fall at her sides.

Greg still looks stunned, all the colour washed from his face. "Jo—" he says. "I swear to God. I swear to God, I never hurt her. I had nothing to do with it. I miss her every day. Every second. I'd gladly kill myself if it meant she would come back."

Josie raises her eyes and looks into his. He looks pained. Like he's telling the truth. But then, Solomon stood in front of their entire church congregation and pledged to be faithful to her until death. And there's a body in Fish Creek Park. "I need to know," she says, "that I did everything...that it wasn't..." the words come in gulping sobs. "...my fault."

Abby sounds confused. "Why would it be *your* fault?"

Summer hovers in the doorway. "Hi, Mom," she says to Abby, but her eyes dart between them, and she bites her lower lip. "What's going on?"

"Nothing, nothing," Abby says, and starts walking towards the door, so Josie follows, and then Greg, too.

Abby gives Summer a hug. "We have to go down to the station after this. Reuben needs to talk to me about the, uh, about Auntie's case. But the three of us—" she gestures at Josie and Greg "—need to talk a little bit first, okay?"

"Okay," Summer says, chewing on a fingernail. She descends the stairs back into the basement.

Josie moves into the living room and Abby and Greg follow her. She sinks onto the edge of one of the sofas, and Abby sits on the other side. Greg stays standing at first, then eventually lowers onto the arm of the loveseat.

It comes out all at once. "The last time I saw her, we had a fight," Josie says. "She was—she was so stressed, she got upset—she said, 'Do you want me to have a complete breakdown?'" She holds out her fingers, the way Natasha did, an inch apart. "She said she was *this* close." She can't look at either Greg or Abby. "What if...?" She fiddles with her fingers in her lap.

Abby shifts on the other side of the couch, moves a little closer. "Jo, they found her watch. She didn't take off on her own."

"Even so," Josie says, "she was so stressed, and the last time I saw her, I made it worse. Maybe she wasn't thinking clearly when whatever happened...maybe she let her guard down because of me."

Abby shakes her head. "If she was stressed about anything, it was me. I basically moved into her house, pregnant, moody...she paid for everything, took care of everything. And, trust me, the two of us argued all the time. I mean, we loved each other, but it wasn't easy."

Josie says quietly, "I feel *so* guilty!"

"I do, too," Greg admits. "I go over and over it every day. Maybe if we hadn't broken up, or maybe if I'd checked in more..."

Summer appears at the top of the stairs again. "Can I get a glass of water?"

"Sure," Josie says, and hops up off the couch to go retrieve one. Is Summer actually thirsty? Or just worried about what's going on with the adults, making excuses to come upstairs? When she comes back out of the kitchen with the glass, Finn has emerged, too. He's introducing himself to Greg.

"What time are we going to see Reuben?" Summer wants to know.

Abby glances over at Josie. It's like she's saying, *are you okay?* Josie nods. She has no choice.

"Why don't we all go?" Greg suggests. "We can take two cars."

"Can Finn ride with us?" Summer asks her mom.

Yes, Josie thinks, they should all go. They all need answers. It's time.

ABBY

THEY NEVER FOUND THE SKULL.

Just the left clavicle, some metatarsals of the foot, three ribs, and the pelvis. But it was enough to exclude them as yours.

"I'm sorry," Reuben said. As though it was his fault the bones were male. Somebody else's loved one. Somebody's father. Somebody's brother. Somebody's son.

Looking out the window now, you can't even tell there was a storm. You have to go closer to the river to find it, or go down into people's basements to see the damage. The broken windows, the thick sewage, the soggy books, the rotting walls.

When we finally got back home from the station, it was pitch black outside, but Summer wanted to check on her garden. She was sure the rain would have damaged the flowers she and Greg had carefully planted that spring. No way was I letting her go outside in the dark alone. So I followed her around the side of the house to the little patch of dirt along the back fence. I couldn't see much in the dark. Summer knelt right there in the wet soil.

"How are they?" I asked, holding my breath.

Quietly, she said, "They're bent. The storm got them. But—I think they'll be okay."

The garden was one of Summer's bucket list items. Summer's had this bucket list for awhile now, I think it started with Greg and Sylvie. You would like Sylvie, by the way. At least, I think you would. She isn't *you* though. Just so you know.

That's how it all started, me going to Edinburgh. Summer decided I needed a bucket list, too. She made me list a bunch of places that I might like to go, and then we pulled one out of a bowl. I was pronouncing it wrong for awhile—Ed-in-berg, rhyming with Pittsburgh—before Sylvie corrected me—apparently it's Ed-in-bruh. Who knew? There's a lot of things I still don't know. You were never big on travelling, and it wasn't like I could just go off on my own after Summer was born. Maybe had none of this happened, we would have travelled together someday, you and me. I'd decided to go alone—but then, when I asked Josie if she'd help Cam with Summer while I was gone, she said, "What if I came, too?" Yesterday, the twenty-four-hour cancellation period on our flights ended. This means we're actually going. Two whole weeks without Summer. If I think about it too much, I want to puke. Sylvie says it rains a lot in the UK. "Bring a raincoat," she said. It sounded like something you would say.

Dad and I decided it's time to put your house on the market. It's going to involve a lot of legal mumbo jumbo. I'll let Dad take care of that. When I get back from Scotland, Summer and I will go look at some apartments, find a place I can afford without Dad's help. Hopefully the landlord will let me paint Summer's room orange. It's her favourite colour, too, you know. Her room at her dad's house is pink (gag). Maybe Cam and Jessica will work things out, now that I called it off with him. Or maybe they won't. Maybe they'll have a baby. Or maybe someday, I'll meet someone and have a baby.

Maybe someday, Summer will have a sister.

NATASHA

JULY 6, 2002

Natasha has seen Jason's son in pictures, but pictures don't do the little boy justice. The truck reeks of cigarettes. Jay has smoked on and off since they were teenagers. She and Josie have told him more than once that he should quit. Seizure risks are higher in smokers. She wrinkles her nose. It's one thing if he inhales the toxins into his own body, but does he have to expose Finn's tiny lungs to it?

"Hi!" Finn chirps, from the back seat with a giant smile. And Natasha smiles back, a reflex, and doesn't realize at first that they are driving.

Jason says, "I need to show you something."

"Where? I have to—"

Finn says, "Go, Daddy!" and Natasha's eyes dart back to him.

"I know you think I'm just this big fuck-up," Jason says. The truck picks up speed. Whose truck is this, anyway? She thinks he's a fuck-up? Maybe. He tends to make bad decisions, for sure. But Jay has always been family. "I don't think that," she sputters.

"I grew up a lot, you know." His eyes focus ahead of him, on the road.

"I know," she says. "You seem really upset. Is everything okay?"

"When you have a kid, life changes. I pulled my shit together. Even Angie could see that."

"That's good," she says. With one more turn, he's on the highway. The speedometer picks up. 80, 90, 100, 110. "Jason, I'm worried—"

"Everyone could see it," he says. "Except you."

Natasha's throat closes. Her heart skips in her ears. Jason seems so agitated. Has he been having seizures again? If he's smoking heavily, he's increasing his risk. Maybe his neurologist changed his medication. Antiseizure meds can have behavioural side effects—restlessness, hyperactivity, agitation, psychosis…

"I was always a convenience for you, wasn't I?" Jason practically spits the words.

"Daddy," Finn babbles from the back, and he fusses, strains against the car seat straps that bind across his chest and up over his shoulders, reaches forwards. "Daddy."

Natasha's throat is so dry. "Jay—" she says, but she doesn't know what she really means. Does she mean stop? Does she mean please? Both?

"Like when your dad knocked up your stepmom and you ran away from home and you wanted someone to listen. Or when you wanted to bitch about your loser boyfriend at Jo's wedding. Or when you wanted your Internet fixed and your baby monitors installed. Jason will do it. Sure, why not?"

"Jay—" she says again. He's driving well above the speed limit. She's never seen him so angry, something is really, really wrong.

In the rearview, she can see Finn fussing in his car seat. Could she pull the door handle and leap out? How fast are they going? If she jumps, she leaves Finn behind. Is Jason going to hurt her? Is he going to hurt his son? She has known Jason her whole life. He would never hurt his child. Not intentionally. But he's clearly unstable right now. Finn is not safe. Maybe this outburst is part of a prodromal phase, the period leading up to a seizure. If he has a spell while driving, it could be deadly for all three of them. The speed he's going at alone…

Her heart thuds faster and faster. Where are they going? West, she thinks. Her hands have formed fists. She uncurls her frozen fingers and realizes that one of her hands is inside the pocket of her running jacket, and before her run she'd slid a slip of paper inside, the fortune from the cookie she'd broken in half at her lunch break with Pav. It read, *It is not what they take away from you that counts. It is what you do with what you have left.* Not really a fortune. Pav had joked that he would have preferred his cookie to say *You will live a long time and be very rich.* But she'd liked her little quote, and so she'd held onto it and tucked it inside her jacket. Now, she closes the fingers of that hand around the small slip of paper.

"I have to make sure he grows up in the right kind of world," Jay rants. There's something in the road. Garbage? Roadkill? He swerves to avoid it, turning the truck sharply to the right, sliding her up against the passenger door.

She forces herself to speak. "I'm sorry if—if I hurt you, in some way."

He doesn't look at her, keeps his eyes on the road. Small flecks begin to speckle the windshield. It's raining. "Oh now you're sorry," he says.

"I am," she says. "I never meant to take you for granted. Maybe it came across that way, but I've always thought of you as…as family."

Jason scoffs. "Family. Yeah." And he turns off the main road. Maybe if she just keeps talking. Sometimes that works when Josie is upset—just talk and talk, in a calm, logical way.

"Do you remember that time, in the ravine?" she starts. Does he remember his first seizure? Of course he does! What a stupid thing to say! "I was so scared. I thought—I thought you were going to die. I didn't want to lose you."

Jay glances at her.

"I still think about it, you know, and maybe—maybe I have taken you for granted, maybe—you know, that's my fault, for not seeing—I mean, until you came over for the monitors, I didn't know how—how you felt about me." Her mouth moves faster than her brain can catch up. "I didn't realize…"

Finn starts crying, and Jason's voice changes. "It's okay, Buddy! We're going for a drive! We'll be there soon."

There? Where is there? Where are they going?

Jason glances up at the rearview. "I'm a race car, Buddy! Zoom! Zoom!"

And the little guy quiets, looks out the window, inserts the nipple end of his blue soother in his mouth, but upside down.

Natasha keeps going. "I'm so messed up right now, because of Greg. You know what that feels like, right? When you and Angie—"

Jay snaps, "Don't!" He glances in the rearview. "That's his mother. Just shut up. Shut up!"

She presses her lips together. How far are they? He's going 120, 130. She can't see anyone else on this rural road. She squeezes her fist around the fortune. She can feel her fingernails digging into her palm, her heart throbbing.

How long do they drive for? Twenty minutes? Thirty? The clock in the truck is broken, hours ahead. She has no idea what time it really is. She doesn't dare look at her watch. She feels frozen in the seat. Her headphones dangle around her neck.

If she starts talking again, will he snap? But it's too quiet. "I'm sorry," she blurts, "I just mean—" What does she mean? Don't cry, don't cry. "It's all a façade," she says, and she means this, she's not just telling him what he wants to hear. "Maybe I make it look good on the outside, but really, I'm just as broken as everyone else. Probably even more. I'm sorry I haven't been a better—" The tears come, streaming hot down her face, and she puts her palms to her cheeks, covers her eyes.

The truck veers and then squeals to a stop, jolting Natasha forward, thrusting her hands forward onto the dash. Her wrist stings with the impact. Finn wails. Jason pushes the driver side door open and leaps out, slams it behind him, and Finn stops crying suddenly. In the rearview mirror, his eyes are wide. A thin line of drool dangles from his bottom lip onto his shirt.

Rain splatters hard against the windshield. Natasha watches Jason's blurry figure pace away. Where is he going? She cranes her neck slightly to look at Finn while still watching Jason as he moves further from the truck.

"It's okay," she whispers to the little boy. "You're okay." Finn looks a lot like Jason. No question of who his father is. He looks a lot like Josie, too.

Josie. Beautiful Josie, who always loved her brother, even when the two were squabbling. Timid, sunny side up Josie would never let anyone else speak negatively of her twin, despite his shortcomings. But then, Josie loved everyone with fierce loyalty like that. At Jo's wedding, the priest had read that traditional Corinthians verse and Natasha had thought, gag, how cliché. But how else to describe Josie? *Love is not easily angered, it keeps no record of wrongs. It always protects, always trusts, always hopes, always perseveres.*

Had she loved Greg this way? *Always patient, always kind?* Or had she been too focused on her own needs, her own wants, her simmering resentment? At once, she is flooded by a memory of Greg in bed beside her, his bare shoulder and the slope of his back. Oh, to wrap her arms around him, to sidle up close, to breathe him in. To trace each of his lines and curves, every freckle, every scar.

Natasha can no longer see Jason—he has moved too far away, and the rain streams too heavily. She could outrun him, easily—on her own. But she doesn't know where they are, and she cannot leave Finn behind. Could she make a break for it with Finn? In the rain? They can't be too far from the highway—she could find help, they just have to get away first. Where the hell is Jason?

She doesn't think. She unstraps her watch. She almost never takes her watch off anymore, even to shower. If someone finds it, they'll know she was here, right? She reaches up, pinches a piece of hair, about a quarter of an inch thick, twists it around her index finger. Grits her teeth and pulls. Gasps a little as the strands rip away from her scalp. She can hear her own rapid breath. She twists the dark strands around the strap of the watch. She doesn't need to be doing this, right? He's not actually going to hurt her. He would never.

Still, she nudges the floor mat up with her sneaker, then bends forward, places the torn pieces of herself on the dirty floor of the truck. Covers them up.

Should she wait? No, she should not wait. She doesn't know what the hell is going on with Jason but it's not good. This could be her only chance.

She leans back in the truck, tries to reach—maybe if she

unbuckles Finn inside the truck, lifts him to the front, or maybe gets him to climb forward, she can just open the one door and run. She tries to lean between the console, reach across for Finn's buckles. "You're okay, you're okay," she whispers.

There's no way she's going to be able to reach.

Has Abby noticed that she's gone? Abby, Abby, Abby—her heart pulses Abby's name with each surge against her rib-cage. She has to get back. Abby needs her. And she needs Abby. She thinks of all the nights she snuck into Abby's nursery, lifted her sweet-smelling baby sister from her crib and rocked her, stroking the soft fluff along Abby's downy head. Abby's tiny metronome heart against hers.

Now! She leaps from the truck. Her feet hit the ground. The rain pounds hard against her head, her back. She fumbles with the truck handle, slips, pulls again. There, it's open! Finn reaches for her. She gropes at his buckles, successfully undoes the one that crosses his chest, but the one that buckles between his legs is tighter. She can't breathe. Almost, almost!

"Don't touch him, you slut!"

Jason shoves her roughly in the side, away from the vehicle, and she slams hard onto the gravel. Heat rips from her wrist up her elbow. Is her arm broken? The skin on her palm and wrist has been torn away and blood has sprouted in the raw pink flesh. She reaches and touches her elbow and feels a sticky wetness there. Her heart screams inside her, trying to escape, pushing out of her ribcage, pushing pushing out, pushing, pushing, pushing, pushing—

He takes a step forward. "Girls like you…"

From inside the truck, Jason's son starts to cry.

SUMMER

WHILE MY MOM AND AUNTIE JOSIE AND MY GRANDPA AND UNCLE Greg and Auntie Sylvie set everything up for the annual balloon release in memory of my Auntie Natasha, Finn and I sit on the grass in the park near my house, which used to be Auntie Natasha's house. I ask Finn, "Do you think it's possible to miss someone you never met?"

Finn brought his skateboard and tried to teach me some tricks, but I sucked at it. Finn is really good at sports. He's starting at my school in September. Celeste is probably going to have a crush on him, except I might have a crush on him first.

Finn reaches into the bag of Doritos he brought with him, takes a few chips, then offers me the bag. "I don't know," he says. "I miss my Dad. He was really fun. My mom only talks about the bad stuff. I think sometimes she's glad he's dead."

I think part of me remembers Auntie Natasha. My mom says when she was pregnant, Auntie Natasha would read me Dr. Seuss. *One Fish, Two Fish, Red Fish, Blue Fish.* Is that her voice saying those words in my head?

Finn pulls a clump of grass out of the ground, then scatters the blades. "He was really good at computers," Finn says. "And he loved nachos. And music from the '80s. When he picked me up for dinner, he would play '80s music on a CD in the car and have a smoke when we were driving. He had a whole bunch of '80s CDs. My mom would have killed him if she knew he smoked in the car with me in there."

I roll over onto my belly on the grass. "My Auntie Natasha loved '80s music, too. I guess that's from when they grew up. CDs are so old school."

Here comes Aunt Sylvie. She's not technically my real aunt, but then, neither is Auntie Jo. A family doesn't have to be blood. You can have blood family that's not good for you, and you can have people who are not related to you, but who love you more than anything. Auntie Jo and Uncle Greg love me as much as Auntie Natasha would have. That's the truth.

"Hey, guys," says Sylvie. "What're you guys talking about?"

"Music," says Finn.

"From your generation," I add. Is it weird that I *love* Sylvie? Because I love Auntie Natasha, too, even though we didn't meet, and my mom says Auntie Natasha and Uncle Greg were each other's destinies. But isn't everything that happens to you your destiny? So was it Auntie Natasha's destiny to end up with Uncle Greg if it was also her destiny to go missing? How does that work?

"Oh yeah?" Sylvie says, grinning at us and sitting down on the grass beside Finn. "Us old fogies, hey?" Sylvie is older than my mom but I think younger than Uncle Greg, but also Uncle Greg's hair went super grey so he looks older than he is, which is forty. We had a big fortieth birthday party for him and I did the invitations on my computer. I asked my mom for a picture of him from when he was a teenager, cuz I thought that would be funny to put in. But it had Auntie Natasha in it, and I had to crop her out, and that felt weird.

"Do you love '80s music?" Finn asks her.

Sylvie shakes her head. "No, but I have weird taste in music. I love classical stuff, no lyrics. Bach, Beethoven."

"Boring!" I say, and roll onto my back. The sun is so bright. I put my hand up over my eyes.

Sylvie laughs. "Which one of you is the '80s fan?"

"Neither," says Finn. "My dad was. And Natasha. We were just saying how weird it was that they both used to keep CDs from the '80s in their cars."

Sylvie's eyes get really big. "Like burned CDs?"

"What's a burnt CD?" I ask.

"Like, homemade," Sylvie says. "Ones where you make the playlist."

"Oh," says Finn. "That's what my dad had, yeah."

The sun is making black spots in front of my eyes. I should ask Finn to borrow his baseball cap.

"I'll be right back," Sylvie says, getting up. "Stay here."

Where else would we go? I roll over onto my stomach and push up onto my elbows. Hey, there's my dad! This is the first time my dad has come to a memorial for Auntie Natasha. I see him across the field. He goes to where my mom is and starts tying strings onto balloons with her. I like it when they get along. Don't get me wrong, it's not like I want them to get back together. That'd be totally weird. But maybe they could be friends.

Sylvie is talking to Reuben and they look over at us, and Reuben shakes his head and Sylvie nods and crosses her arms. Reuben looks over at me and Finn. He's like, staring at us. He takes a step forward.

But now here comes my mom, with a big fistful of orange and white balloons tied to ribbons. It's time for the balloon release! There are so many! Could we ever get so many balloons that it would lift my mom right up off the ground? She hands me and Finn each a handful. I hold onto mine and look up at the bright orange and shiny white dancing against the pale blue sky.

In three days, I am going to be eleven, which is the age my Auntie Natasha was when my mom was born. My mom says we can get a kitten! Finally! Another thing crossed off my bucket list. I picked an orange tabby one from the SPCA website but he's not old enough to come home with us yet. He has to stay with his mother another couple weeks.

This is the first time I'm going to be away from my mom for two whole weeks when she and Auntie Jo go to Scotland. I'm happy for her but also it makes my tummy feel like flies are buzzing around in there. My mom says it's okay to have both feelings, and she's happy and scared about it, too. We're going to Skype each other every day.

The truth about balloons is that you're not supposed to let go of them, because they don't actually float off to Heaven, they just run out of helium and come back down and damage the environment. An animal could choke on them, or they could cause pollution in the river. Uncle Greg taught me this. You're supposed to pop them and put them in the garbage.

I let go of my handful and watch the orange and white turn into specks in the sky and then disappear.

This time, I'll make an exception.

ACKNOWLEDGEMENTS

Gratitude sprinkles to everyone who helped this novel grow from idea to story (in no particular order):

The staff at NeWest Press—my agent, editor, Anne Nothof; general manager, Matt Bowes; book designer, Kate Hargreaves; and marketing and production coordinator, Claire Kelly.

Those who read early drafts and provided feedback along the way—Carrie Mumford, Rachelle Pinnow, Stefanie Barton, Tania Jacobs, Meghan Doraty, Henry Campbell, Nicole Blaszczak, Robin van Eck, Andrew Wilmot, Cecilia Ekbäck; Nicole Petrowski and Topher McFarlane Palumbo.

My early writing instructors—Suzette Mayr, Nicole Markotić and Helen Humphreys.

Stefanie Barton, friend/photographer extraordinare (as evidenced by author photo).

And a bunch of other people I love/who supported my writing career—my husband, David Gishler; Alyssa Adair; Ashlee Ellerbruch Young; Elena Meekhoff; my parents; Sue McDermott Taylor; Dave Taylor; Darby and Flynn Taylor; Katie Hyde; John Siddons; Tyler Hellard; Felicia Zuniga; Cherinne Banister; Ashley Sperling; Nicole Ko; Naomi Lewis; and Dwayne Clayden.

Special thank you to the Alberta Foundation for the Arts grants for funding the writing and revision of this novel.

THEANNA BISCHOFF is a novelist from Calgary, Alberta. Her first novel, *Cleavage* (NeWest Press, 2008), was shortlisted for both the 2009 Commonwealth Writers Prize for Best First Book (Canada/the Caribbean), and the 2009 Re-Lit Awards. Her second novel, *Swallow* (NeWest Press, 2012), was shortlisted for the 2013 City of Calgary W.O. Mitchell Book Prize. Theanna holds a Concentration in Creative Writing from the University of Calgary (2006) and a Ph.D. in Educational Psychology (2012).